Pokémon Horizon: Sun & Moon

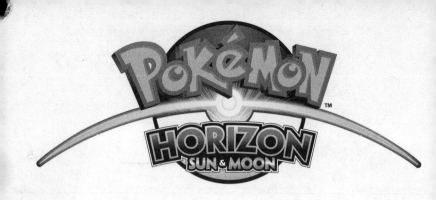

02

Story & Art
TENYA YABUNO

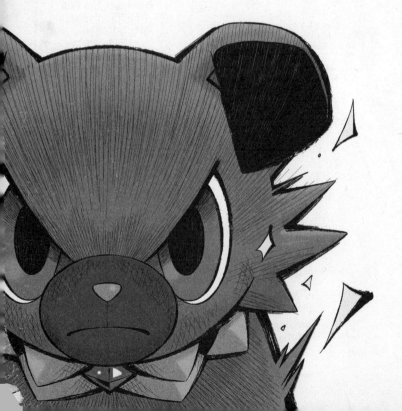

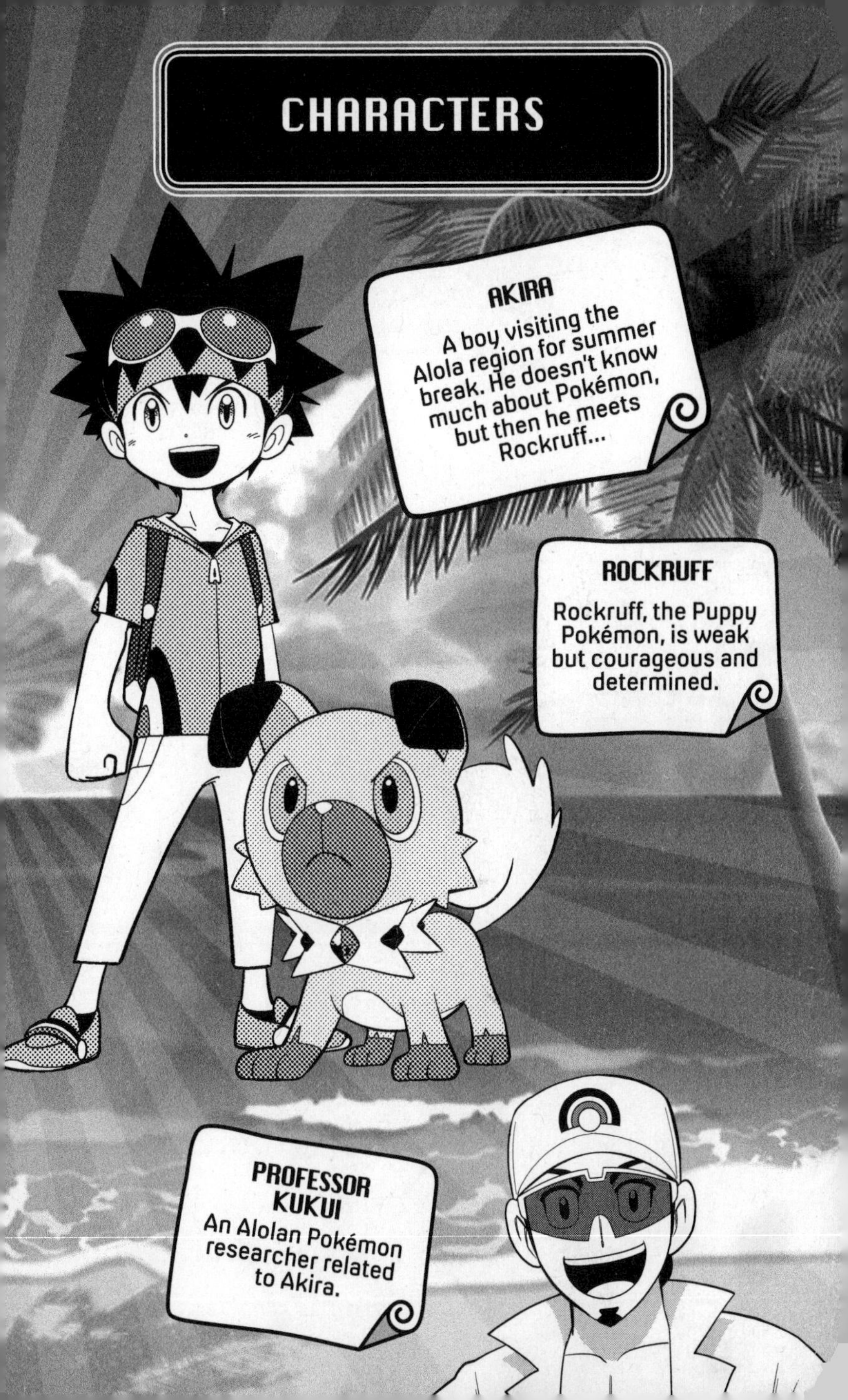
CHARACTERS
AKIRA
A boy visiting the Alola region for summer break. He doesn't know much about Pokémon, but then he meets Rockruff...
ROCKRUFF
Rockruff, the Puppy Pokémon, is weak but courageous and determined.
PROFESSOR KUKUI
An Alolan Pokémon researcher related to Akira.

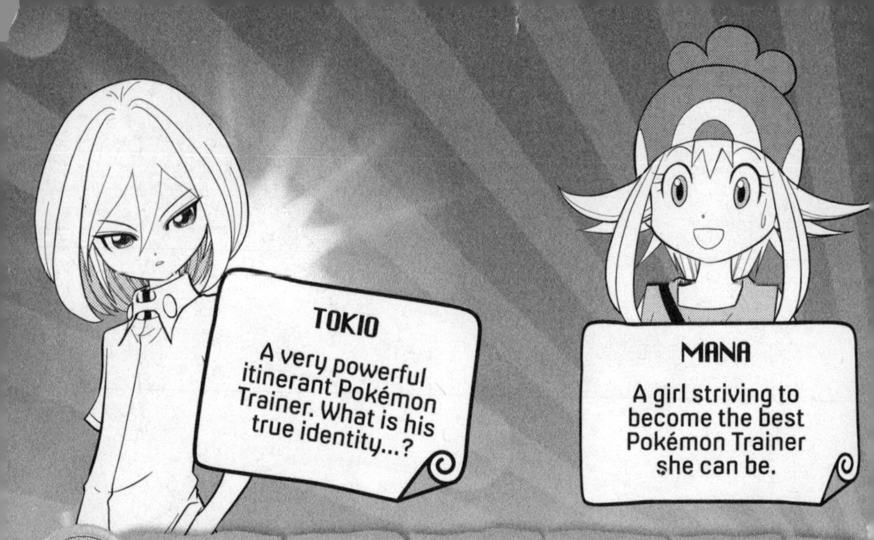
TOKIO
A very powerful itinerant Pokémon Trainer. What is his true identity...?
MANA
A girl striving to become the best Pokémon Trainer she can be.

THE STORY SO FAR

On his summer vacation in the Alola region, Akira meets a Rockruff with a mysterious red gemstone. The two become partners. Together, Akira hopes they can achieve his dream of becoming a first-rate Pokémon Trainer. First he must earn a Trainer Passport. After he accomplishes that, the pair set off to win the Island Challenge. But Team Kings—an evil organization with plans for world domination—stands in their way. They try to kidnap Rockruff, but in the midst of battle, Rockruff evolves into Lycanroc...

EVENT HORIZON

Event 6: Lycanroc Evolution!

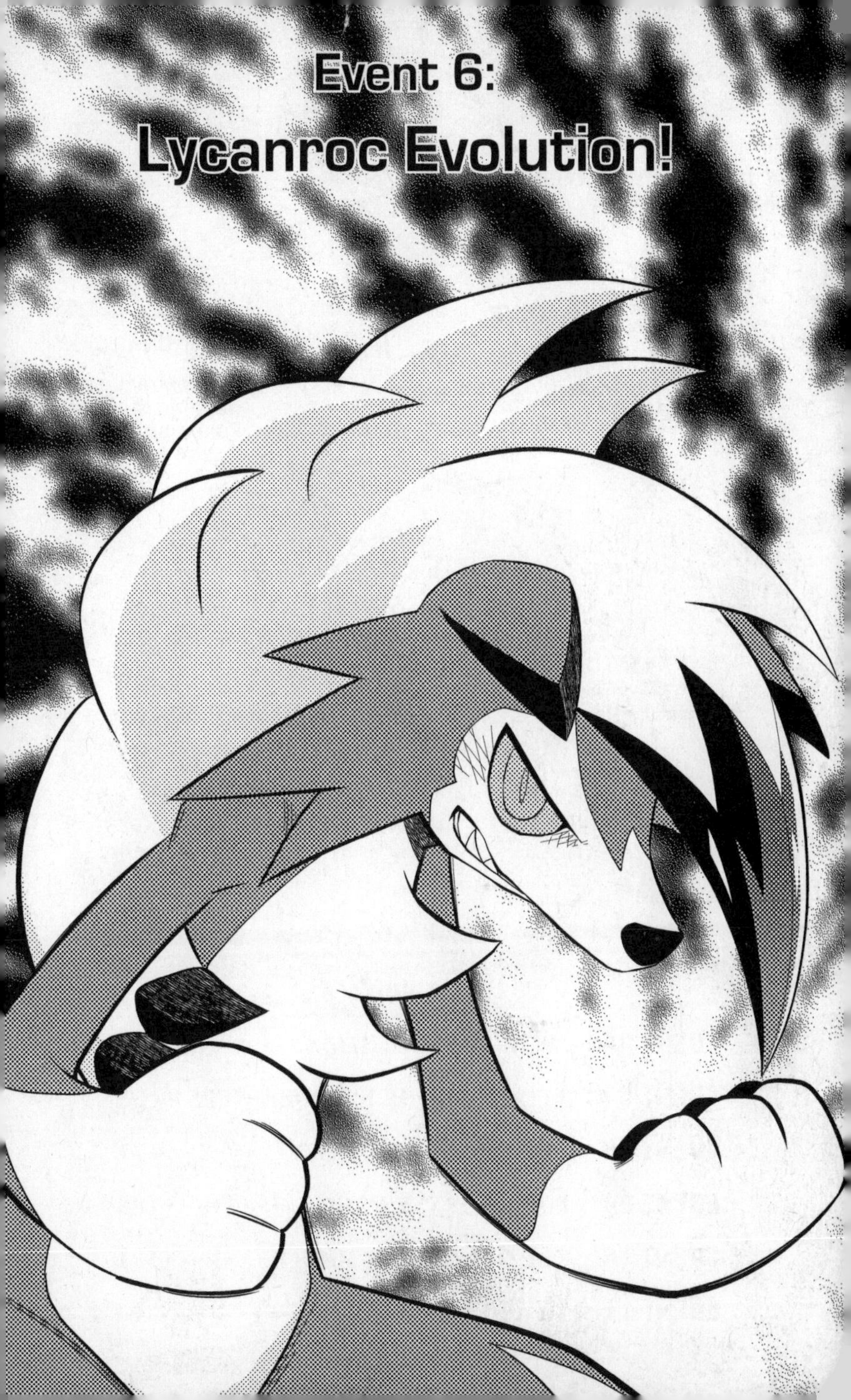

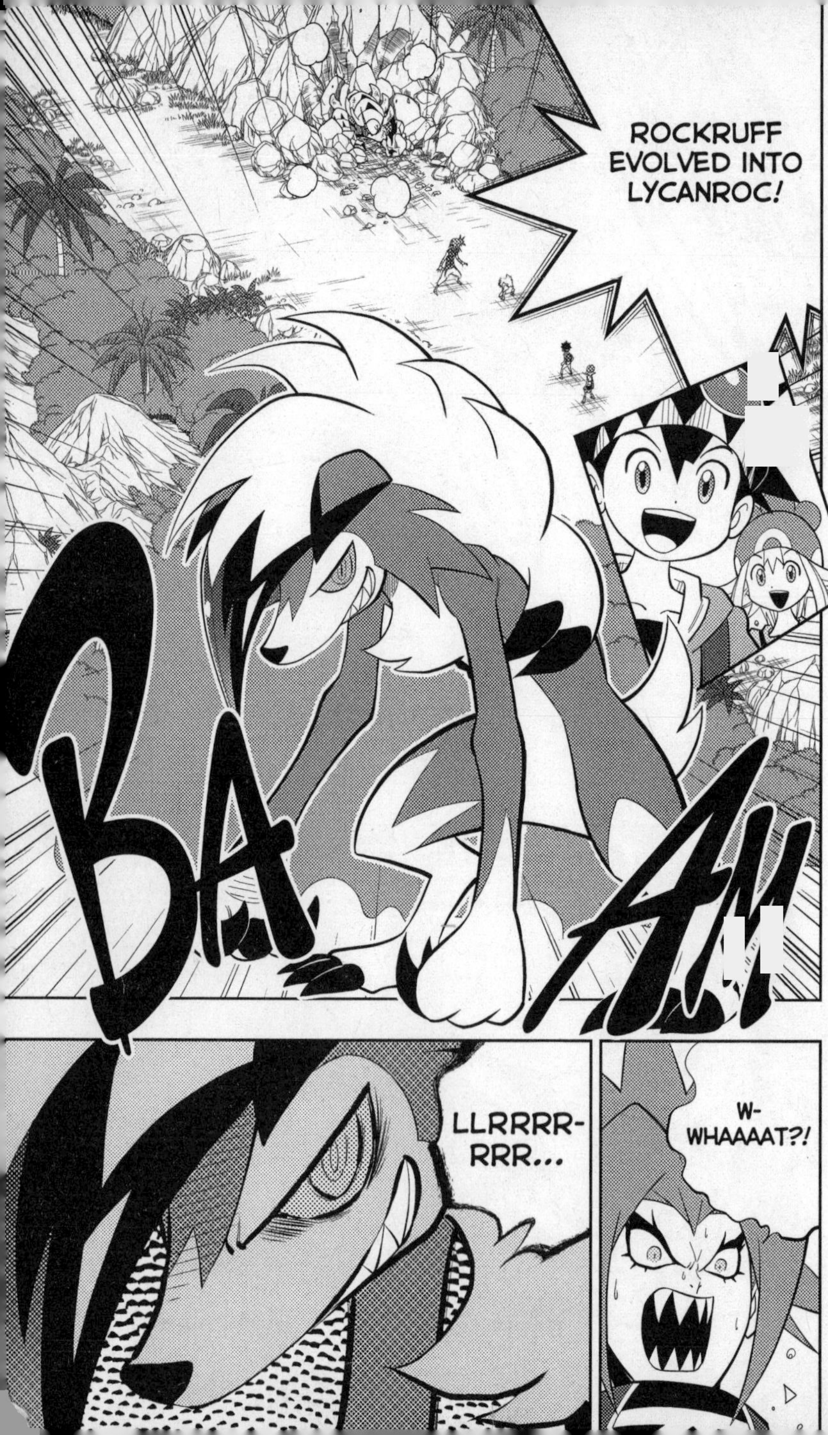
ROCKRUFF EVOLVED INTO LYCANROC!
BAAM
W-WHAAAAT?!
LLRRRR-RRR...

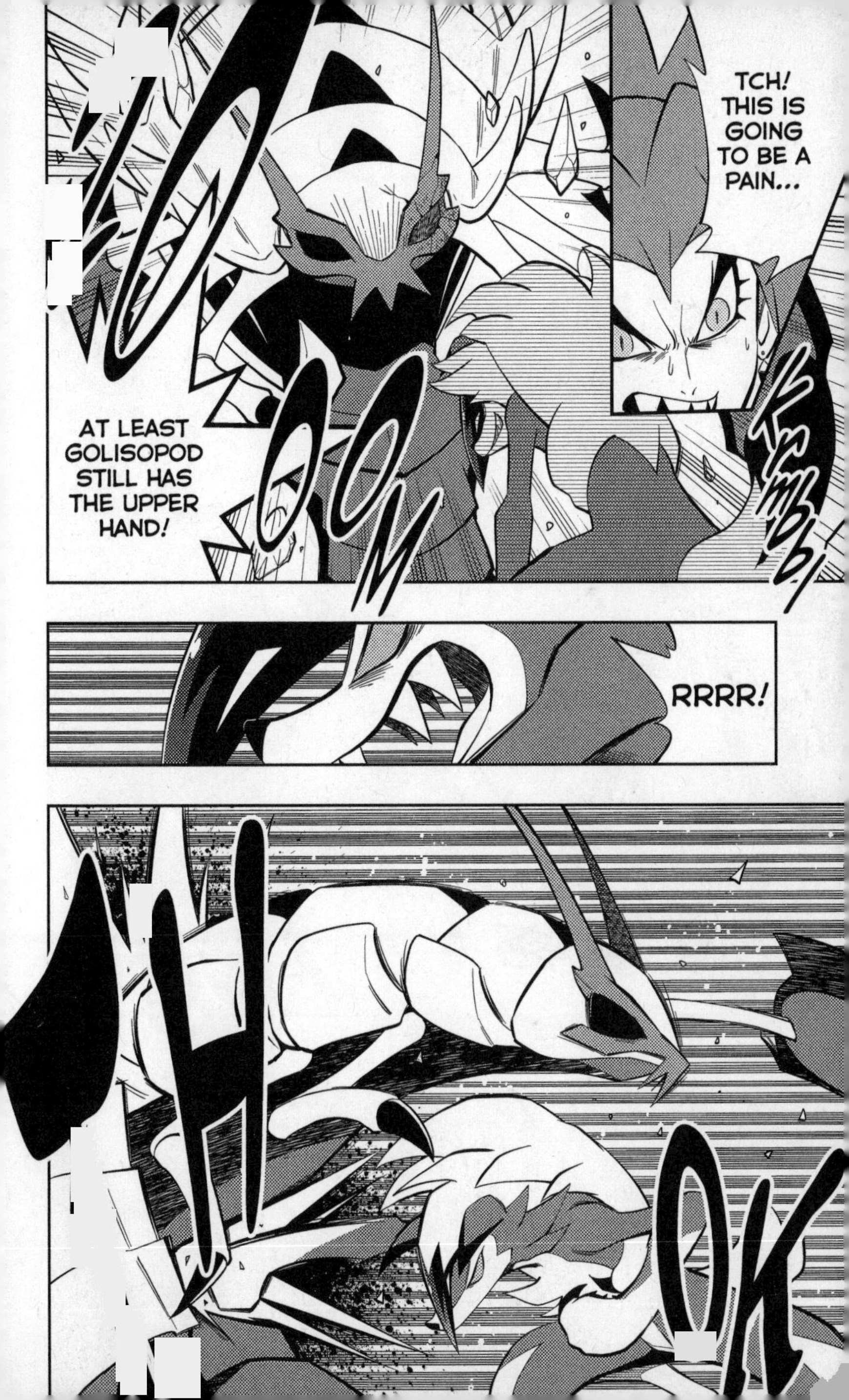
TCH! THIS IS GOING TO BE A PAIN...
AT LEAST GOLISOPOD STILL HAS THE UPPER HAND!
RRRR!

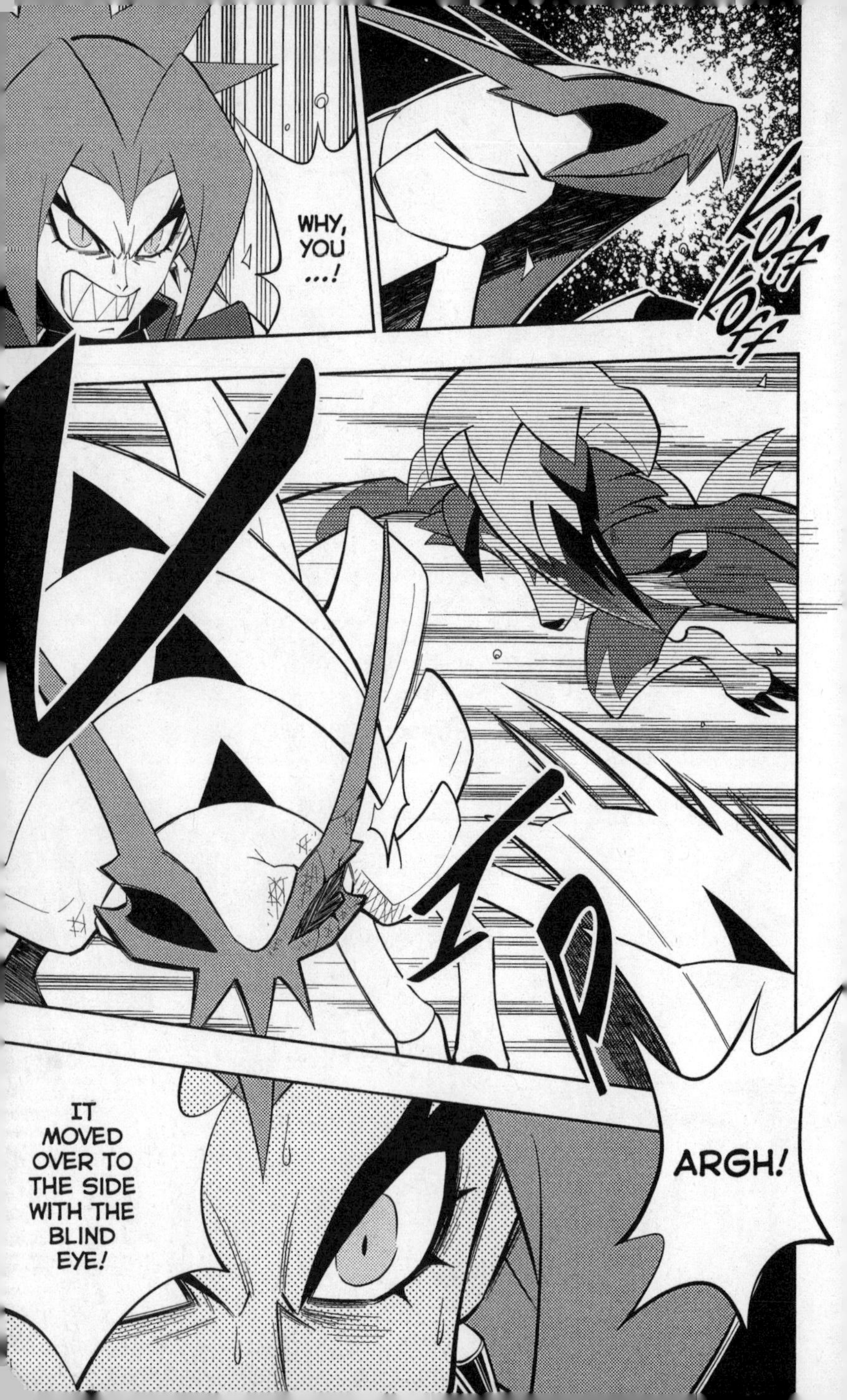
KOFF KOFF
WHY, YOU ...!
ARGH!
IT MOVED OVER TO THE SIDE WITH THE BLIND EYE!

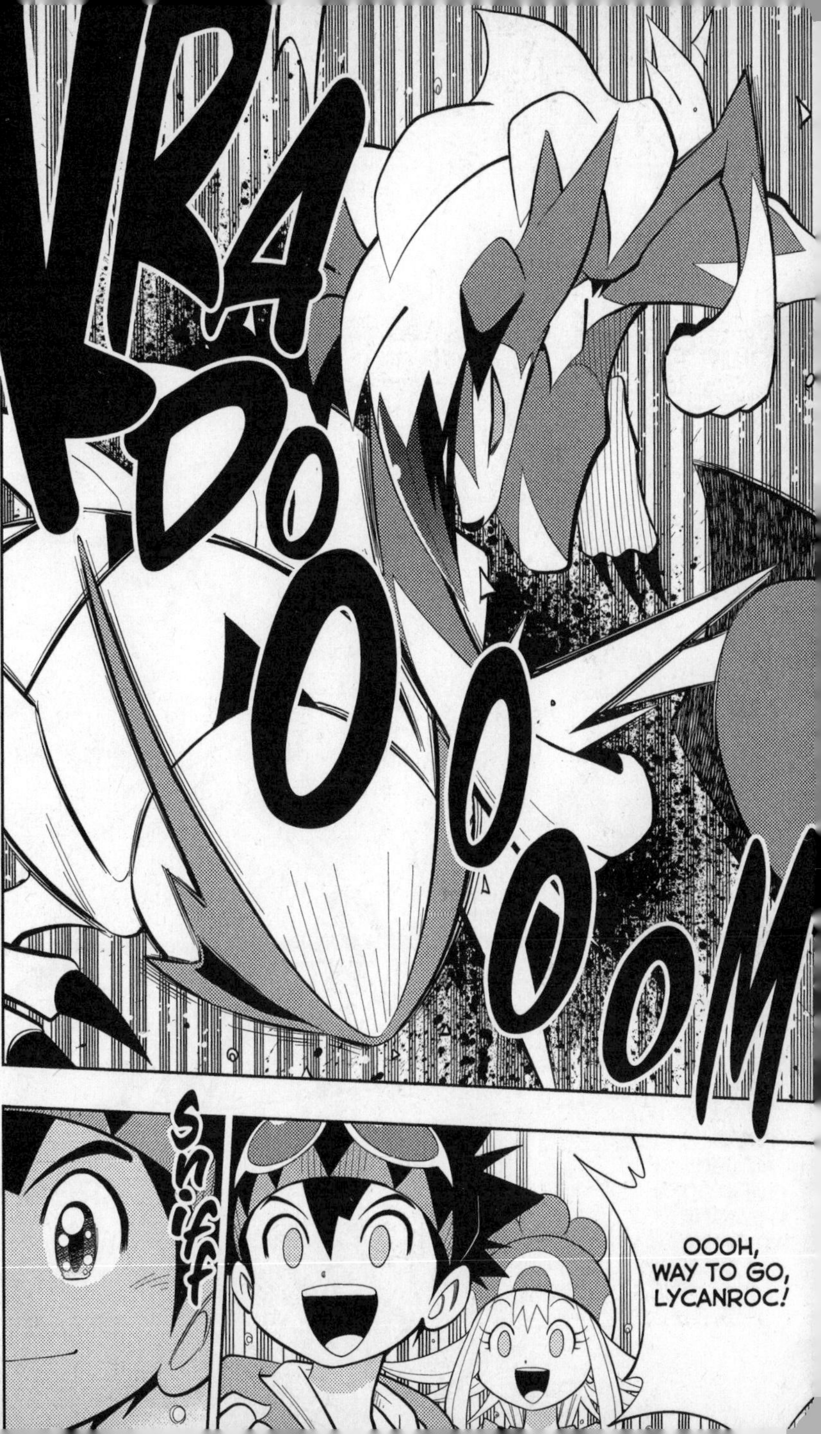
KADOOOOOOM
OOOH, WAY TO GO, LYCANROC!
Sniff

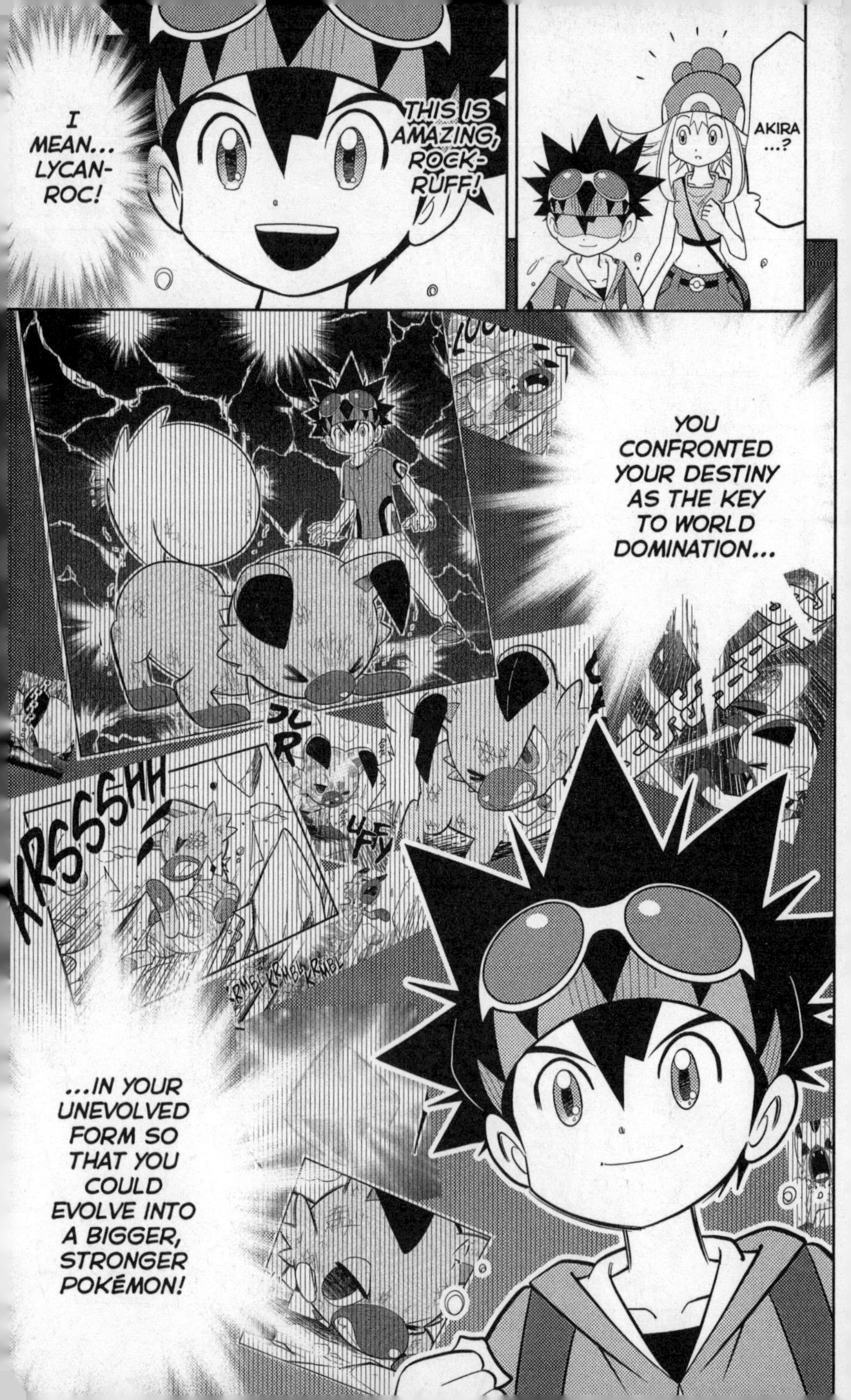
AKIRA ...?
THIS IS AMAZING, ROCK-RUFF!
I MEAN... LYCAN-ROC!
YOU CONFRONTED YOUR DESTINY AS THE KEY TO WORLD DOMINATION...
KRSSSHH
...IN YOUR UNEVOLVED FORM SO THAT YOU COULD EVOLVE INTO A BIGGER, STRONGER POKÉMON!

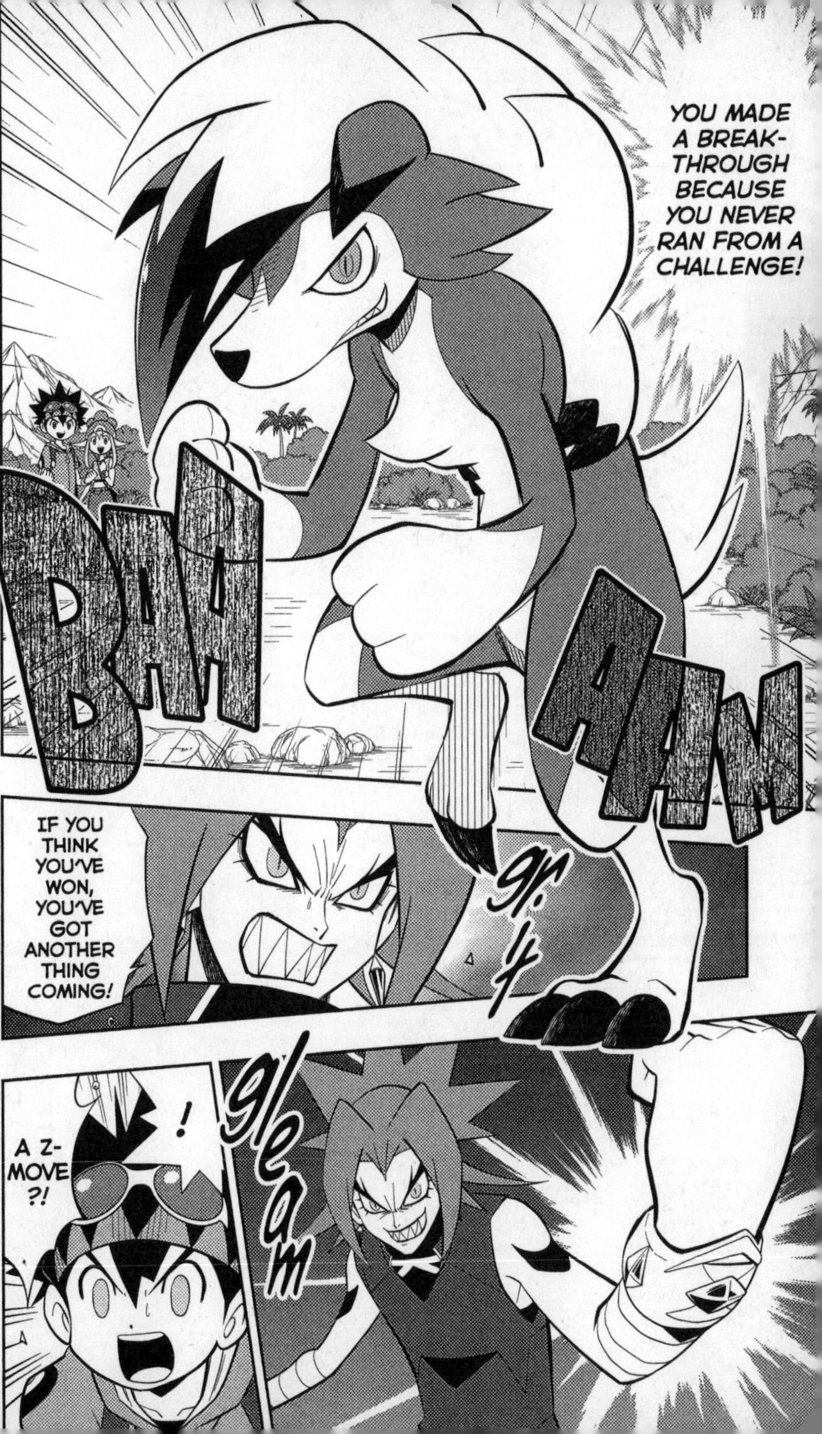
YOU MADE A BREAK-THROUGH BECAUSE YOU NEVER RAN FROM A CHALLENGE!
BAAAAM
gr: it
IF YOU THINK YOU'VE WON, YOU'VE GOT ANOTHER THING COMING!
gleam
!
A Z-MOVE?!

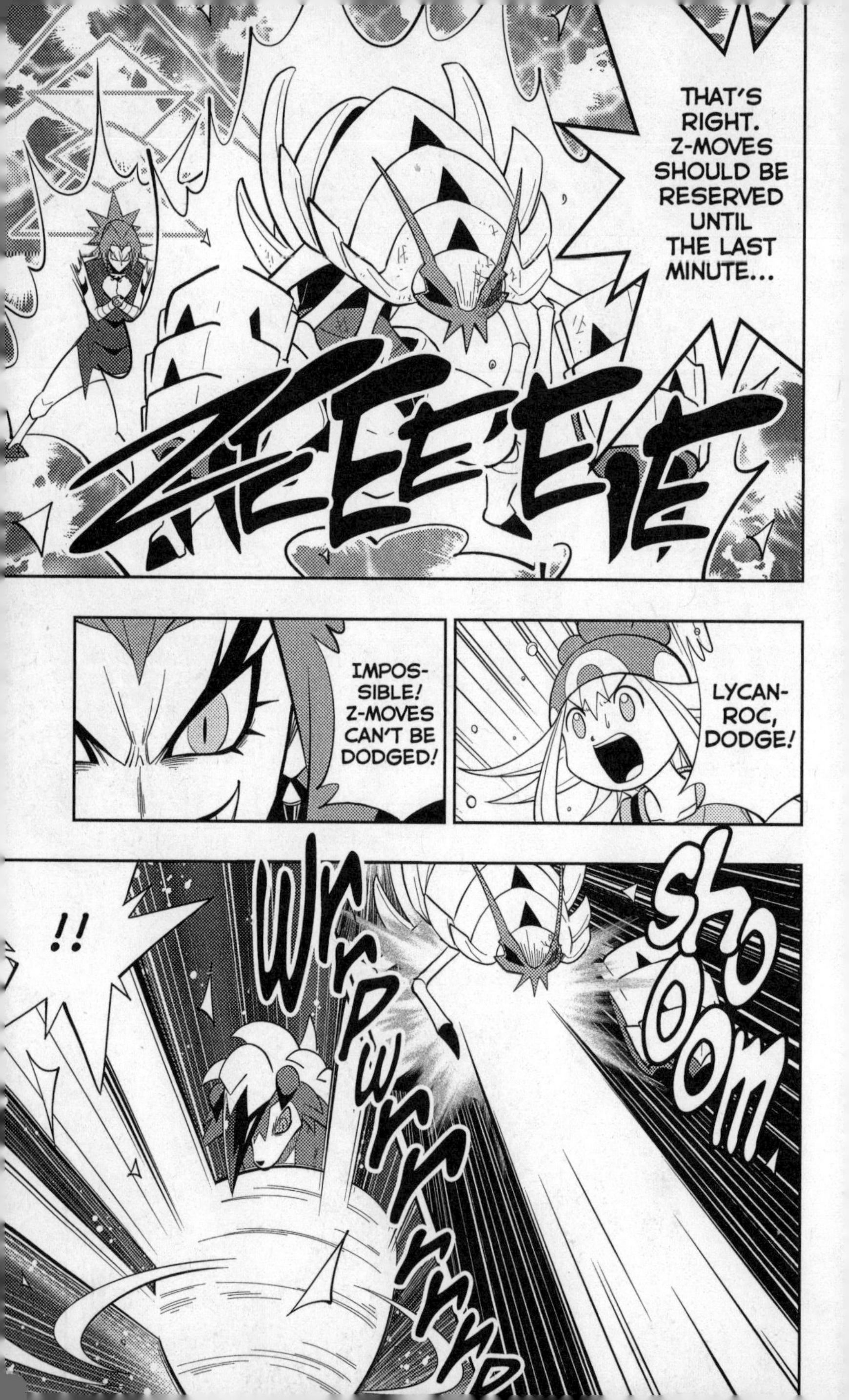
THAT'S RIGHT. Z-MOVES SHOULD BE RESERVED UNTIL THE LAST MINUTE...
LYCAN-ROC, DODGE!
IMPOS-SIBLE! Z-MOVES CAN'T BE DODGED!
SHOOOM
!!

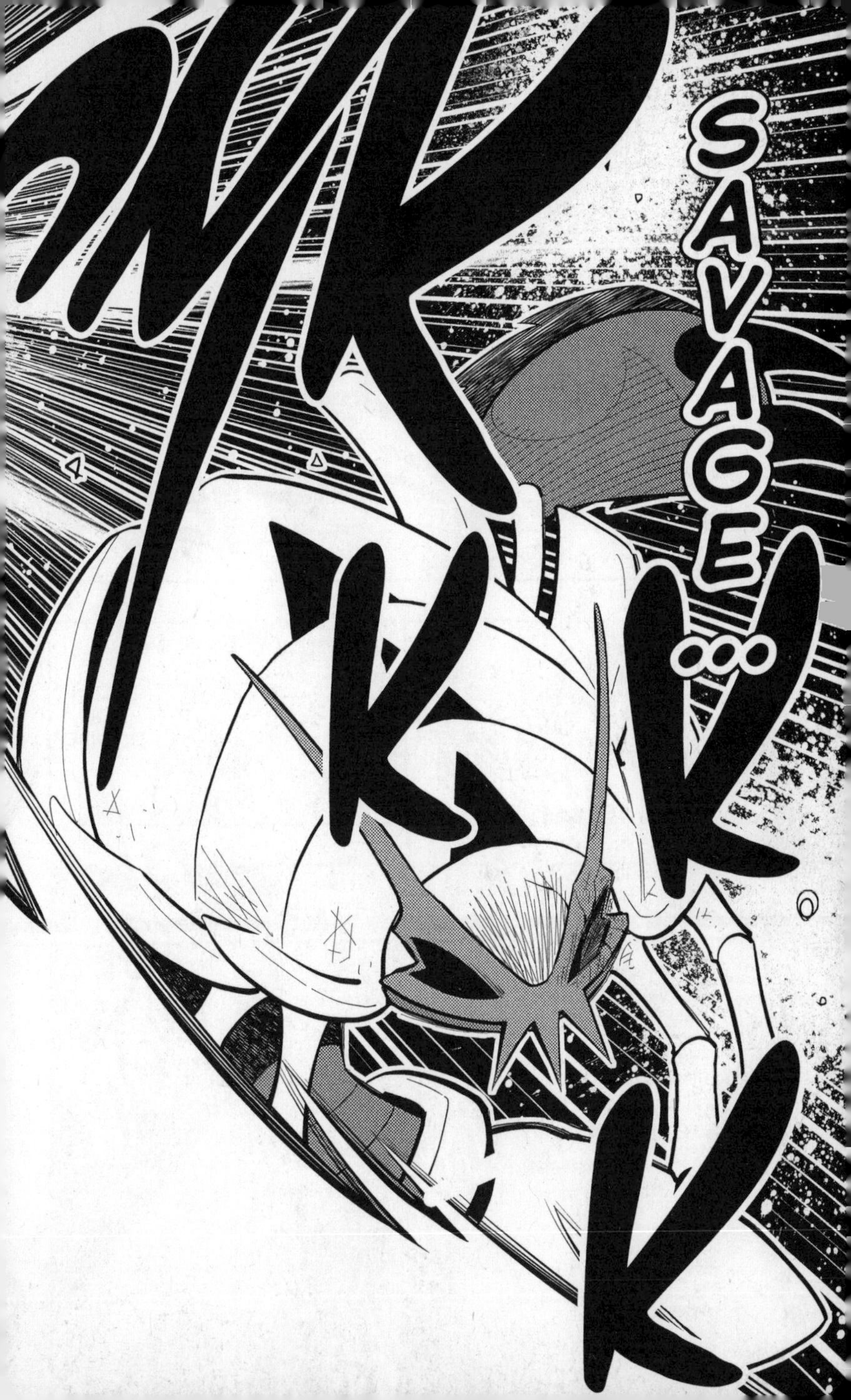
SAVAGE...

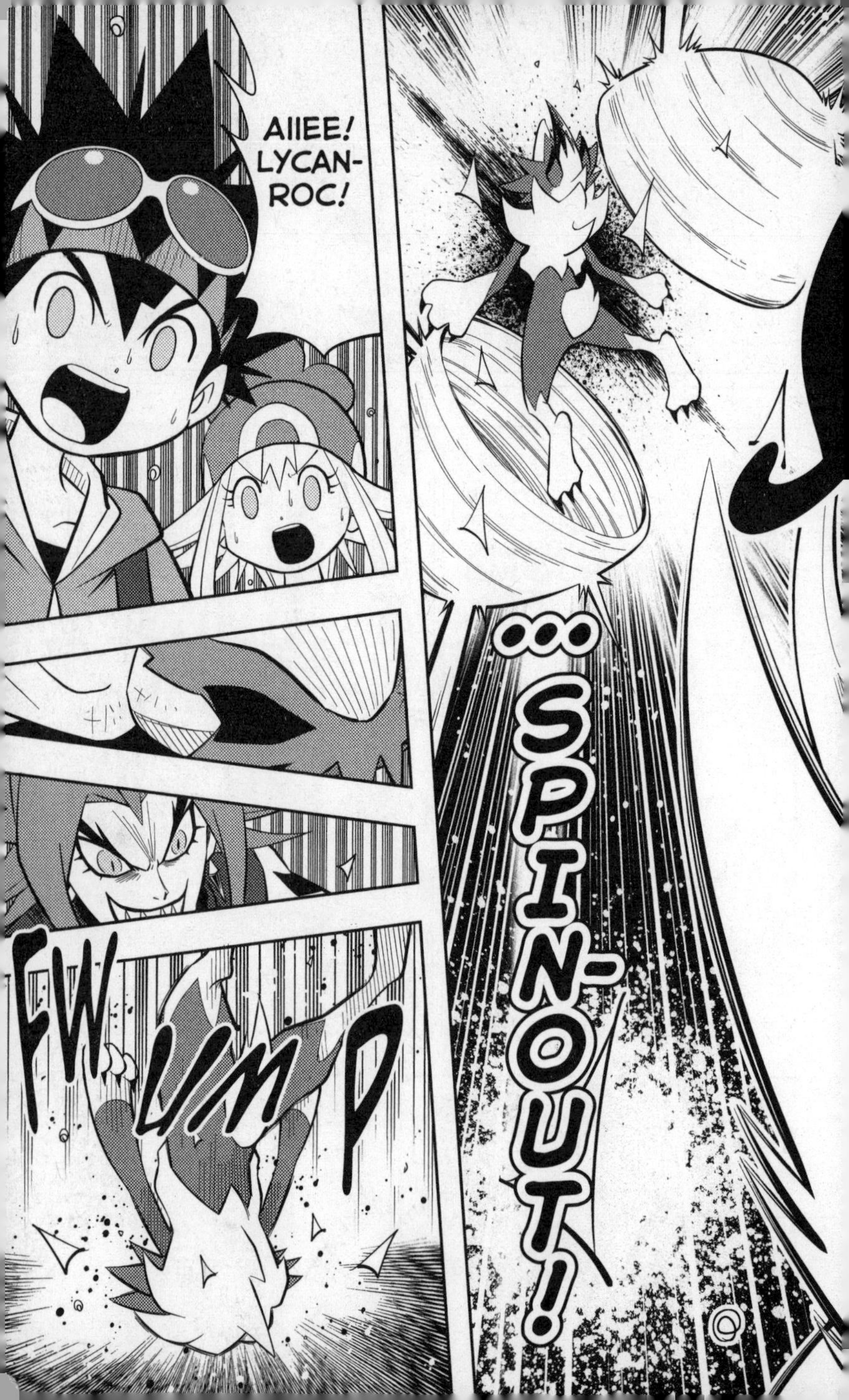
...SPIN-OUT!
AIIEE! LYCAN-ROC!
FWUMP

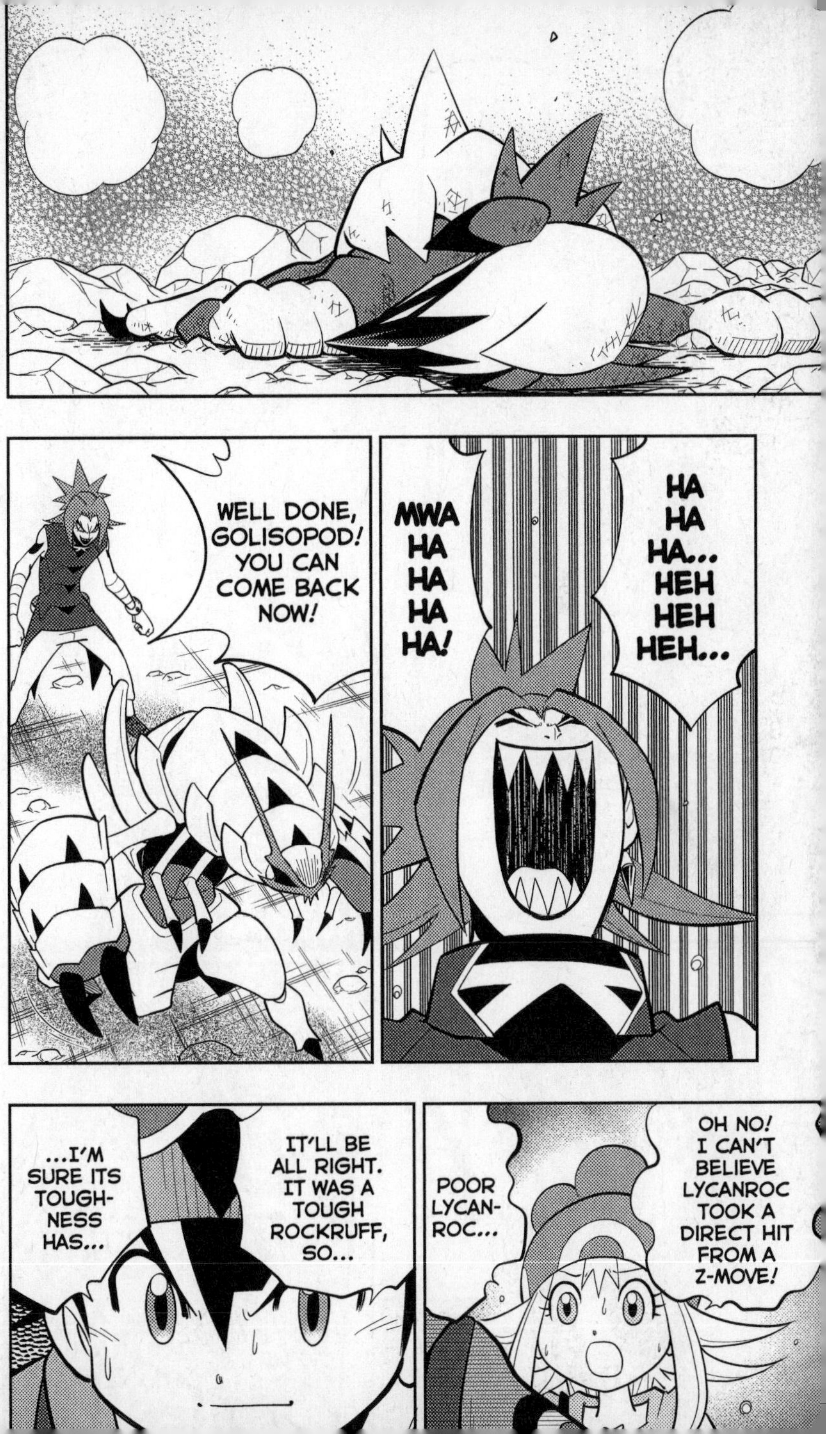
HA HA HA... HEH HEH HEH...
MWA HA HA HA HA!
WELL DONE, GOLISOPOD! YOU CAN COME BACK NOW!
OH NO! I CAN'T BELIEVE LYCANROC TOOK A DIRECT HIT FROM A Z-MOVE!
POOR LYCAN-ROC...
IT'LL BE ALL RIGHT. IT WAS A TOUGH ROCKRUFF, SO...
...I'M SURE ITS TOUGH-NESS HAS...

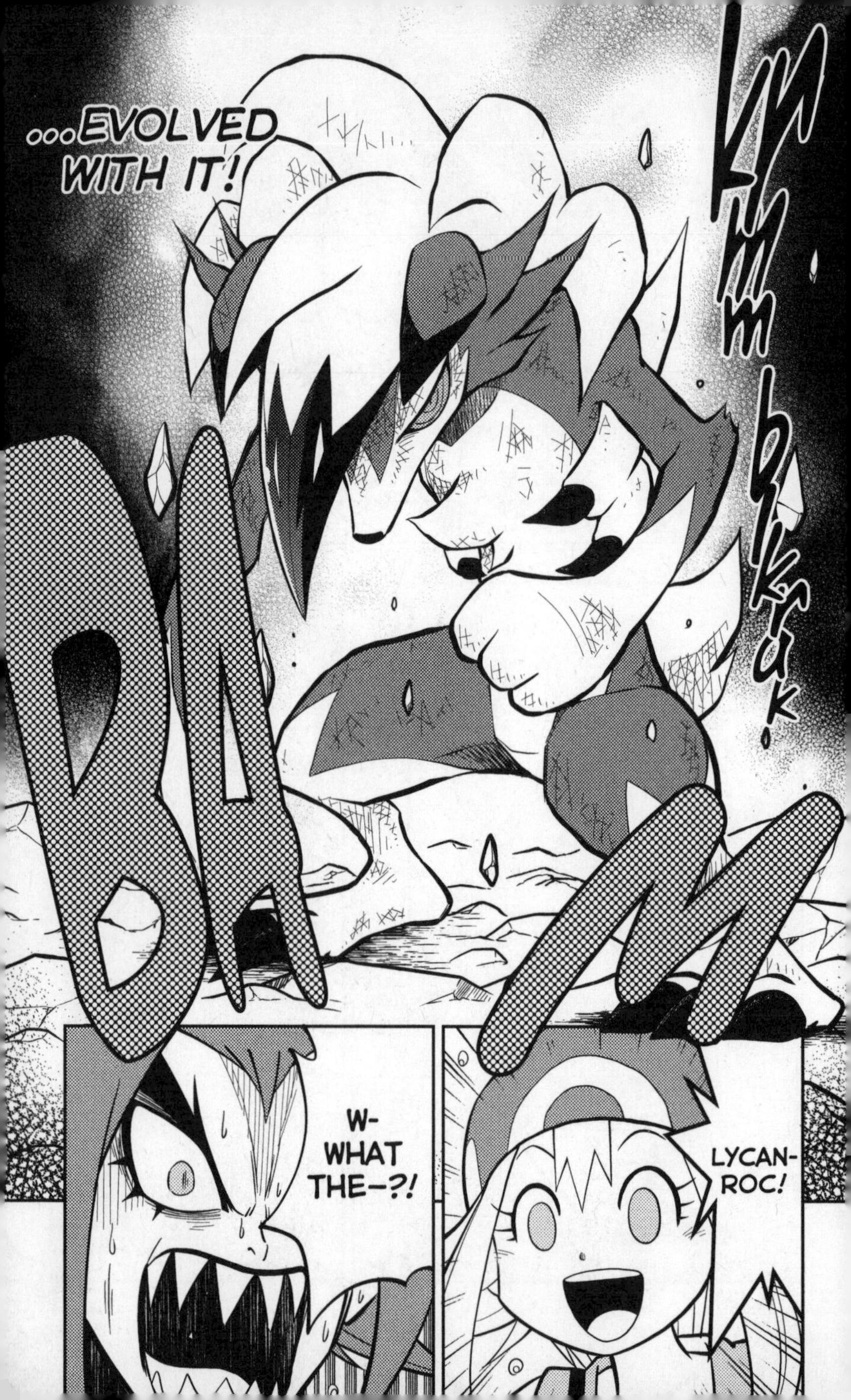
...EVOLVED WITH IT!
BAM
LYCAN-ROC!
W-WHAT THE-?!

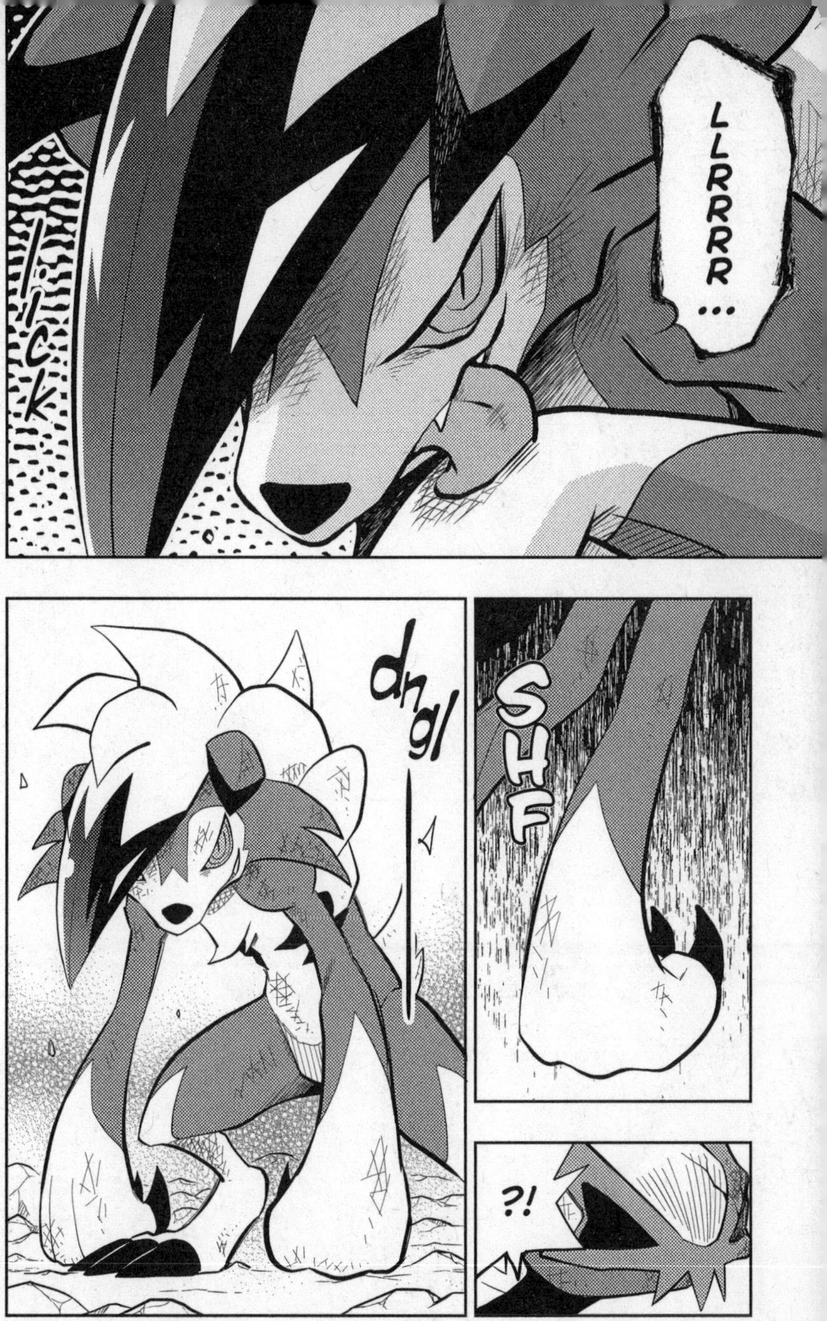
LLRRRR...
lick
SHF
?!
dngl

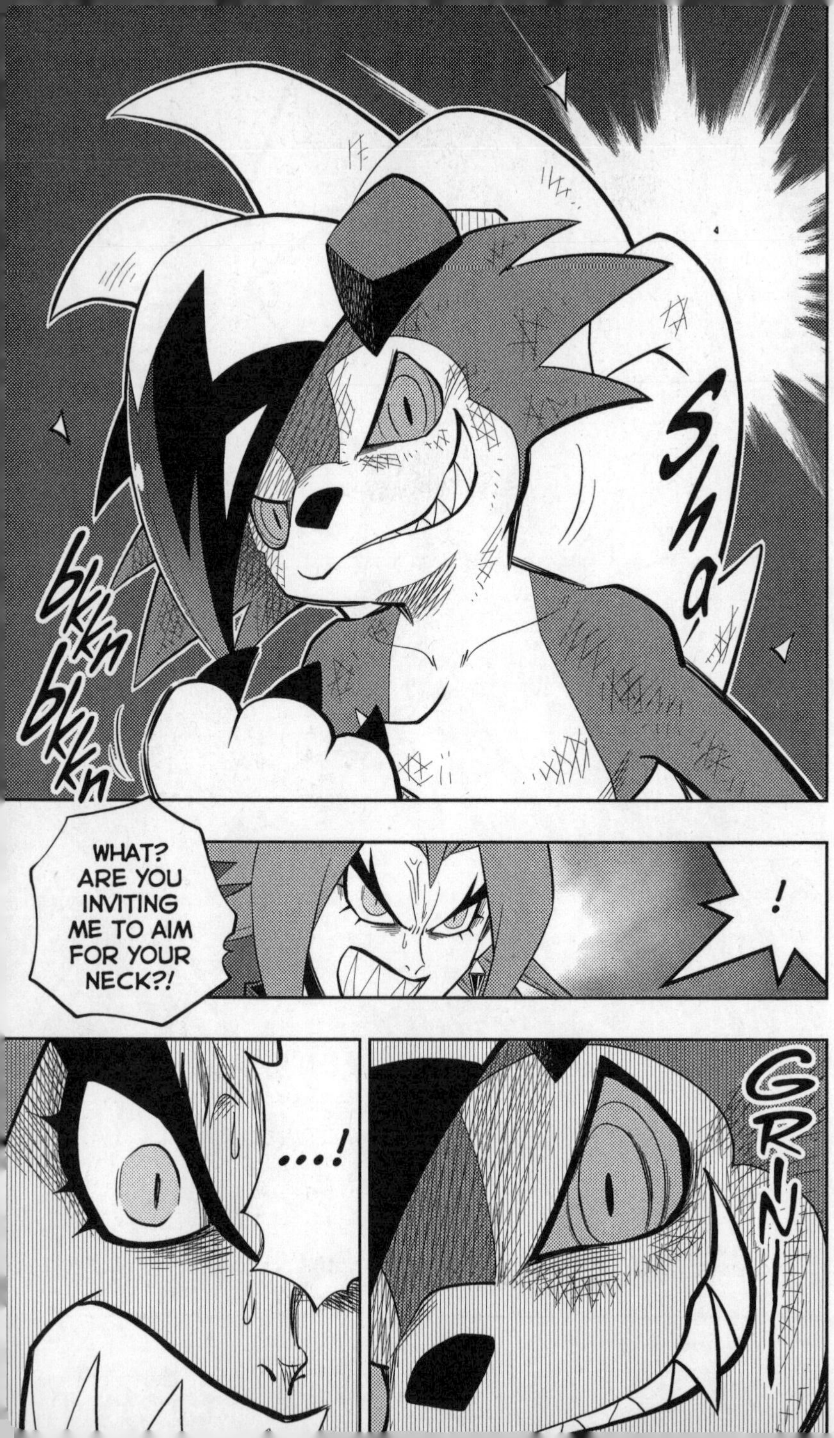
Sha
bkkn bkkn
!
WHAT? ARE YOU INVITING ME TO AIM FOR YOUR NECK?!
GRIN
...!

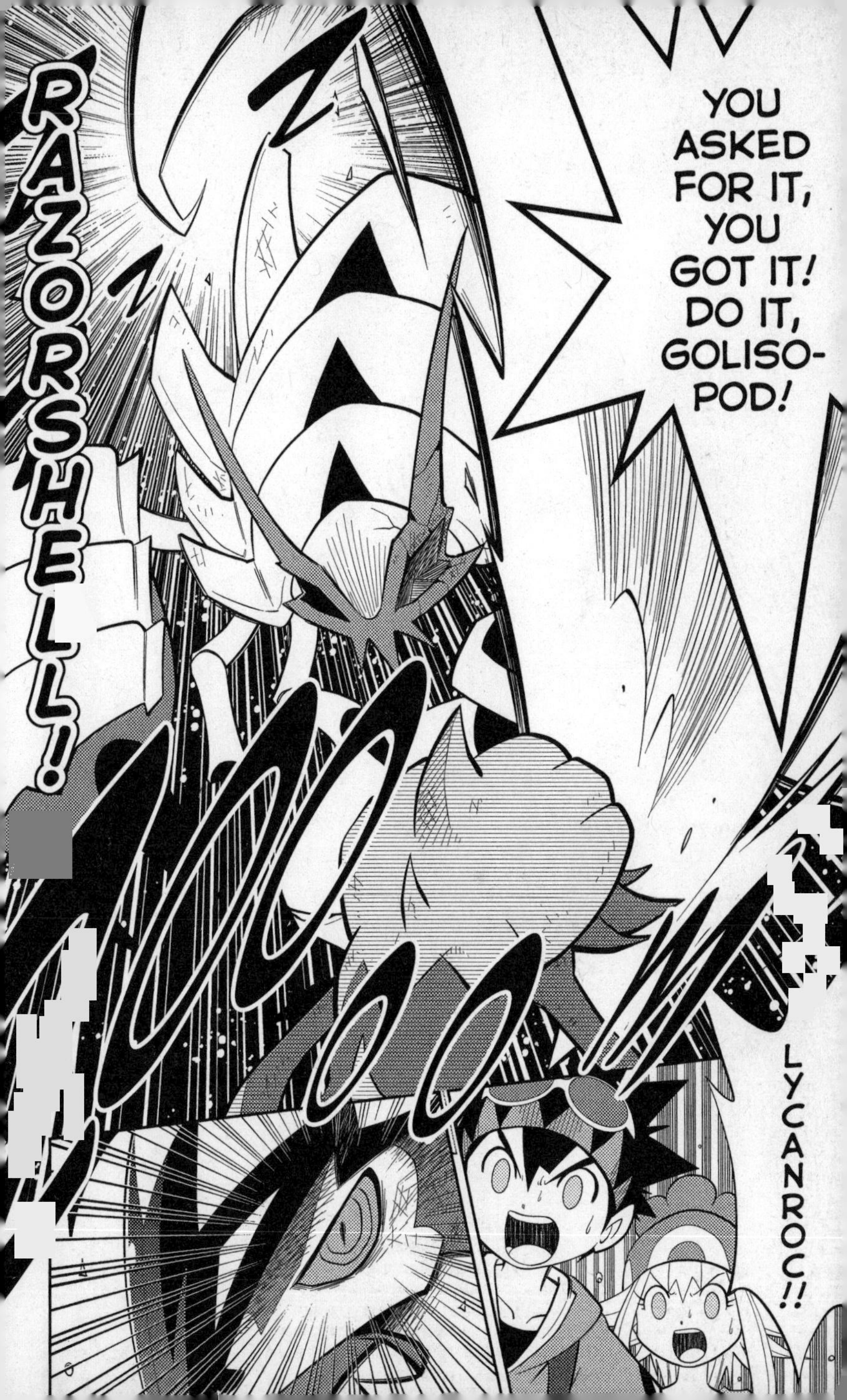
YOU ASKED FOR IT, YOU GOT IT! DO IT, GOLISO-POD!
RAZOR SHELL!
LYCANROC!!

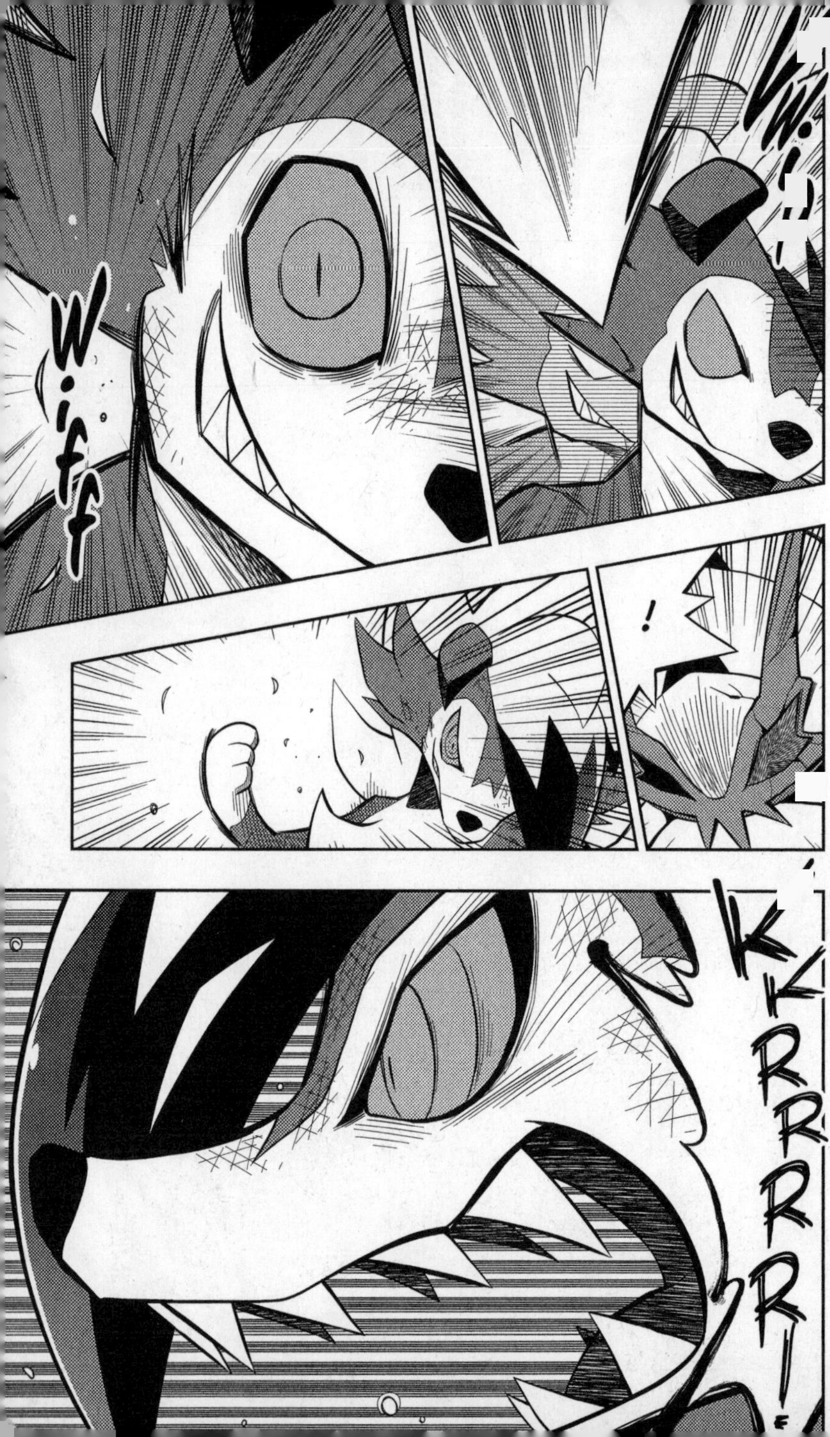
Wi!!
Wiff
!
KKRRRRR!

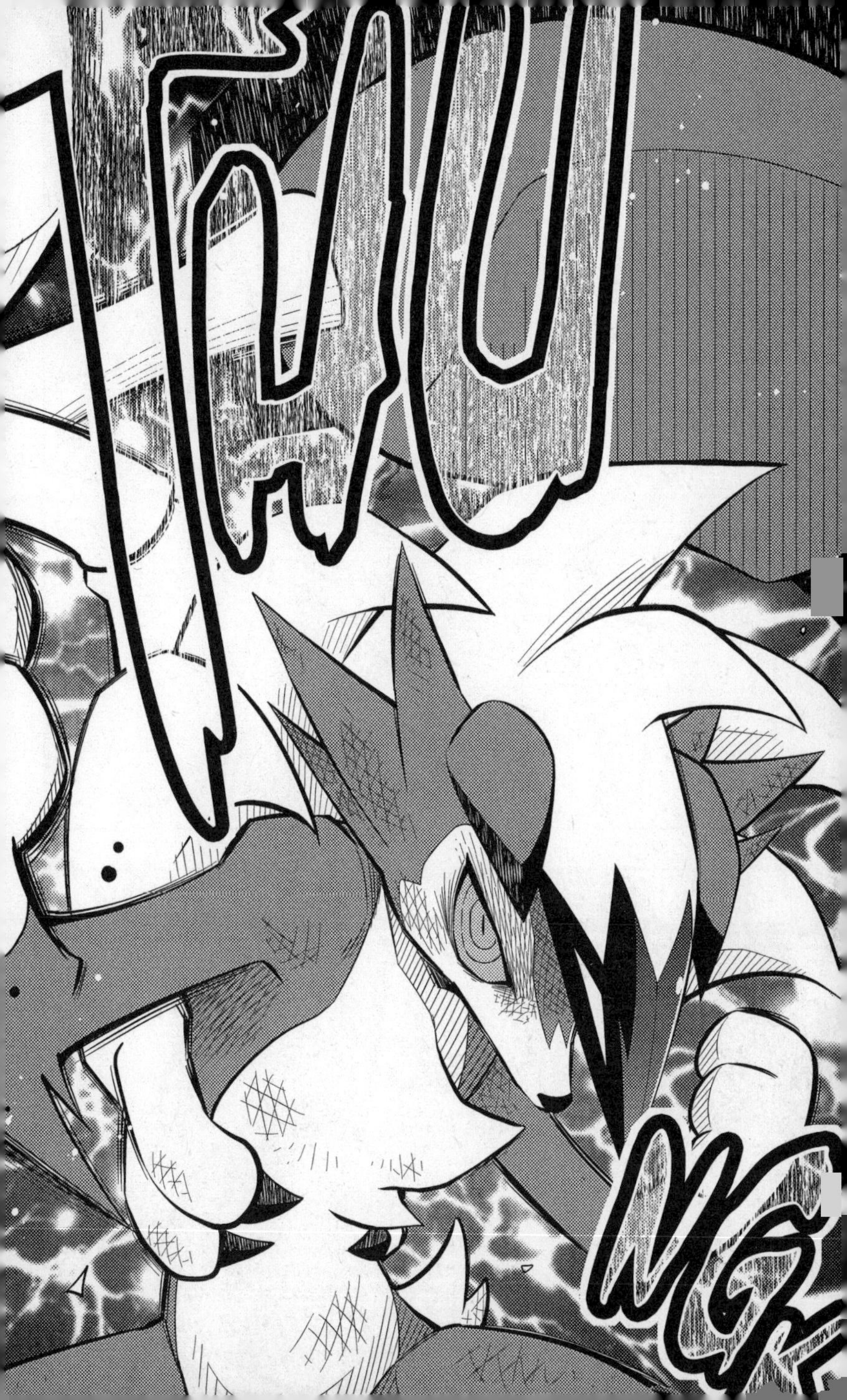

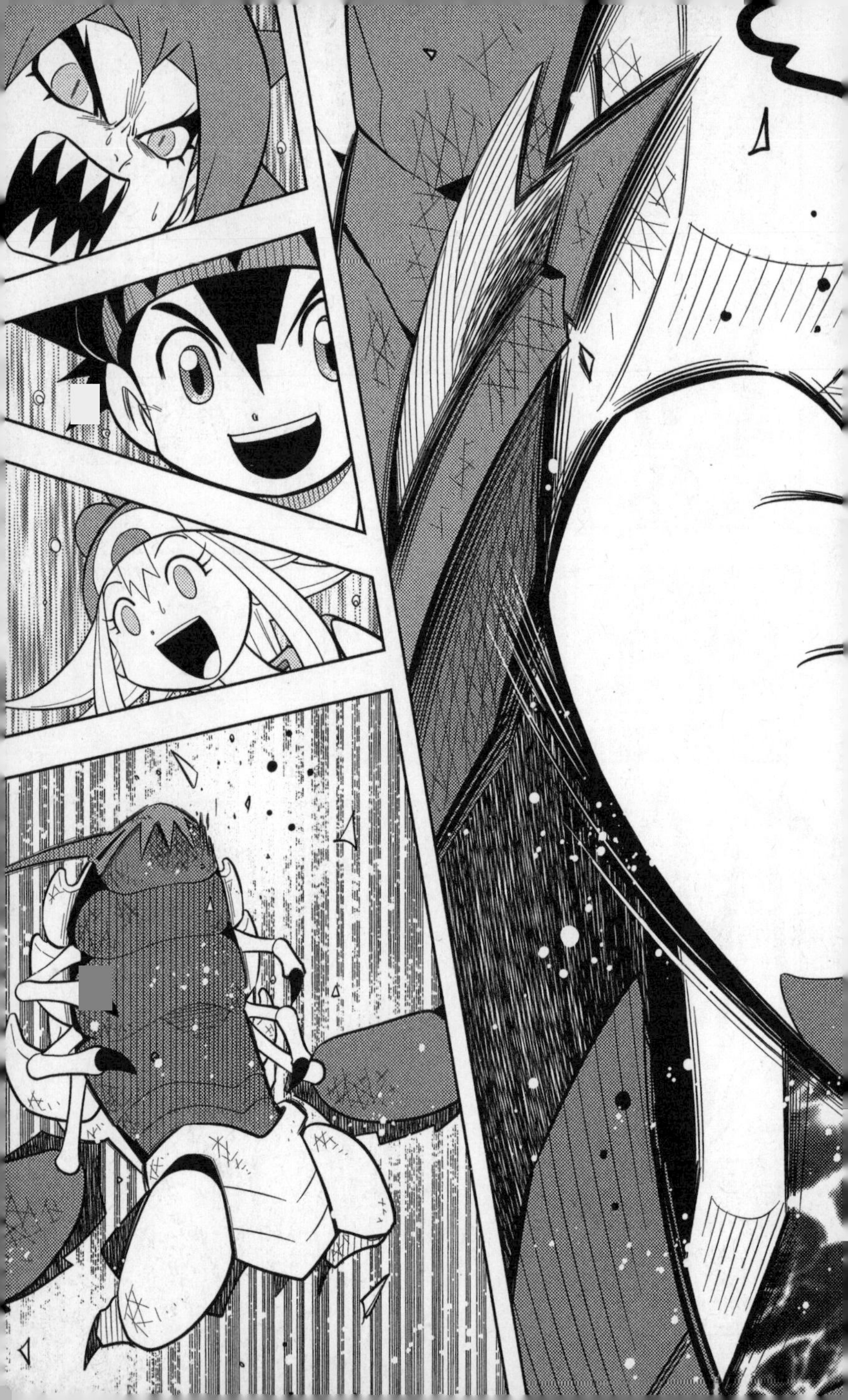

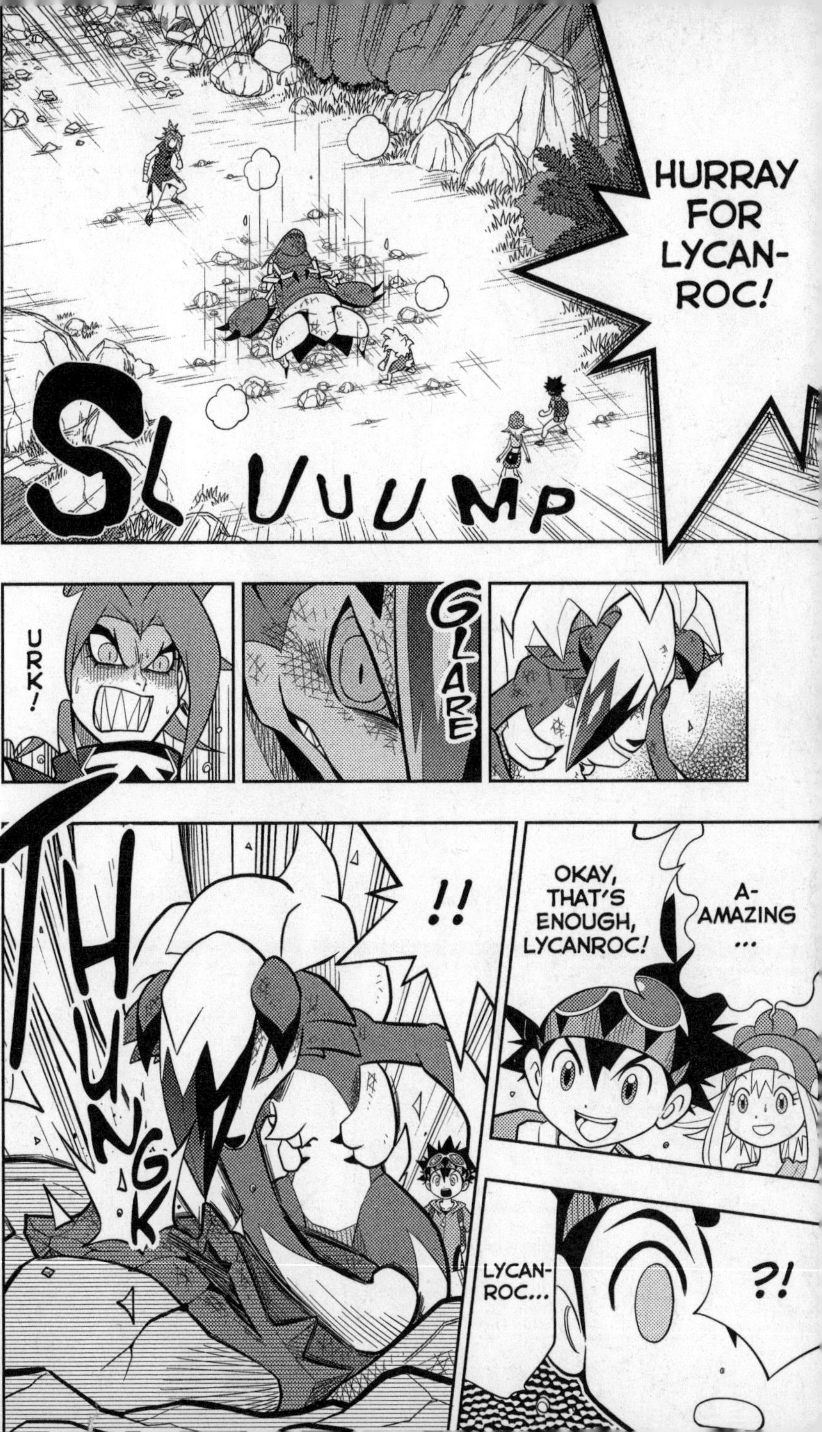
HURRAY FOR LYCAN-ROC!
SLUUUMP
GLARE
URK!
A-AMAZING...
OKAY, THAT'S ENOUGH, LYCANROC!
?!
LYCAN-ROC...
!!
THUNGK

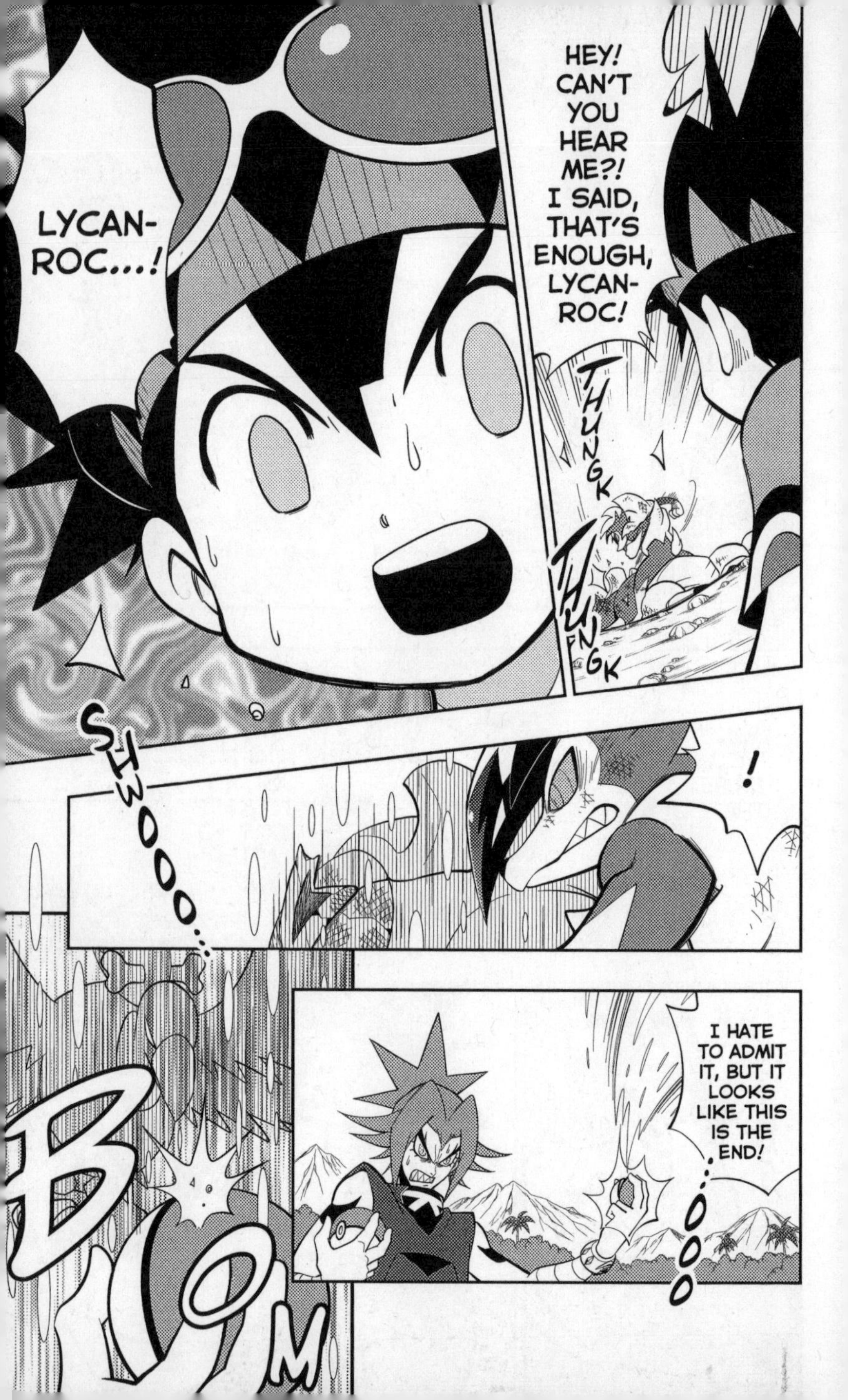
HEY! CAN'T YOU HEAR ME?! I SAID, THAT'S ENOUGH, LYCANROC!
THUNGK
THUNGK
LYCAN-ROC...!
SHWOOO...
!
I HATE TO ADMIT IT, BUT IT LOOKS LIKE THIS IS THE END!
...OOOO
BOOM

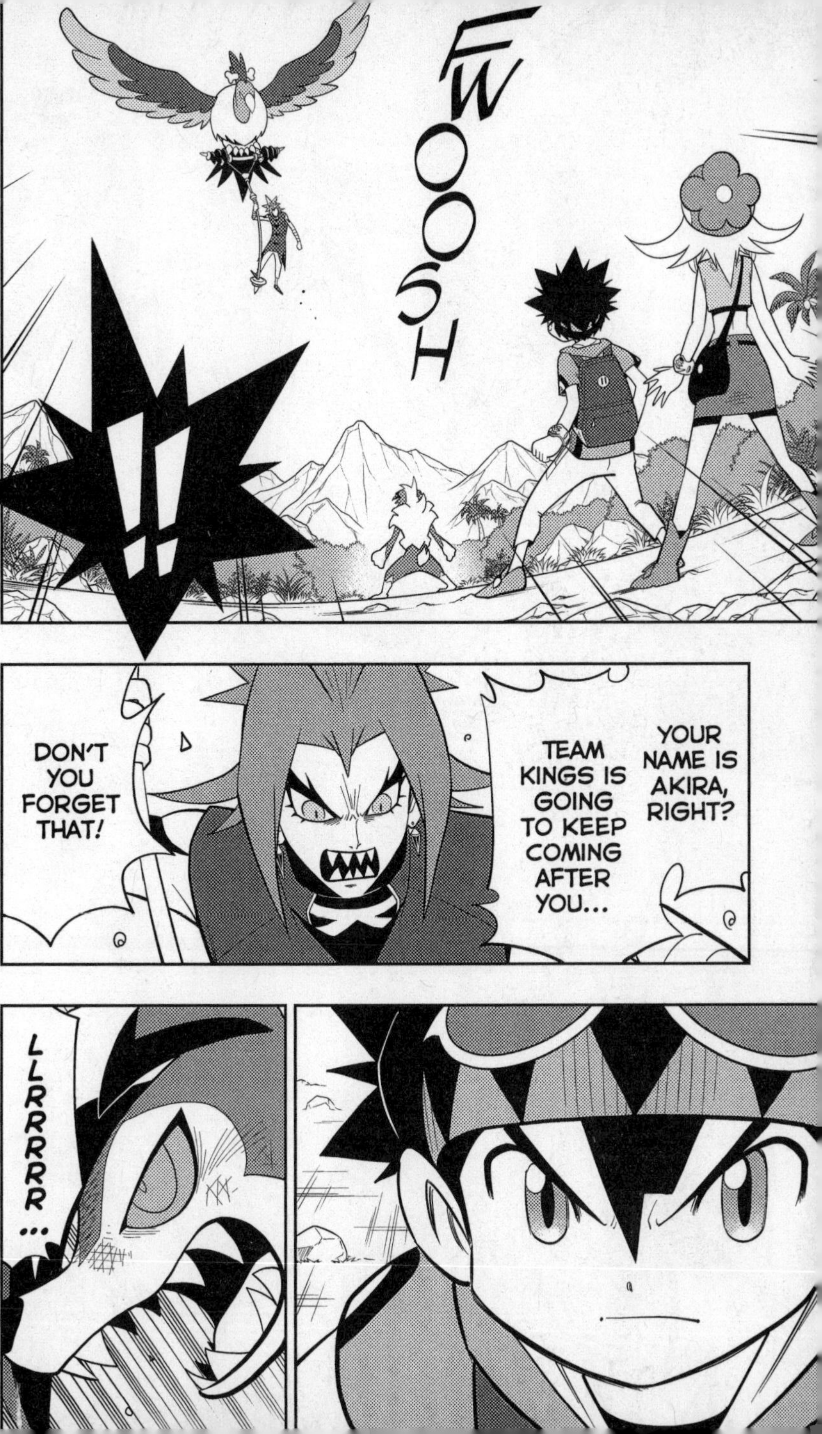
FWOOSH
!!
YOUR NAME IS AKIRA, RIGHT?
TEAM KINGS IS GOING TO KEEP COMING AFTER YOU...
DON'T YOU FORGET THAT!
LLRRRRR...

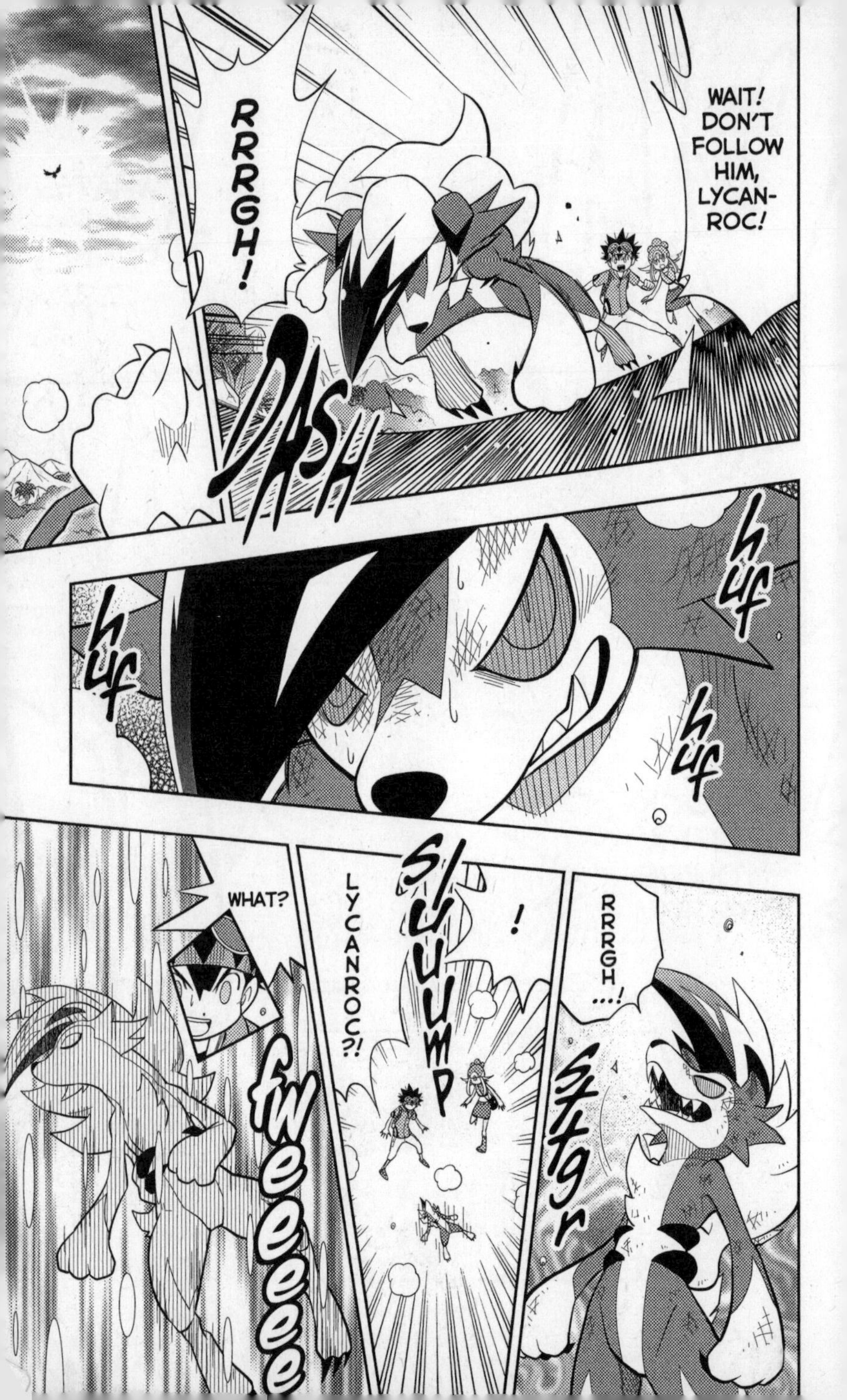
WAIT! DON'T FOLLOW HIM, LYCANROC!
RRRGH!
DASH
huf
huf
huf
RRRGH...!
stgr
!
SLUUUMP
LYCANROC?!
WHAT?
fweeeee

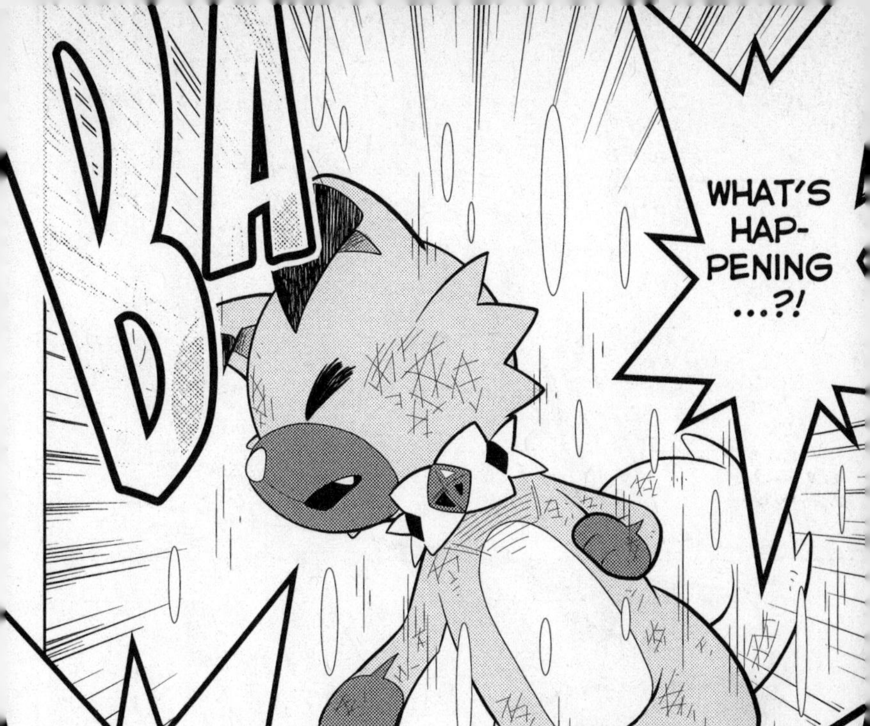
BAM
WHAT'S HAP-PENING...?!
R-ROCK-RUFF?! YOU'RE BACK?!

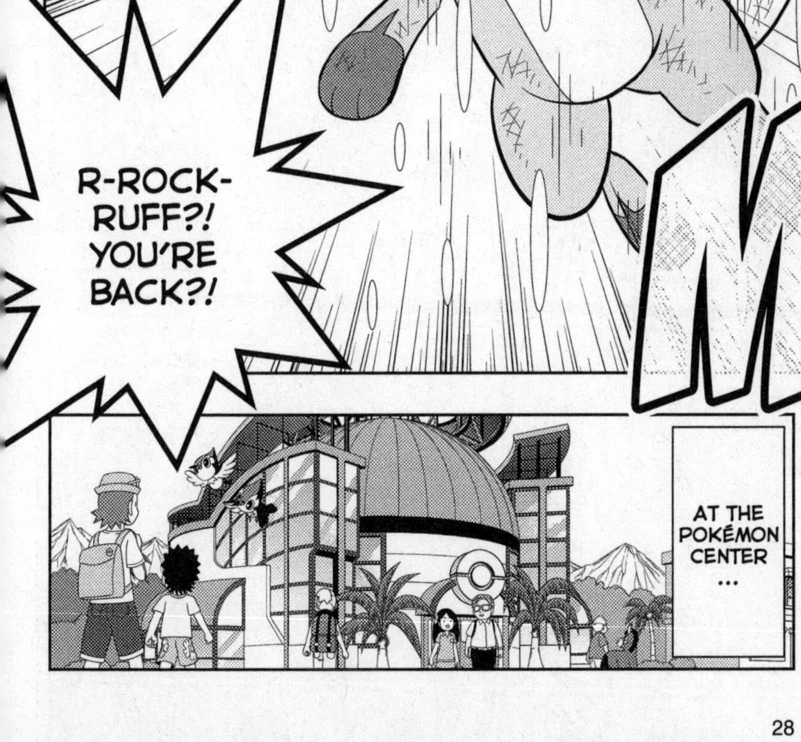
AT THE POKÉMON CENTER ...

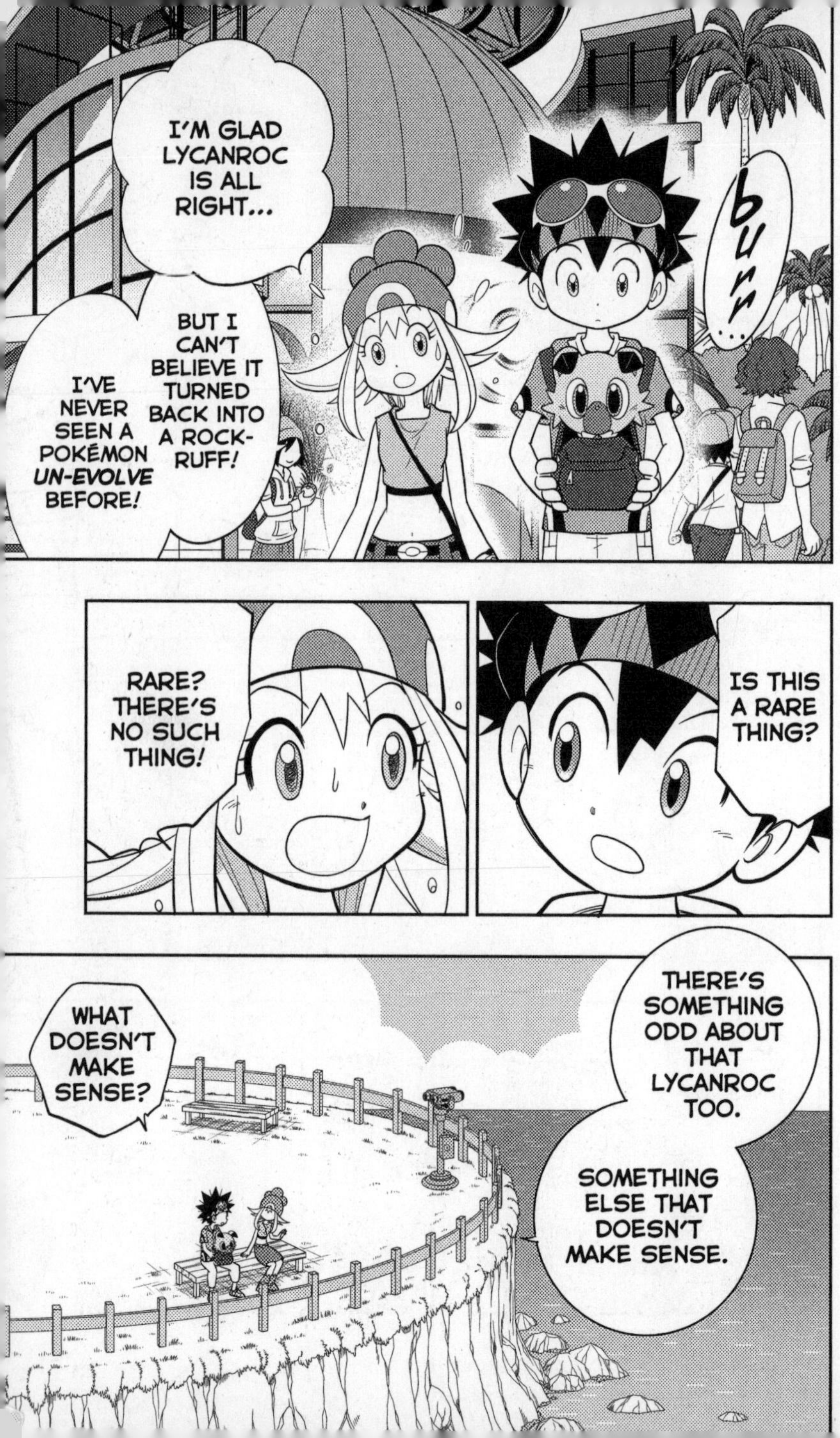
burr...
I'M GLAD LYCANROC IS ALL RIGHT...
BUT I CAN'T BELIEVE IT TURNED BACK INTO A ROCK-RUFF!
I'VE NEVER SEEN A POKÉMON *UN-EVOLVE* BEFORE!
IS THIS A RARE THING?
RARE? THERE'S NO SUCH THING!
THERE'S SOMETHING ODD ABOUT THAT LYCANROC TOO.
SOMETHING ELSE THAT DOESN'T MAKE SENSE.
WHAT DOESN'T MAKE SENSE?

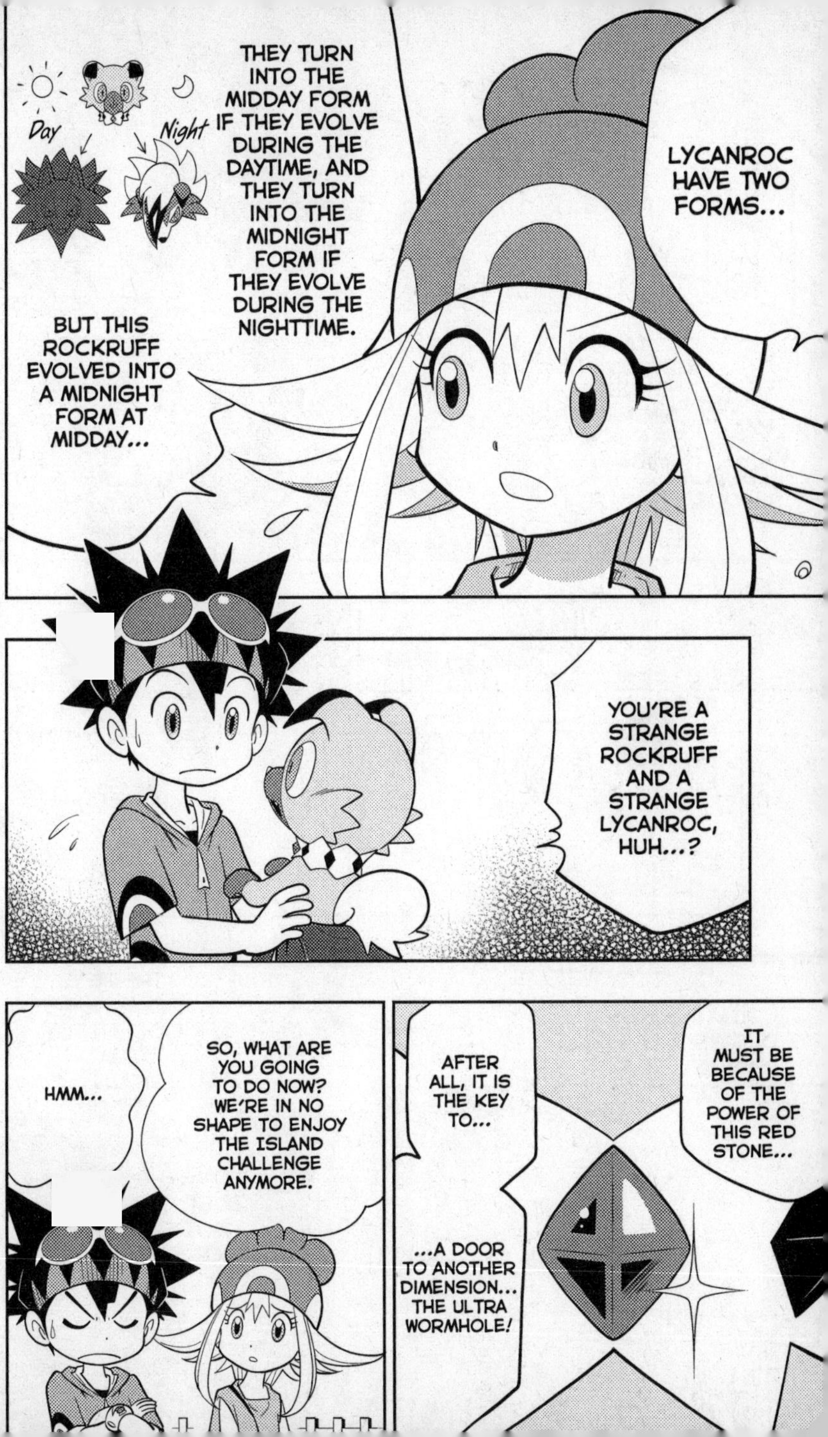
LYCANROC HAVE TWO FORMS...
THEY TURN INTO THE MIDDAY FORM IF THEY EVOLVE DURING THE DAYTIME, AND THEY TURN INTO THE MIDNIGHT FORM IF THEY EVOLVE DURING THE NIGHTTIME.
Day
Night
BUT THIS ROCKRUFF EVOLVED INTO A MIDNIGHT FORM AT MIDDAY...
YOU'RE A STRANGE ROCKRUFF AND A STRANGE LYCANROC, HUH...?
IT MUST BE BECAUSE OF THE POWER OF THIS RED STONE...
AFTER ALL, IT IS THE KEY TO...
...A DOOR TO ANOTHER DIMENSION... THE ULTRA WORMHOLE!
SO, WHAT ARE YOU GOING TO DO NOW? WE'RE IN NO SHAPE TO ENJOY THE ISLAND CHALLENGE ANYMORE.
HMM...

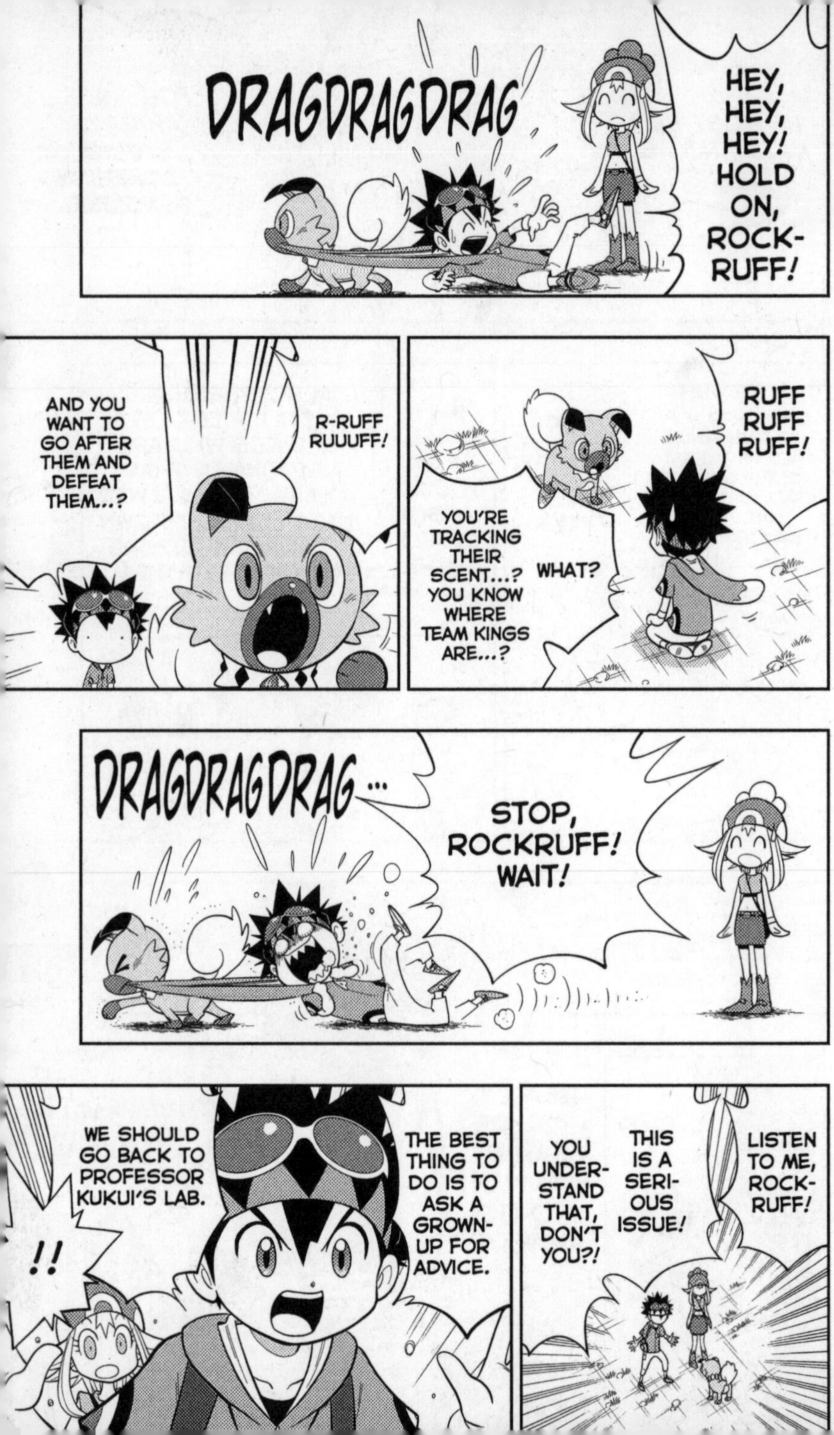
HEY, HEY, HEY! HOLD ON, ROCK-RUFF!
DRAGDRAGDRAG
RUFF RUFF RUFF!
WHAT?
YOU'RE TRACKING THEIR SCENT...? YOU KNOW WHERE TEAM KINGS ARE...?
R-RUFF RUUUFF!
AND YOU WANT TO GO AFTER THEM AND DEFEAT THEM...?
STOP, ROCKRUFF! WAIT!
DRAGDRAGDRAG...
LISTEN TO ME, ROCK-RUFF!
THIS IS A SERI-OUS ISSUE!
YOU UNDER-STAND THAT, DON'T YOU?!
THE BEST THING TO DO IS TO ASK A GROWN-UP FOR ADVICE.
WE SHOULD GO BACK TO PROFESSOR KUKUI'S LAB.
!!

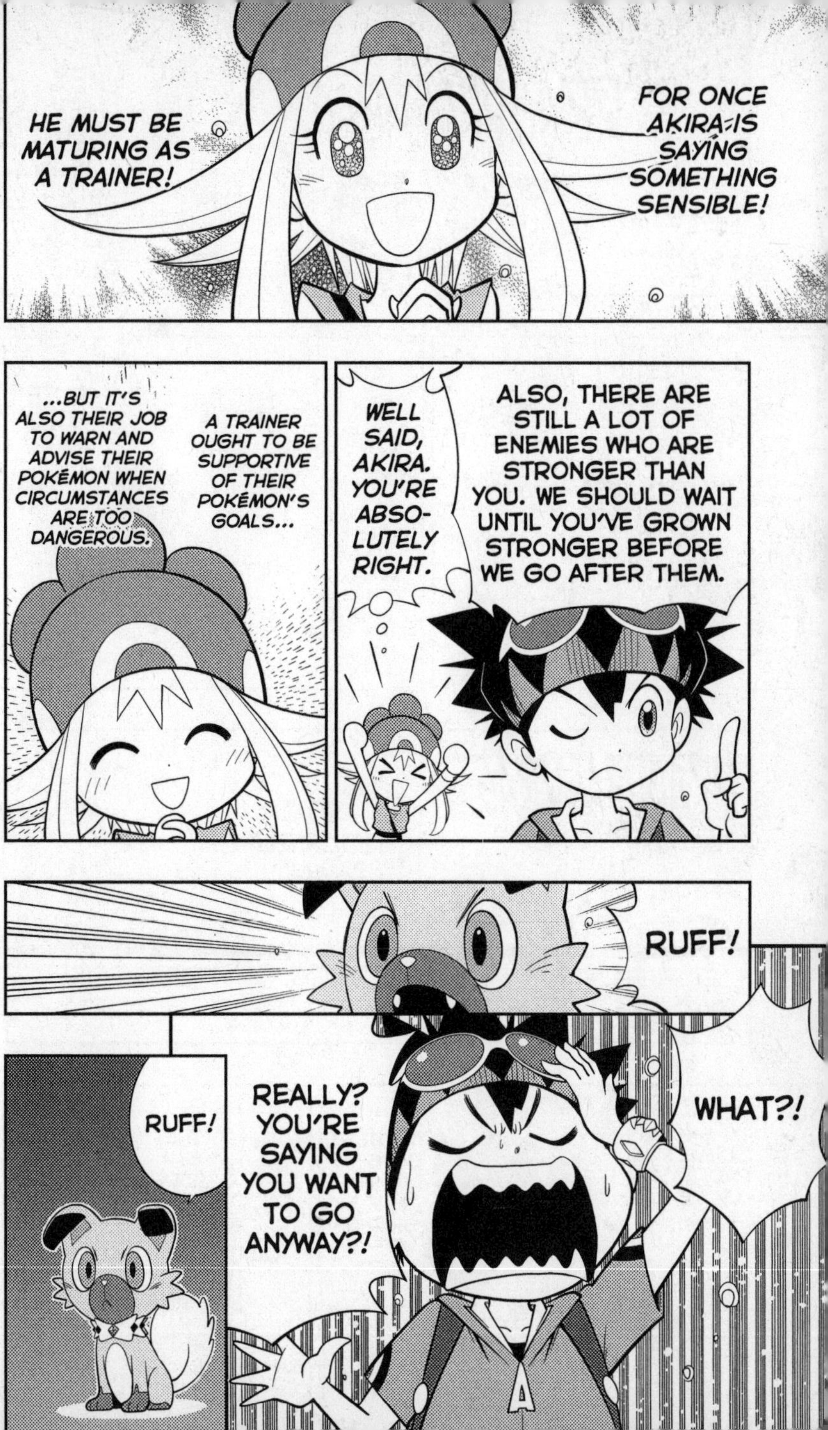
FOR ONCE AKIRA IS SAYING SOMETHING SENSIBLE!
HE MUST BE MATURING AS A TRAINER!
ALSO, THERE ARE STILL A LOT OF ENEMIES WHO ARE STRONGER THAN YOU. WE SHOULD WAIT UNTIL YOU'VE GROWN STRONGER BEFORE WE GO AFTER THEM.
WELL SAID, AKIRA. YOU'RE ABSO-LUTELY RIGHT.
A TRAINER OUGHT TO BE SUPPORTIVE OF THEIR POKÉMON'S GOALS...
...BUT IT'S ALSO THEIR JOB TO WARN AND ADVISE THEIR POKÉMON WHEN CIRCUMSTANCES ARE TOO DANGEROUS.
RUFF!
WHAT?!
REALLY? YOU'RE SAYING YOU WANT TO GO ANYWAY?!
RUFF!

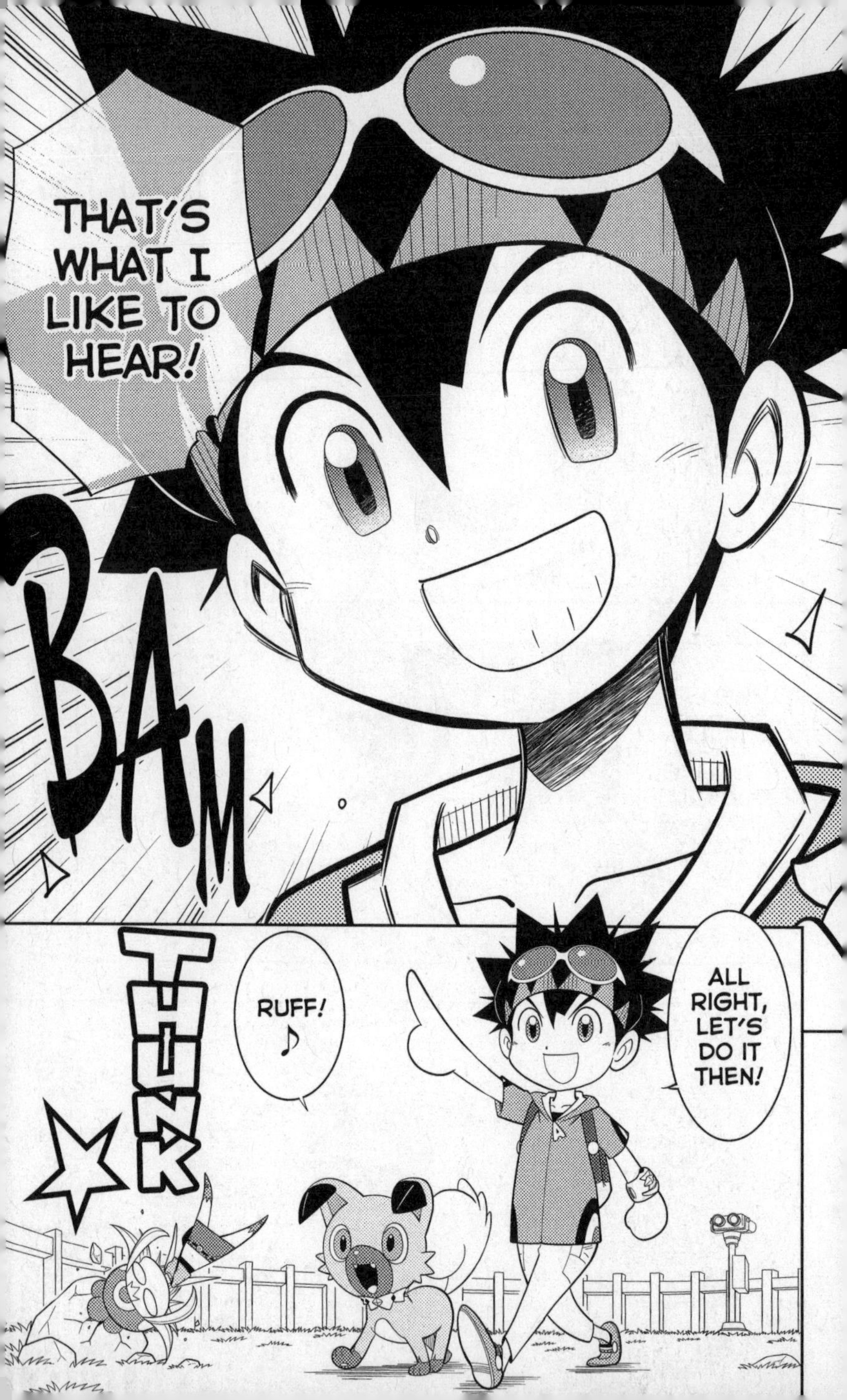
THAT'S WHAT I LIKE TO HEAR!
BAM
ALL RIGHT, LET'S DO IT THEN!
RUFF! ♪
THUNK

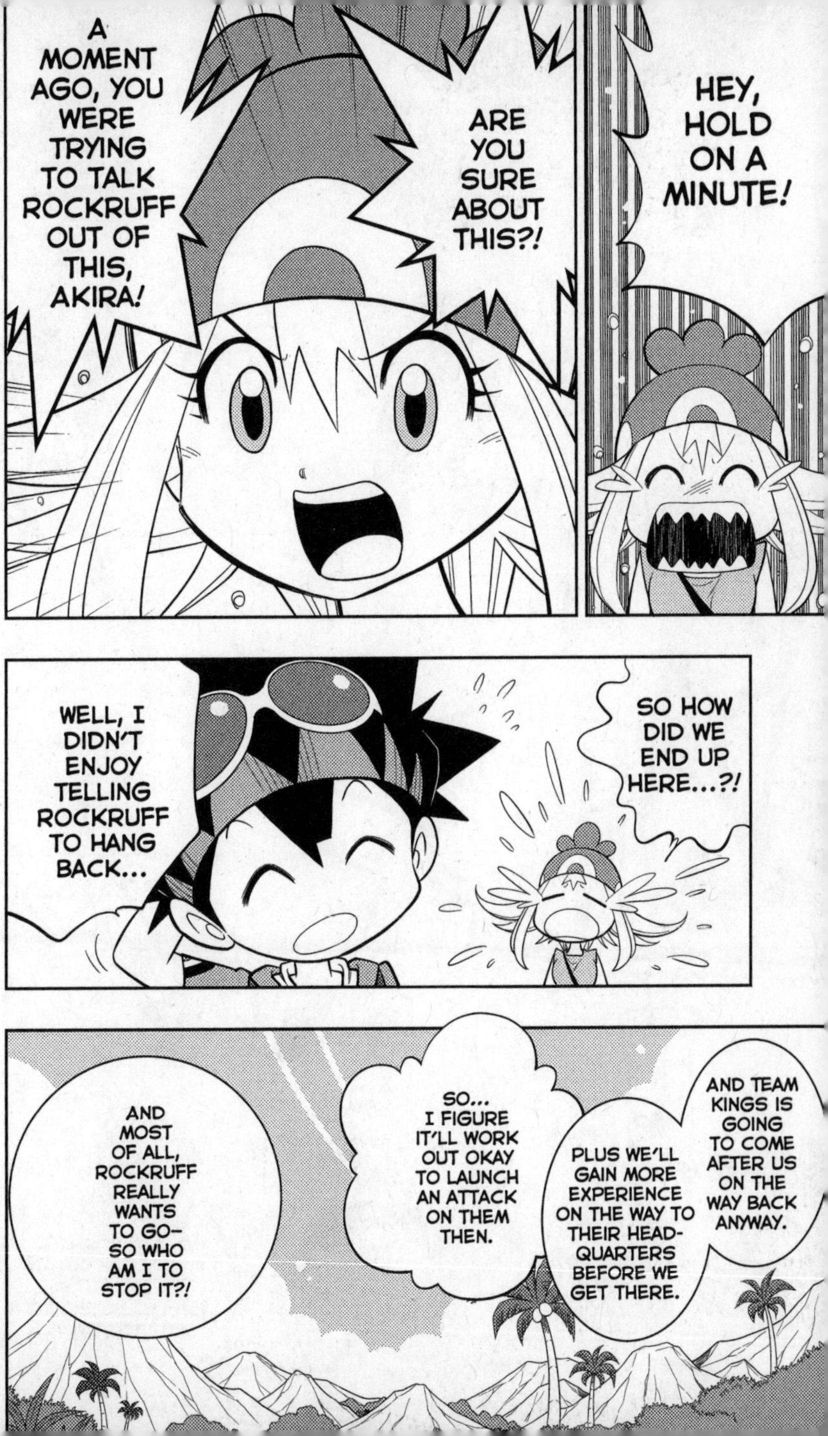
HEY, HOLD ON A MINUTE!
ARE YOU SURE ABOUT THIS?!
A MOMENT AGO, YOU WERE TRYING TO TALK ROCKRUFF OUT OF THIS, AKIRA!
SO HOW DID WE END UP HERE...?!
WELL, I DIDN'T ENJOY TELLING ROCKRUFF TO HANG BACK...
AND TEAM KINGS IS GOING TO COME AFTER US ON THE WAY BACK ANYWAY.
PLUS WE'LL GAIN MORE EXPERIENCE ON THE WAY TO THEIR HEAD-QUARTERS BEFORE WE GET THERE.
SO... I FIGURE IT'LL WORK OUT OKAY TO LAUNCH AN ATTACK ON THEM THEN.
AND MOST OF ALL, ROCKRUFF REALLY WANTS TO GO– SO WHO AM I TO STOP IT?!

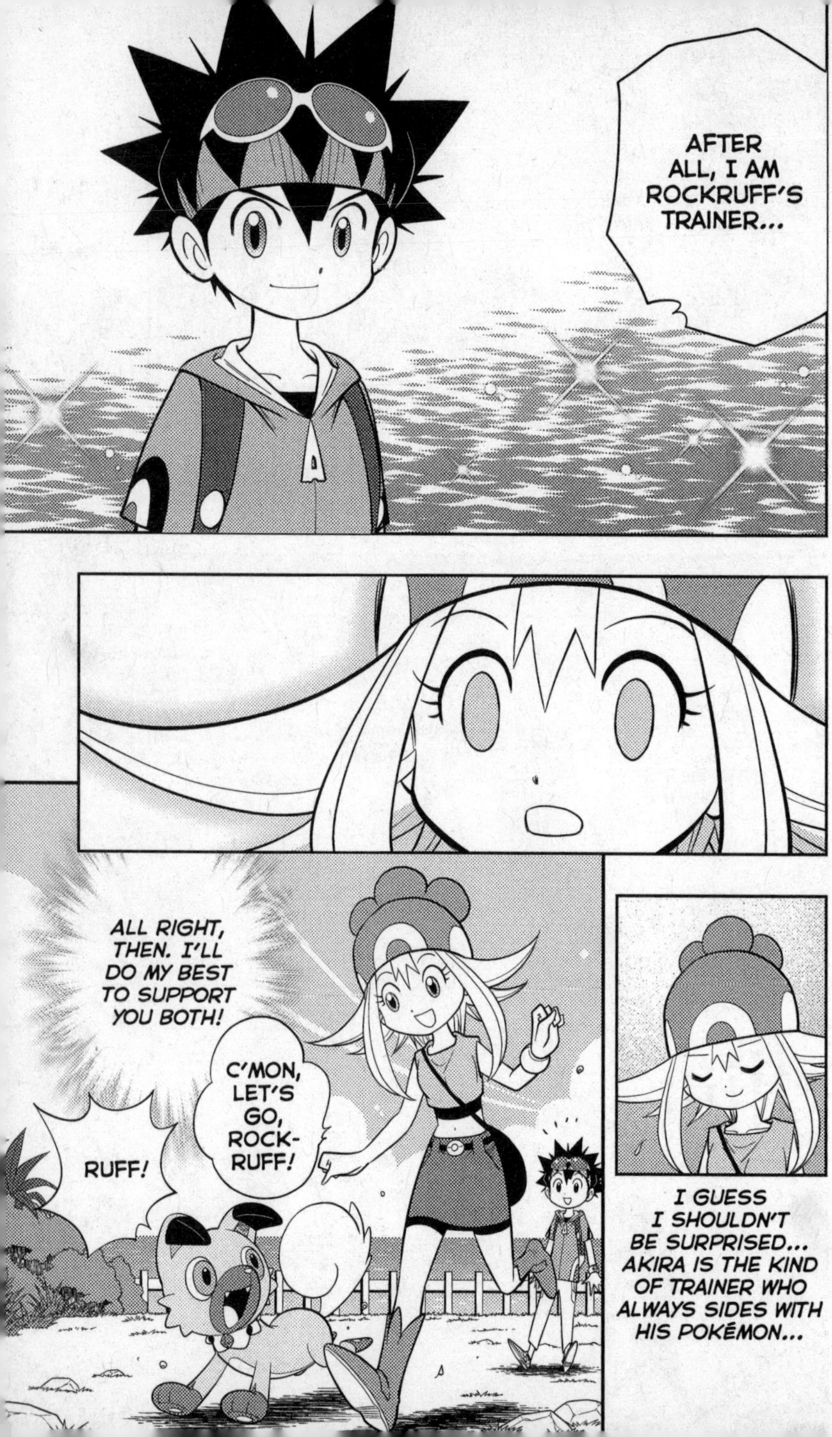
AFTER ALL, I AM ROCKRUFF'S TRAINER...
I GUESS I SHOULDN'T BE SURPRISED... AKIRA IS THE KIND OF TRAINER WHO ALWAYS SIDES WITH HIS POKÉMON...
ALL RIGHT, THEN. I'LL DO MY BEST TO SUPPORT YOU BOTH!
C'MON, LET'S GO, ROCK-RUFF!
RUFF!

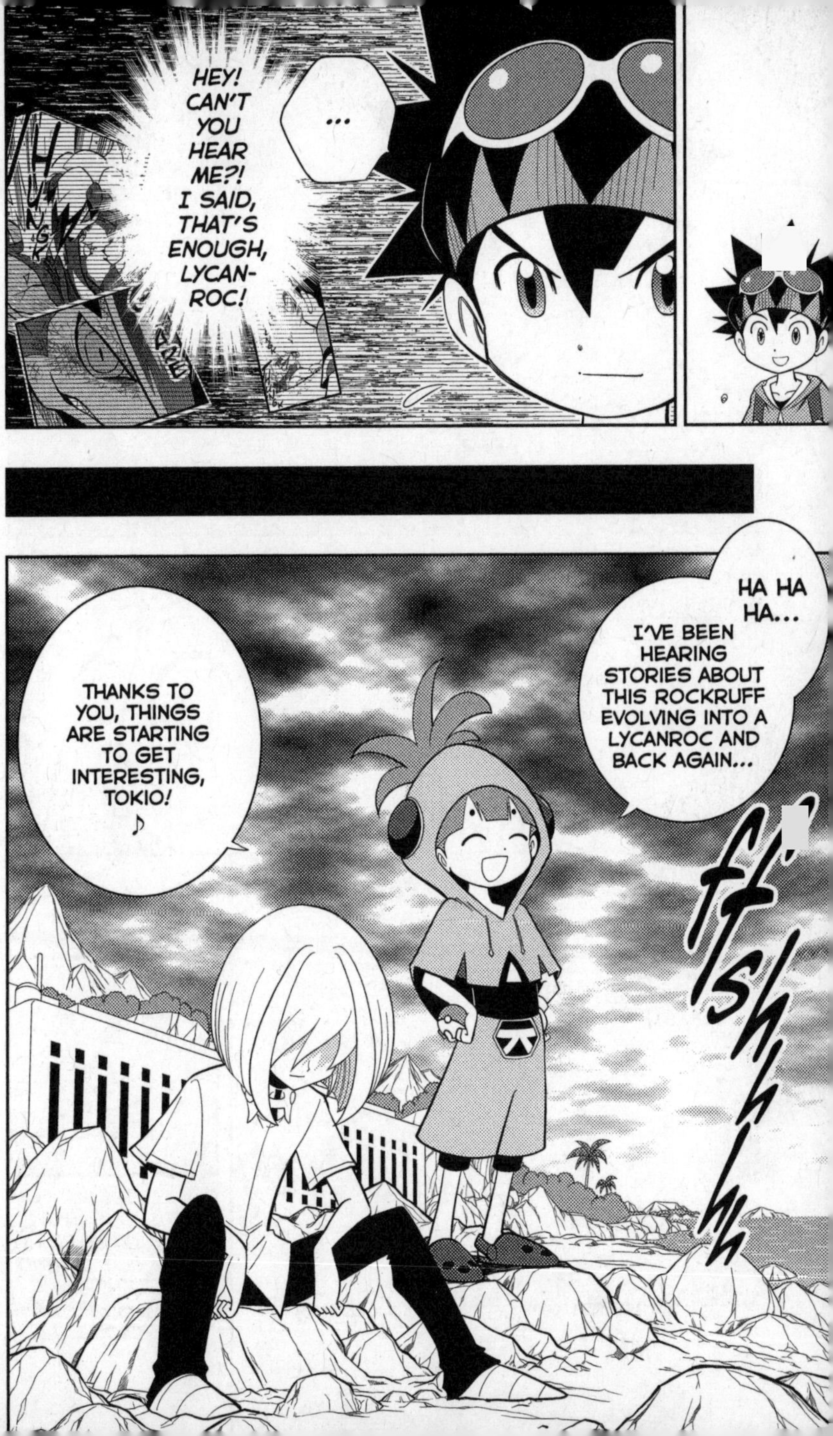
...
HEY! CAN'T YOU HEAR ME?! I SAID, THAT'S ENOUGH, LYCANROC!
HA HA HA... I'VE BEEN HEARING STORIES ABOUT THIS ROCKRUFF EVOLVING INTO A LYCANROC AND BACK AGAIN...
THANKS TO YOU, THINGS ARE STARTING TO GET INTERESTING, TOKIO! ♪

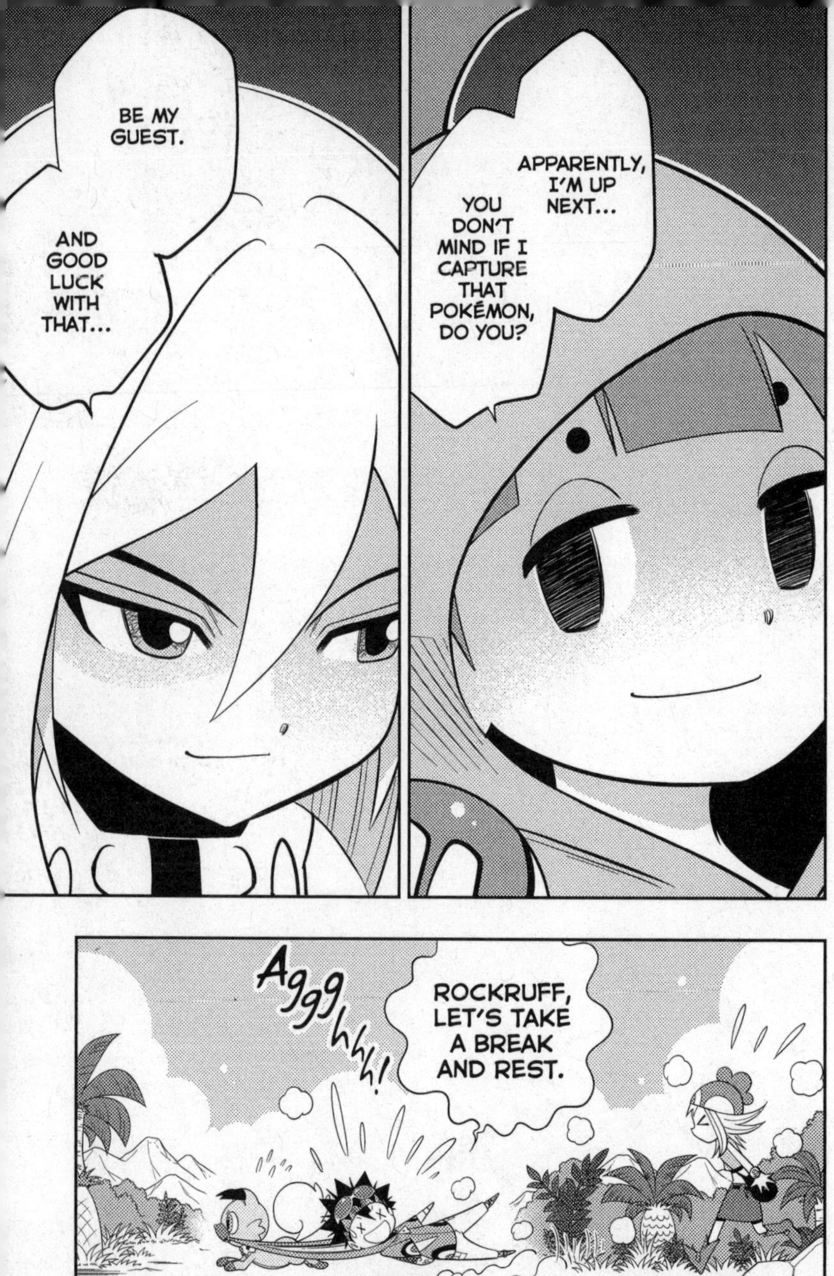
APPARENTLY, I'M UP NEXT...
YOU DON'T MIND IF I CAPTURE THAT POKÉMON, DO YOU?
BE MY GUEST.
AND GOOD LUCK WITH THAT...
ROCKRUFF, LET'S TAKE A BREAK AND REST.
Aggghhh!

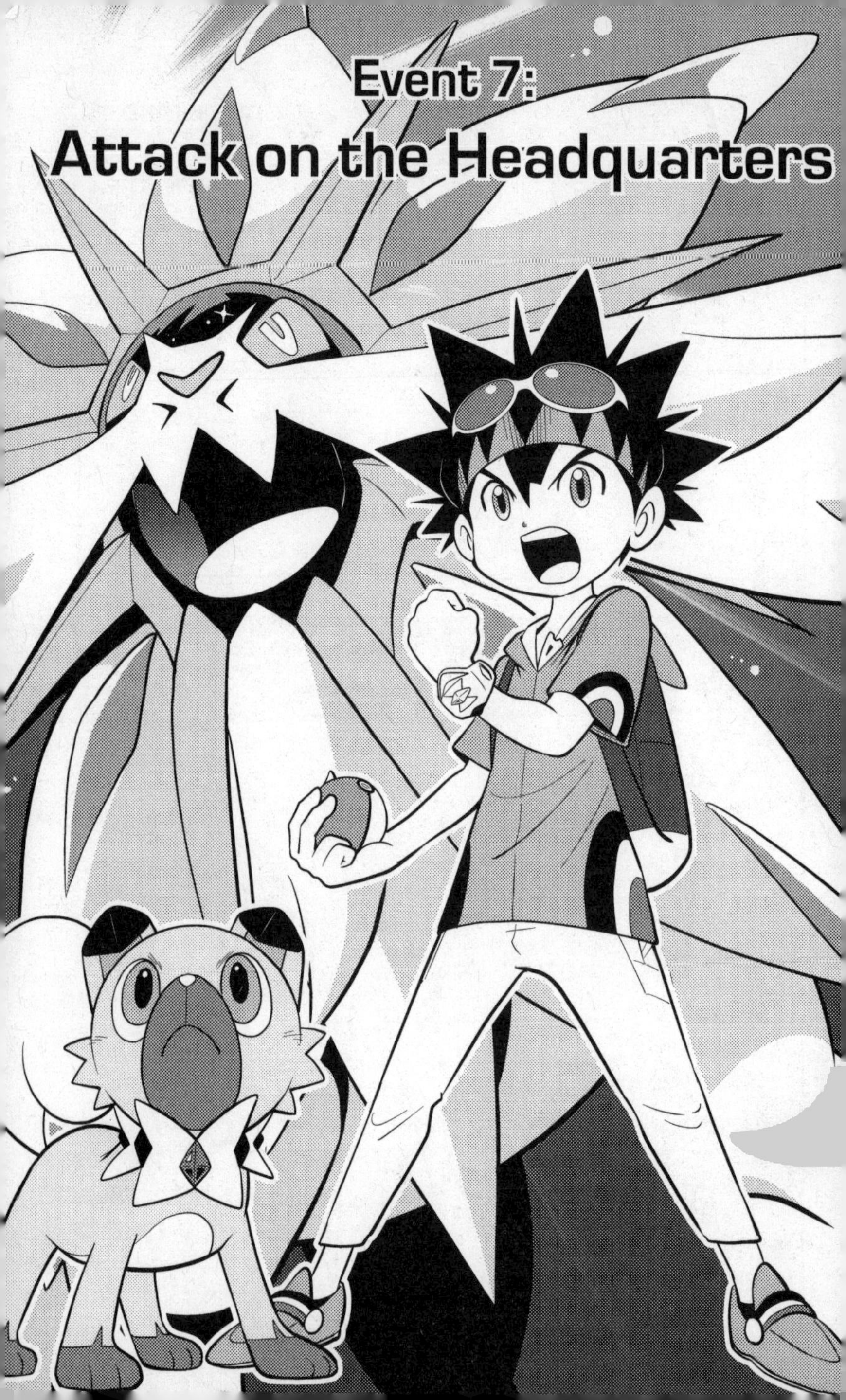
Event 7:
Attack on the Headquarters

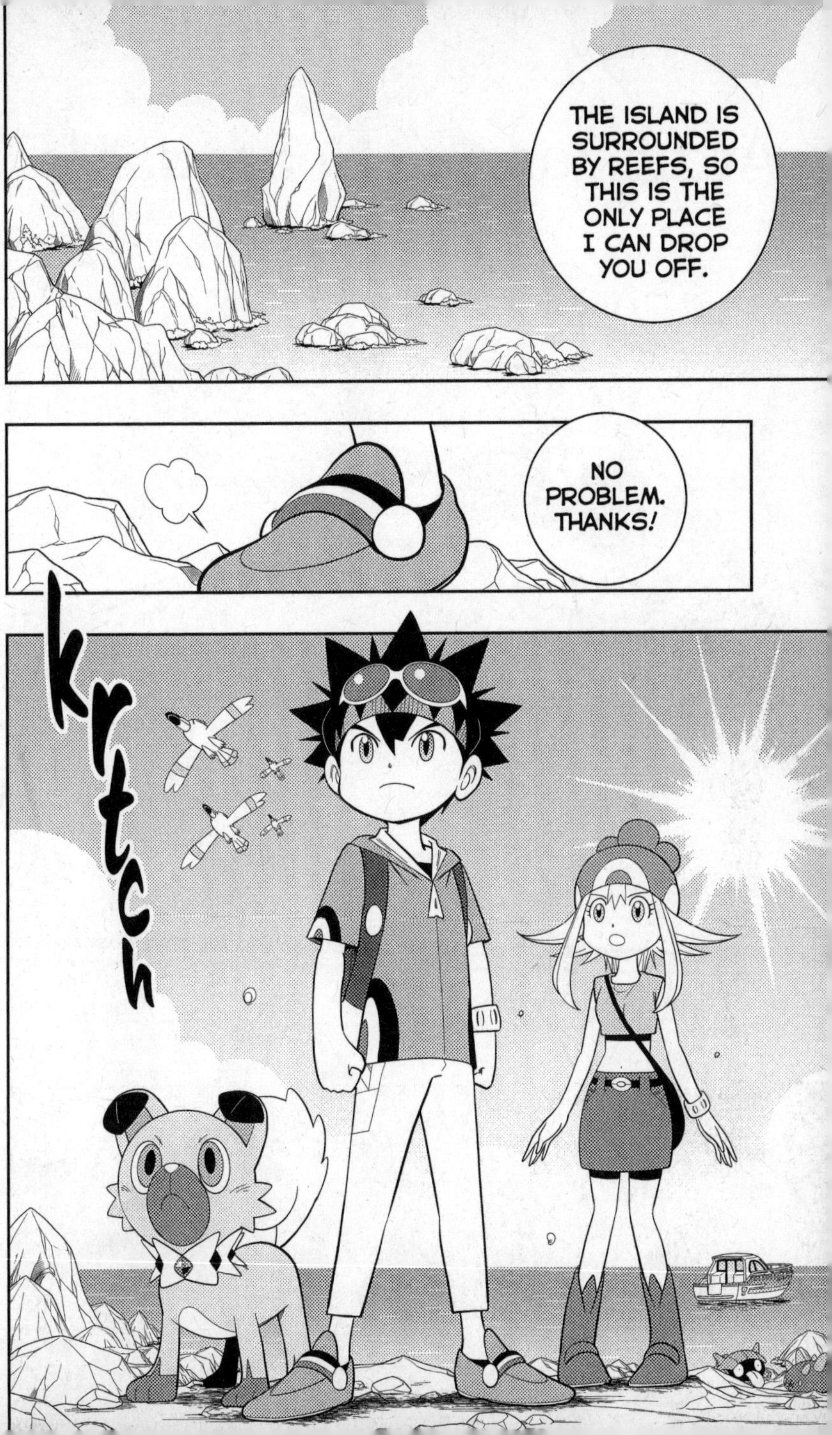
THE ISLAND IS SURROUNDED BY REEFS, SO THIS IS THE ONLY PLACE I CAN DROP YOU OFF.
NO PROBLEM. THANKS!
krtch

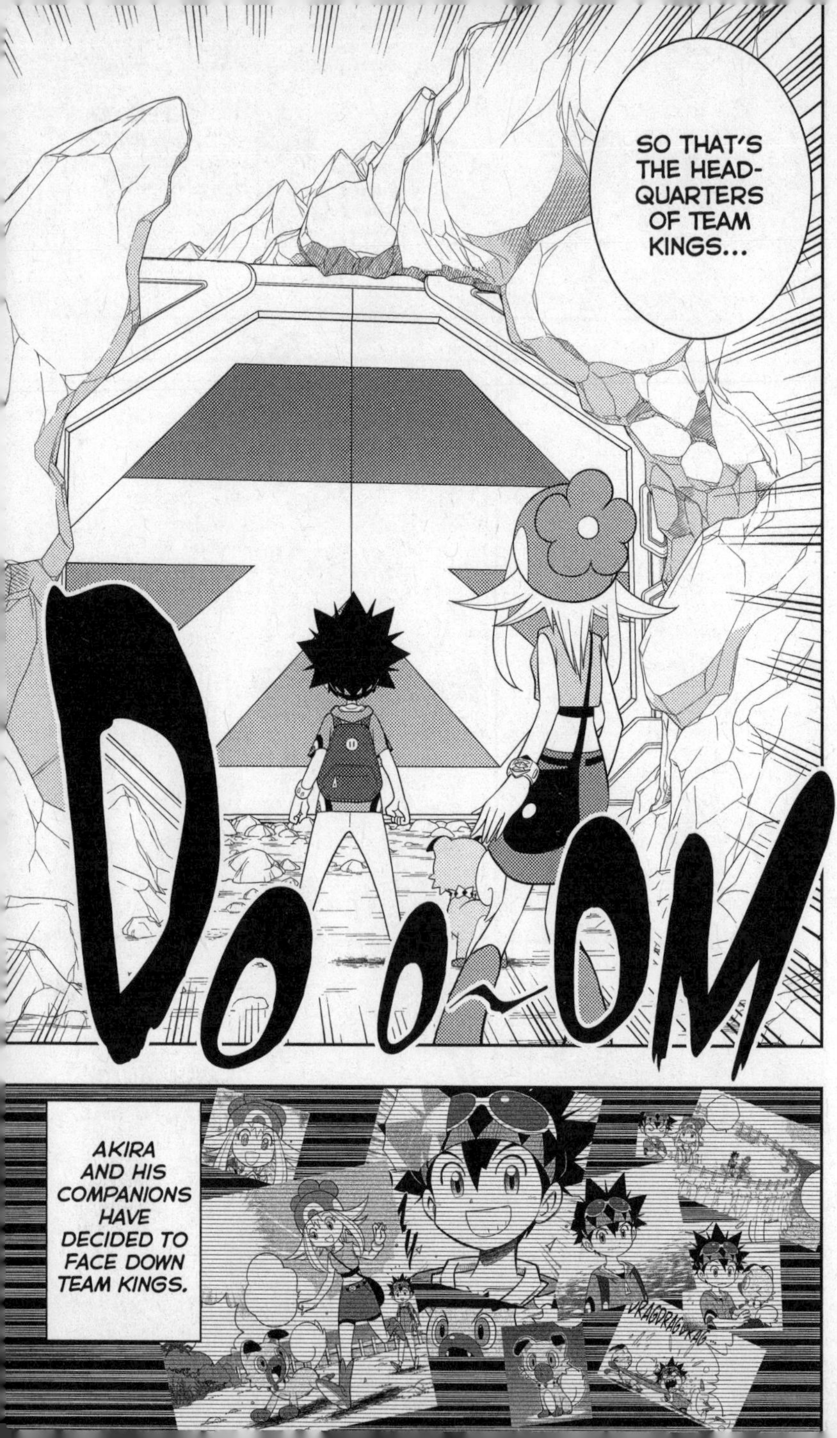
SO THAT'S THE HEAD-QUARTERS OF TEAM KINGS...
DOO~OM
AKIRA AND HIS COMPANIONS HAVE DECIDED TO FACE DOWN TEAM KINGS.

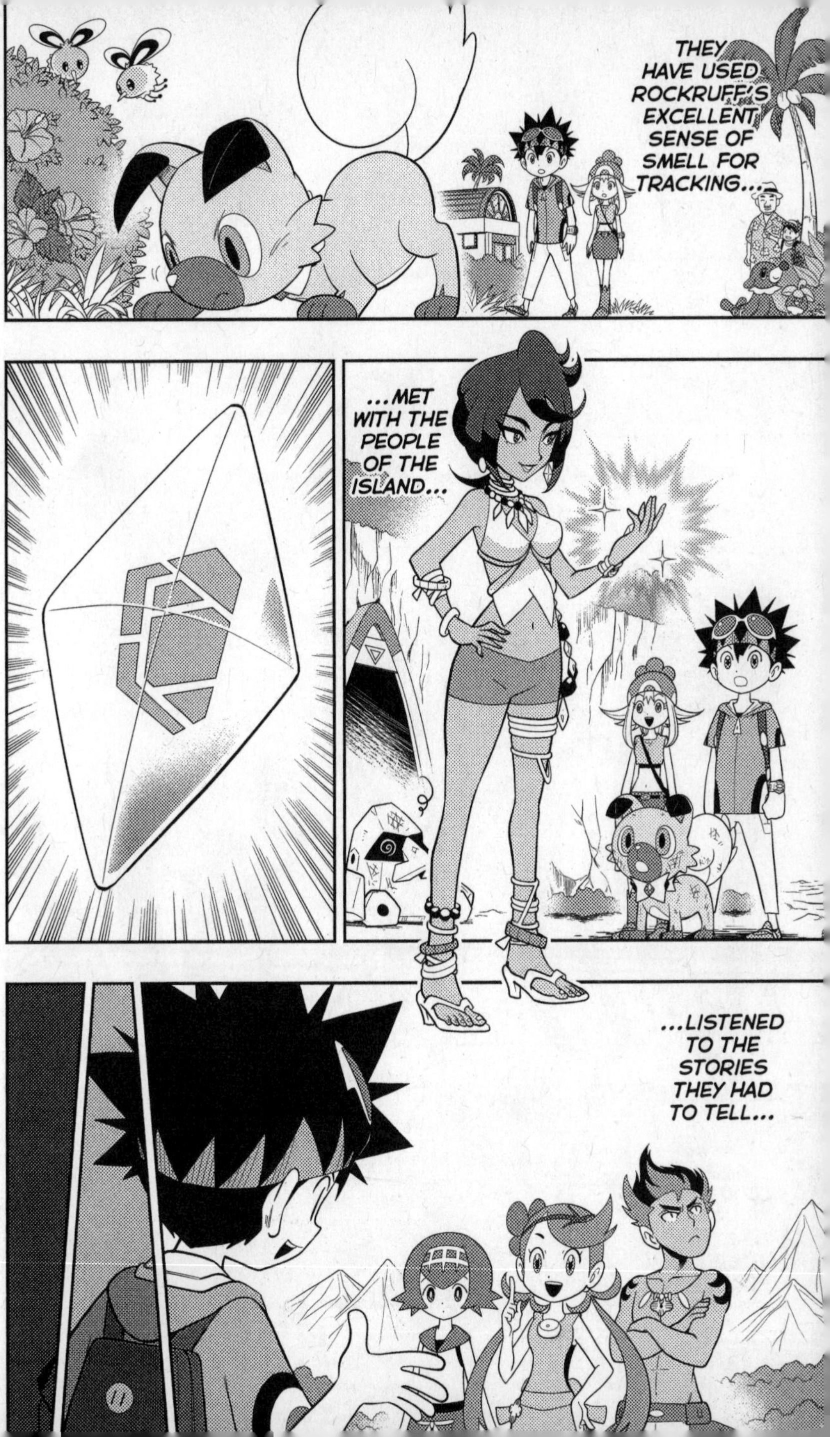
THEY HAVE USED ROCKRUFF'S EXCELLENT SENSE OF SMELL FOR TRACKING...
...MET WITH THE PEOPLE OF THE ISLAND...
...LISTENED TO THE STORIES THEY HAD TO TELL...

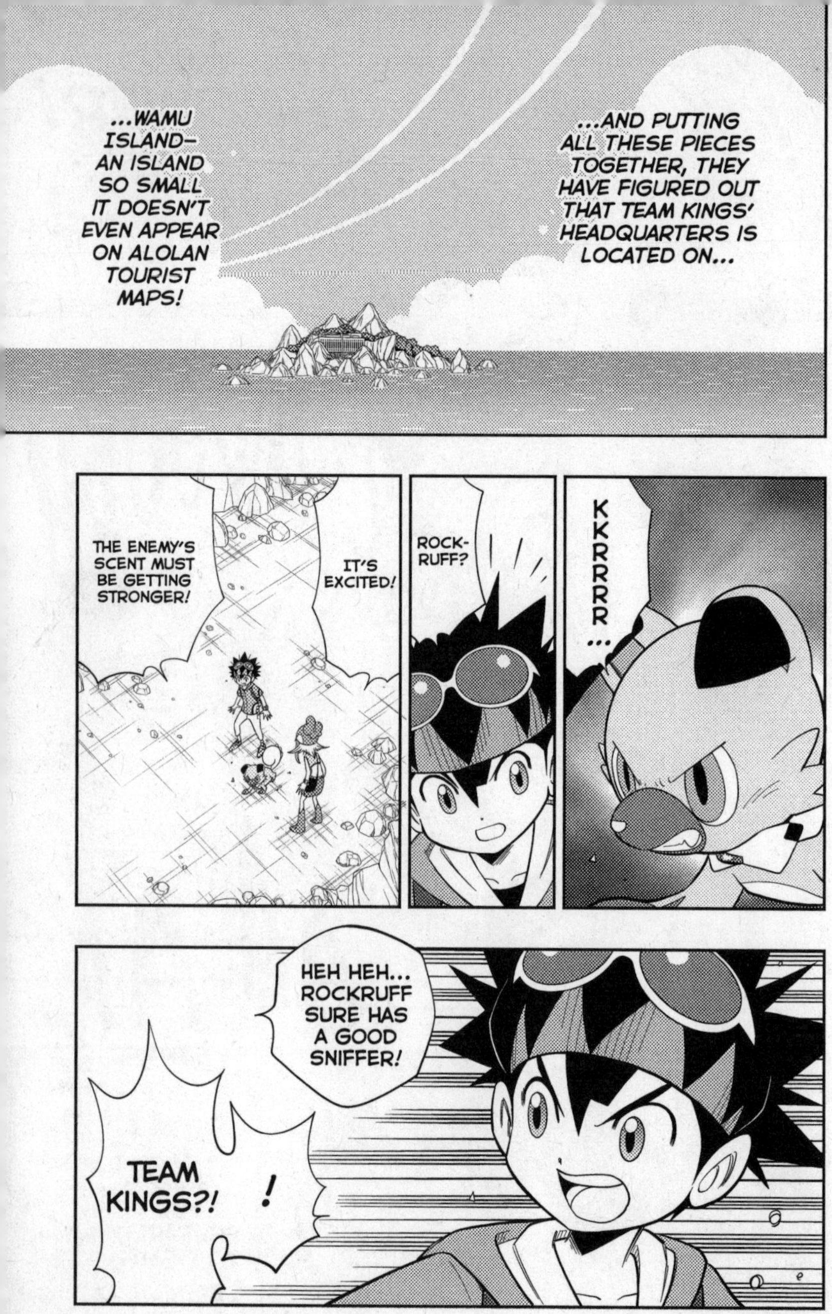
...AND PUTTING ALL THESE PIECES TOGETHER, THEY HAVE FIGURED OUT THAT TEAM KINGS' HEADQUARTERS IS LOCATED ON...
...WAMU ISLAND— AN ISLAND SO SMALL IT DOESN'T EVEN APPEAR ON ALOLAN TOURIST MAPS!
KKRRRR...
ROCK-RUFF?
IT'S EXCITED!
THE ENEMY'S SCENT MUST BE GETTING STRONGER!
HEH HEH... ROCKRUFF SURE HAS A GOOD SNIFFER!
TEAM KINGS?!
!

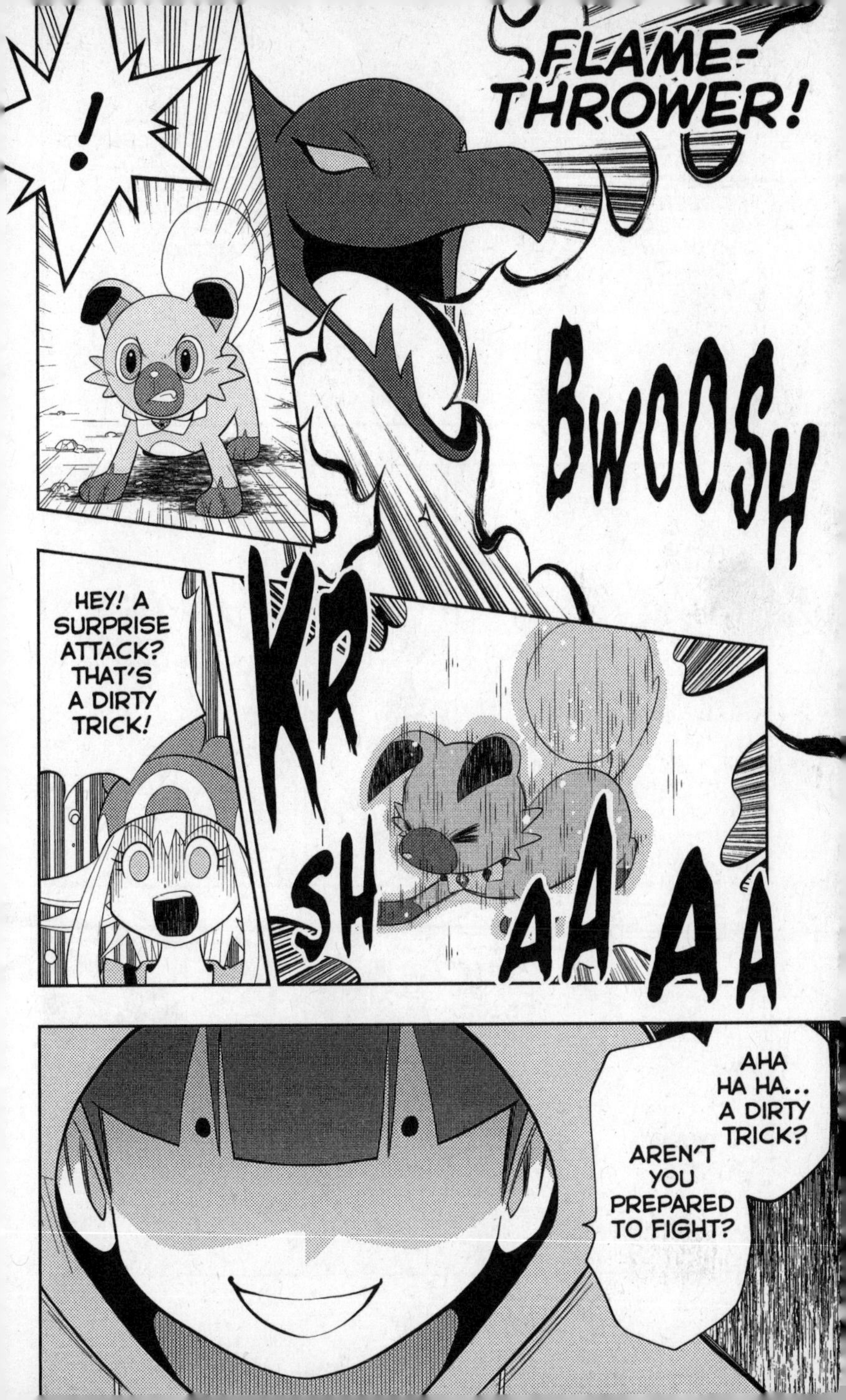
FLAME-THROWER!
BWOOSH
!
KRSHAAAA
HEY! A SURPRISE ATTACK? THAT'S A DIRTY TRICK!
AHA HA HA... A DIRTY TRICK?
AREN'T YOU PREPARED TO FIGHT?

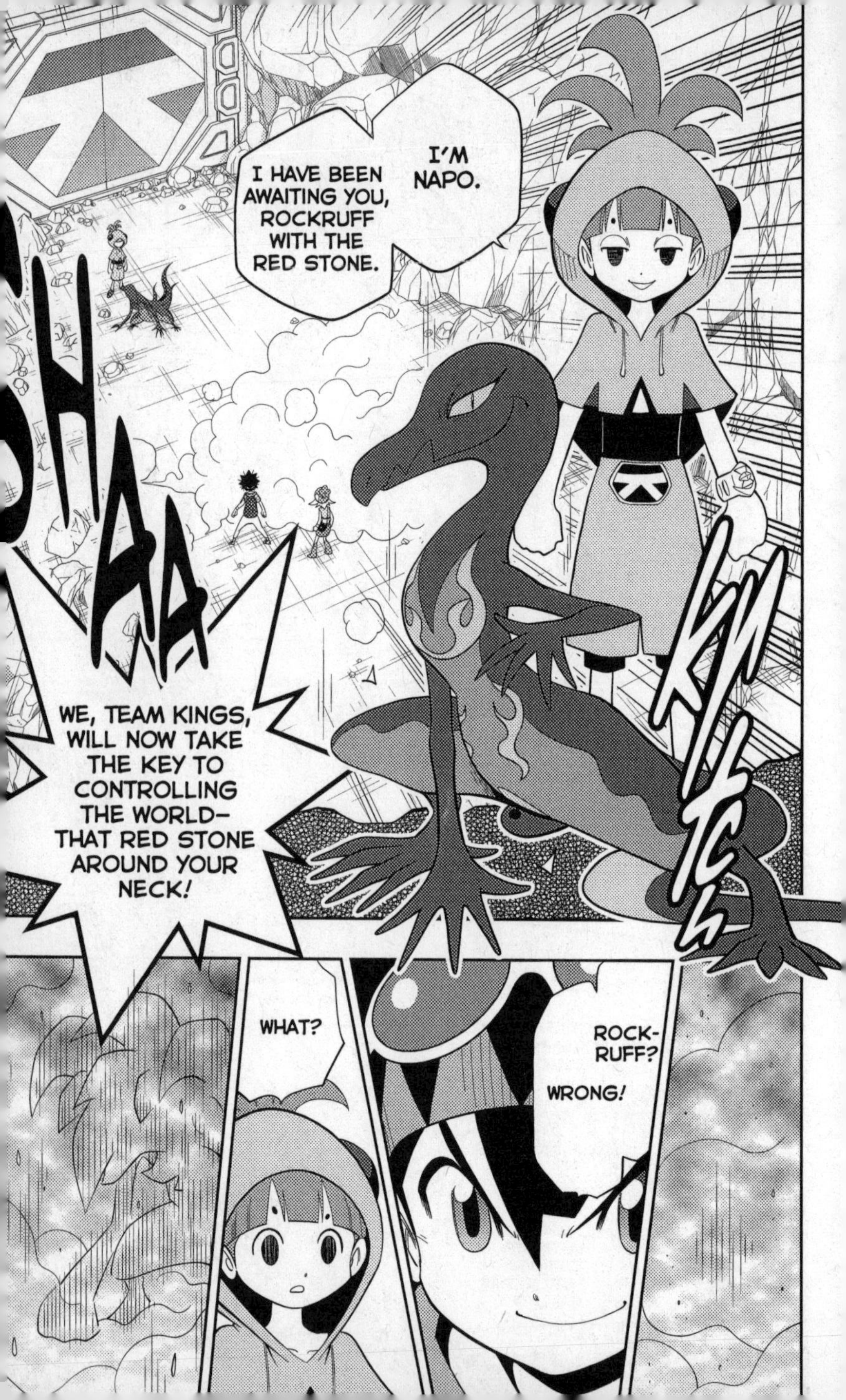
I'M NAPO.
I HAVE BEEN AWAITING YOU, ROCKRUFF WITH THE RED STONE.
WE, TEAM KINGS, WILL NOW TAKE THE KEY TO CONTROLLING THE WORLD–THAT RED STONE AROUND YOUR NECK!
ROCK-RUFF?
WRONG!
WHAT?

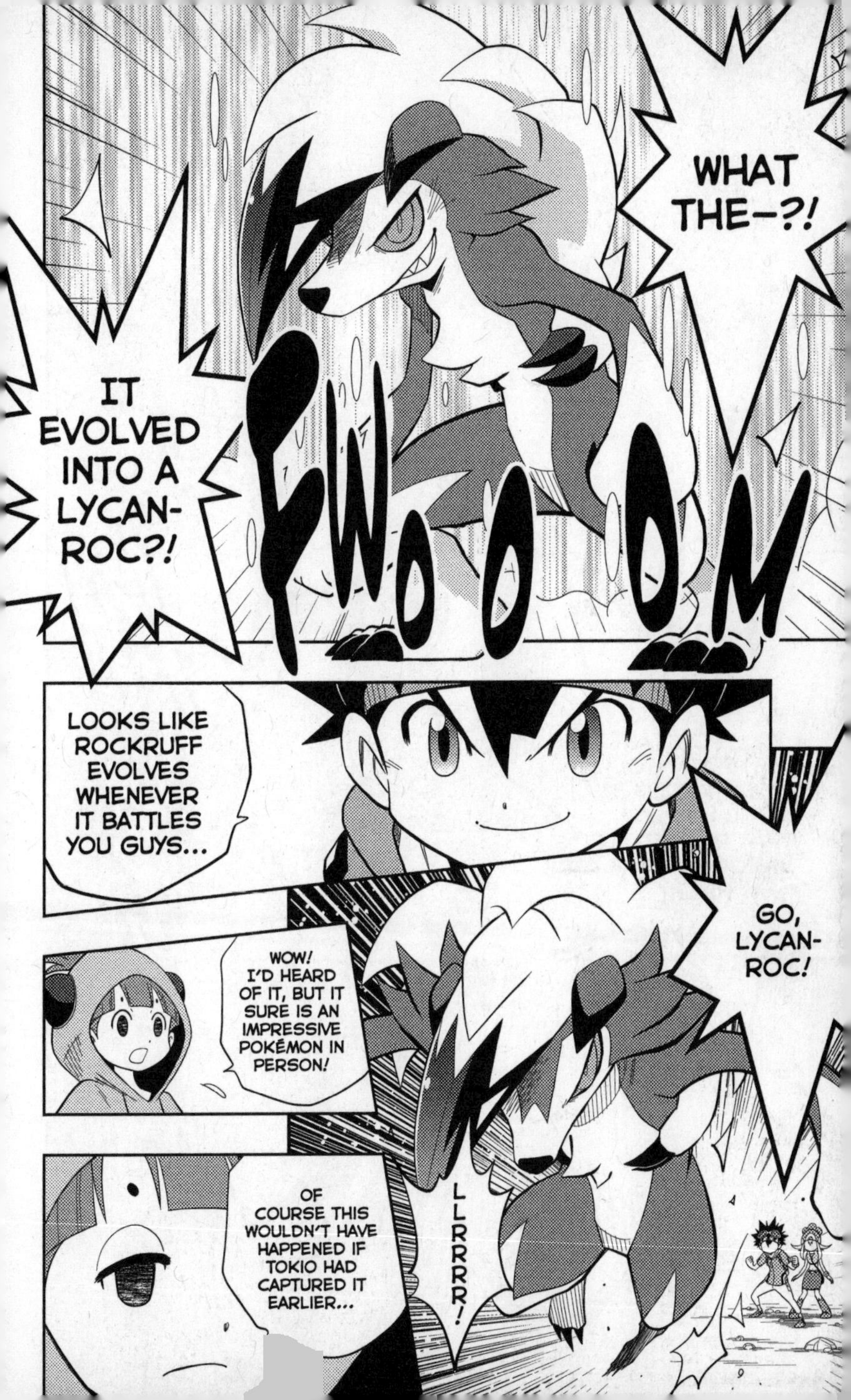

WHAT THE–?!
FWOOOM
IT EVOLVED INTO A LYCAN-ROC?!
GO, LYCAN-ROC!
LLRRRR!
LOOKS LIKE ROCKRUFF EVOLVES WHENEVER IT BATTLES YOU GUYS...
WOW! I'D HEARD OF IT, BUT IT SURE IS AN IMPRESSIVE POKéMON IN PERSON!
OF COURSE THIS WOULDN'T HAVE HAPPENED IF TOKIO HAD CAPTURED IT EARLIER...

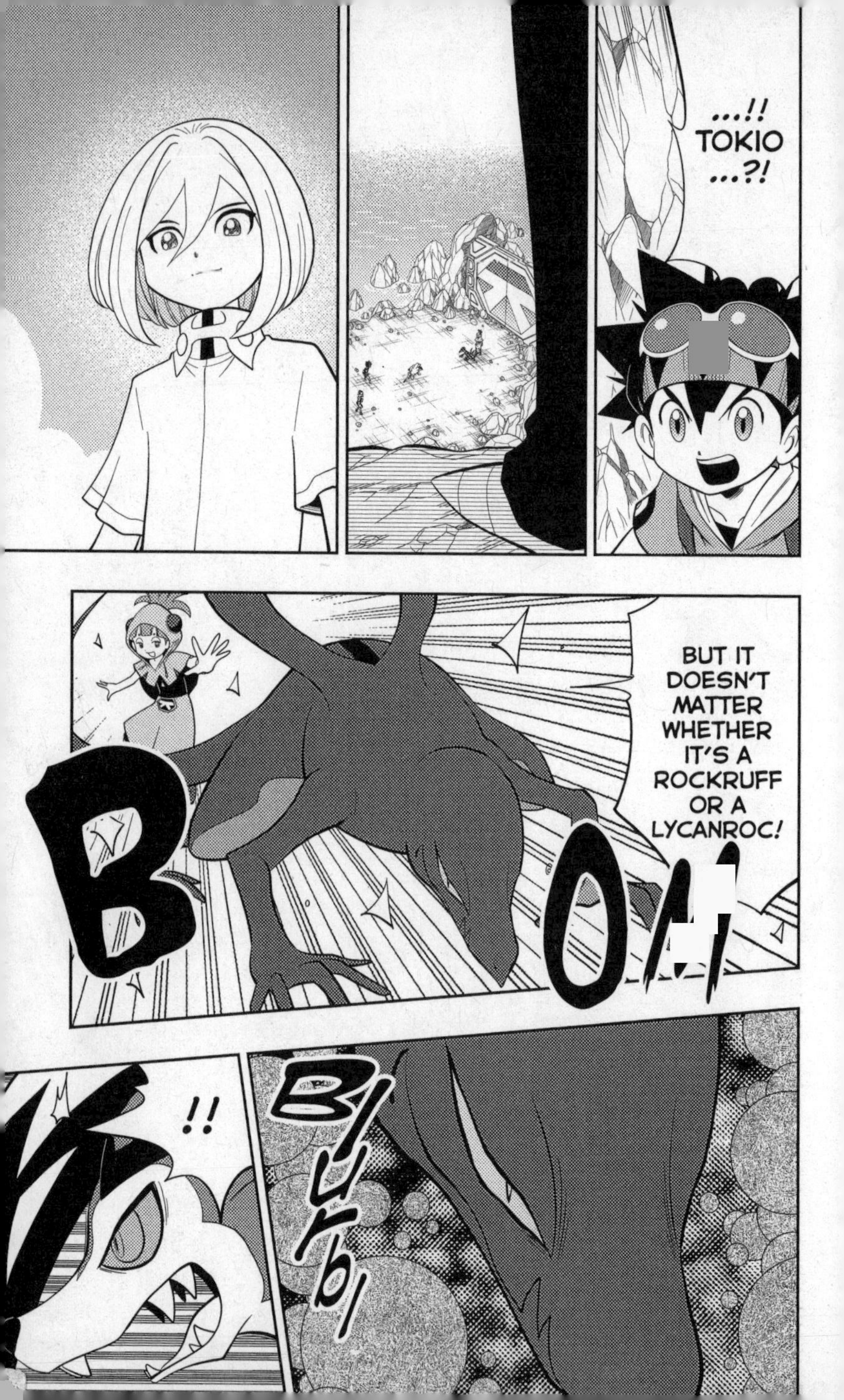
...!! TOKIO ...?!
BUT IT DOESN'T MATTER WHETHER IT'S A ROCKRUFF OR A LYCANROC!
Blurb!
!!

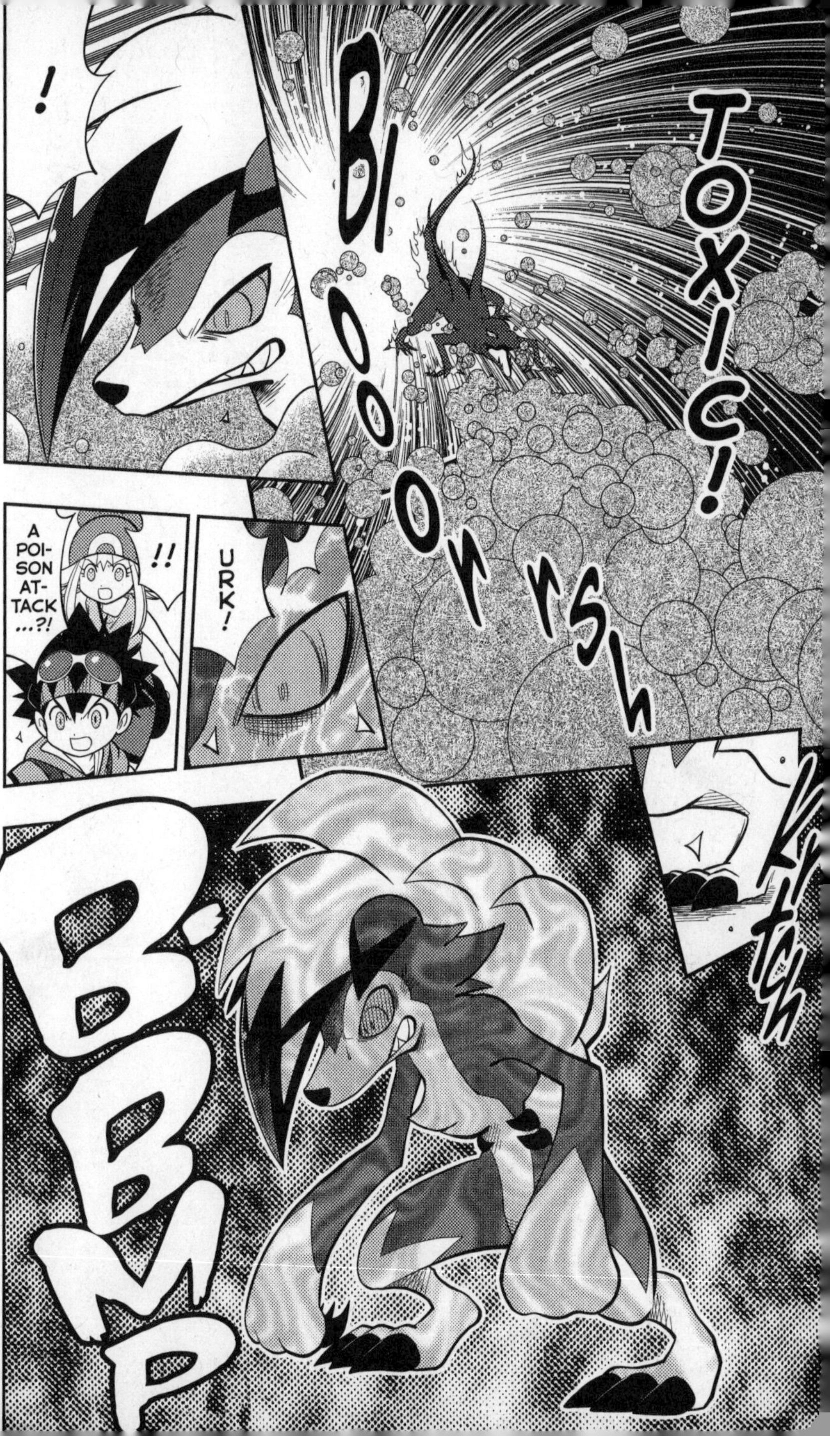
TOXIC!
BLOOOrrsh
!
Krtch
URK!
!!
A POI-SON AT-TACK...?!
BBMP

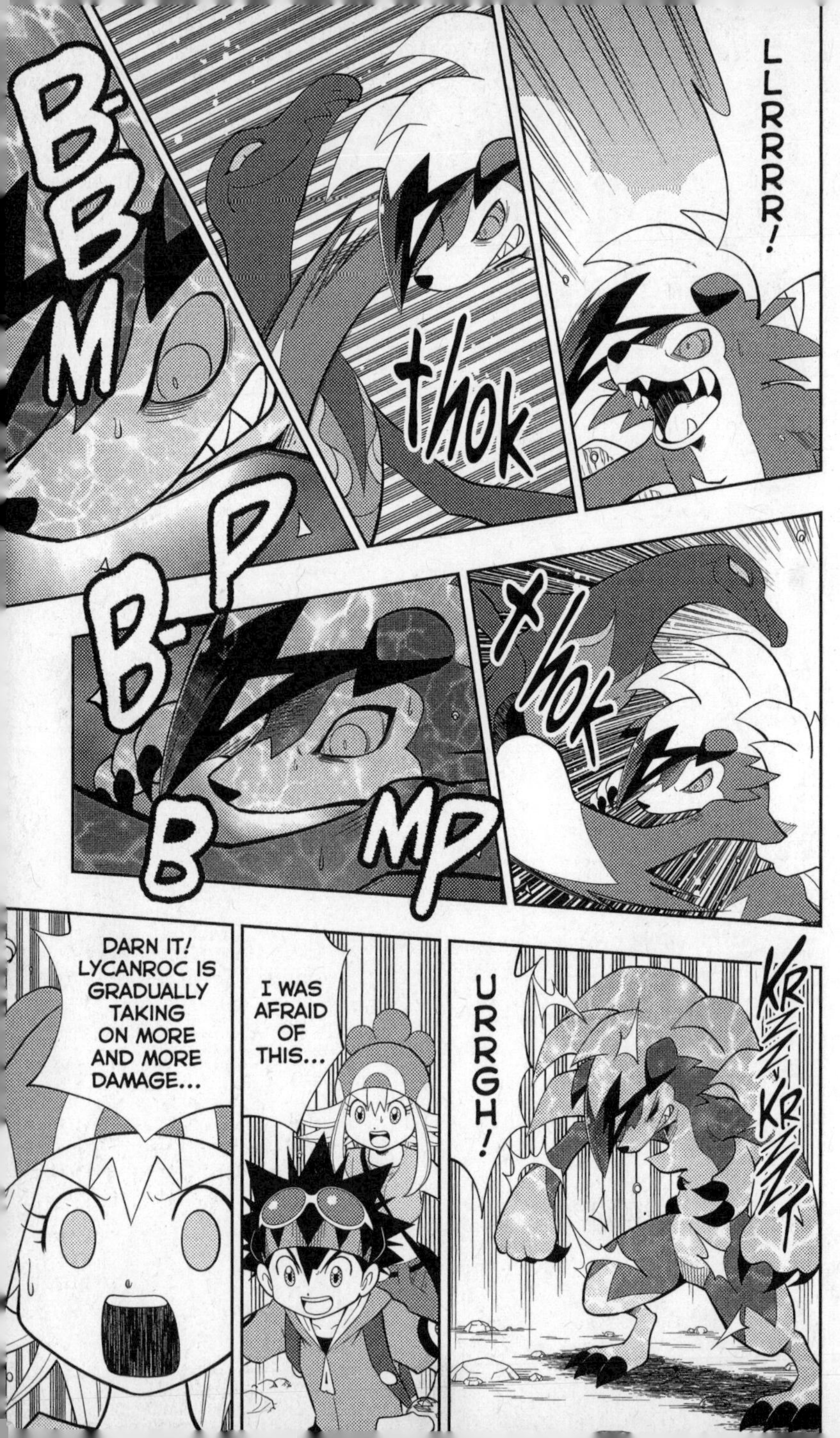

LLRRRR!
thok
B-BM
thok
B-BMP
KRZZ KRZZZT
URRGH!
I WAS AFRAID OF THIS...
DARN IT! LYCANROC IS GRADUALLY TAKING ON MORE AND MORE DAMAGE...

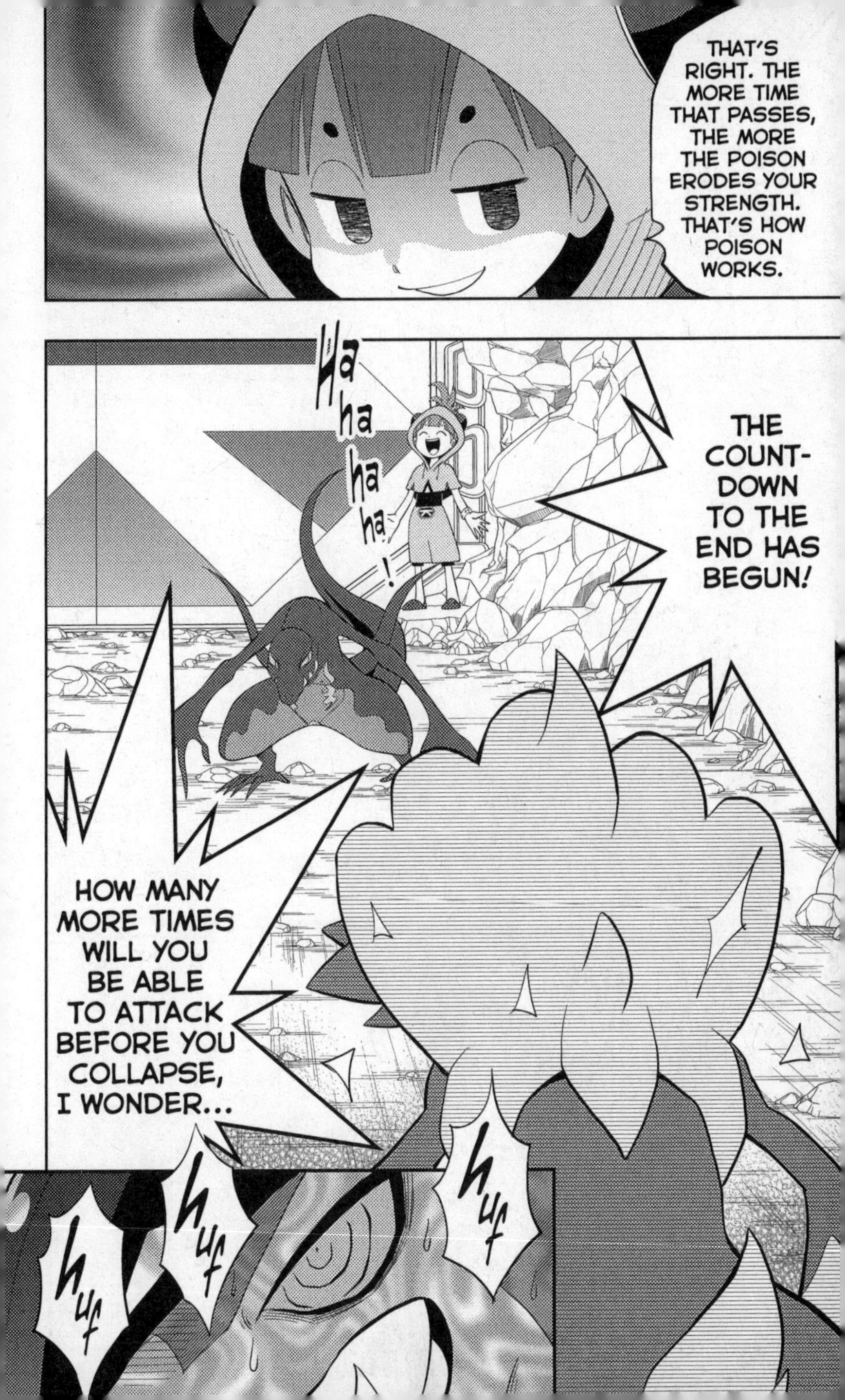
THAT'S RIGHT. THE MORE TIME THAT PASSES, THE MORE THE POISON ERODES YOUR STRENGTH. THAT'S HOW POISON WORKS.
THE COUNT-DOWN TO THE END HAS BEGUN!
Ha ha ha ha!
HOW MANY MORE TIMES WILL YOU BE ABLE TO ATTACK BEFORE YOU COLLAPSE, I WONDER...
huf
huf
huf

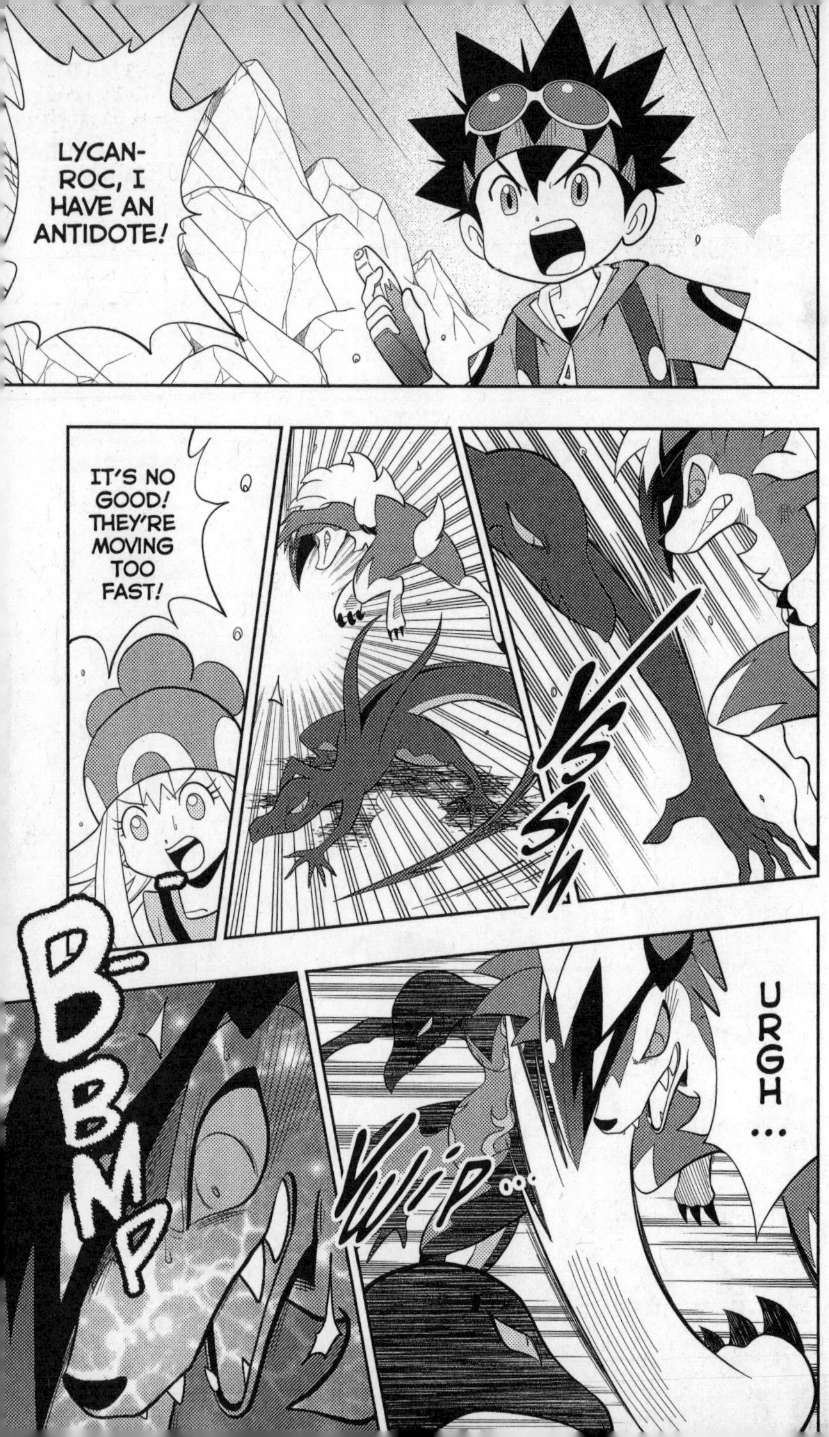
LYCAN-ROC, I HAVE AN ANTIDOTE!
VSSH
IT'S NO GOOD! THEY'RE MOVING TOO FAST!
URGH...
VWIP...
B-BMP

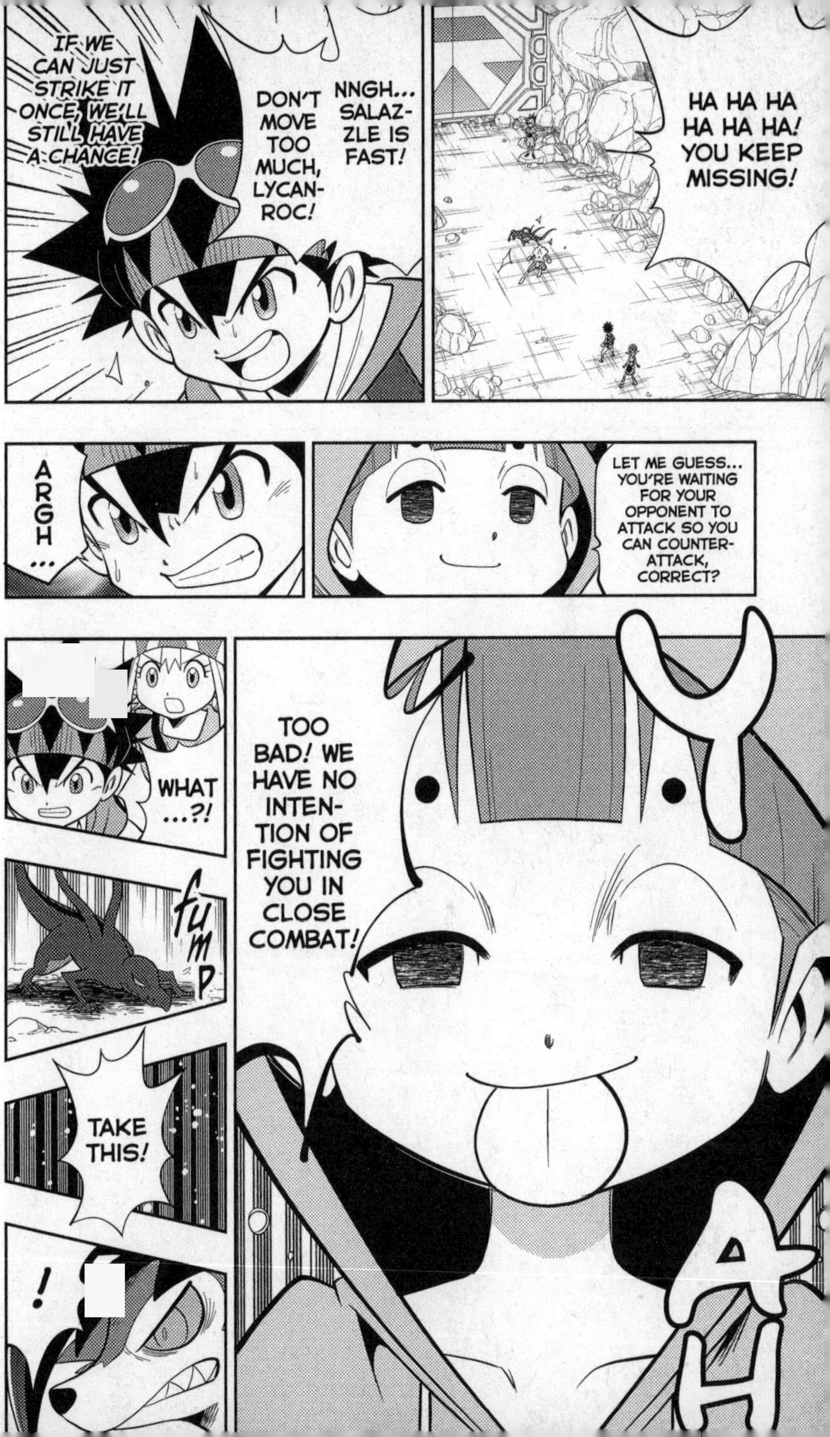
HA HA HA HA HA HA! YOU KEEP MISSING!
NNGH... SALAZ-ZLE IS FAST!
DON'T MOVE TOO MUCH, LYCAN-ROC!
IF WE CAN JUST STRIKE IT ONCE, WE'LL STILL HAVE A CHANCE!
LET ME GUESS... YOU'RE WAITING FOR YOUR OPPONENT TO ATTACK SO YOU CAN COUNTER-ATTACK, CORRECT?
ARGH...
TOO BAD! WE HAVE NO INTEN-TION OF FIGHTING YOU IN CLOSE COMBAT!
HA
WHAT...?!
fump
TAKE THIS!
!

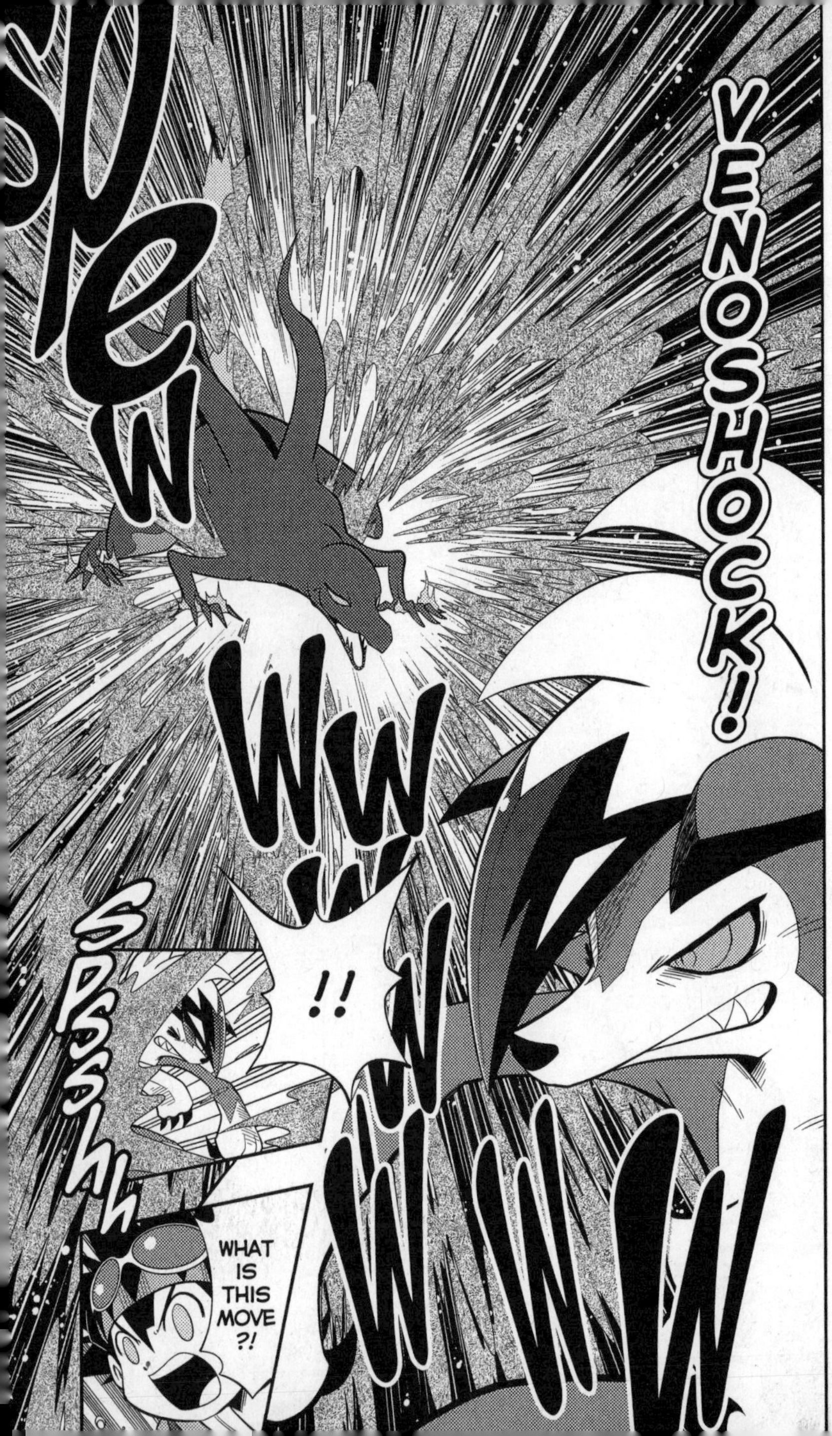
VENOSHOCK!
Shew
!!
Spssshh
WHAT IS THIS MOVE?!

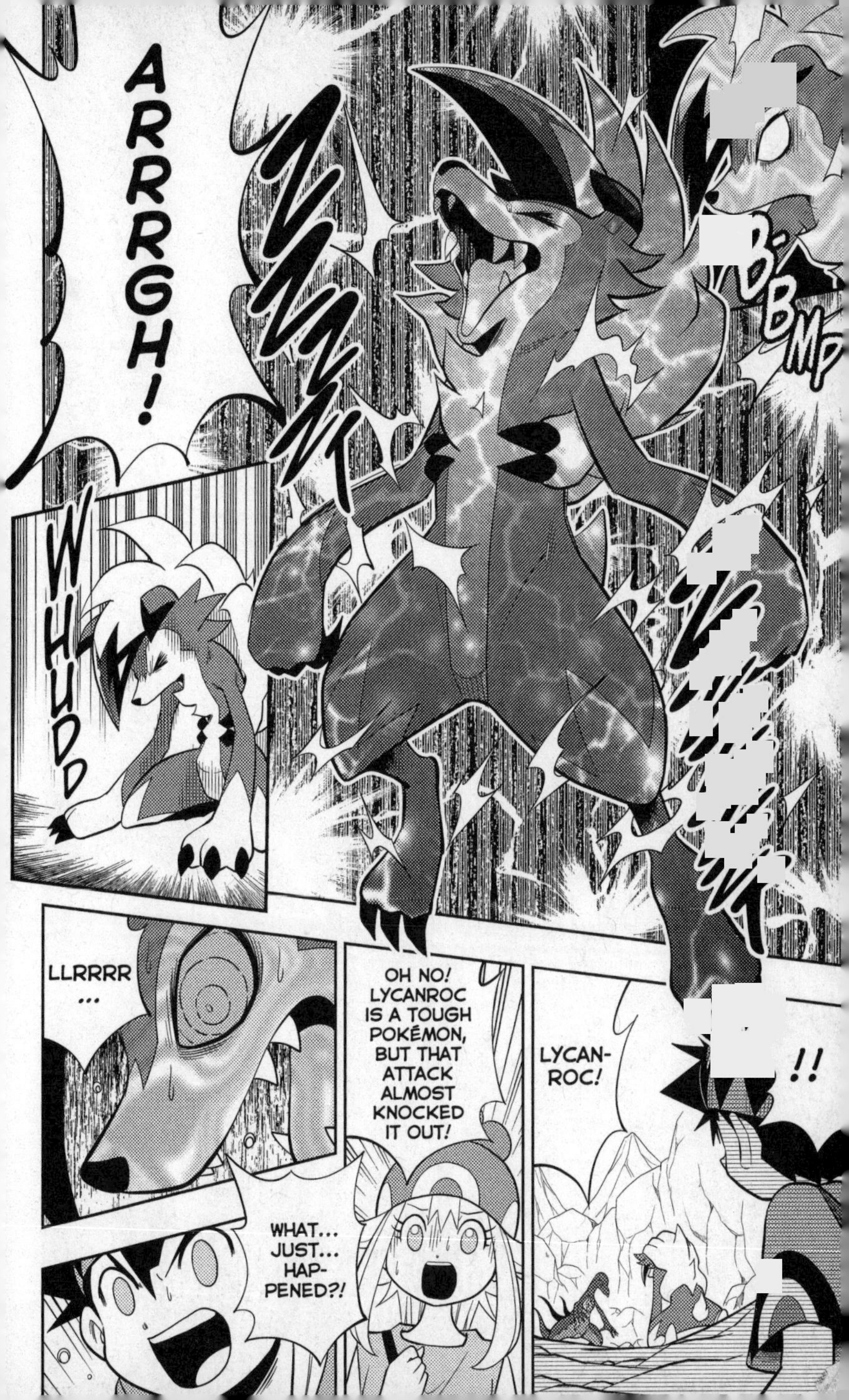
B-BMP
ARRRGH!
WHUDD
!!
LYCAN-ROC!
OH NO! LYCANROC IS A TOUGH POKÉMON, BUT THAT ATTACK ALMOST KNOCKED IT OUT!
WHAT... JUST... HAP-PENED?!
LLRRRR ...

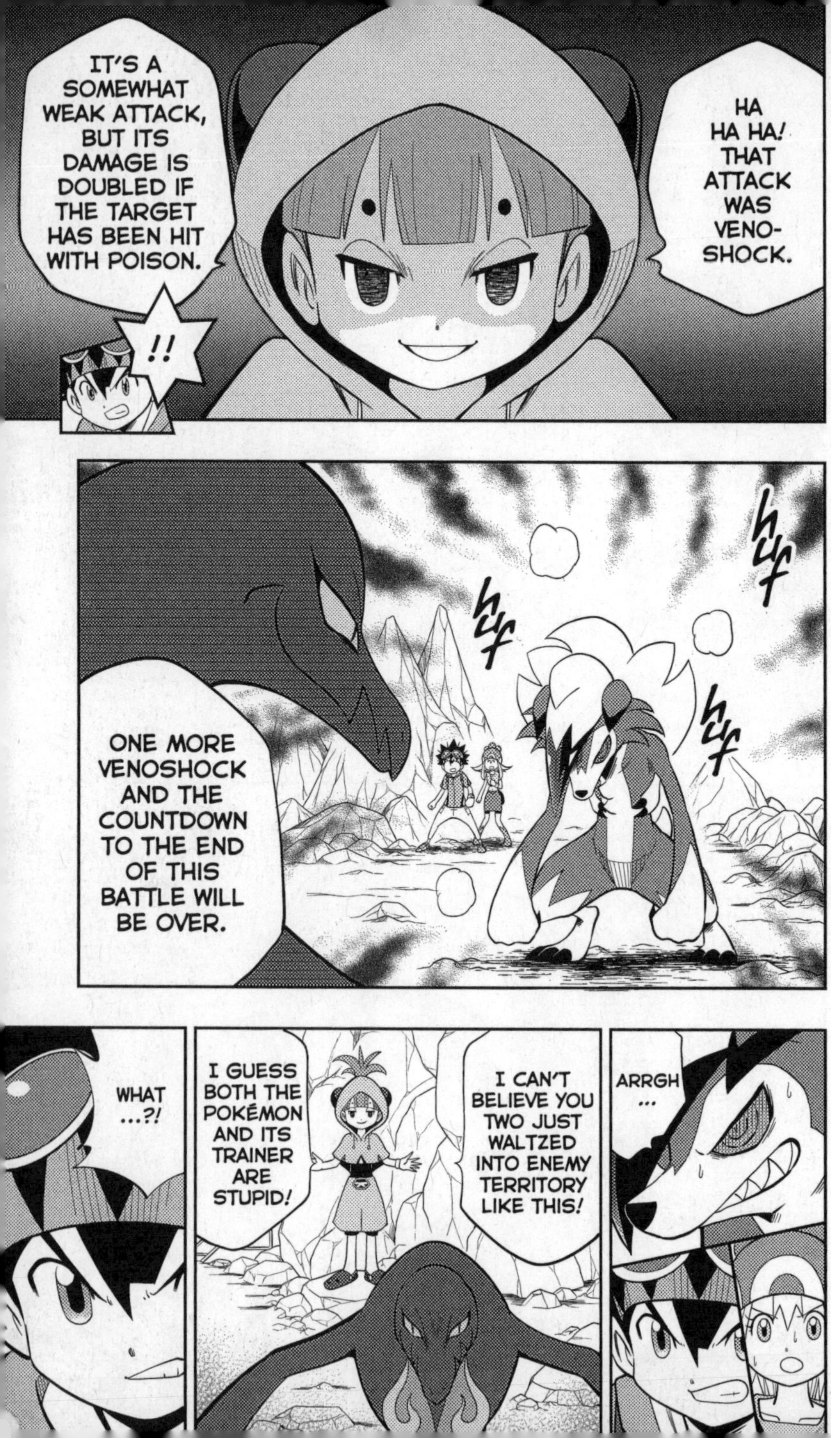
HA HA HA! THAT ATTACK WAS VENO-SHOCK.
IT'S A SOMEWHAT WEAK ATTACK, BUT ITS DAMAGE IS DOUBLED IF THE TARGET HAS BEEN HIT WITH POISON.
!!
huf
huf
huf
ONE MORE VENOSHOCK AND THE COUNTDOWN TO THE END OF THIS BATTLE WILL BE OVER.
ARRGH ...
I CAN'T BELIEVE YOU TWO JUST WALTZED INTO ENEMY TERRITORY LIKE THIS!
I GUESS BOTH THE POKÉMON AND ITS TRAINER ARE STUPID!
WHAT ...?!
WHAT

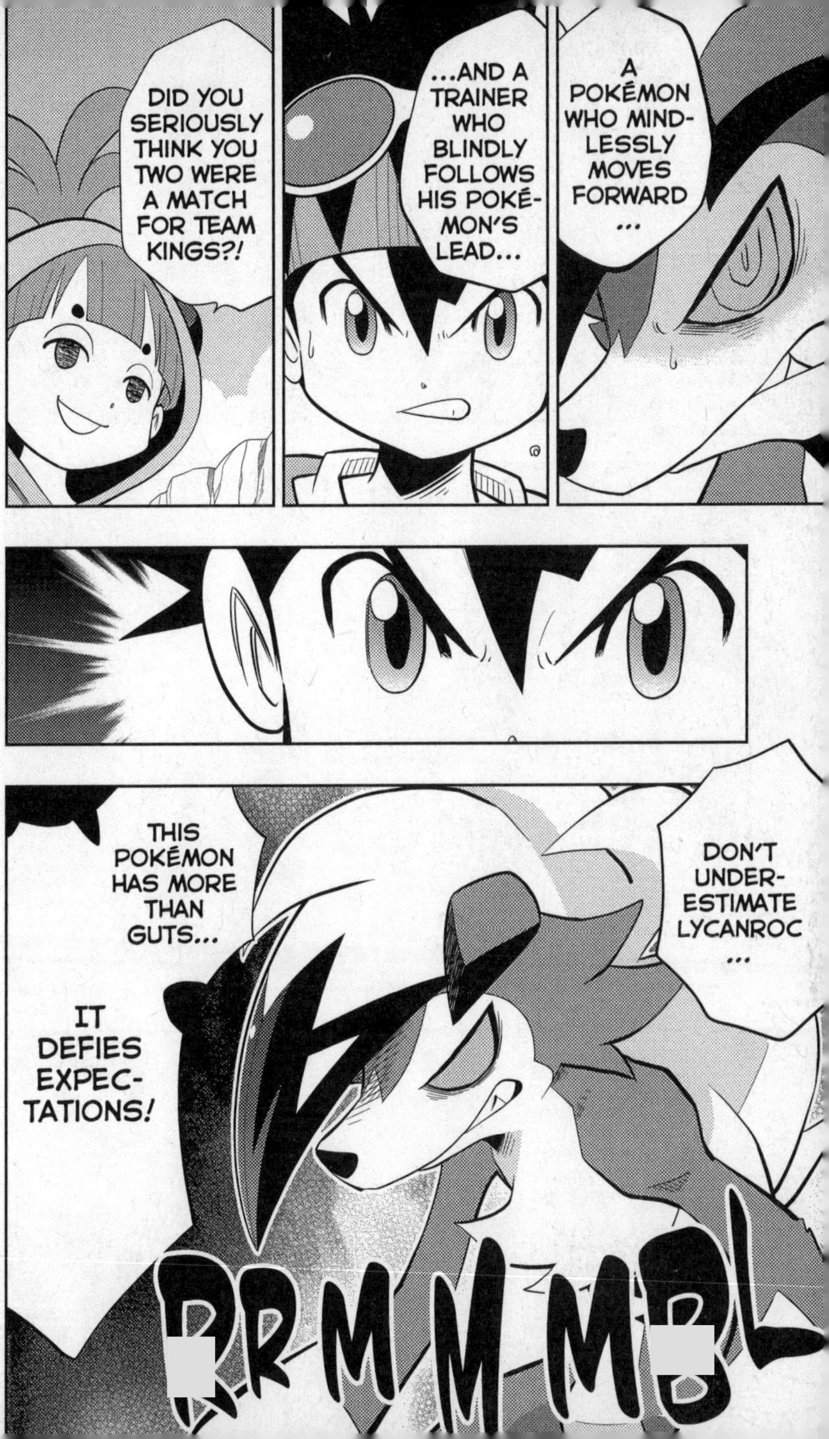
A POKÉMON WHO MINDLESSLY MOVES FORWARD...
...AND A TRAINER WHO BLINDLY FOLLOWS HIS POKÉMON'S LEAD...
DID YOU SERIOUSLY THINK YOU TWO WERE A MATCH FOR TEAM KINGS?!
DON'T UNDERESTIMATE LYCANROC...
THIS POKÉMON HAS MORE THAN GUTS...
IT DEFIES EXPECTATIONS!
RRMMMBL

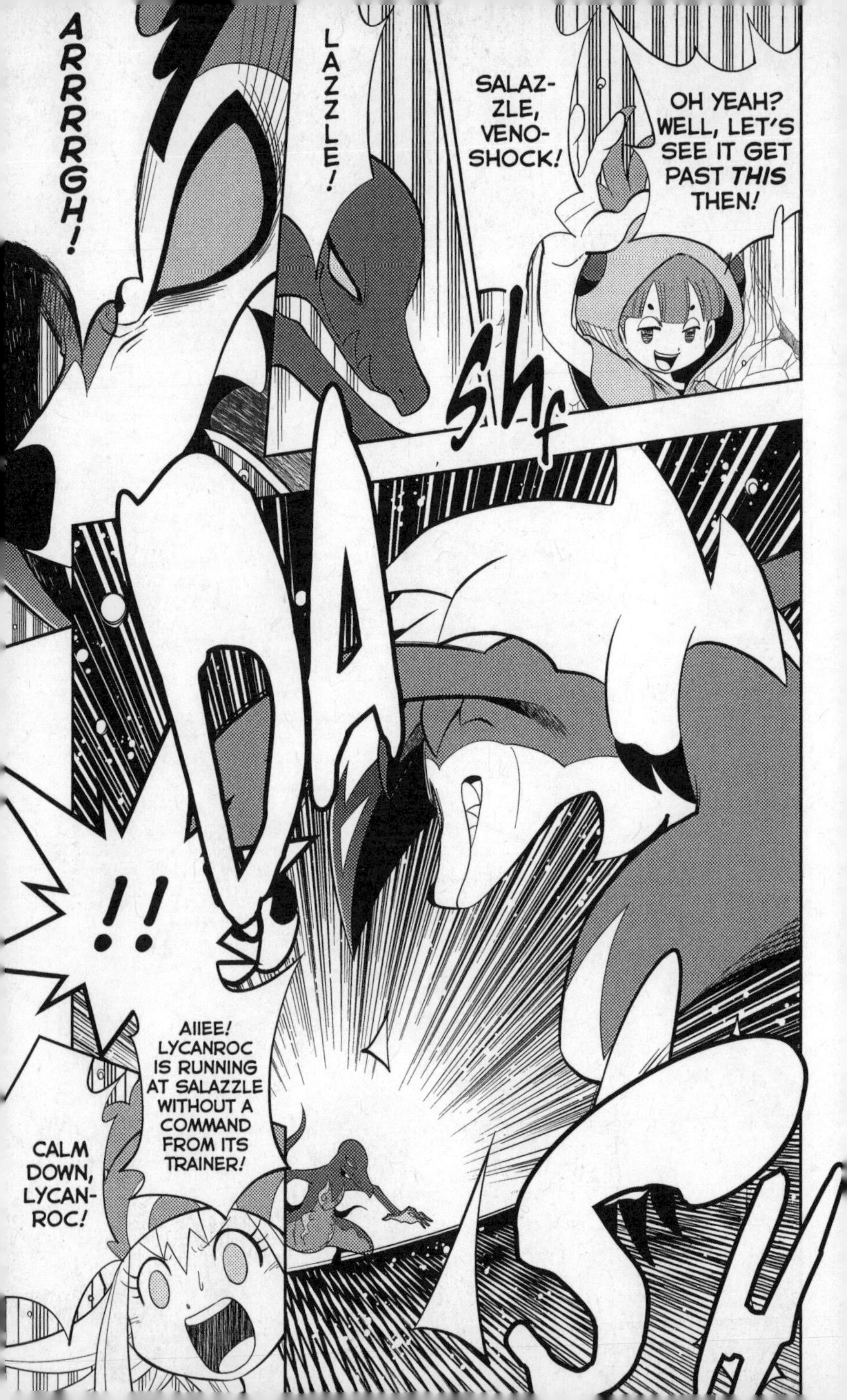
OH YEAH? WELL, LET'S SEE IT GET PAST *THIS* THEN!
SALAZ-ZLE, VENO-SHOCK!
LAZZLE!
Shf
ARRRRGH!
!!
AIIEE! LYCANROC IS RUNNING AT SALAZZLE WITHOUT A COMMAND FROM ITS TRAINER!
CALM DOWN, LYCAN-ROC!

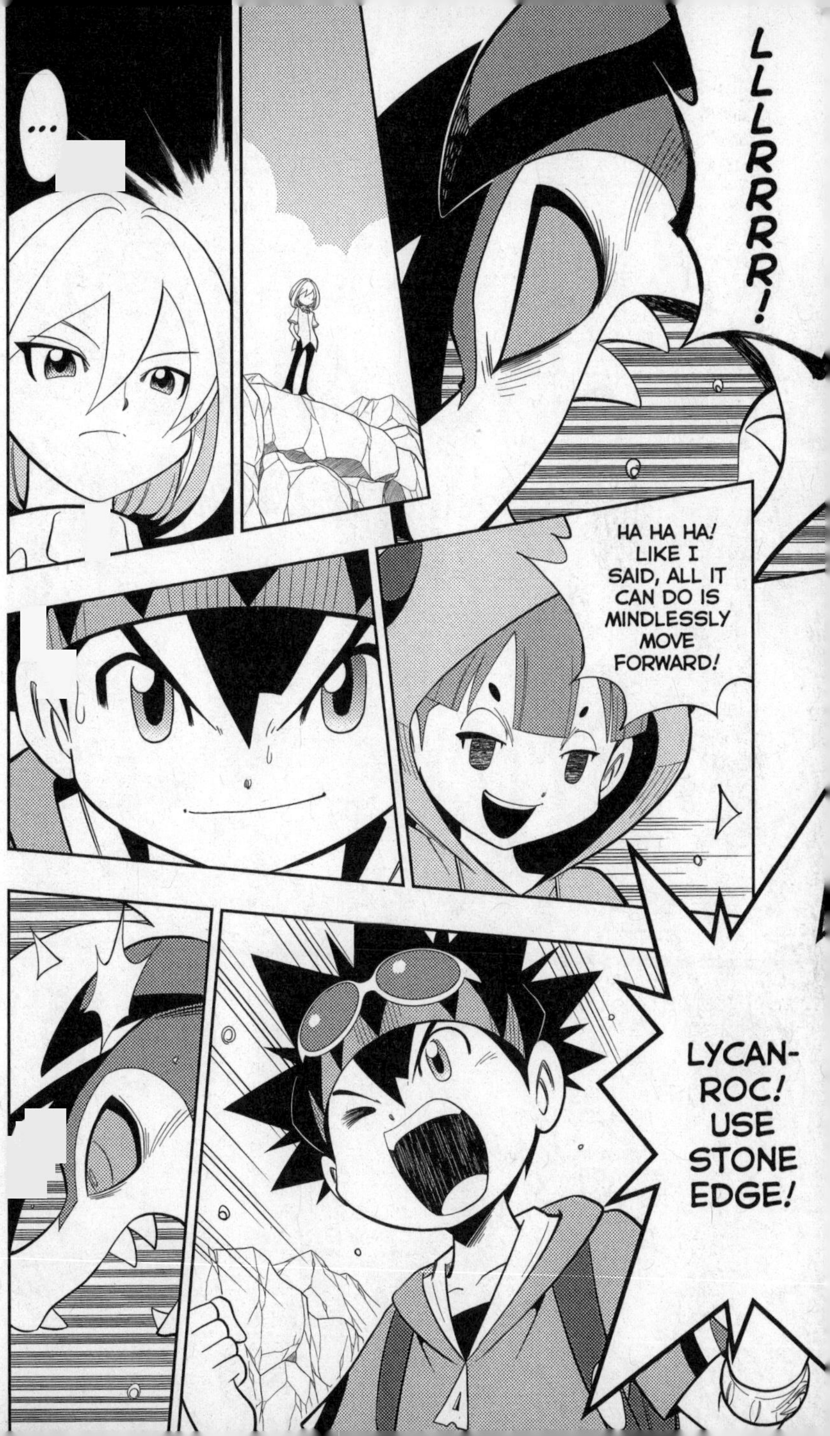
LLLRRRR!
...
HA HA HA! LIKE I SAID, ALL IT CAN DO IS MINDLESSLY MOVE FORWARD!
LYCAN-ROC! USE STONE EDGE!

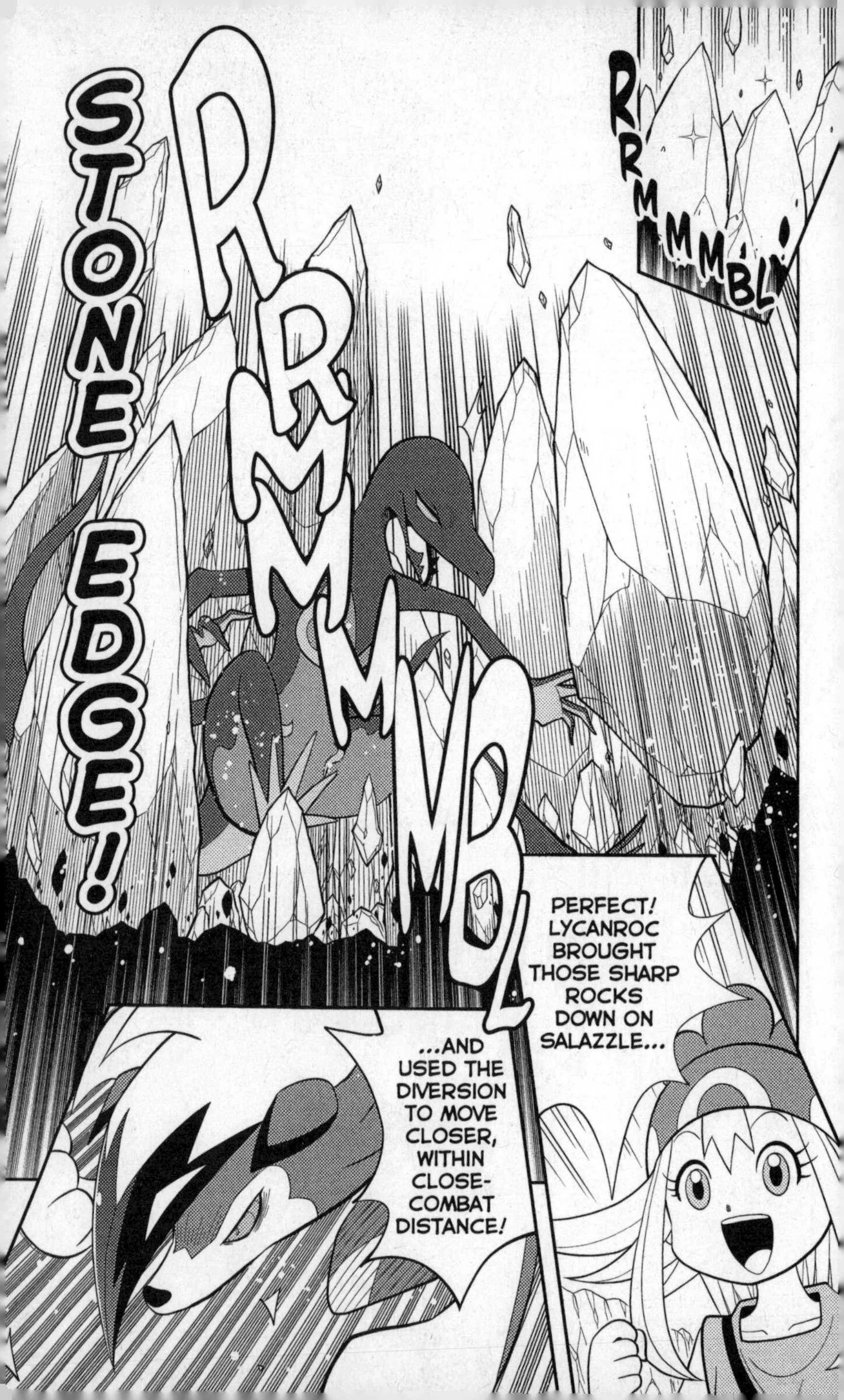

RRMMMBL
RRMMMBL
STONE EDGE!
PERFECT! LYCANROC BROUGHT THOSE SHARP ROCKS DOWN ON SALAZZLE...
...AND USED THE DIVERSION TO MOVE CLOSER, WITHIN CLOSE-COMBAT DISTANCE!

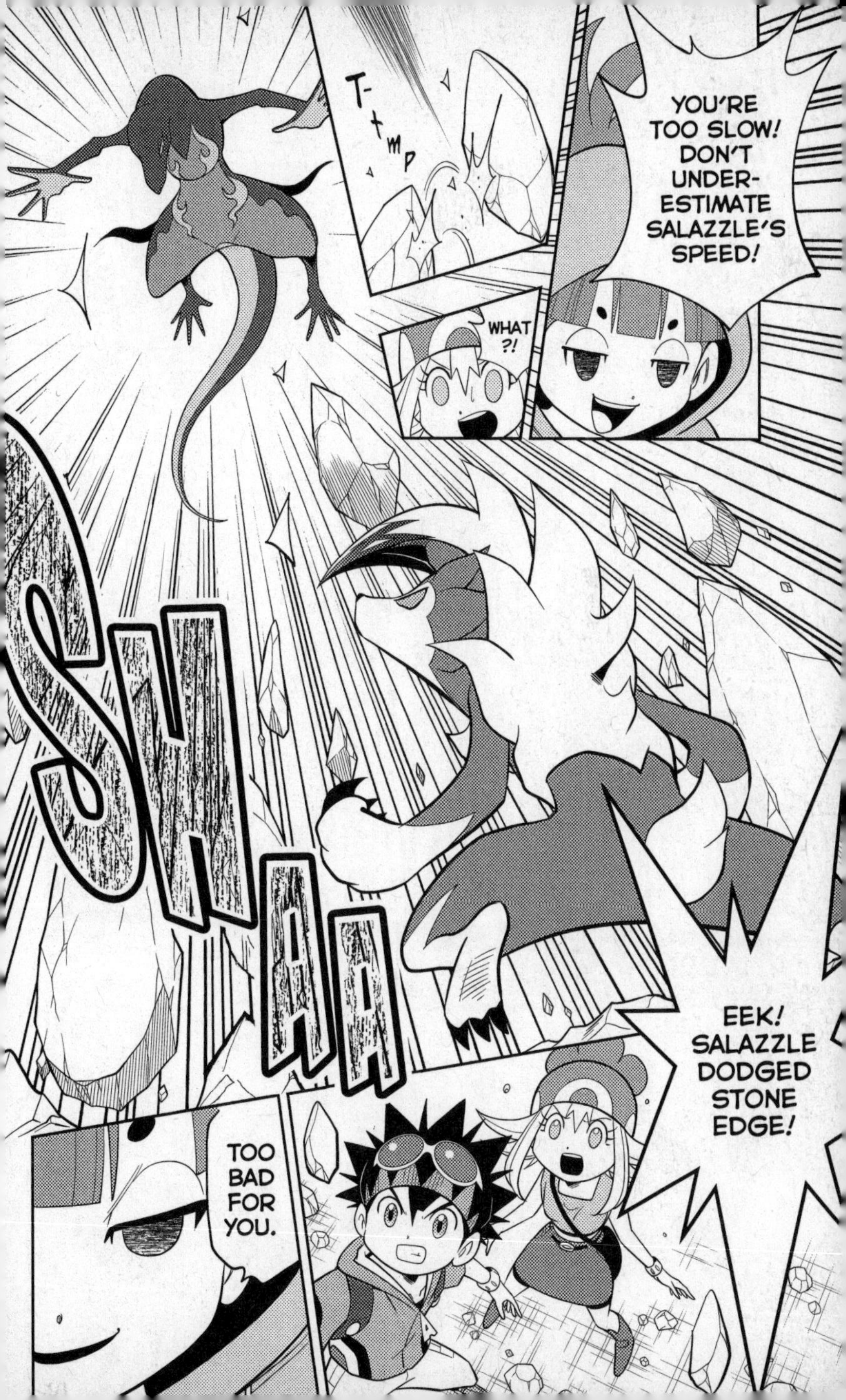
YOU'RE TOO SLOW! DON'T UNDER-ESTIMATE SALAZZLE'S SPEED!
T-tmp
WHAT ?!
SHAAA
EEK! SALAZZLE DODGED STONE EDGE!
TOO BAD FOR YOU.

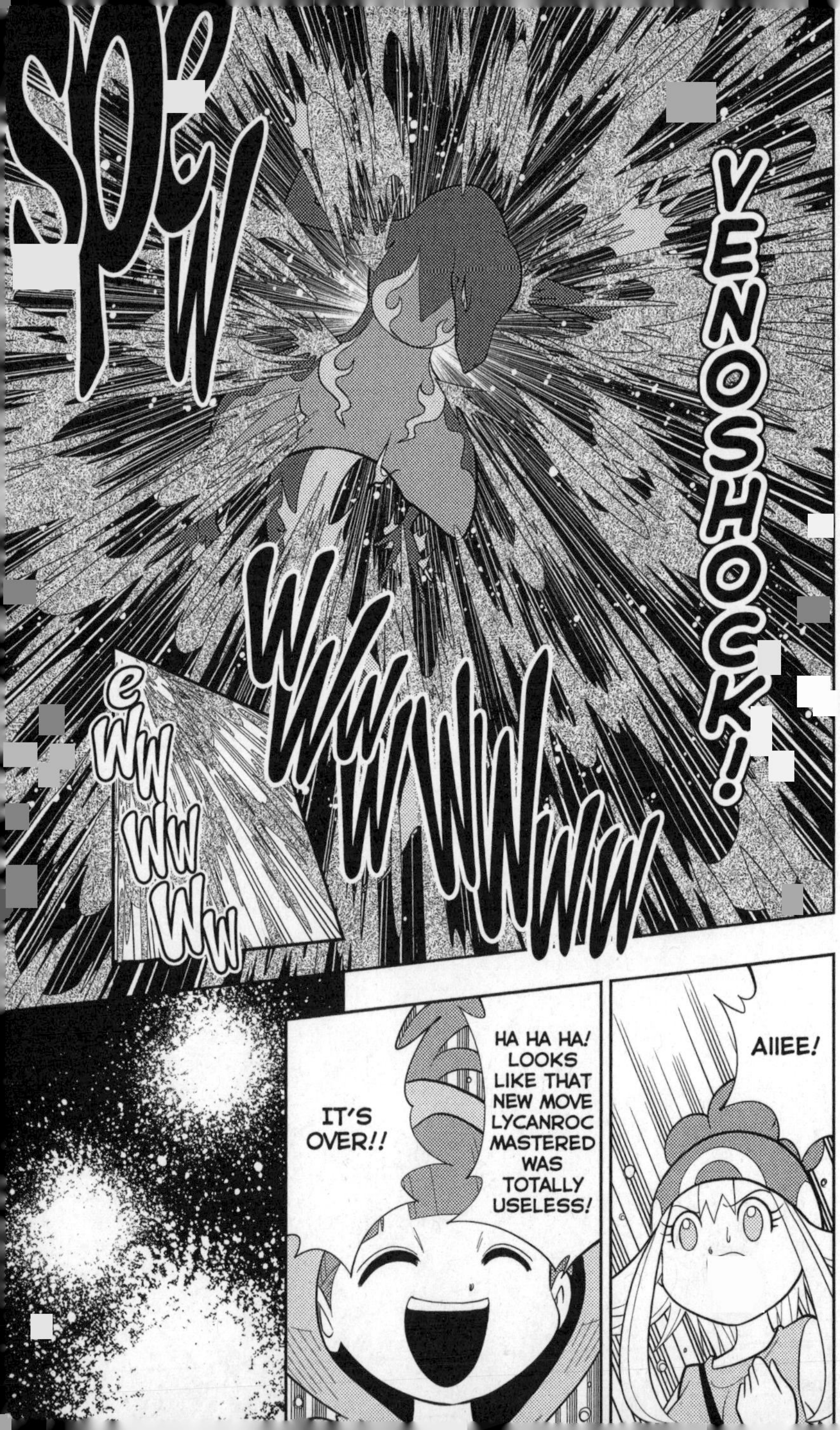
VENOSHOCK!
AIIEE!
HA HA HA! LOOKS LIKE THAT NEW MOVE LYCANROC MASTERED WAS TOTALLY USELESS!
IT'S OVER!!

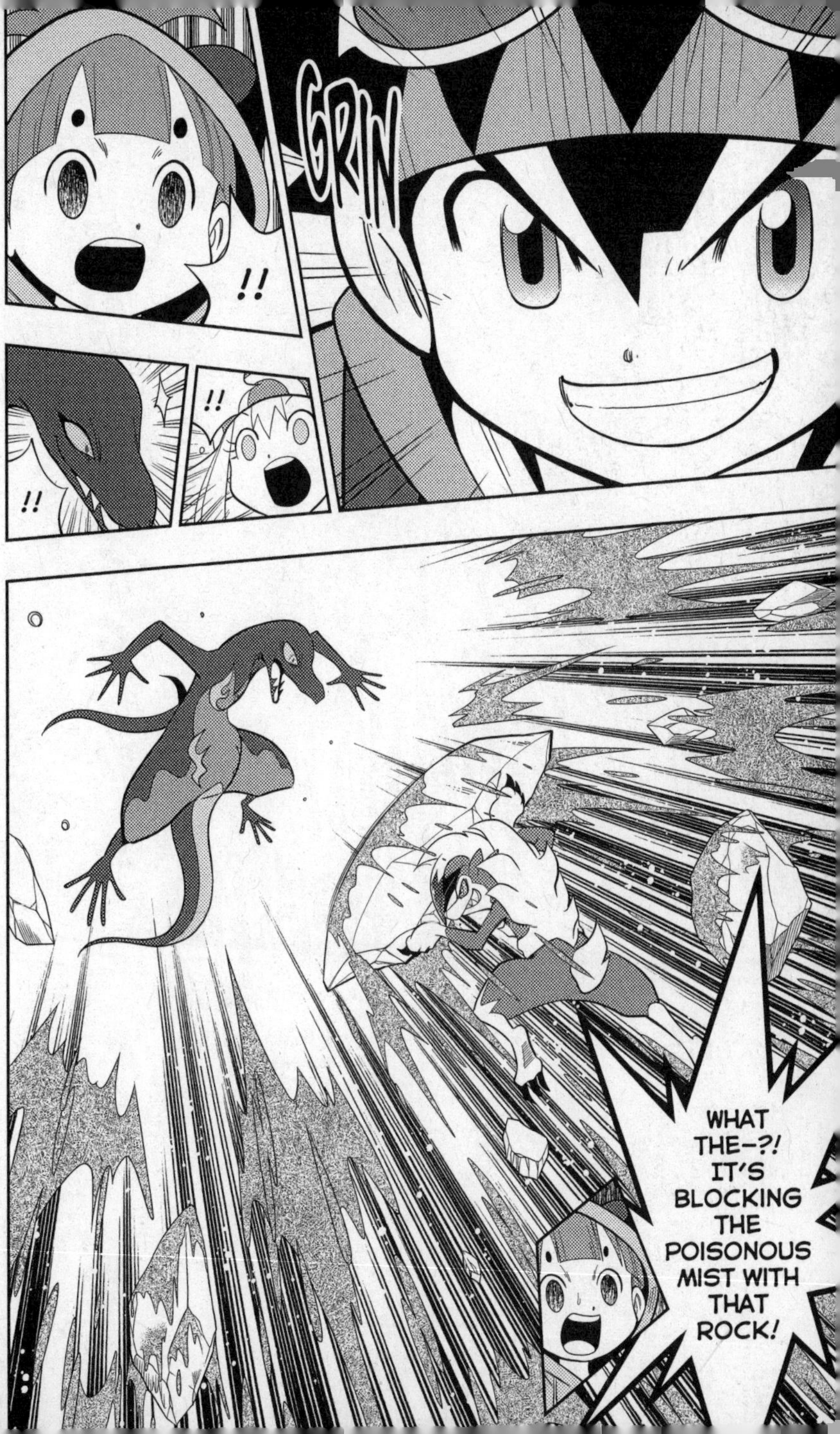
GRIN
!!
!!
!!
WHAT THE--?! IT'S BLOCKING THE POISONOUS MIST WITH THAT ROCK!

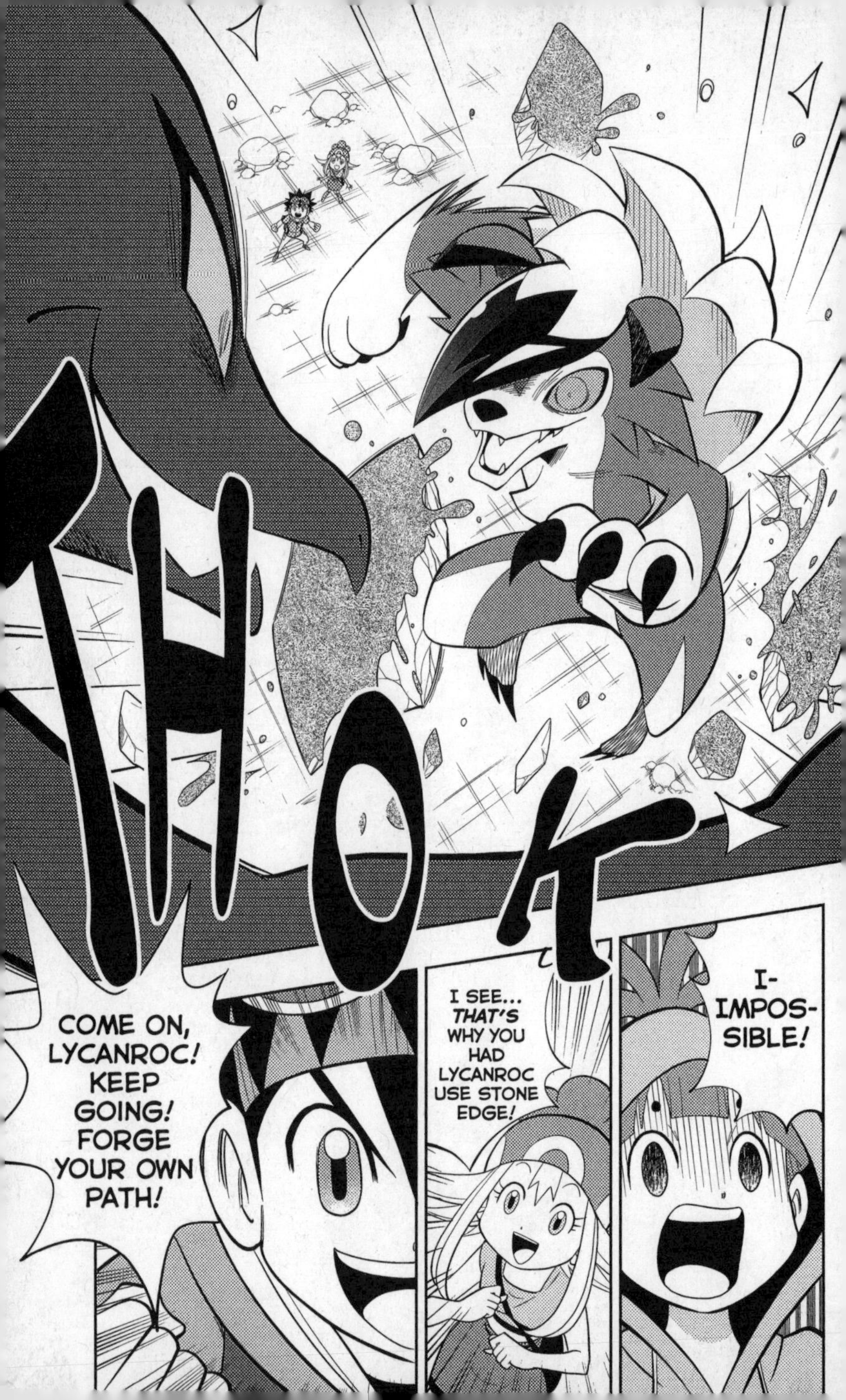
I- IMPOS- SIBLE!
I SEE... *THAT'S* WHY YOU HAD LYCANROC USE STONE EDGE!
COME ON, LYCANROC! KEEP GOING! FORGE YOUR OWN PATH!

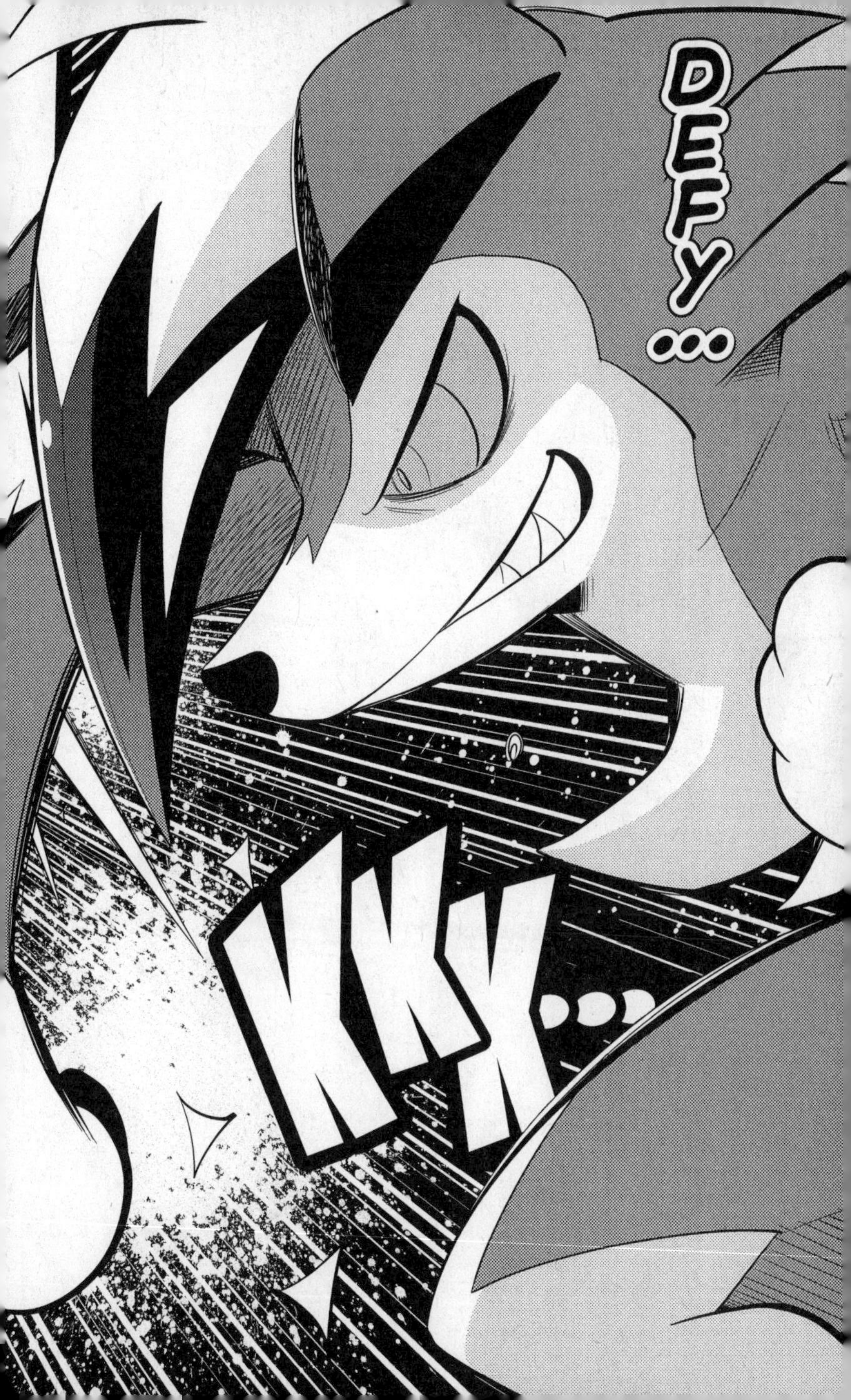
DEFY...
KKK...

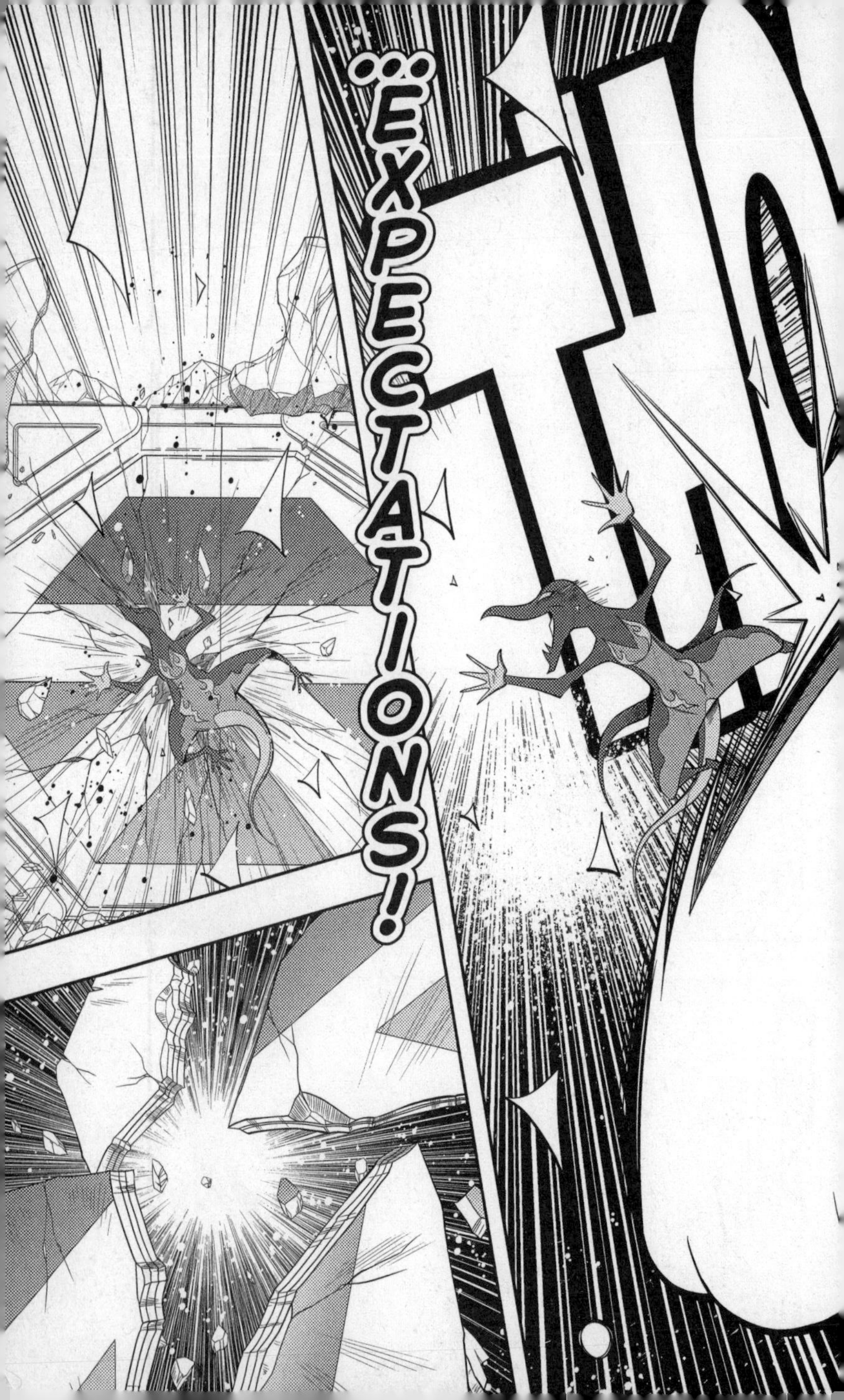
...EXPECTATIONS!

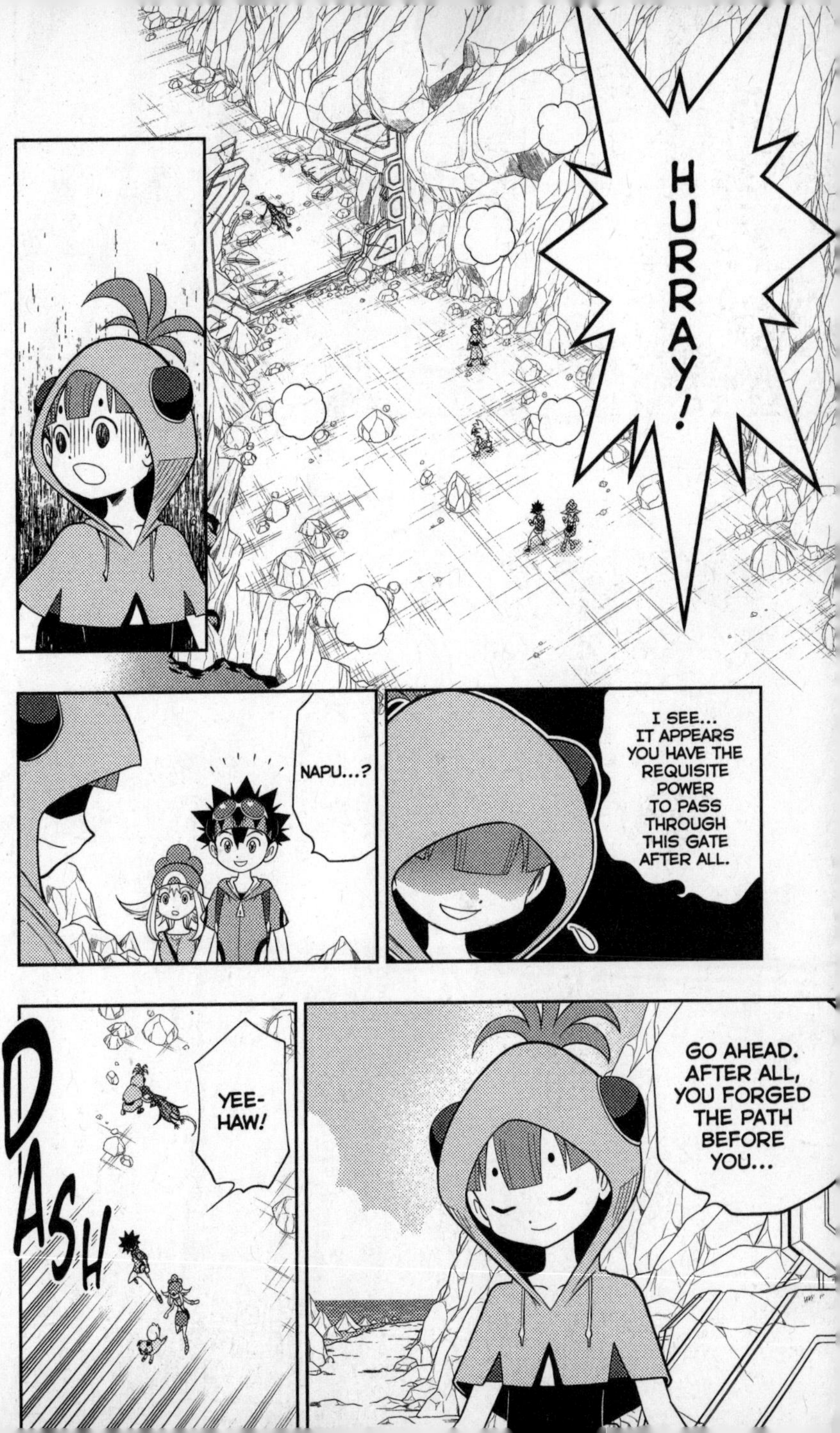
HURRAY!
I SEE... IT APPEARS YOU HAVE THE REQUISITE POWER TO PASS THROUGH THIS GATE AFTER ALL.
NAPU...?
GO AHEAD. AFTER ALL, YOU FORGED THE PATH BEFORE YOU...
YEE-HAW!
DASH

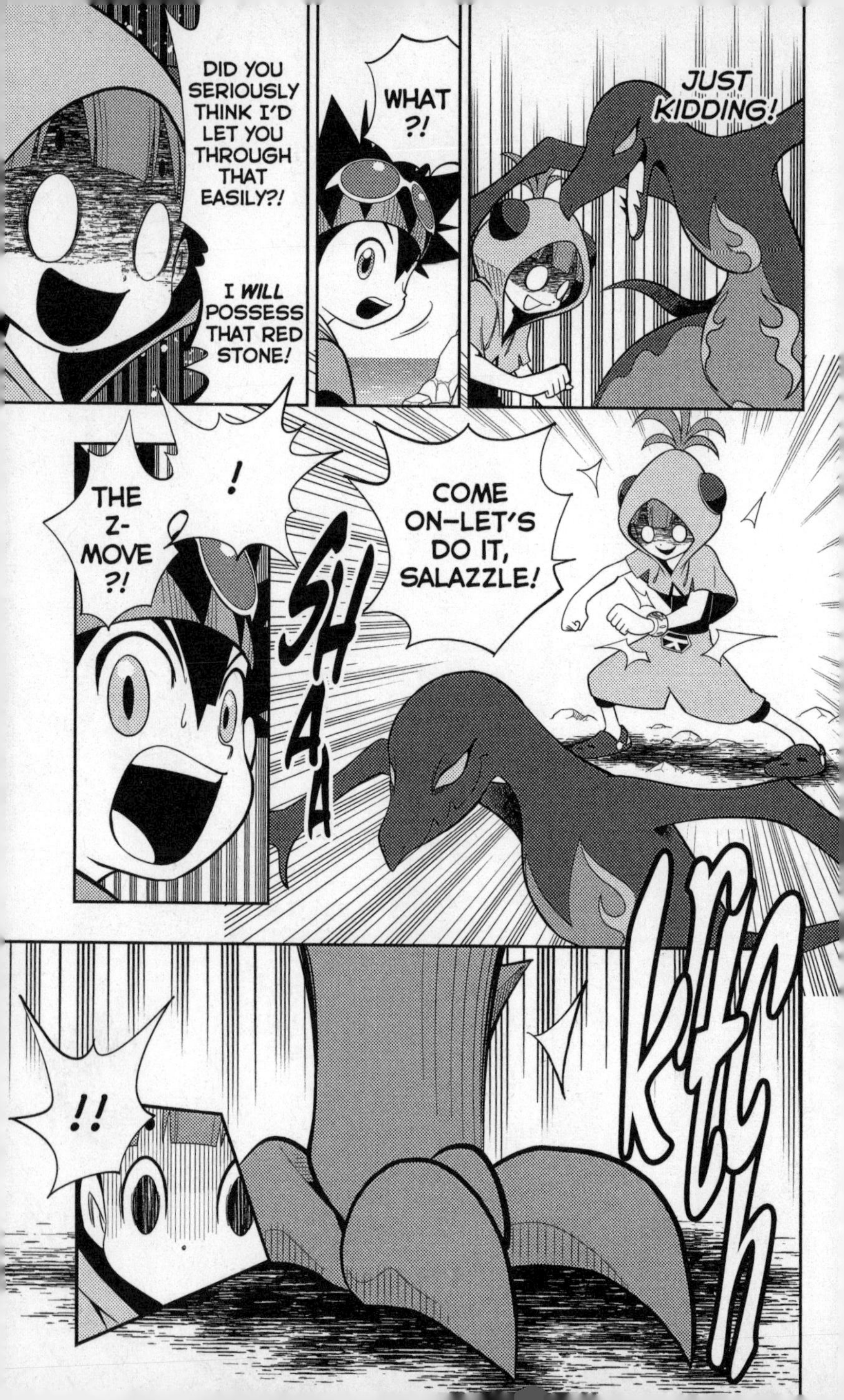
JUST KIDDING!
WHAT ?!
DID YOU SERIOUSLY THINK I'D LET YOU THROUGH THAT EASILY?!
I WILL POSSESS THAT RED STONE!
COME ON—LET'S DO IT, SALAZZLE!
SHAA
!
THE Z-MOVE ?!
!!

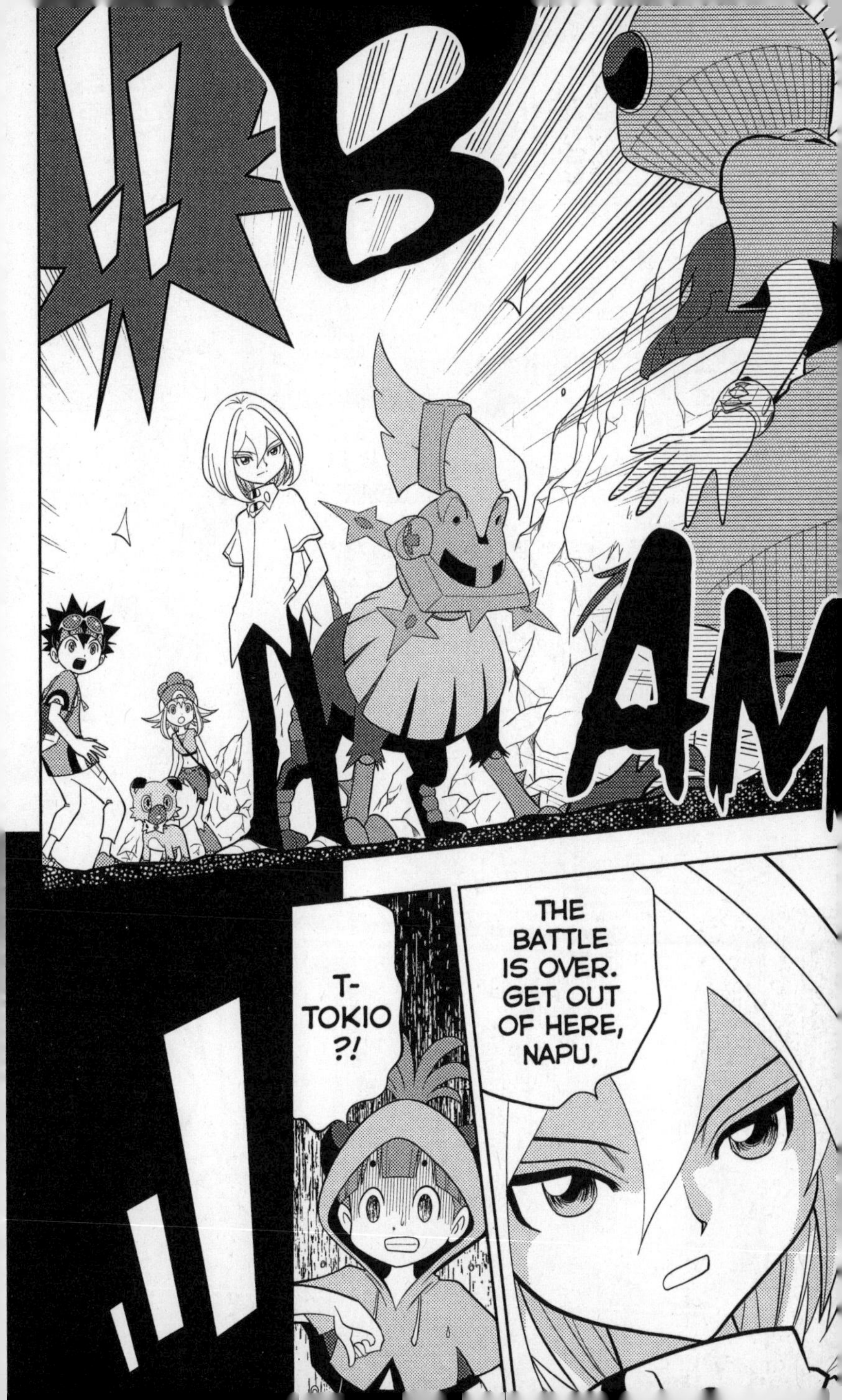
BAM
!!
THE BATTLE IS OVER. GET OUT OF HERE, NAPU.
T-TOKIO?!
..!!

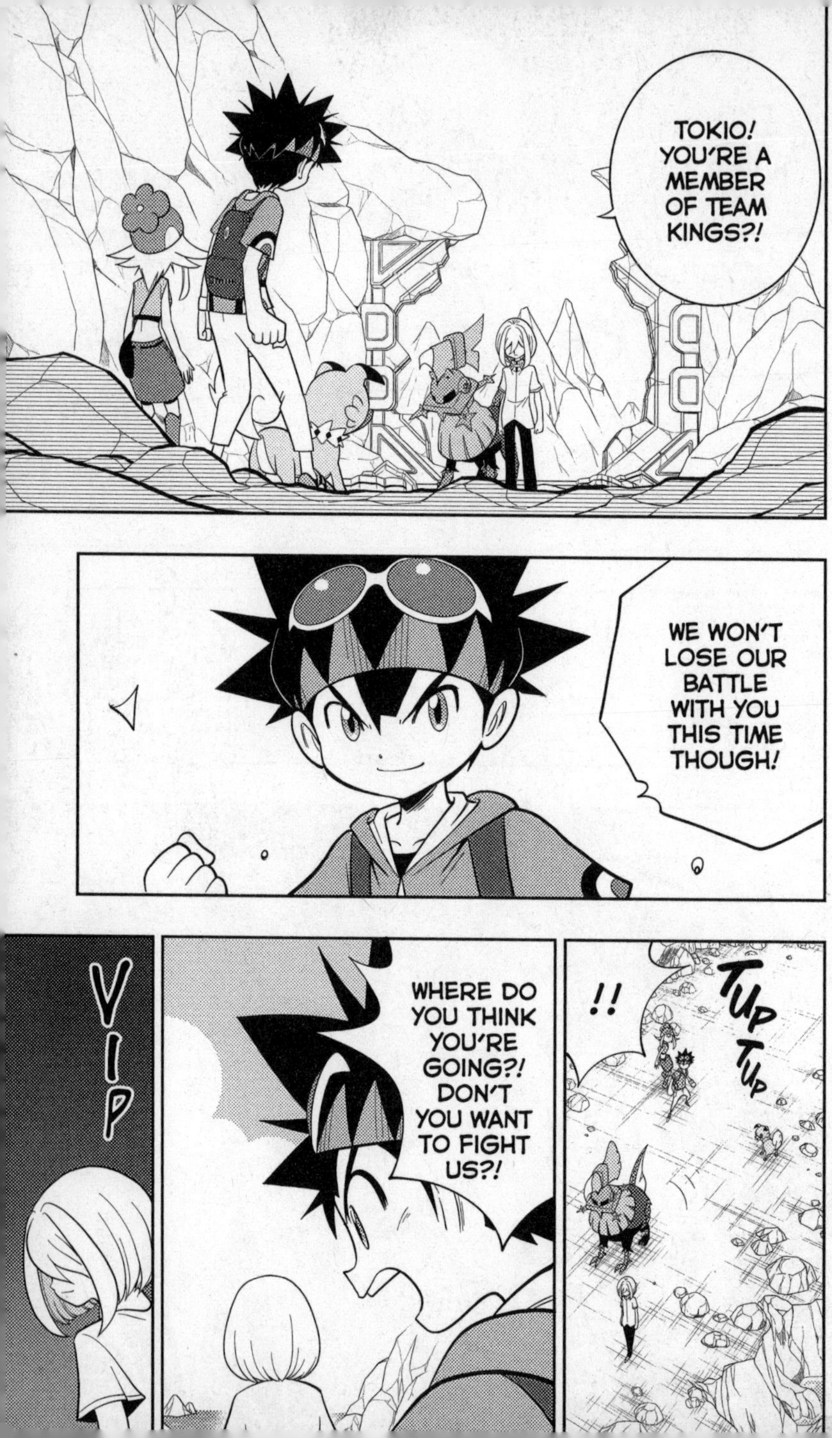
TOKIO! YOU'RE A MEMBER OF TEAM KINGS?!
WE WON'T LOSE OUR BATTLE WITH YOU THIS TIME THOUGH!
!!
TUP TUP
WHERE DO YOU THINK YOU'RE GOING?! DON'T YOU WANT TO FIGHT US?!
VIP

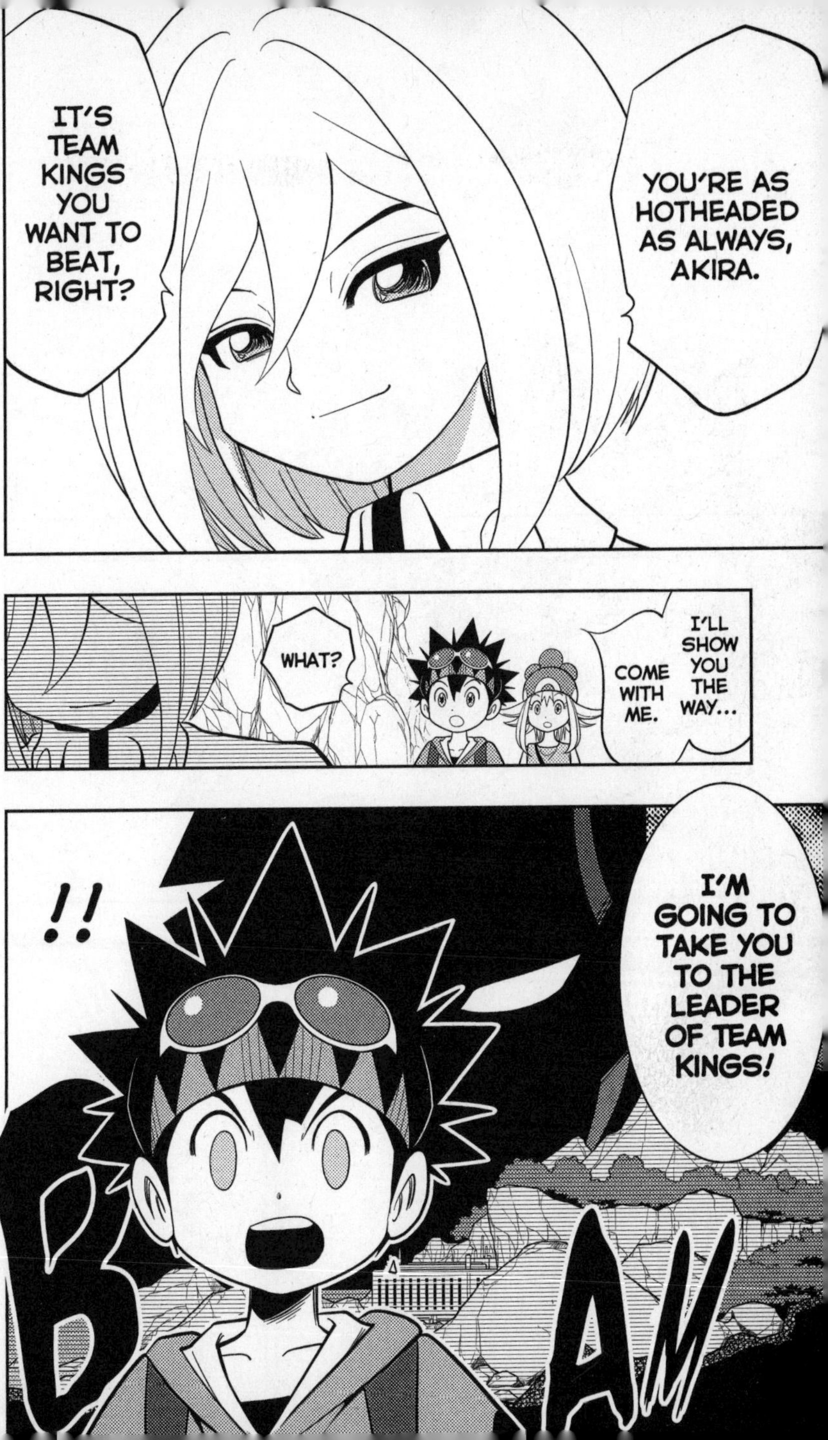
YOU'RE AS HOTHEADED AS ALWAYS, AKIRA.
IT'S TEAM KINGS YOU WANT TO BEAT, RIGHT?
I'LL SHOW YOU THE WAY...
COME WITH ME.
WHAT?
I'M GOING TO TAKE YOU TO THE LEADER OF TEAM KINGS!
!!
BAM

Event 8: The Legend Revealed

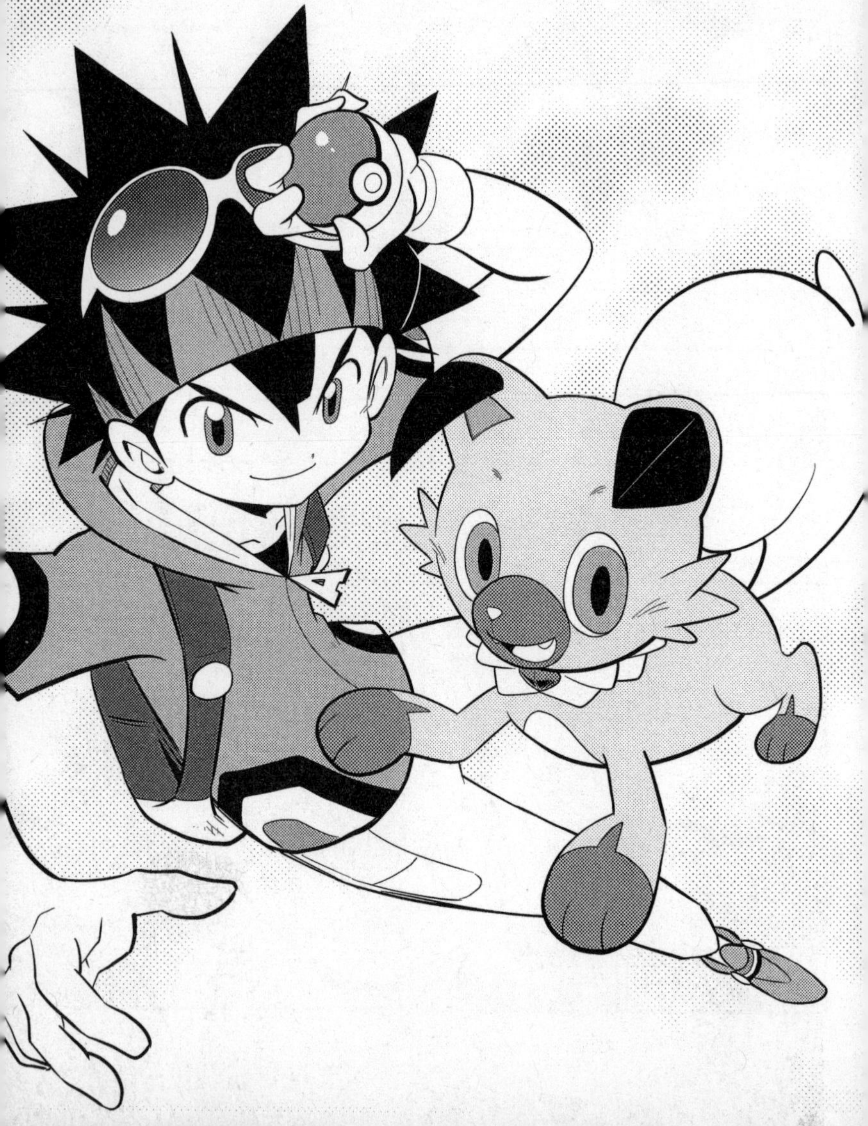

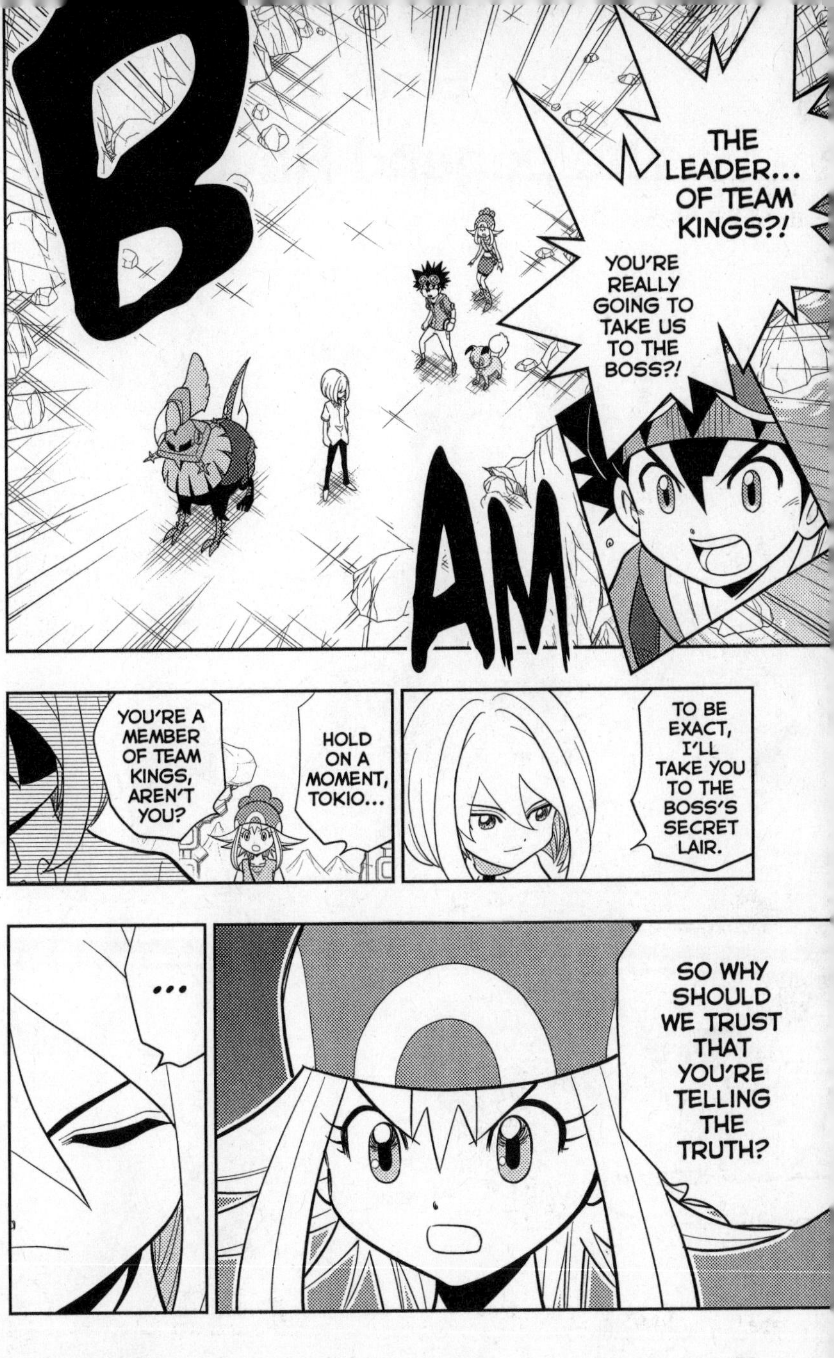
THE LEADER... OF TEAM KINGS?!
YOU'RE REALLY GOING TO TAKE US TO THE BOSS?!
BAM
TO BE EXACT, I'LL TAKE YOU TO THE BOSS'S SECRET LAIR.
HOLD ON A MOMENT, TOKIO...
YOU'RE A MEMBER OF TEAM KINGS, AREN'T YOU?
SO WHY SHOULD WE TRUST THAT YOU'RE TELLING THE TRUTH?
...

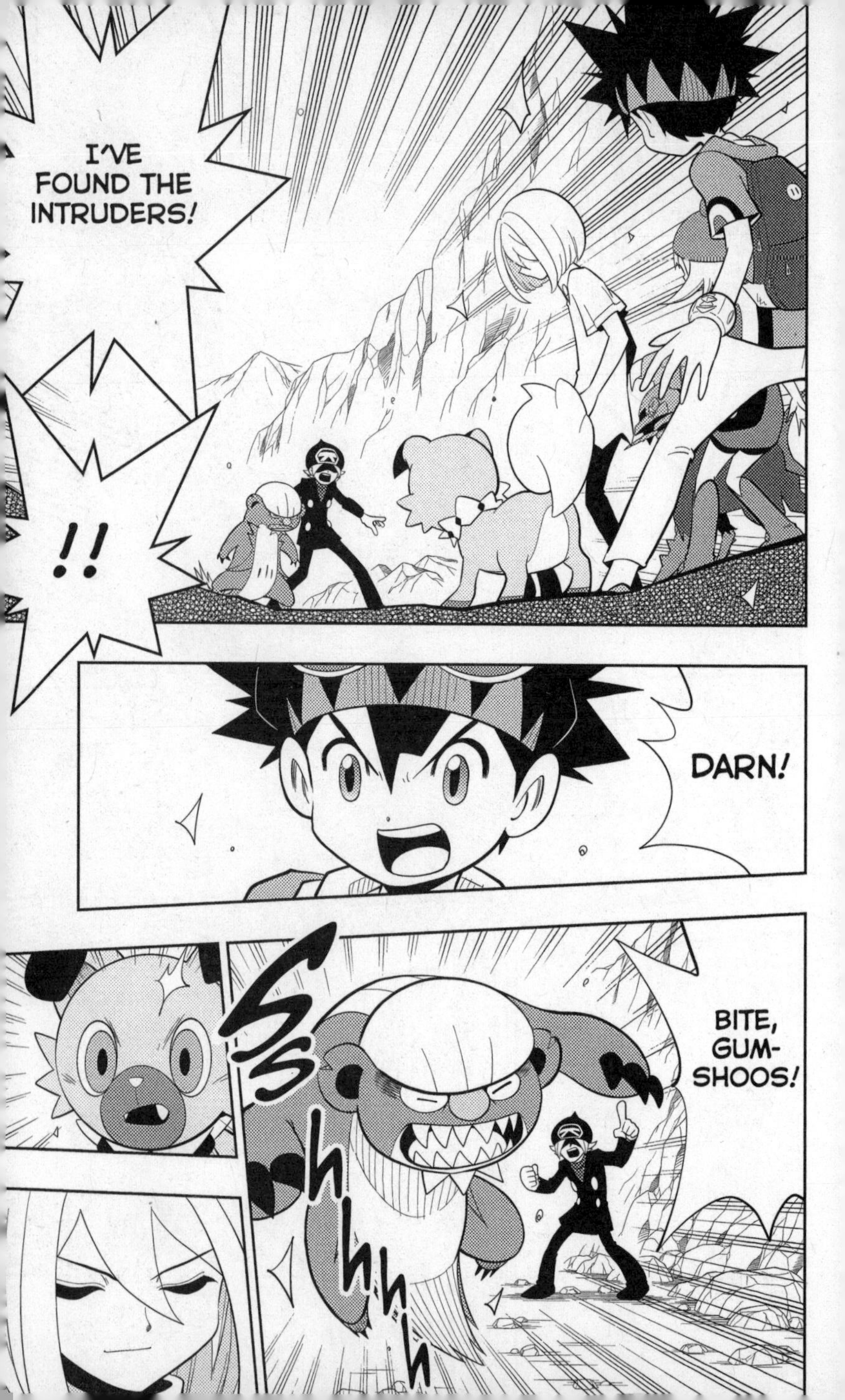
I'VE FOUND THE INTRUDERS!
!!
DARN!
BITE, GUM-SHOOS!
SShhhhh

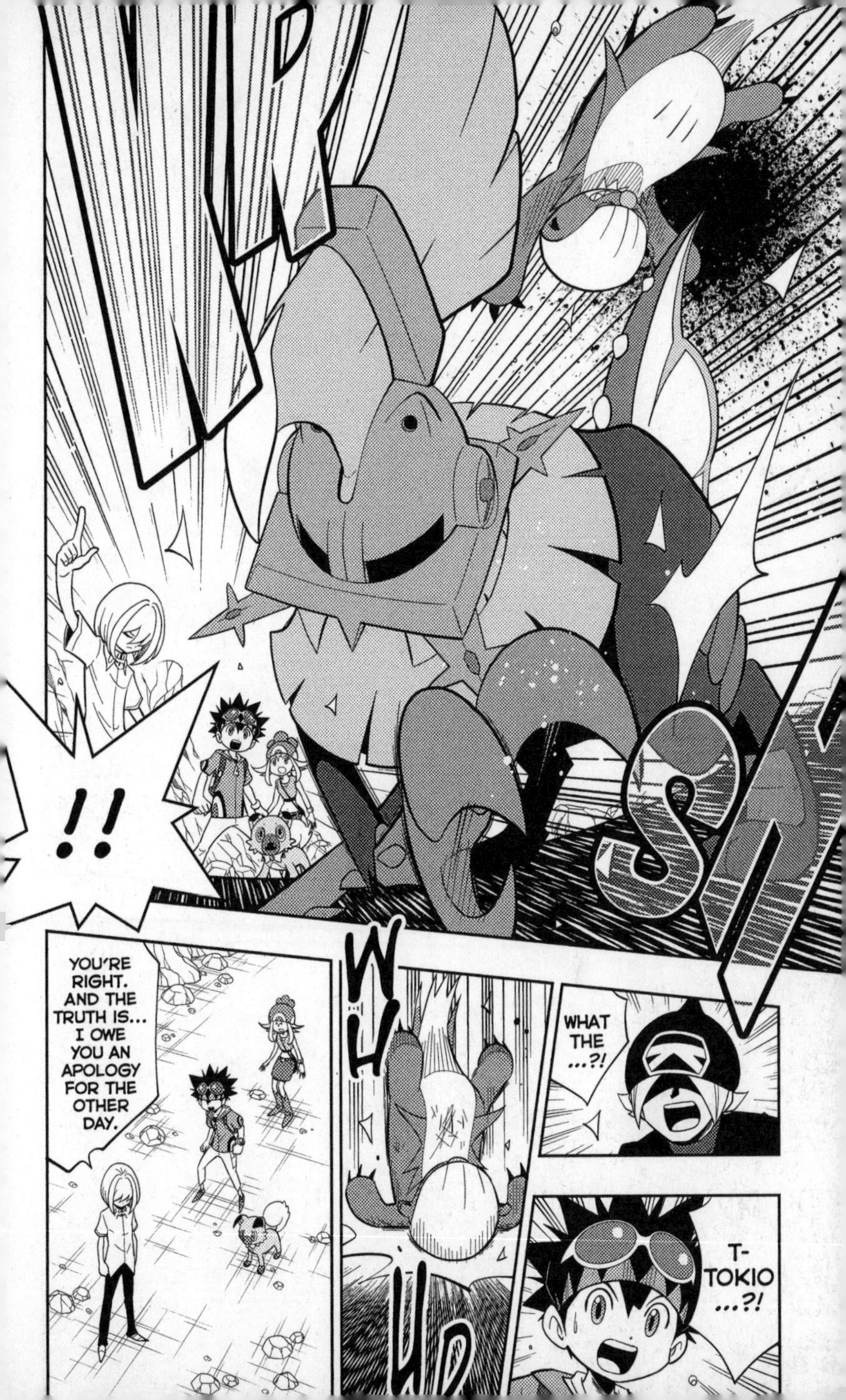
!!
WHAT THE ...?!
T-TOKIO ...?!
YOU'RE RIGHT. AND THE TRUTH IS... I OWE YOU AN APOLOGY FOR THE OTHER DAY.

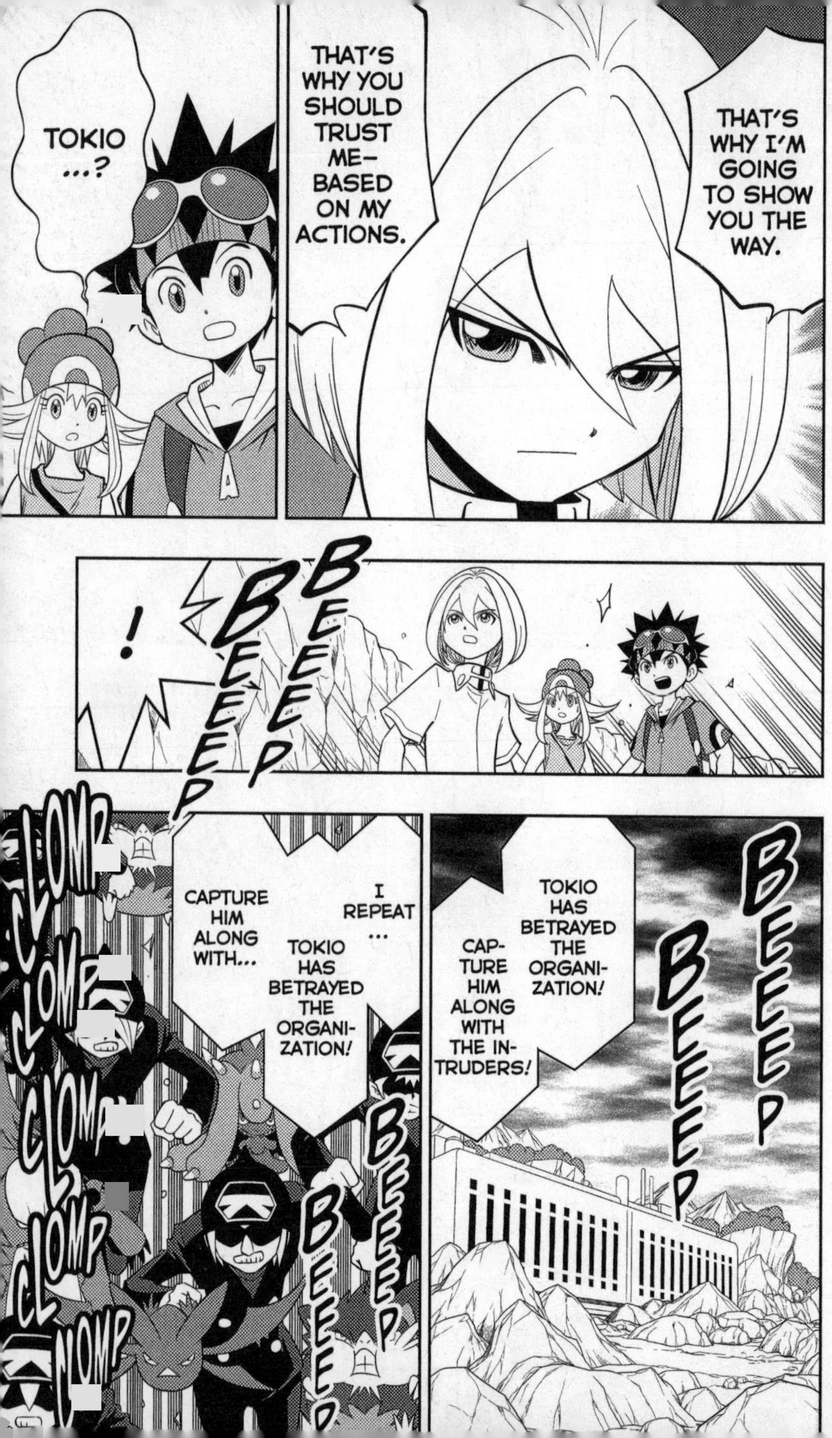
THAT'S WHY YOU SHOULD TRUST ME— BASED ON MY ACTIONS.
THAT'S WHY I'M GOING TO SHOW YOU THE WAY.
TOKIO ...?
BEEEP
BEEEEP
!
BEEEP
BEEEEP
TOKIO HAS BETRAYED THE ORGANIZATION!
CAPTURE HIM ALONG WITH THE INTRUDERS!
I REPEAT...
TOKIO HAS BETRAYED THE ORGANIZATION!
CAPTURE HIM ALONG WITH...
BEEEP
BEEEEP
CLOMP
CLOMP
CLOMP
CLOMP
CLOMP
CLOMP

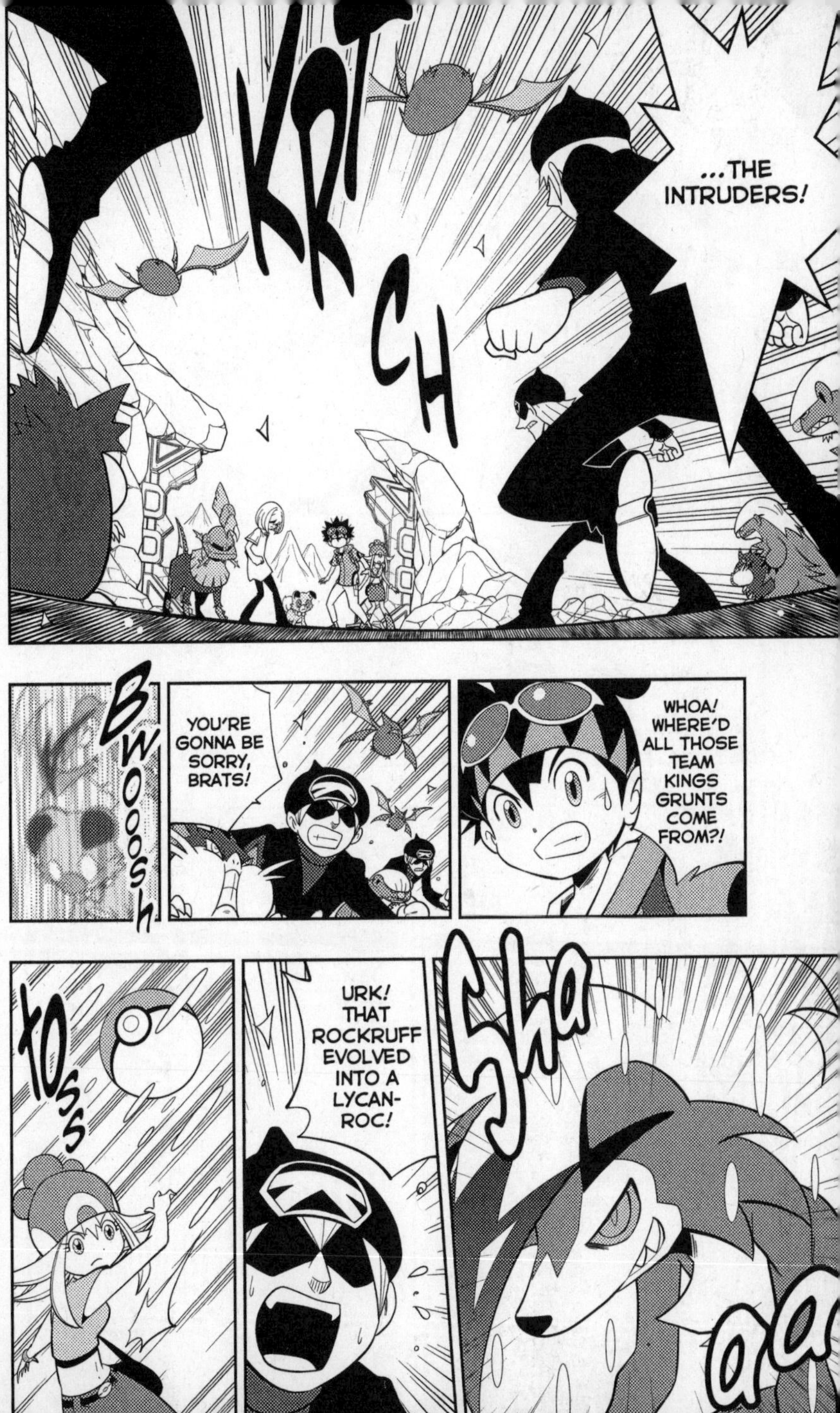
KRTCH
...THE INTRUDERS!
WHOA! WHERE'D ALL THOSE TEAM KINGS GRUNTS COME FROM?!
YOU'RE GONNA BE SORRY, BRATS!
BWOOOSH
Shaaa
URK! THAT ROCKRUFF EVOLVED INTO A LYCAN-ROC!
toss

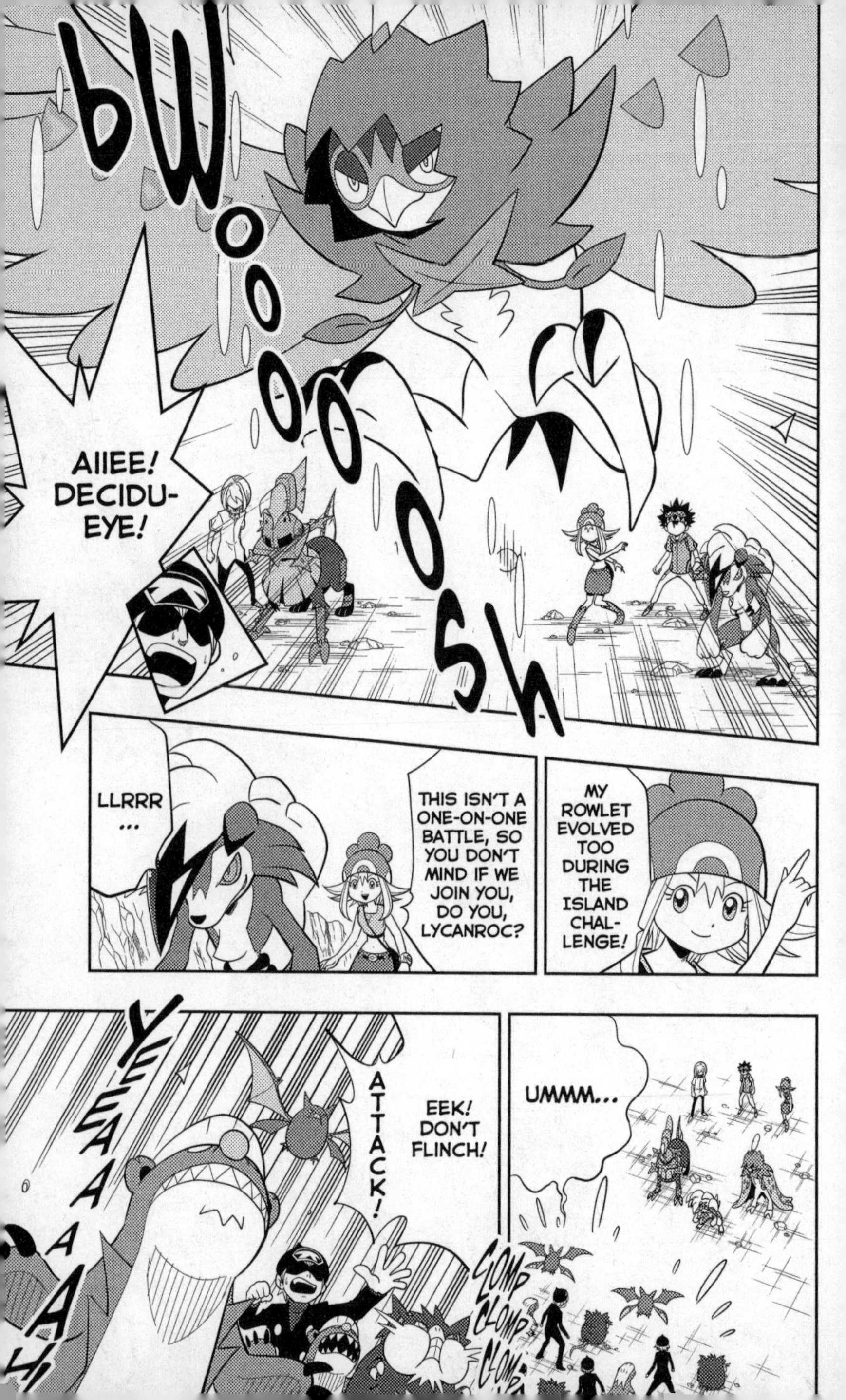
WOOOOOSH
AIIEE! DECIDU-EYE!
MY ROWLET EVOLVED TOO DURING THE ISLAND CHAL-LENGE!
THIS ISN'T A ONE-ON-ONE BATTLE, SO YOU DON'T MIND IF WE JOIN YOU, DO YOU, LYCANROC?
LLRRR...
UMMM...
CLOMP CLOMP CLOMP
EEK! DON'T FLINCH!
ATTACK!
YEEAAAAAH

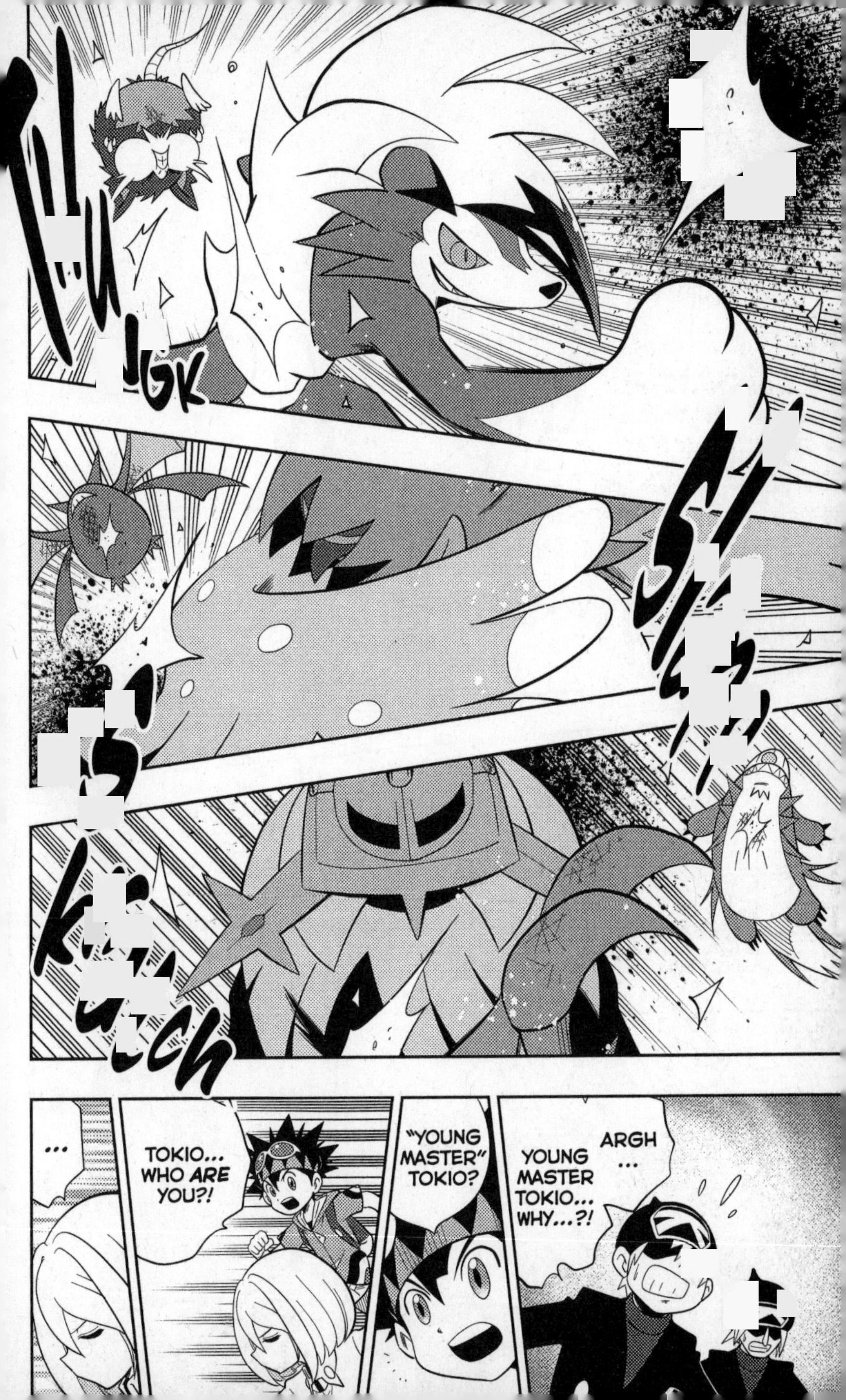
ARGH ...
YOUNG MASTER TOKIO... WHY...?!
"YOUNG MASTER" TOKIO?
TOKIO... WHO ARE YOU?!
...

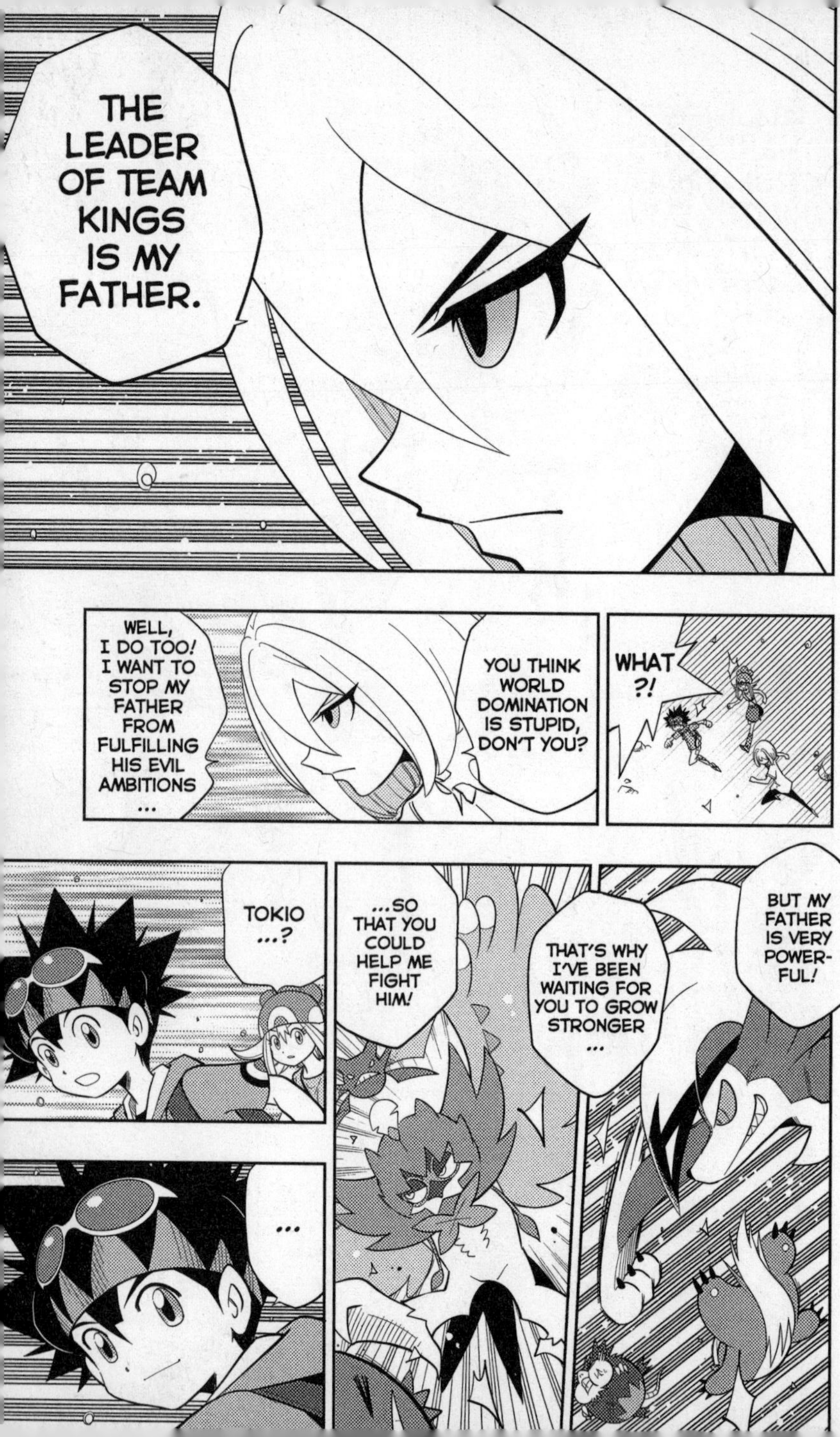
THE LEADER OF TEAM KINGS IS MY FATHER.
WHAT ?!
YOU THINK WORLD DOMINATION IS STUPID, DON'T YOU?
WELL, I DO TOO! I WANT TO STOP MY FATHER FROM FULFILLING HIS EVIL AMBITIONS ...
BUT MY FATHER IS VERY POWER-FUL!
THAT'S WHY I'VE BEEN WAITING FOR YOU TO GROW STRONGER ...
...SO THAT YOU COULD HELP ME FIGHT HIM!
TOKIO ...?
...

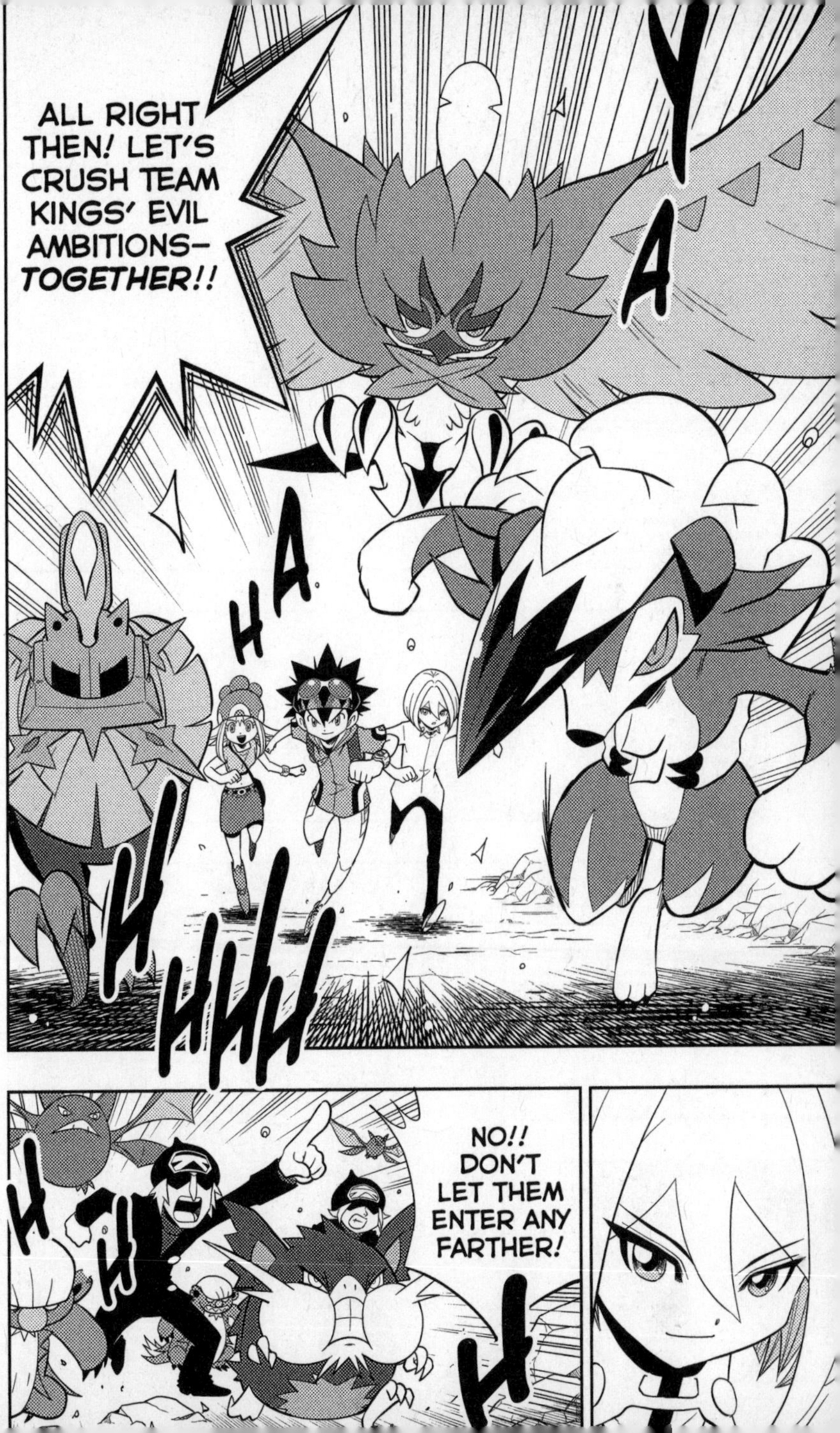
ALL RIGHT THEN! LET'S CRUSH TEAM KINGS' EVIL AMBITIONS—*TOGETHER!!*
YAAH
HHHHH
NO!! DON'T LET THEM ENTER ANY FARTHER!

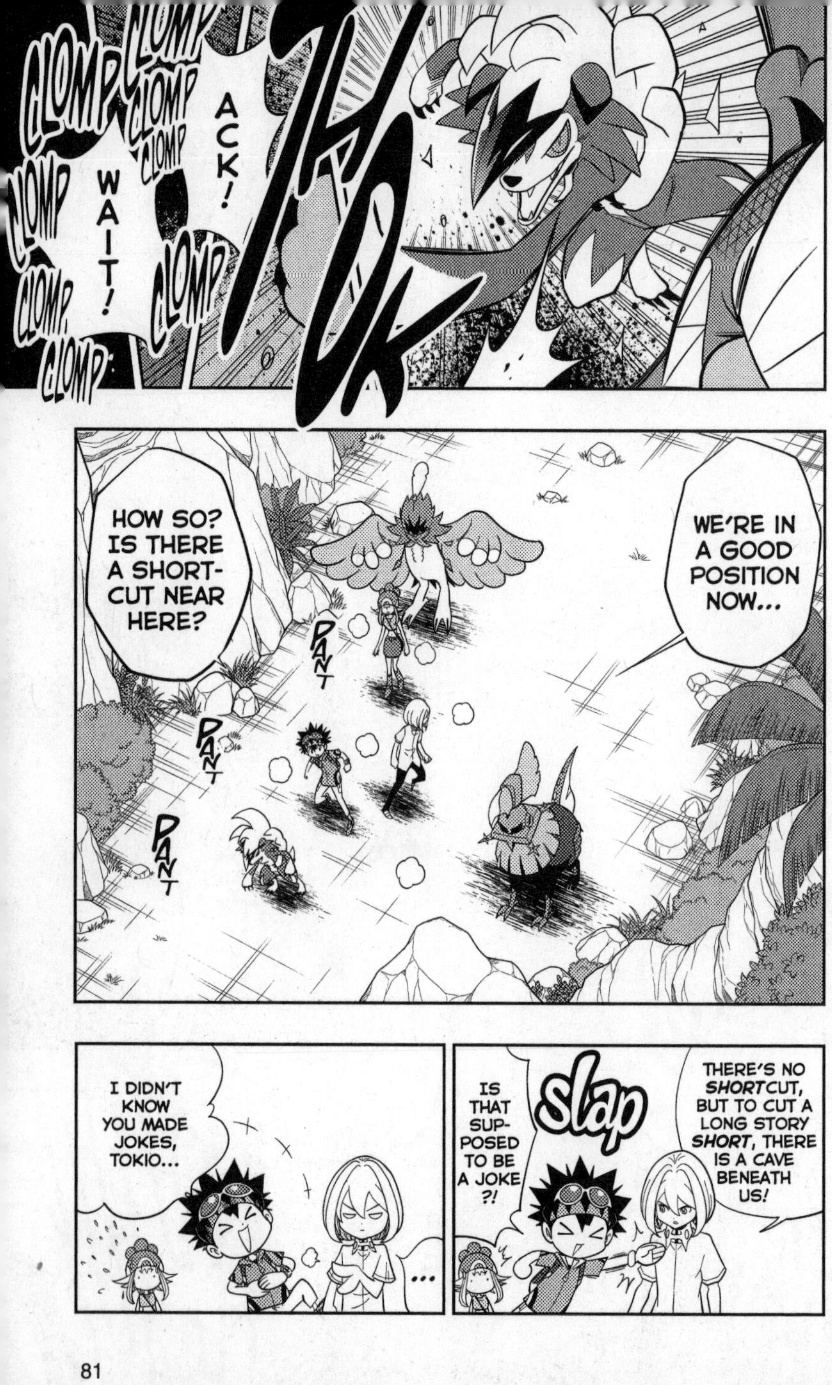
ACK!
WAIT!
CLOMP CLOMP CLOMP CLOMP CLOMP
CLOMP CLOMP CLOMP CLOMP
WE'RE IN A GOOD POSITION NOW...
HOW SO? IS THERE A SHORT-CUT NEAR HERE?
PANT
PANT
PANT
THERE'S NO *SHORT*CUT, BUT TO CUT A LONG STORY *SHORT*, THERE IS A CAVE BENEATH US!
slap
IS THAT SUP-POSED TO BE A JOKE ?!
I DIDN'T KNOW YOU MADE JOKES, TOKIO...
...

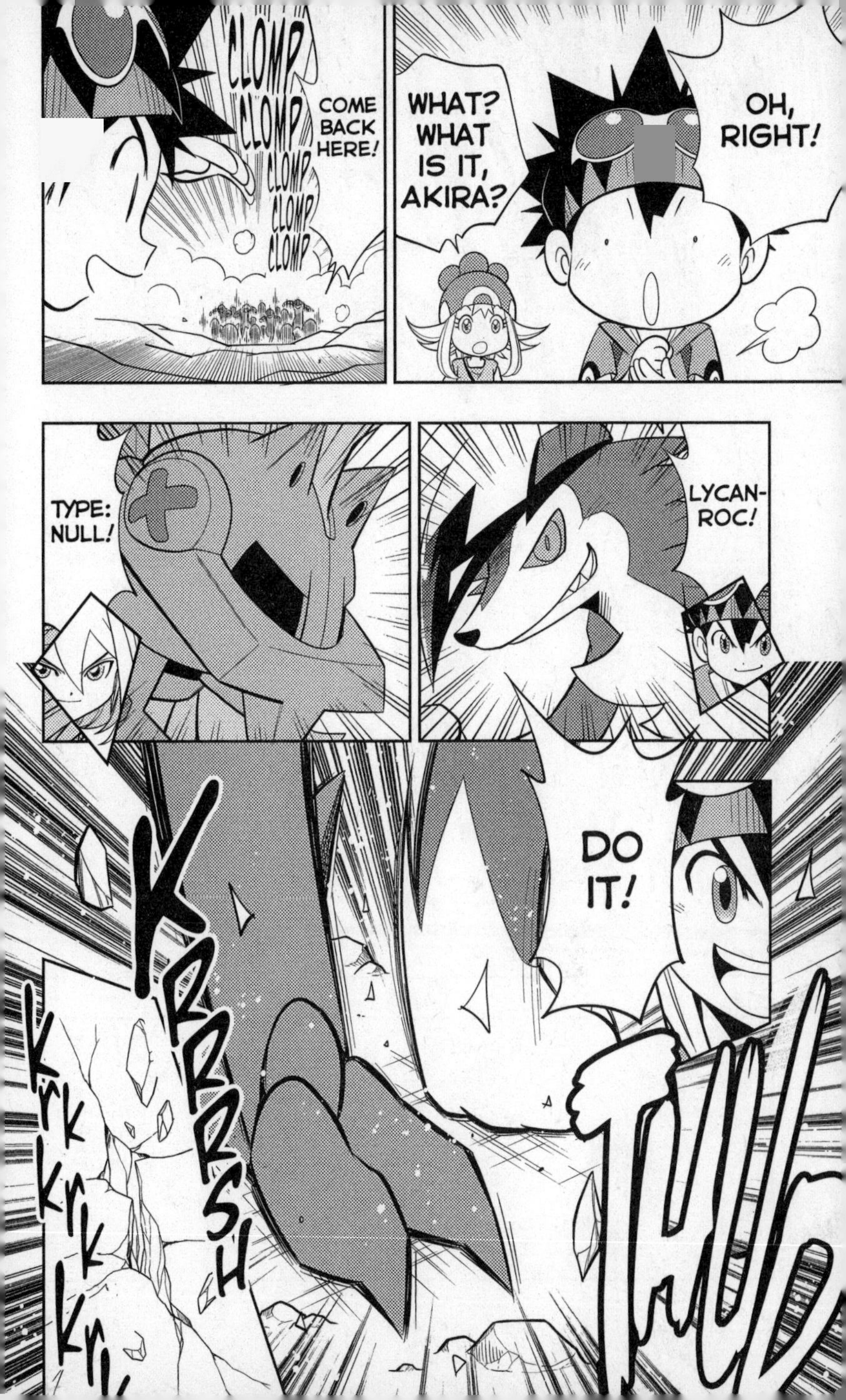
OH, RIGHT!
WHAT? WHAT IS IT, AKIRA?
COME BACK HERE!
CLOMP CLOMP CLOMP CLOMP CLOMP CLOMP
LYCAN-ROC!
TYPE: NULL!
DO IT!
KRRRSH
THUD

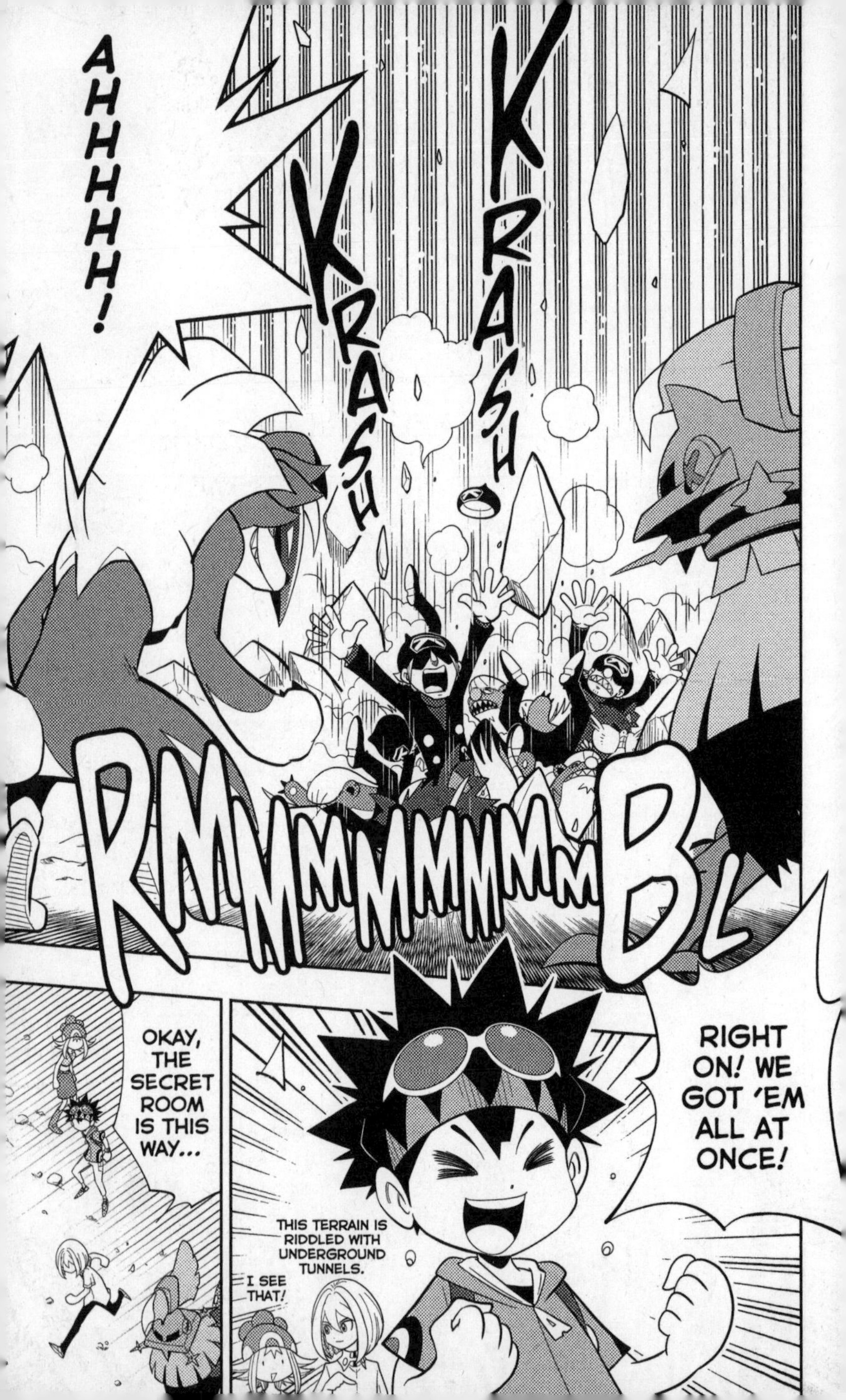
KRASH
KRASH
AHHHHH!
RMMMMMMMMBL
RIGHT ON! WE GOT 'EM ALL AT ONCE!
THIS TERRAIN IS RIDDLED WITH UNDERGROUND TUNNELS.
I SEE THAT!
OKAY, THE SECRET ROOM IS THIS WAY...

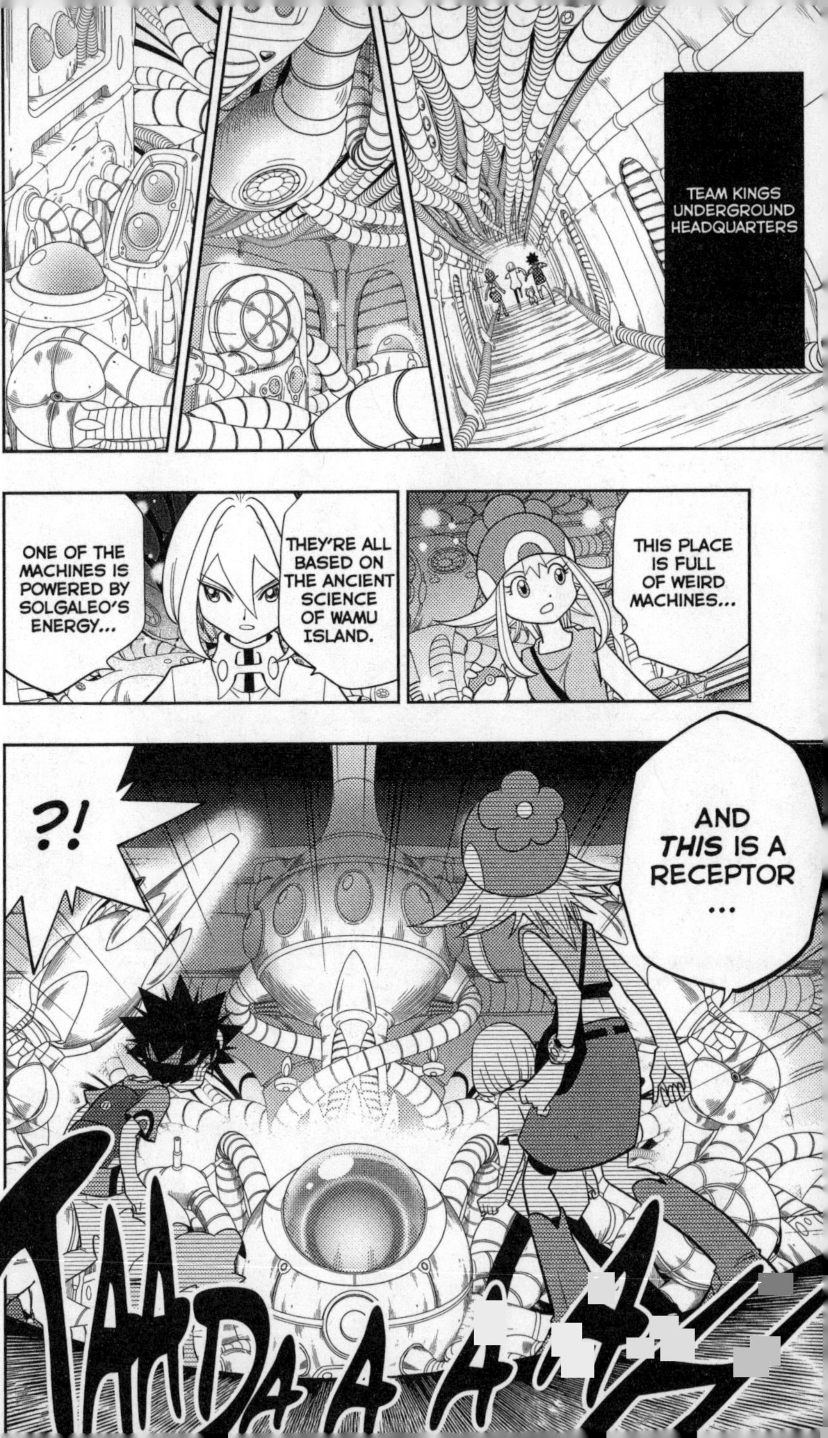
TEAM KINGS UNDERGROUND HEADQUARTERS
THIS PLACE IS FULL OF WEIRD MACHINES...
THEY'RE ALL BASED ON THE ANCIENT SCIENCE OF WAMU ISLAND.
ONE OF THE MACHINES IS POWERED BY SOLGALEO'S ENERGY...
AND *THIS* IS A RECEPTOR ...
?!

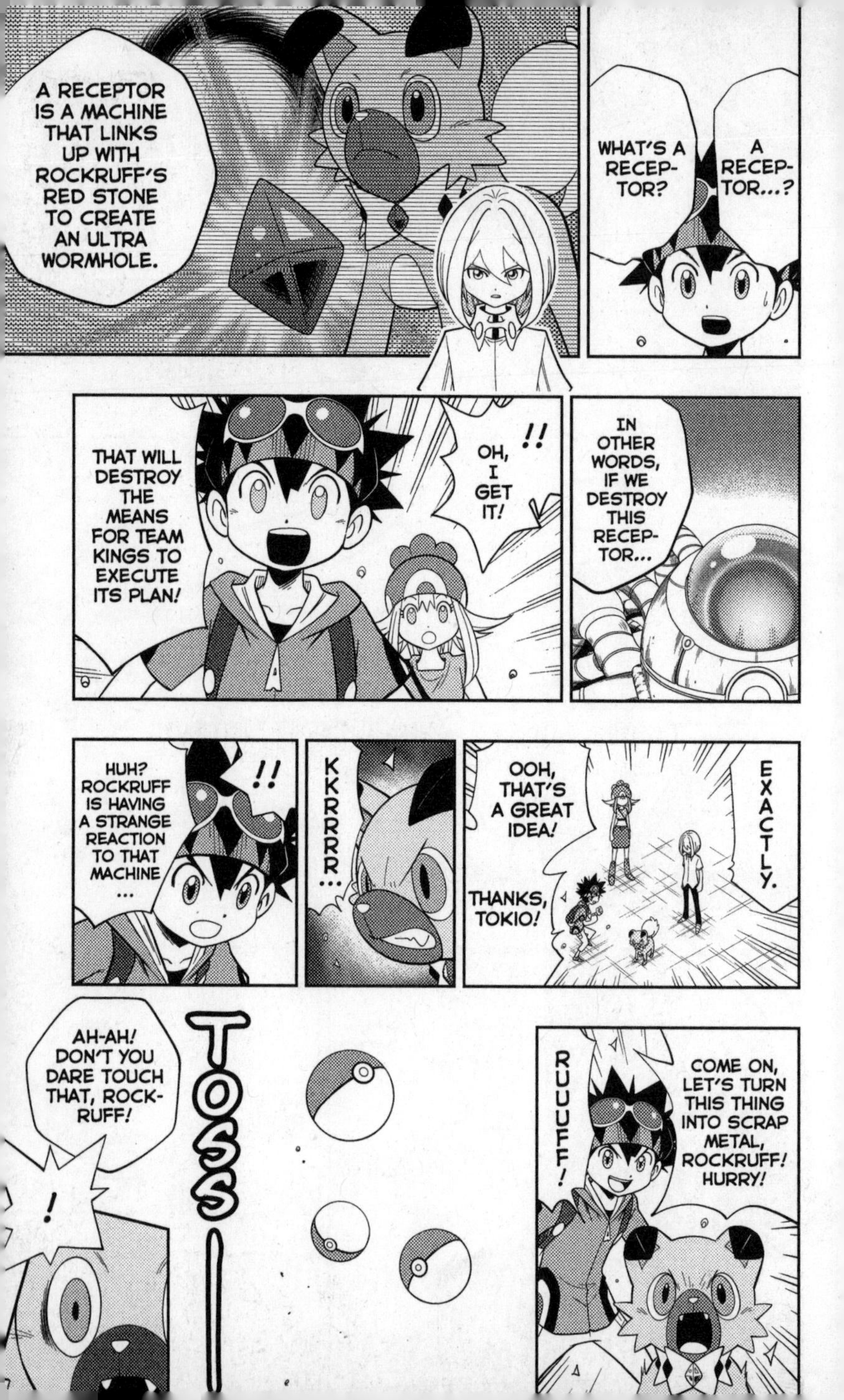
A RECEP-TOR...?
WHAT'S A RECEP-TOR?
A RECEPTOR IS A MACHINE THAT LINKS UP WITH ROCKRUFF'S RED STONE TO CREATE AN ULTRA WORMHOLE.
IN OTHER WORDS, IF WE DESTROY THIS RECEP-TOR...
!!
OH, I GET IT!
THAT WILL DESTROY THE MEANS FOR TEAM KINGS TO EXECUTE ITS PLAN!
EXACTLY.
OOH, THAT'S A GREAT IDEA!
THANKS, TOKIO!
KKRRRR...
!!
HUH? ROCKRUFF IS HAVING A STRANGE REACTION TO THAT MACHINE...
COME ON, LET'S TURN THIS THING INTO SCRAP METAL, ROCKRUFF! HURRY!
RUUUFF!
TOSS
AH-AH! DON'T YOU DARE TOUCH THAT, ROCK-RUFF!
!

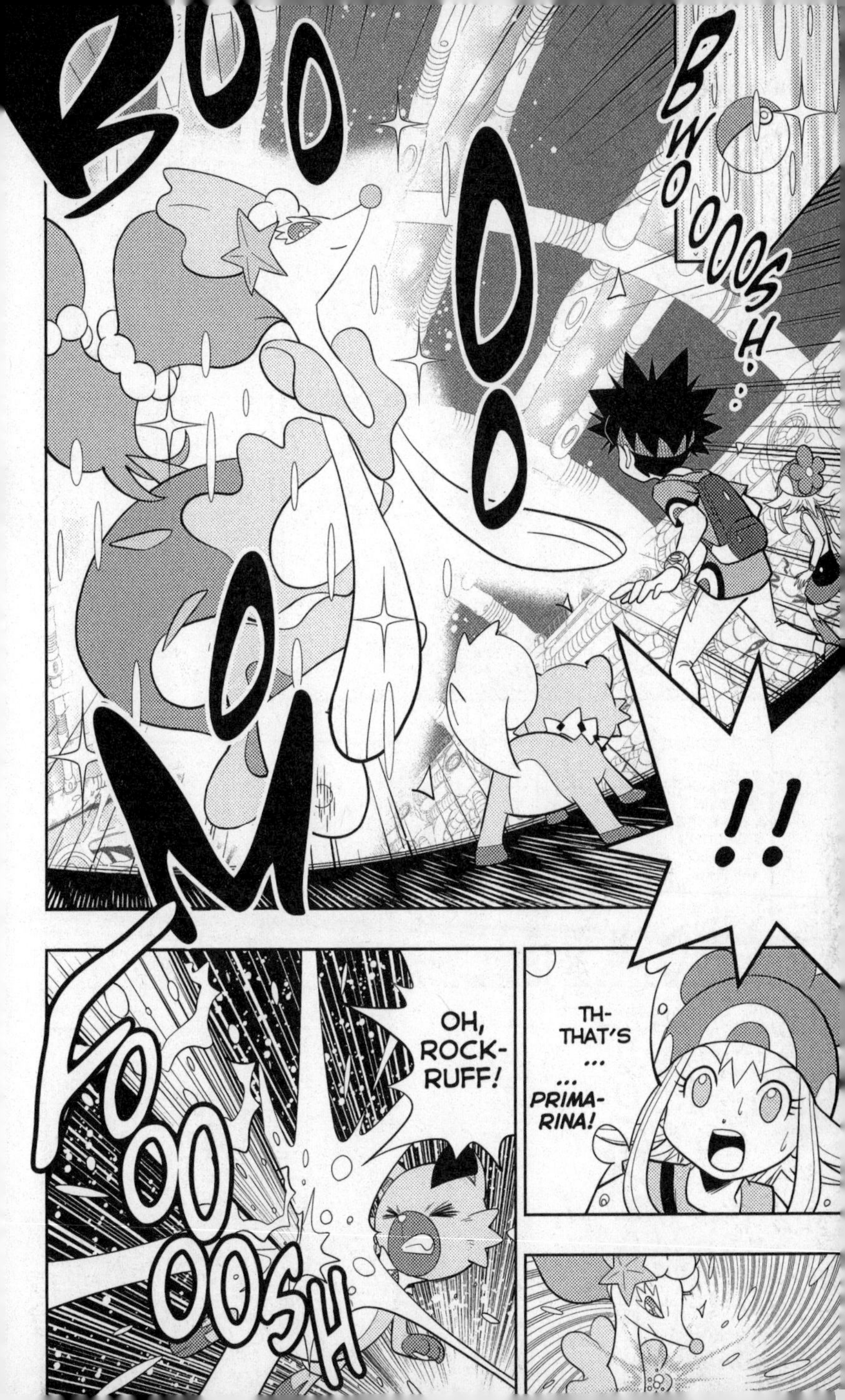
BWOOOOOSH...
BOOOOOOOM
!!
TH-THAT'S... ...PRIMA-RINA!
OH, ROCK-RUFF!
FOOOOOOSH

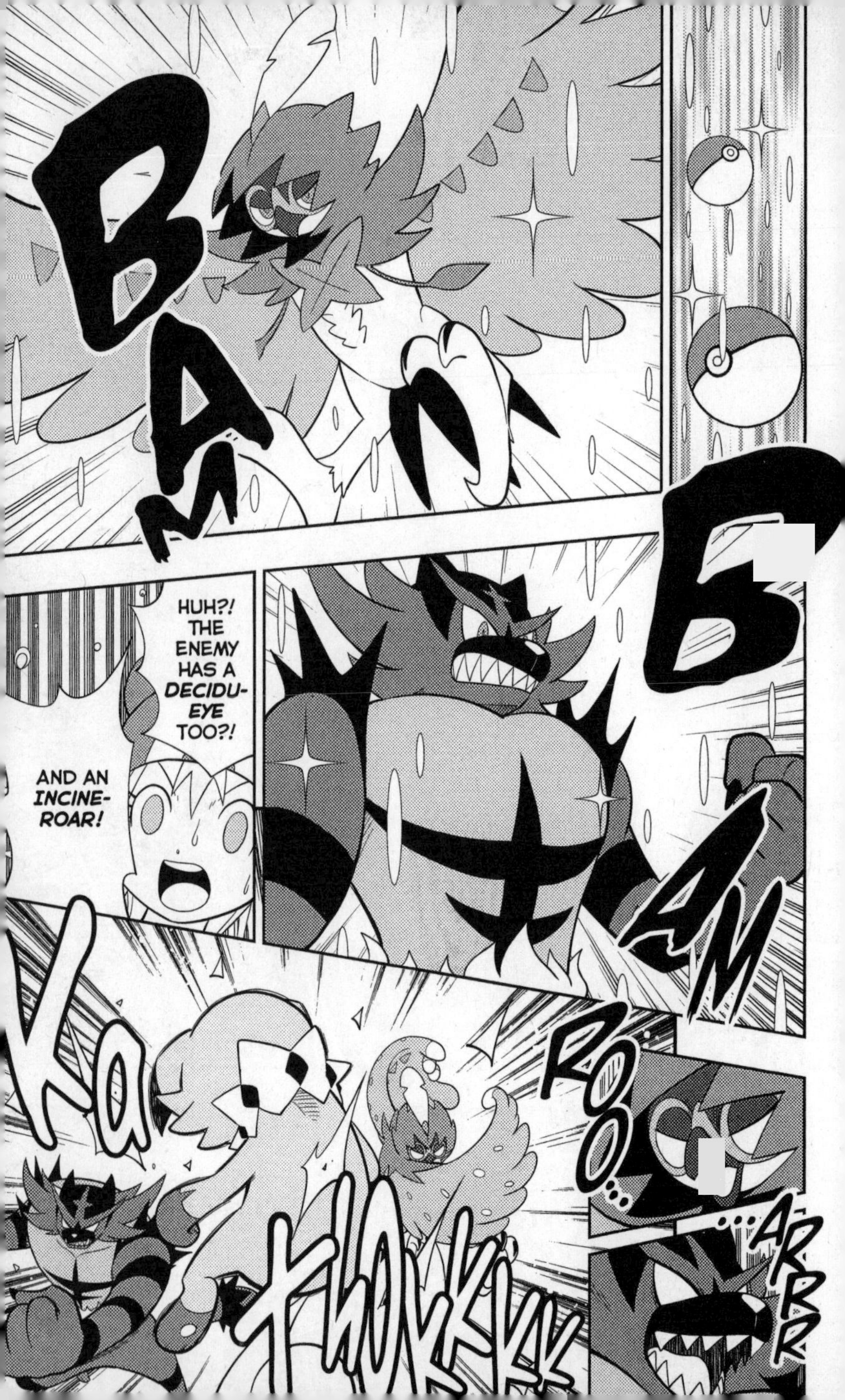
BAM
BAM
HUH?! THE ENEMY HAS A *DECIDUEYE* TOO?!
AND AN *INCINEROAR!*
ROO...
...ARRR

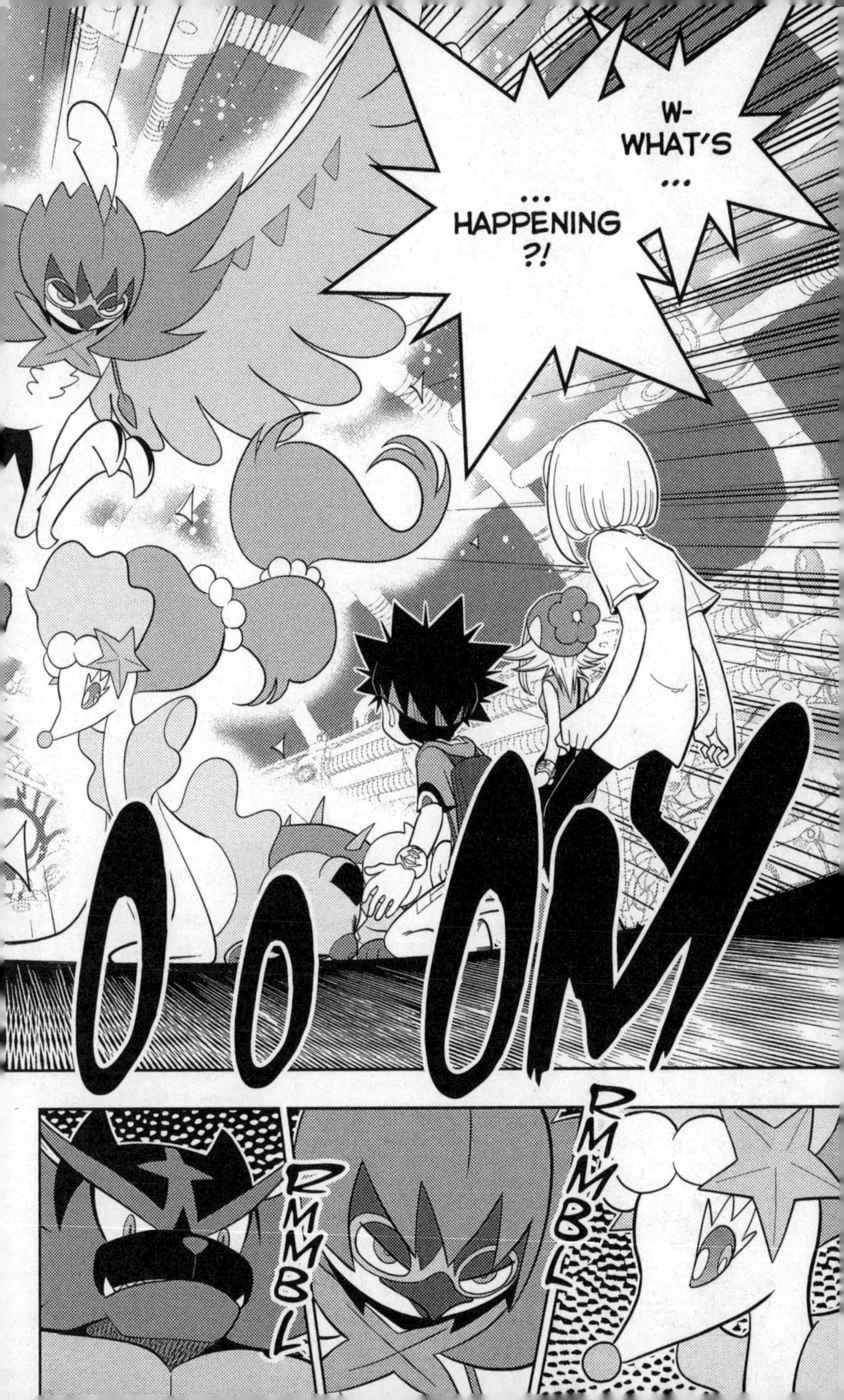
W-
WHAT'S
...
... HAPPENING ?!
OOOM
RMMMBL
RMMBL

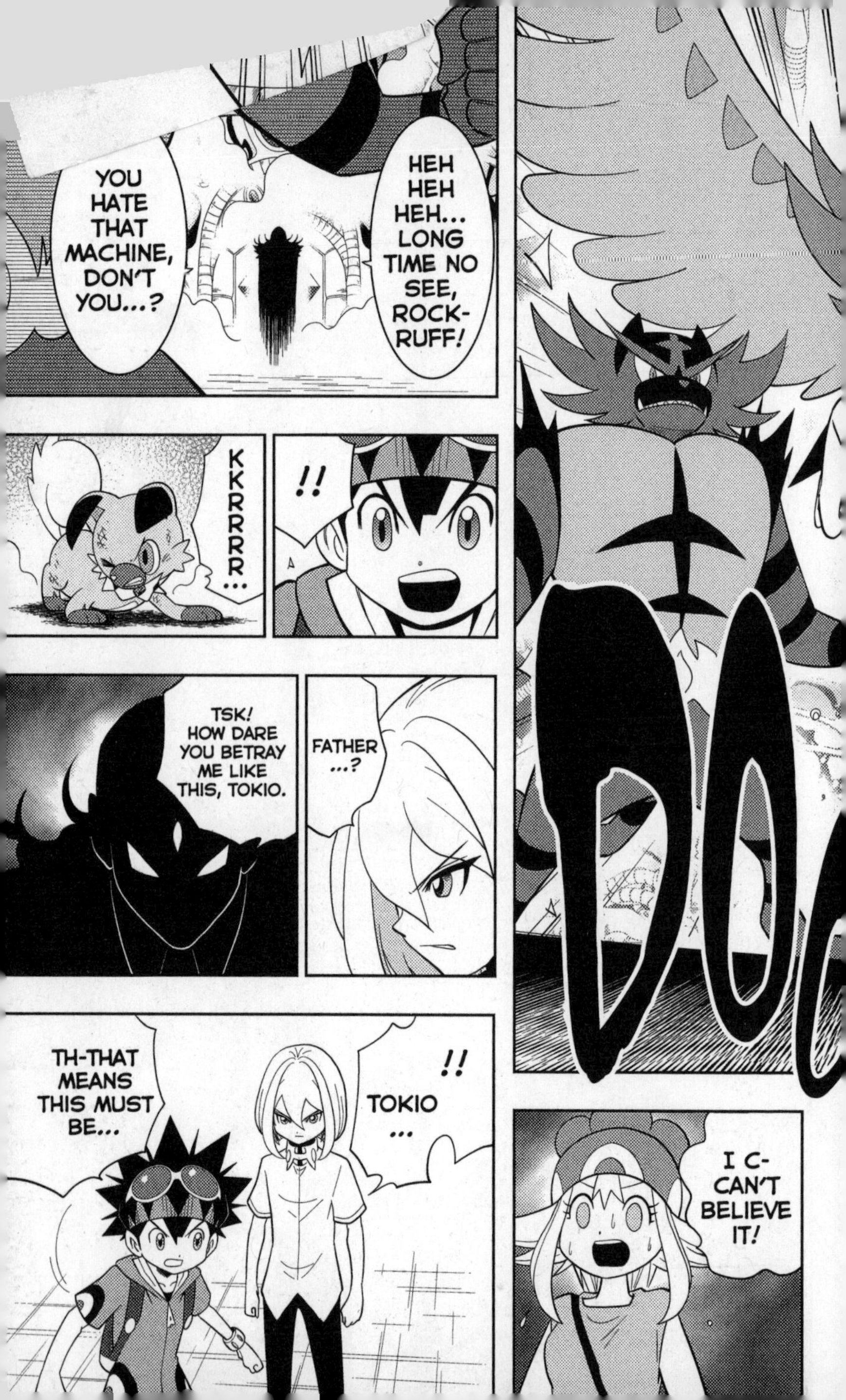
DO
HEH HEH HEH... LONG TIME NO SEE, ROCK-RUFF!
YOU HATE THAT MACHINE, DON'T YOU...?
!!
KKRRRR...
FATHER ...?
TSK! HOW DARE YOU BETRAY ME LIKE THIS, TOKIO.
I C-CAN'T BELIEVE IT!
!!
TOKIO ...
TH-THAT MEANS THIS MUST BE...

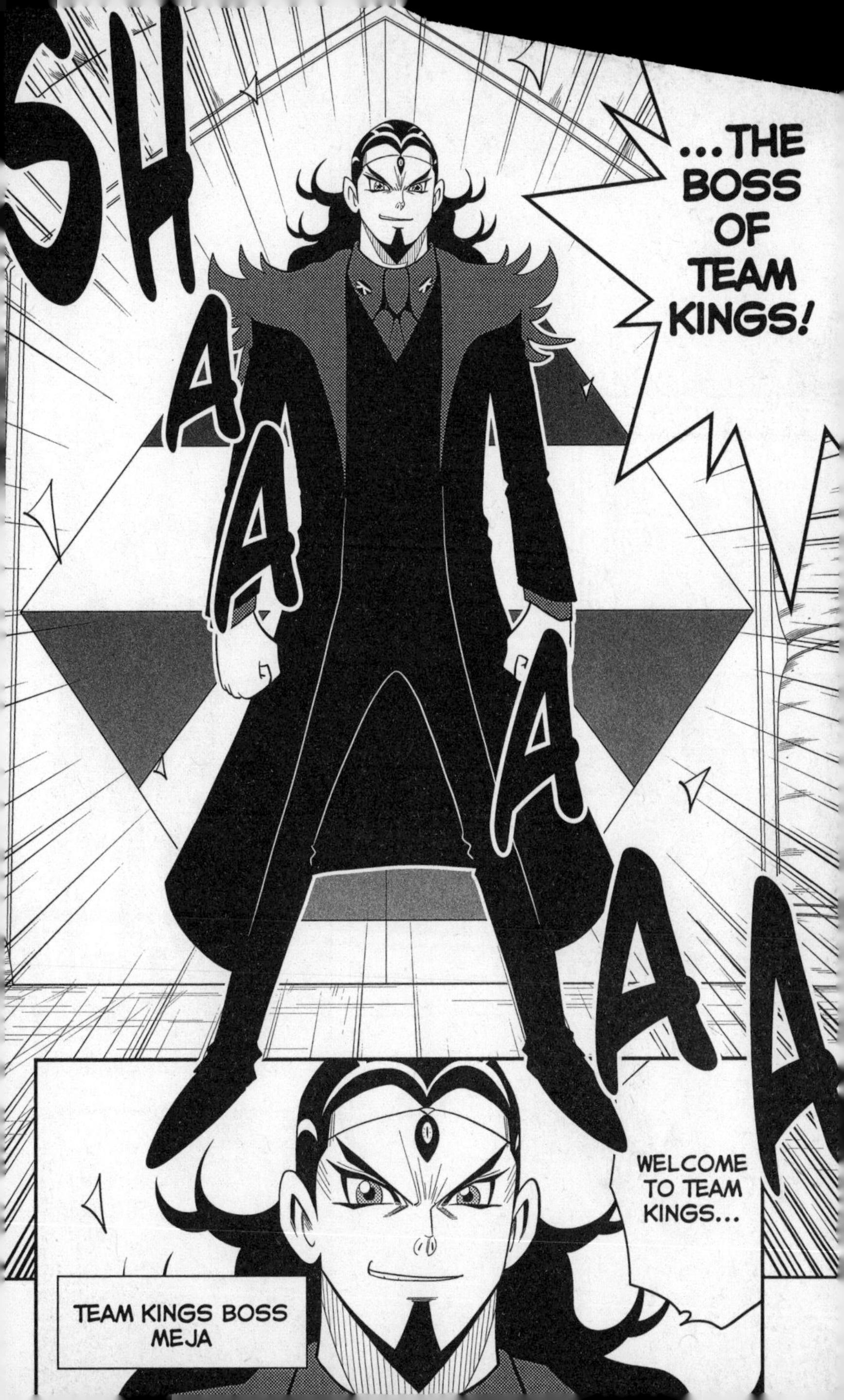
SHAAAAAAA
...THE BOSS OF TEAM KINGS!
WELCOME TO TEAM KINGS...
TEAM KINGS BOSS MEJA

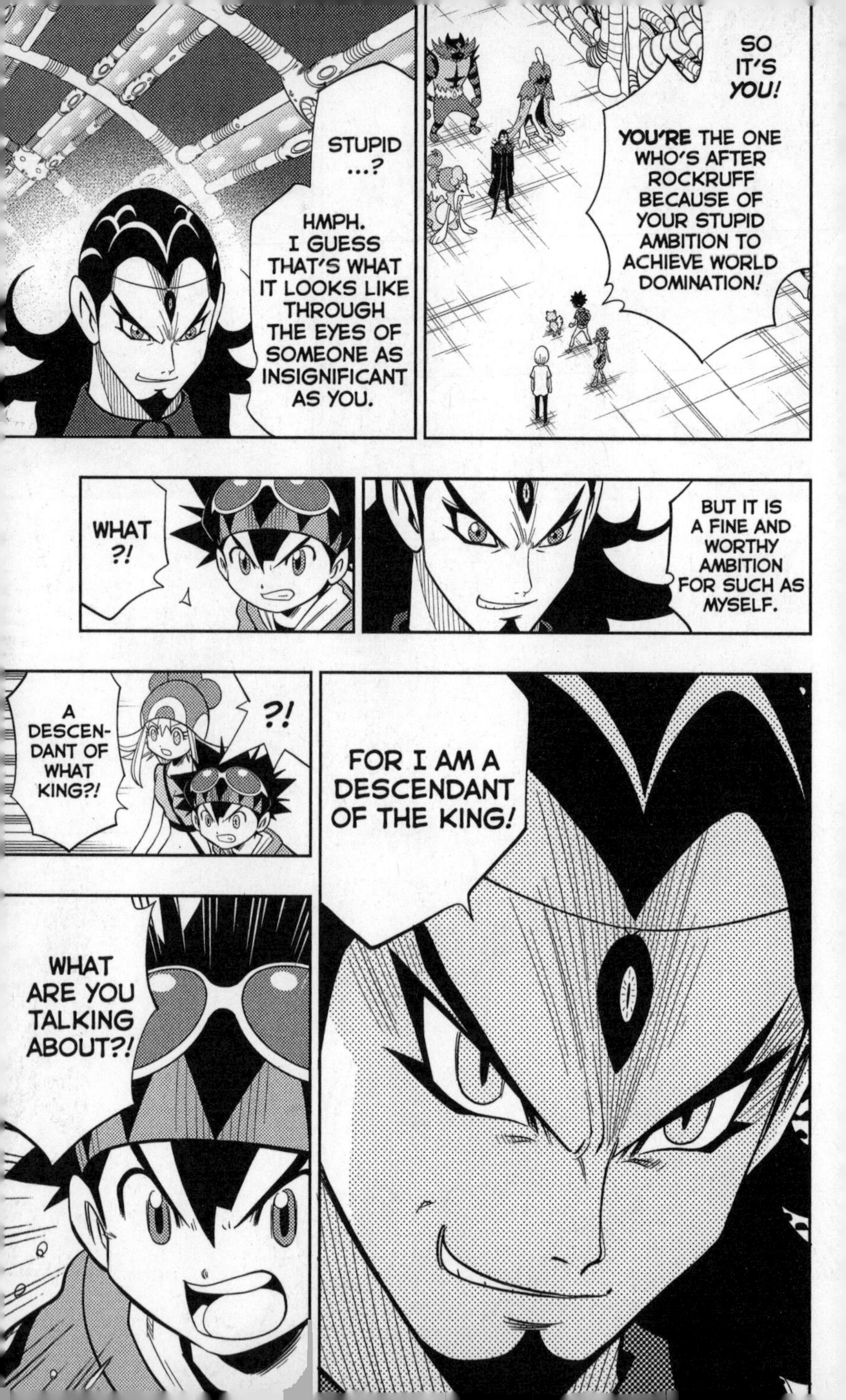
SO IT'S YOU!
YOU'RE THE ONE WHO'S AFTER ROCKRUFF BECAUSE OF YOUR STUPID AMBITION TO ACHIEVE WORLD DOMINATION!
STUPID ...?
HMPH. I GUESS THAT'S WHAT IT LOOKS LIKE THROUGH THE EYES OF SOMEONE AS INSIGNIFICANT AS YOU.
BUT IT IS A FINE AND WORTHY AMBITION FOR SUCH AS MYSELF.
WHAT ?!
FOR I AM A DESCENDANT OF THE KING!
?!
A DESCENDANT OF WHAT KING?!
WHAT ARE YOU TALKING ABOUT?!

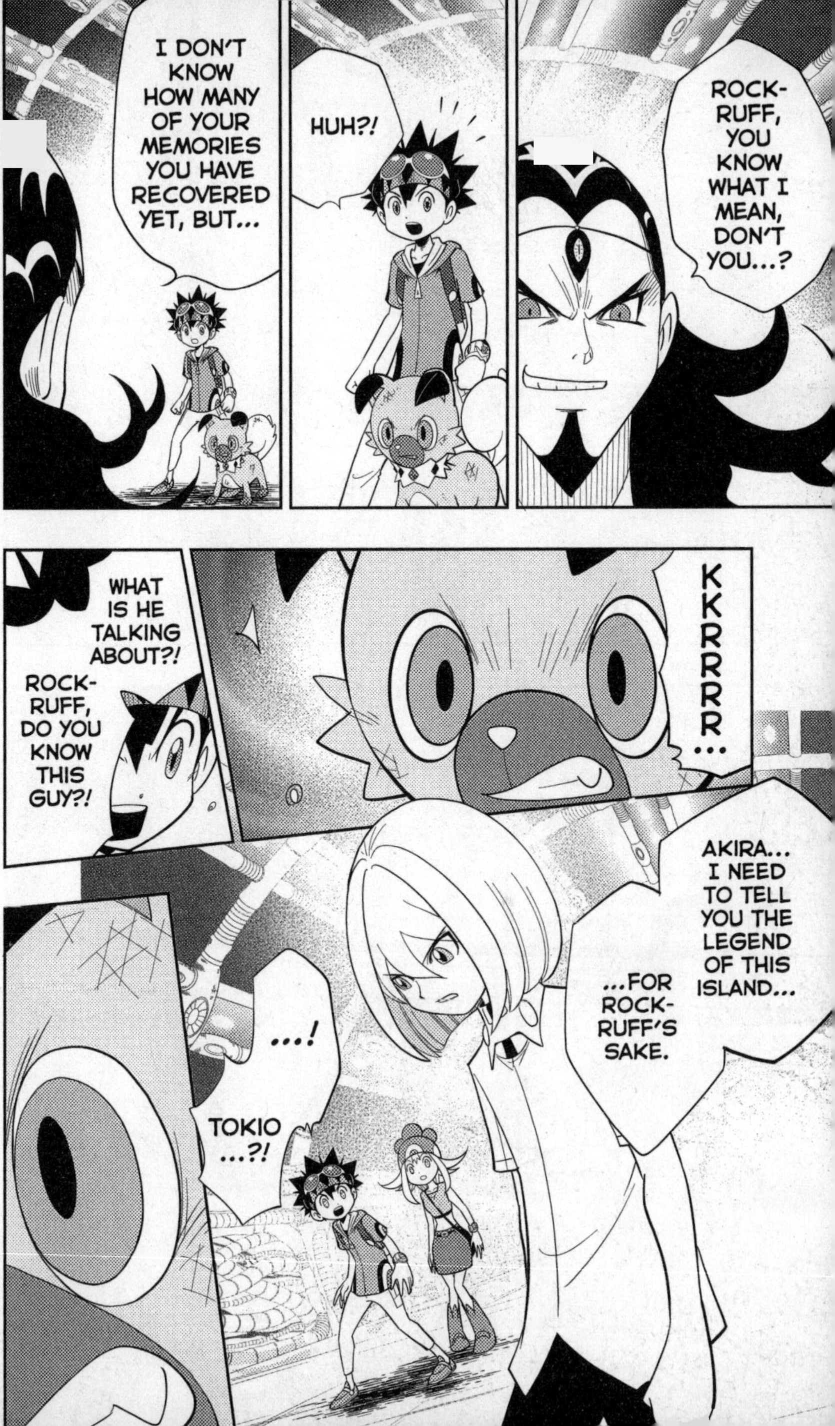
I DON'T KNOW HOW MANY OF YOUR MEMORIES YOU HAVE RECOVERED YET, BUT...
HUH?!
ROCK-RUFF, YOU KNOW WHAT I MEAN, DON'T YOU...?
WHAT IS HE TALKING ABOUT?!
ROCK-RUFF, DO YOU KNOW THIS GUY?!
KKRRRR...
...!
TOKIO ...?!
AKIRA... I NEED TO TELL YOU THE LEGEND OF THIS ISLAND...
...FOR ROCK-RUFF'S SAKE.

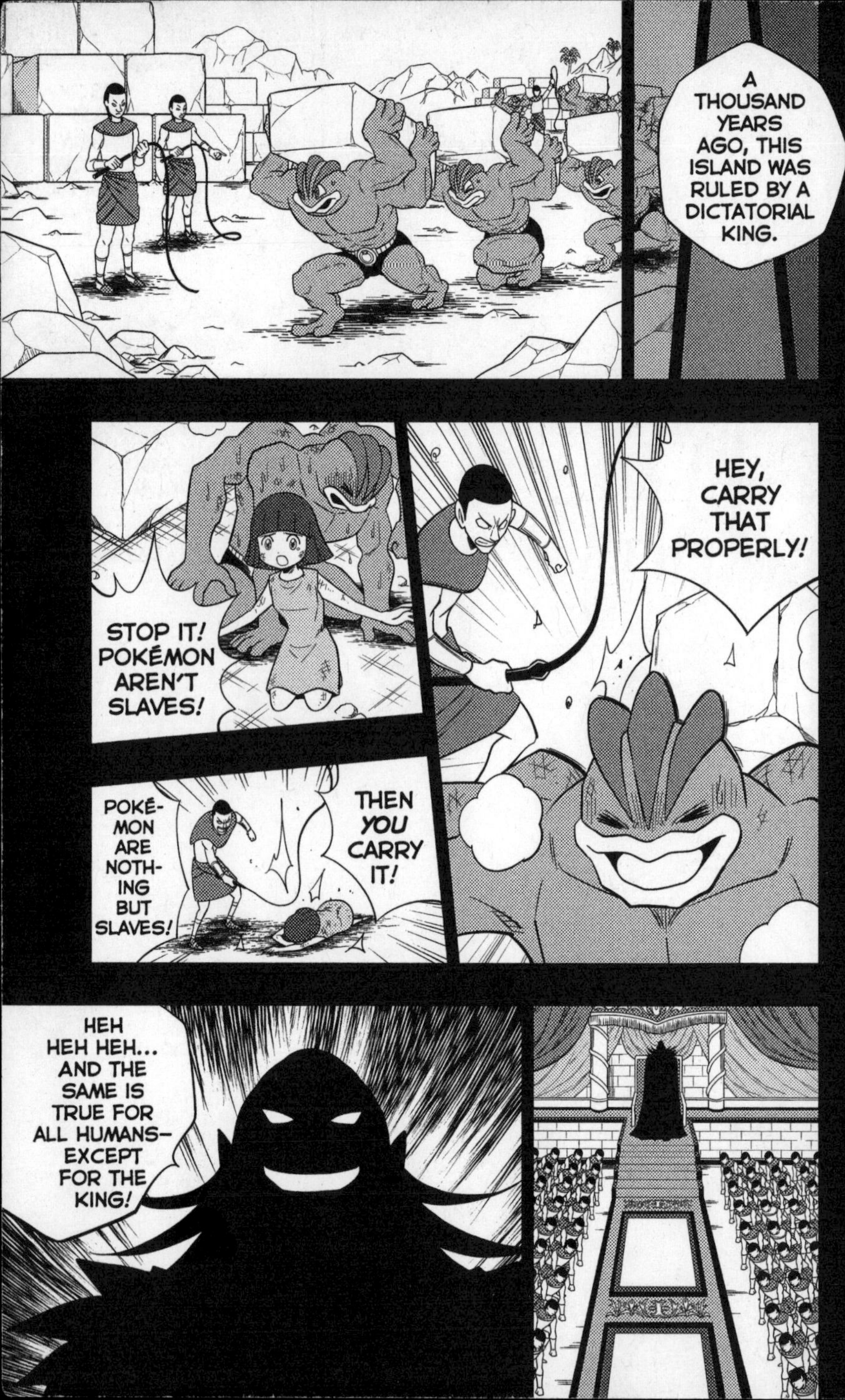
A THOUSAND YEARS AGO, THIS ISLAND WAS RULED BY A DICTATORIAL KING.
HEY, CARRY THAT PROPERLY!
STOP IT! POKÉMON AREN'T SLAVES!
THEN *YOU* CARRY IT!
POKÉ-MON ARE NOTH-ING BUT SLAVES!
HEH HEH HEH... AND THE SAME IS TRUE FOR ALL HUMANS— EXCEPT FOR THE KING!

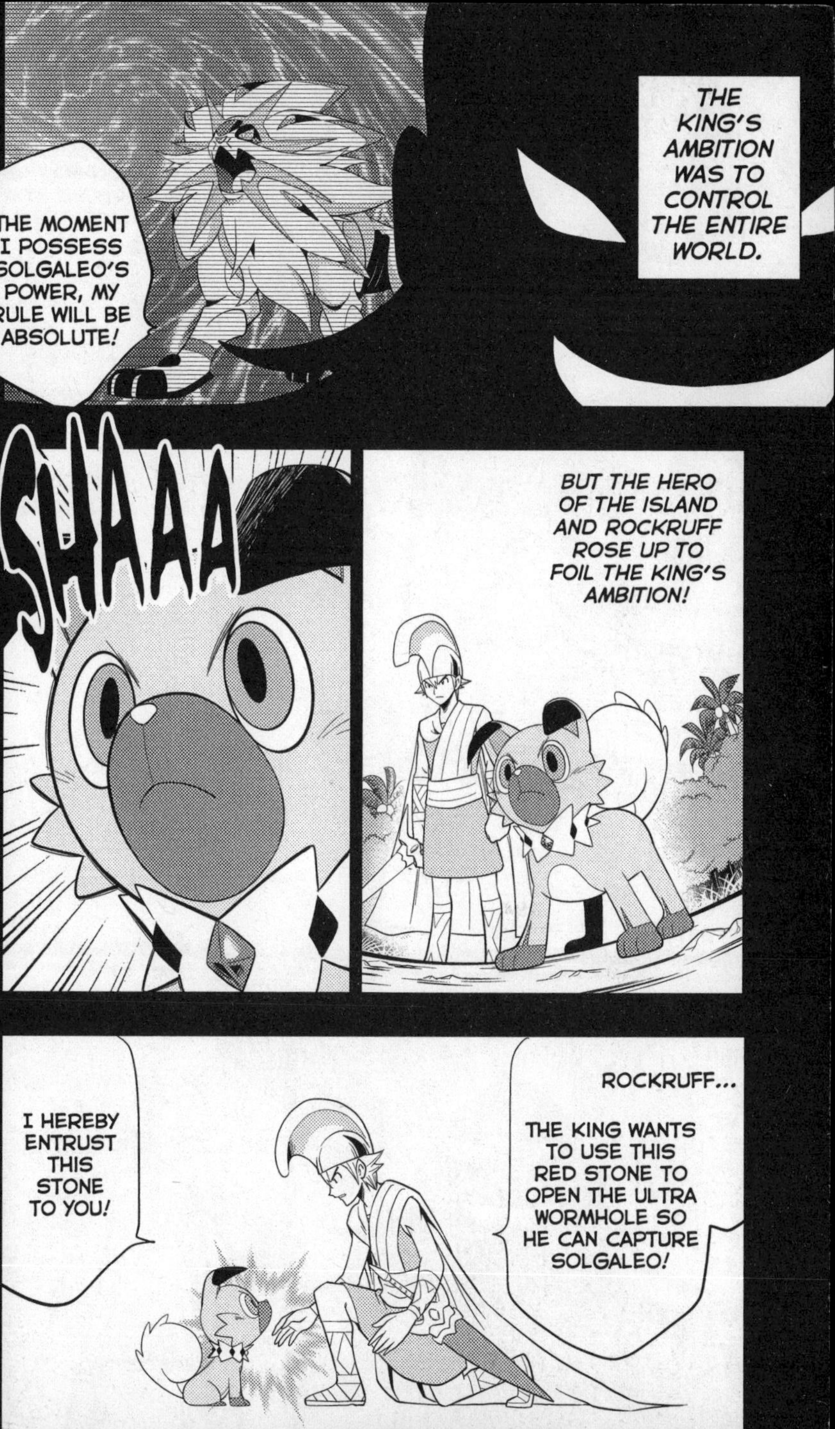
THE KING'S AMBITION WAS TO CONTROL THE ENTIRE WORLD.
THE MOMENT I POSSESS SOLGALEO'S POWER, MY RULE WILL BE ABSOLUTE!
BUT THE HERO OF THE ISLAND AND ROCKRUFF ROSE UP TO FOIL THE KING'S AMBITION!
SHAAA
ROCKRUFF...
THE KING WANTS TO USE THIS RED STONE TO OPEN THE ULTRA WORMHOLE SO HE CAN CAPTURE SOLGALEO!
I HEREBY ENTRUST THIS STONE TO YOU!

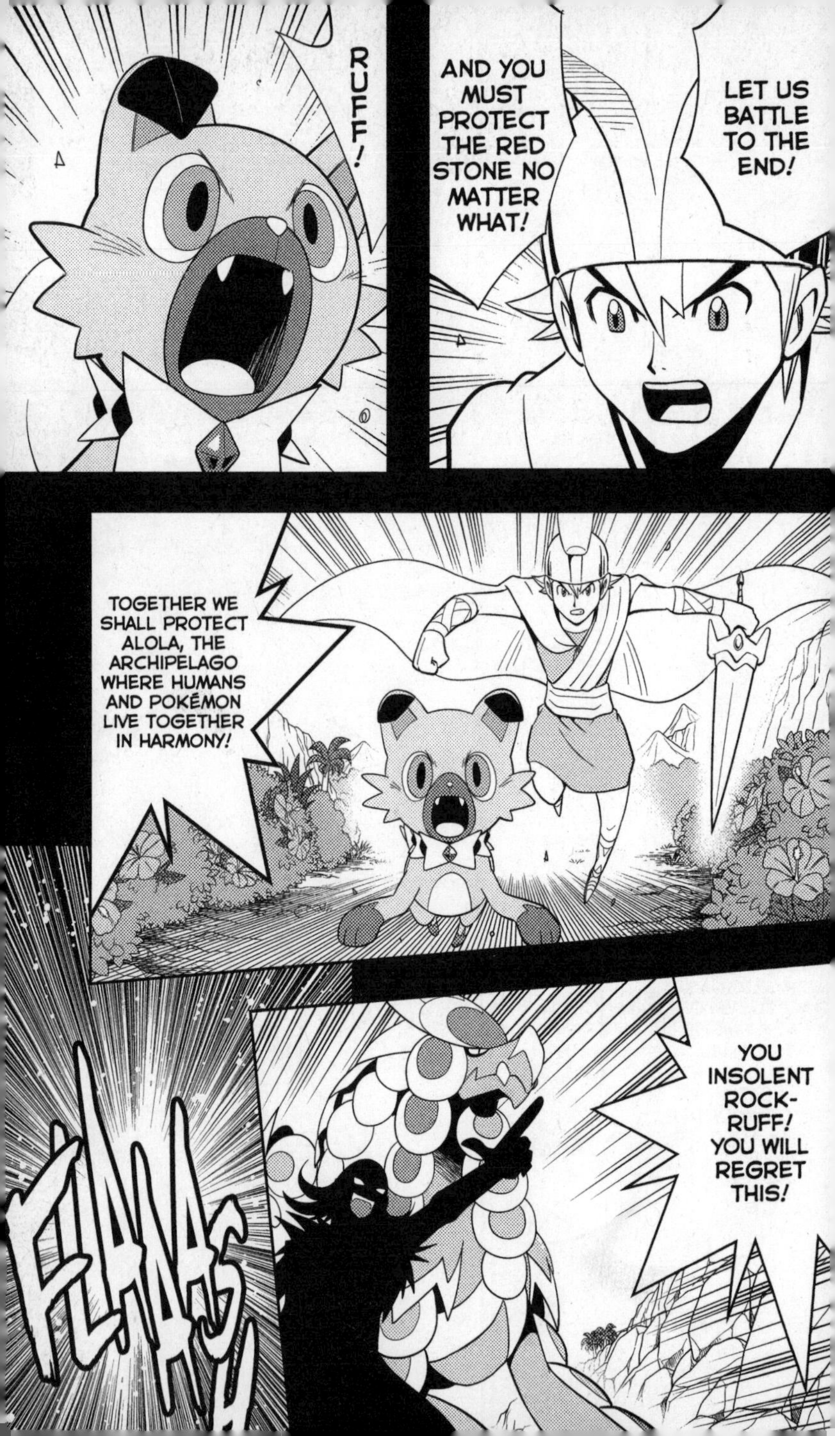
LET US BATTLE TO THE END!
AND YOU MUST PROTECT THE RED STONE NO MATTER WHAT!
RUFF!
TOGETHER WE SHALL PROTECT ALOLA, THE ARCHIPELAGO WHERE HUMANS AND POKÉMON LIVE TOGETHER IN HARMONY!
YOU INSOLENT ROCK-RUFF! YOU WILL REGRET THIS!
FLAAAS

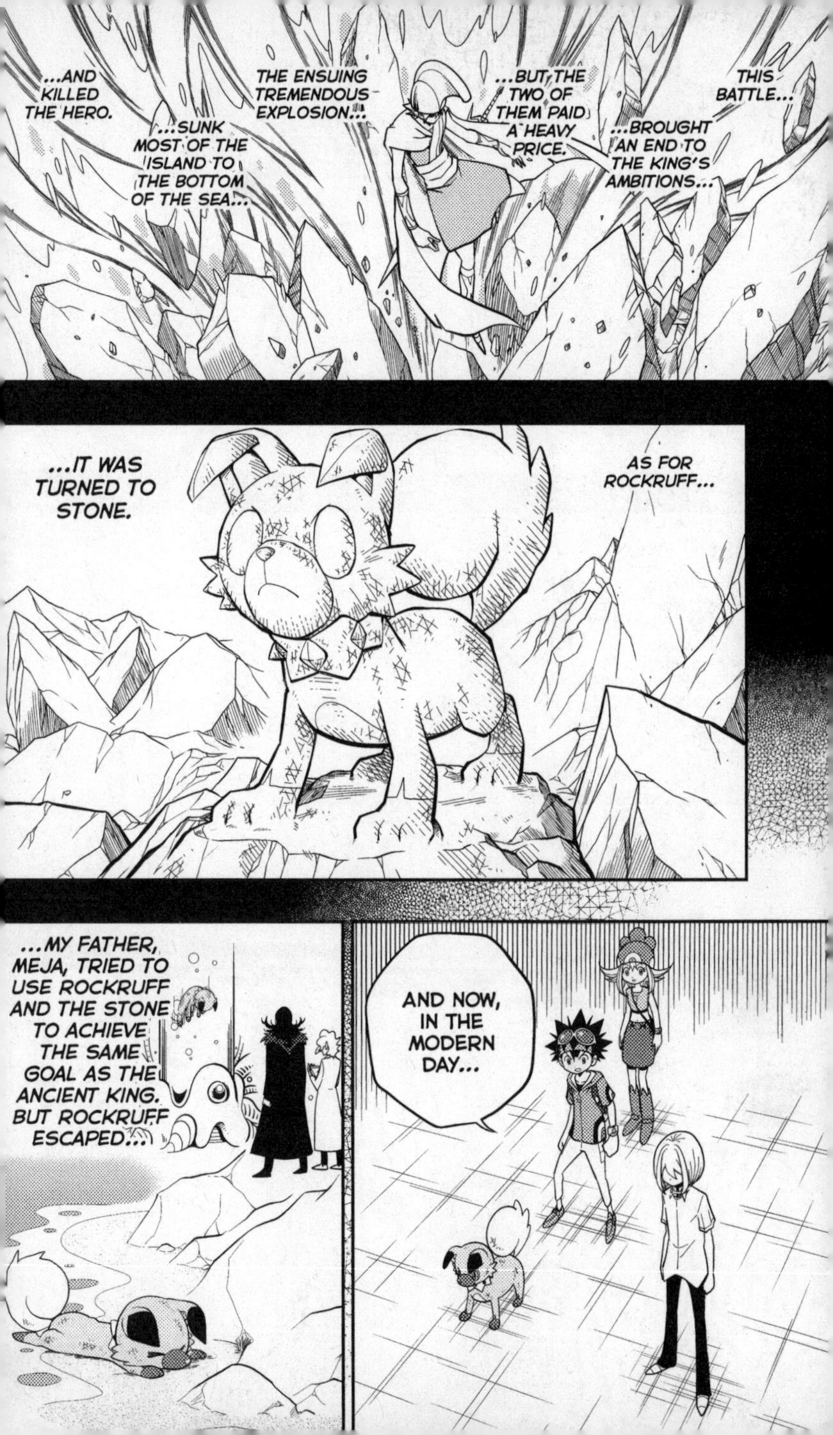
THIS BATTLE...
...BROUGHT AN END TO THE KING'S AMBITIONS...
...BUT THE TWO OF THEM PAID A HEAVY PRICE.
THE ENSUING TREMENDOUS EXPLOSION...
...SUNK MOST OF THE ISLAND TO THE BOTTOM OF THE SEA...
...AND KILLED THE HERO.
AS FOR ROCKRUFF...
...IT WAS TURNED TO STONE.
AND NOW, IN THE MODERN DAY...
...MY FATHER, MEJA, TRIED TO USE ROCKRUFF AND THE STONE TO ACHIEVE THE SAME GOAL AS THE ANCIENT KING. BUT ROCKRUFF ESCAPED...

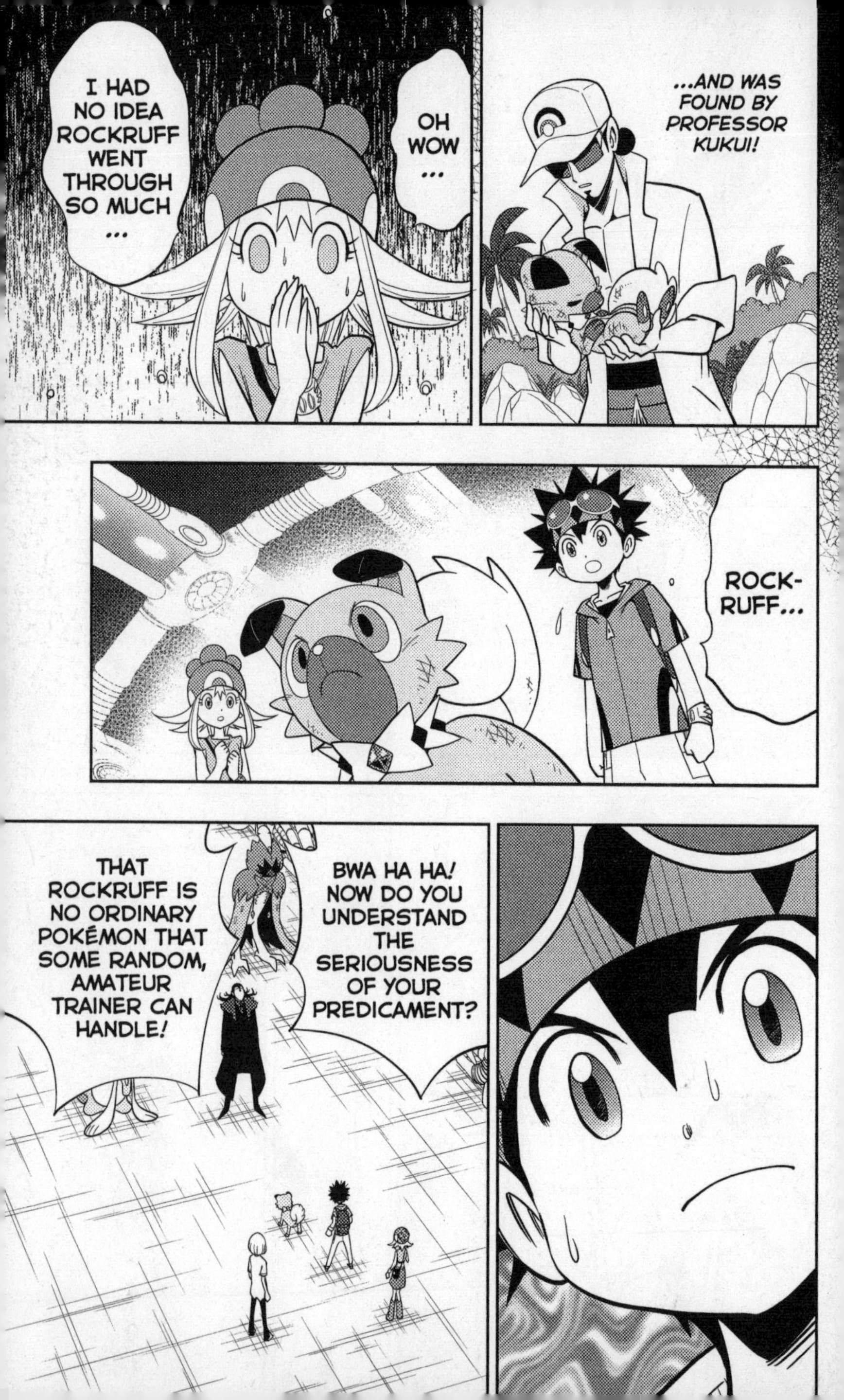
...AND WAS FOUND BY PROFESSOR KUKUI!
OH WOW ...
I HAD NO IDEA ROCKRUFF WENT THROUGH SO MUCH ...
ROCK-RUFF...
BWA HA HA! NOW DO YOU UNDERSTAND THE SERIOUSNESS OF YOUR PREDICAMENT?
THAT ROCKRUFF IS NO ORDINARY POKÉMON THAT SOME RANDOM, AMATEUR TRAINER CAN HANDLE!

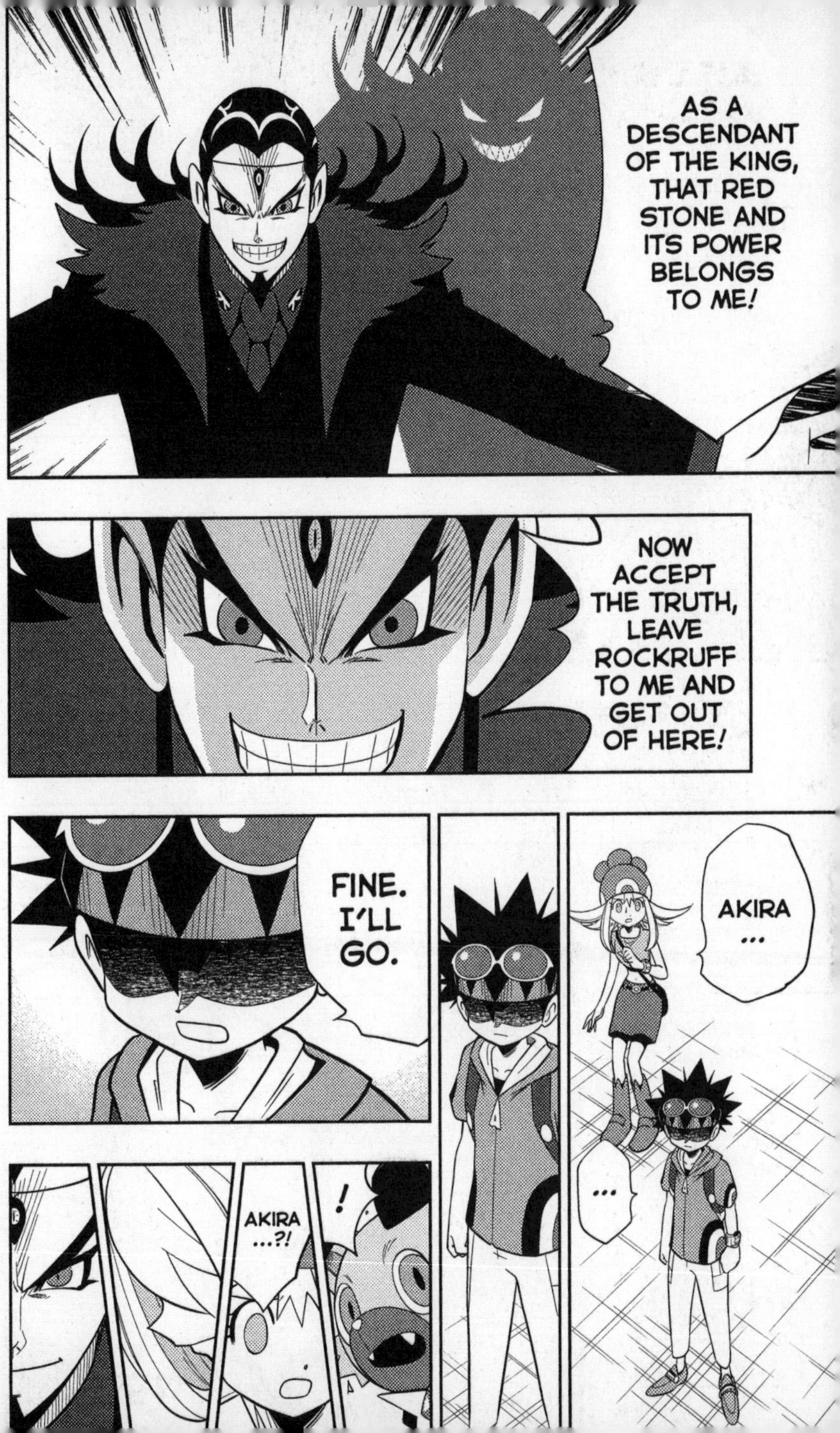
AS A DESCENDANT OF THE KING, THAT RED STONE AND ITS POWER BELONGS TO ME!
NOW ACCEPT THE TRUTH, LEAVE ROCKRUFF TO ME AND GET OUT OF HERE!
AKIRA ...
...
FINE. I'LL GO.
!
AKIRA ...?!

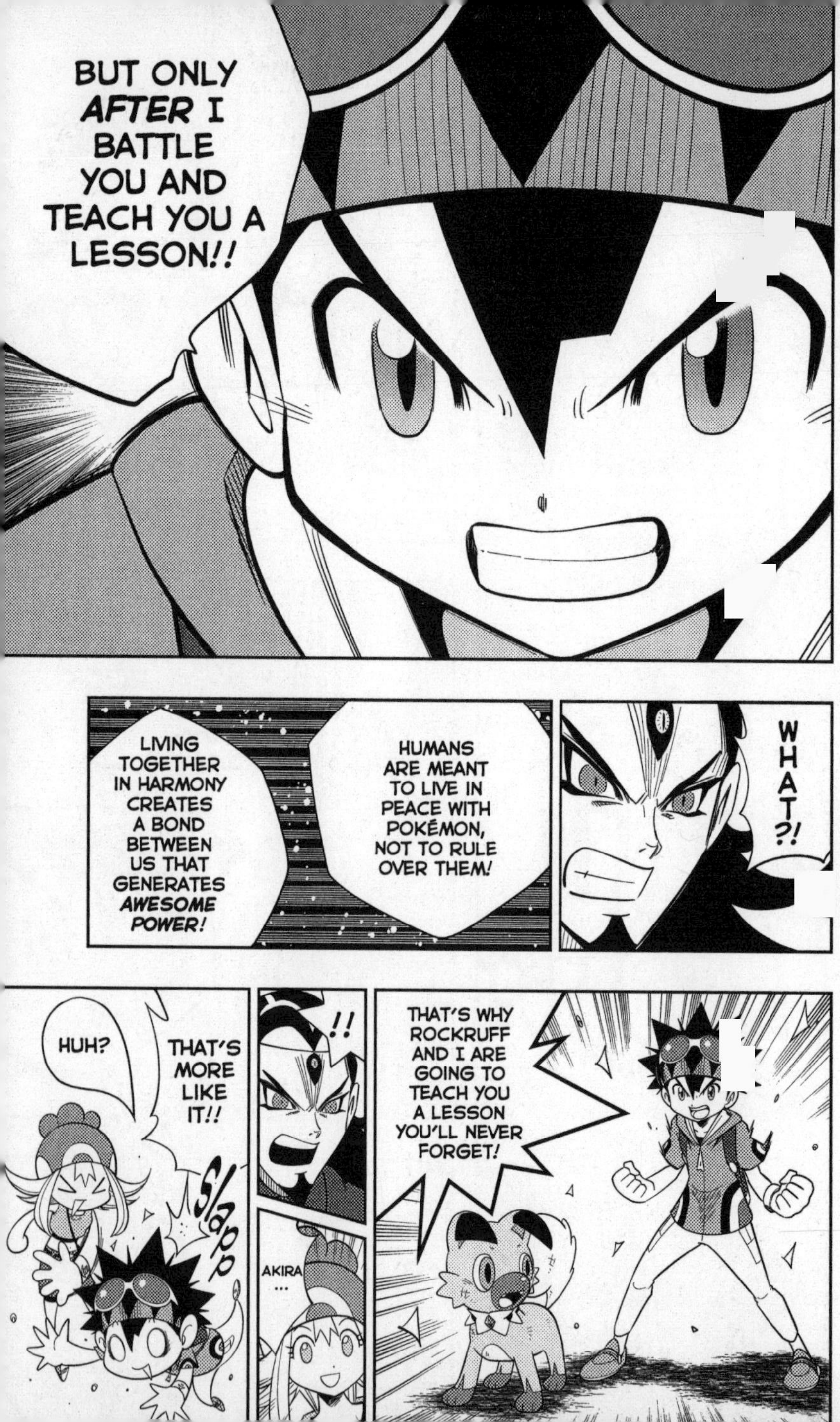
BUT ONLY *AFTER* I BATTLE YOU AND TEACH YOU A LESSON!!
WHAT?!
HUMANS ARE MEANT TO LIVE IN PEACE WITH POKÉMON, NOT TO RULE OVER THEM!
LIVING TOGETHER IN HARMONY CREATES A BOND BETWEEN US THAT GENERATES *AWESOME POWER!*
THAT'S WHY ROCKRUFF AND I ARE GOING TO TEACH YOU A LESSON YOU'LL NEVER FORGET!
!!
AKIRA...
THAT'S MORE LIKE IT!!
HUH?
Slapp

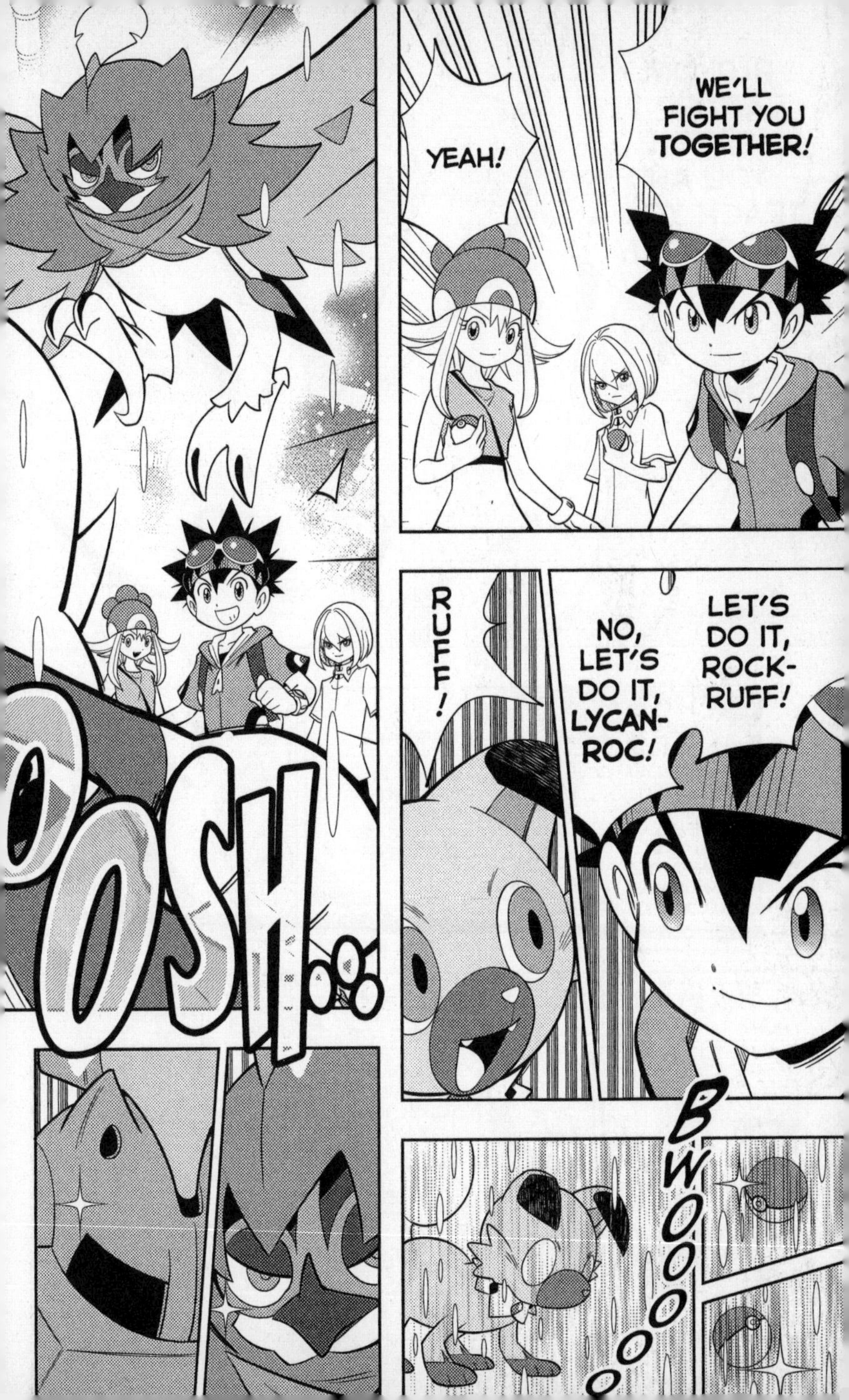
WE'LL FIGHT YOU TOGETHER!
YEAH!
LET'S DO IT, ROCK-RUFF!
NO, LET'S DO IT, LYCAN-ROC!
RUFF!
OOSH...
BWOOOOOOO

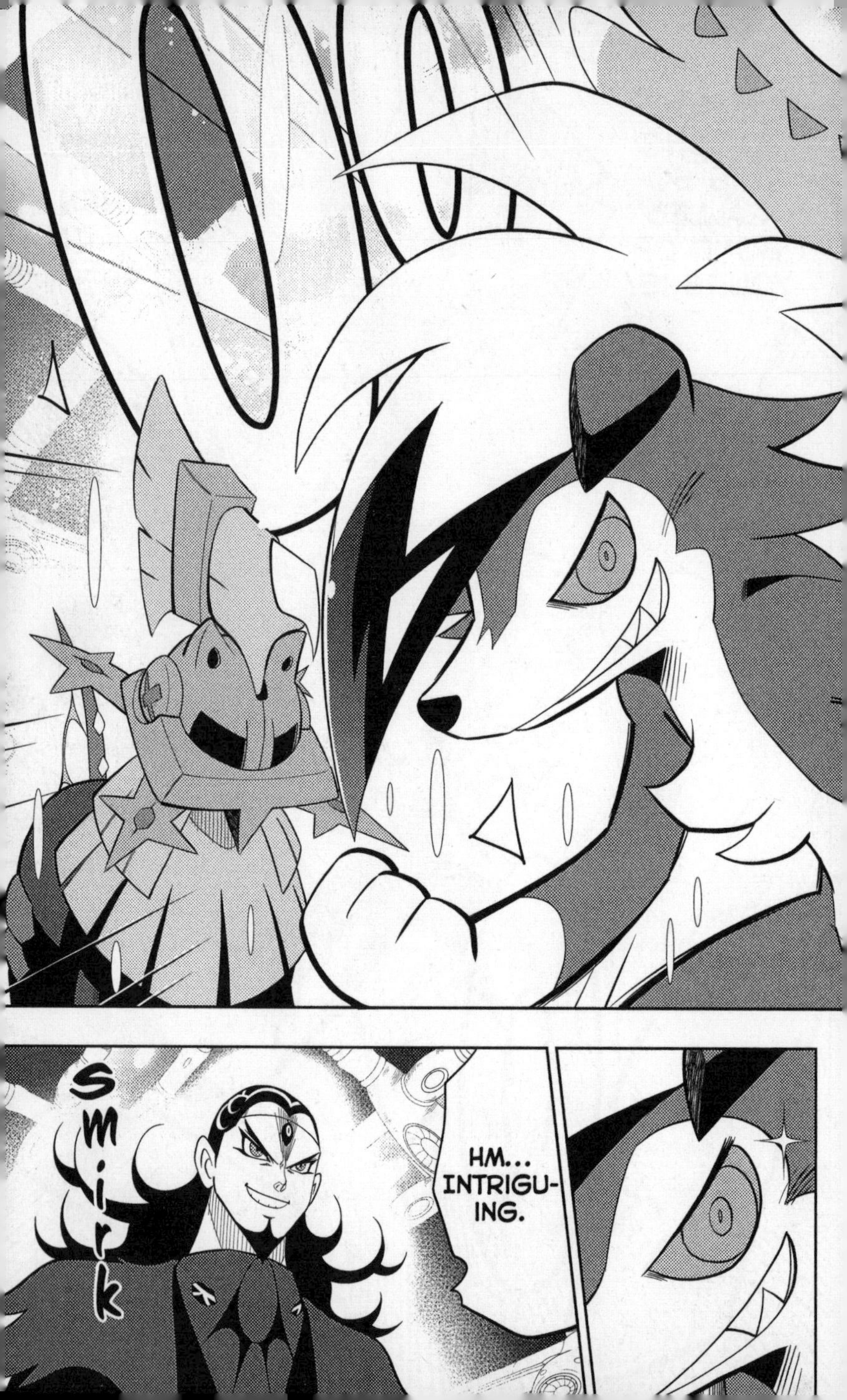
HM... INTRIGU-ING.
Smirk

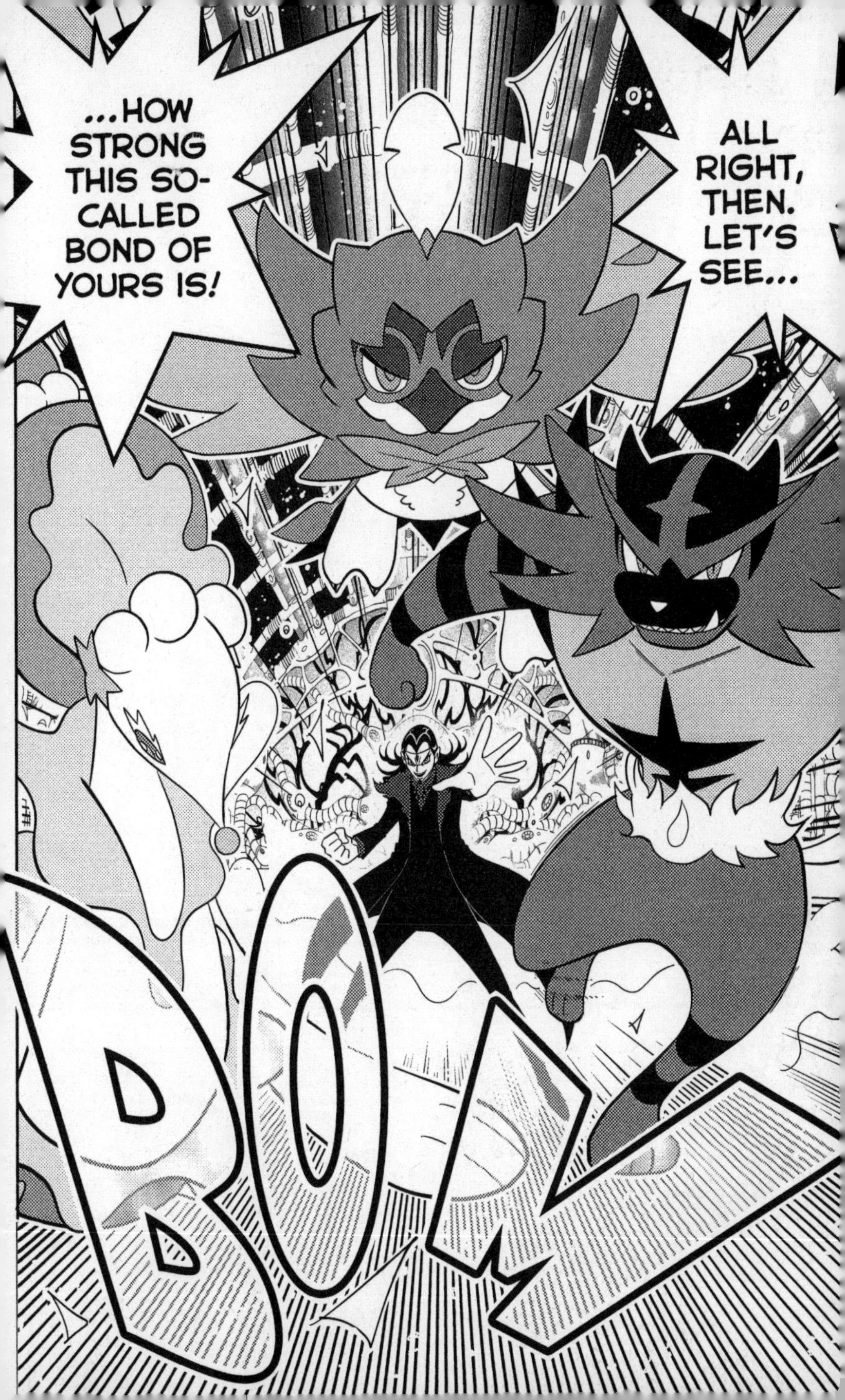
ALL RIGHT, THEN. LET'S SEE...
...HOW STRONG THIS SO-CALLED BOND OF YOURS IS!

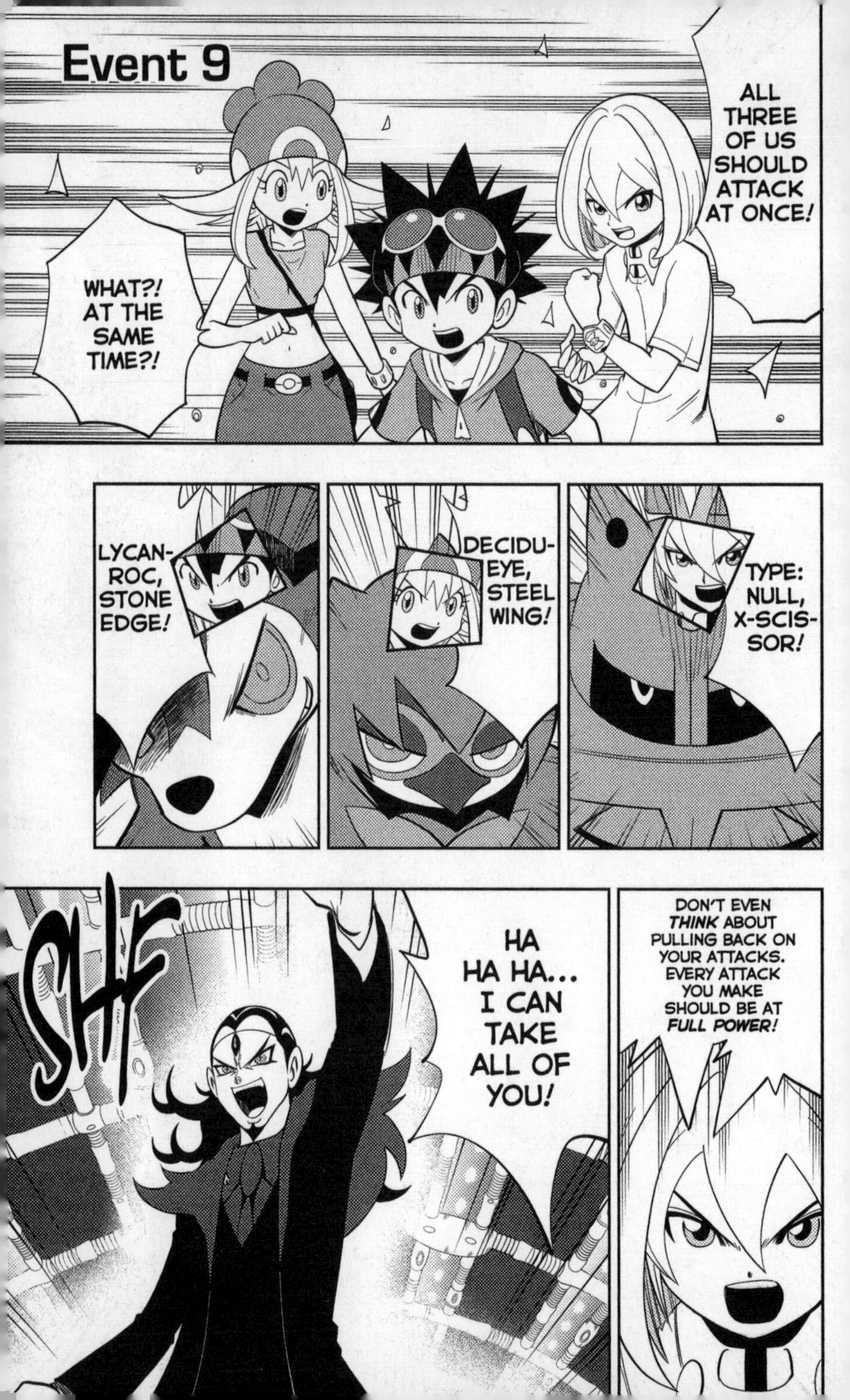
Event 9
ALL THREE OF US SHOULD ATTACK AT ONCE!
WHAT?! AT THE SAME TIME?!
TYPE: NULL, X-SCISSOR!
DECIDUEYE, STEEL WING!
LYCANROC, STONE EDGE!
DON'T EVEN *THINK* ABOUT PULLING BACK ON YOUR ATTACKS. EVERY ATTACK YOU MAKE SHOULD BE AT *FULL POWER!*
HA HA HA... I CAN TAKE ALL OF YOU!
SHF

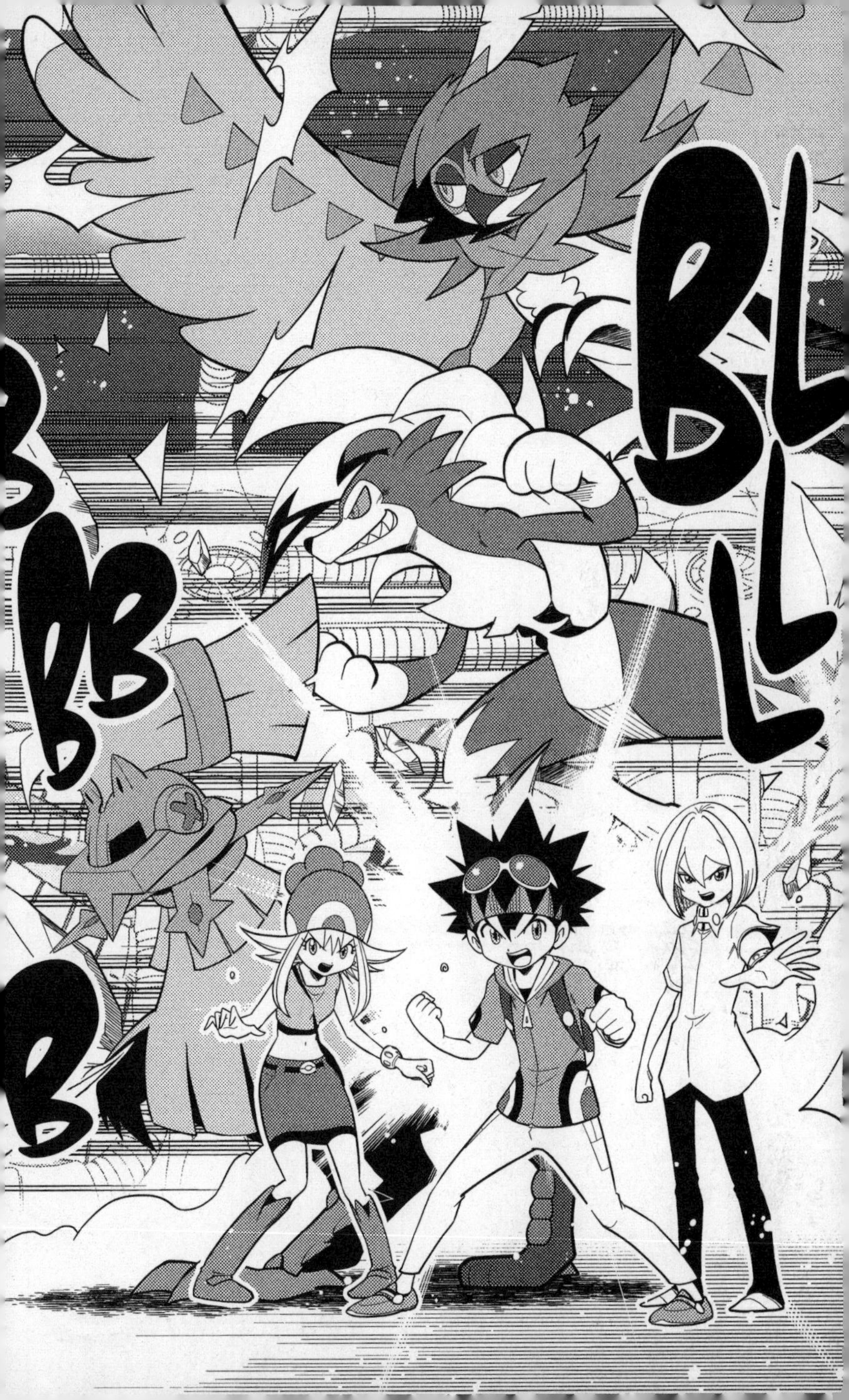
BLLL
BBBB

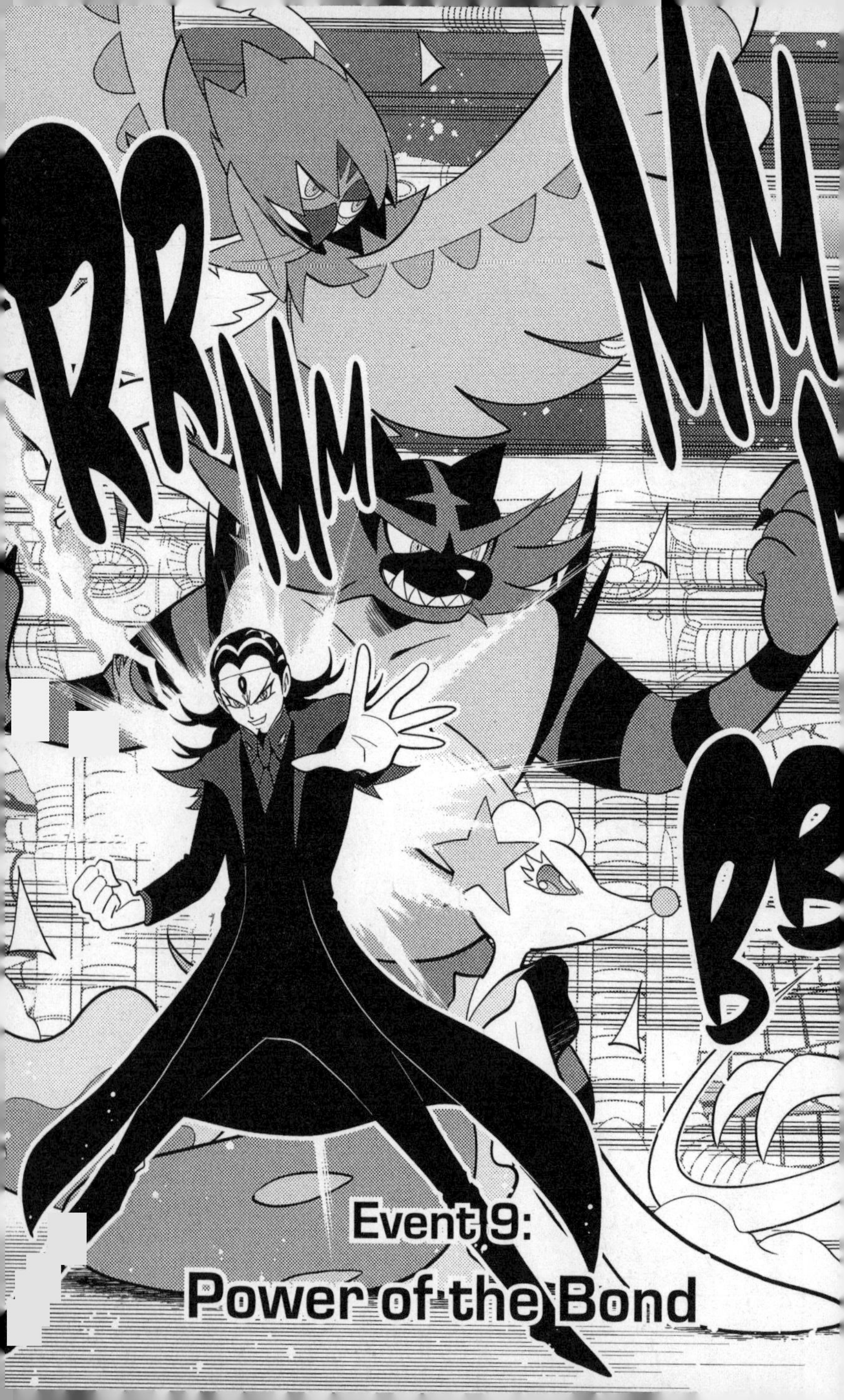

Event 9: Power of the Bond

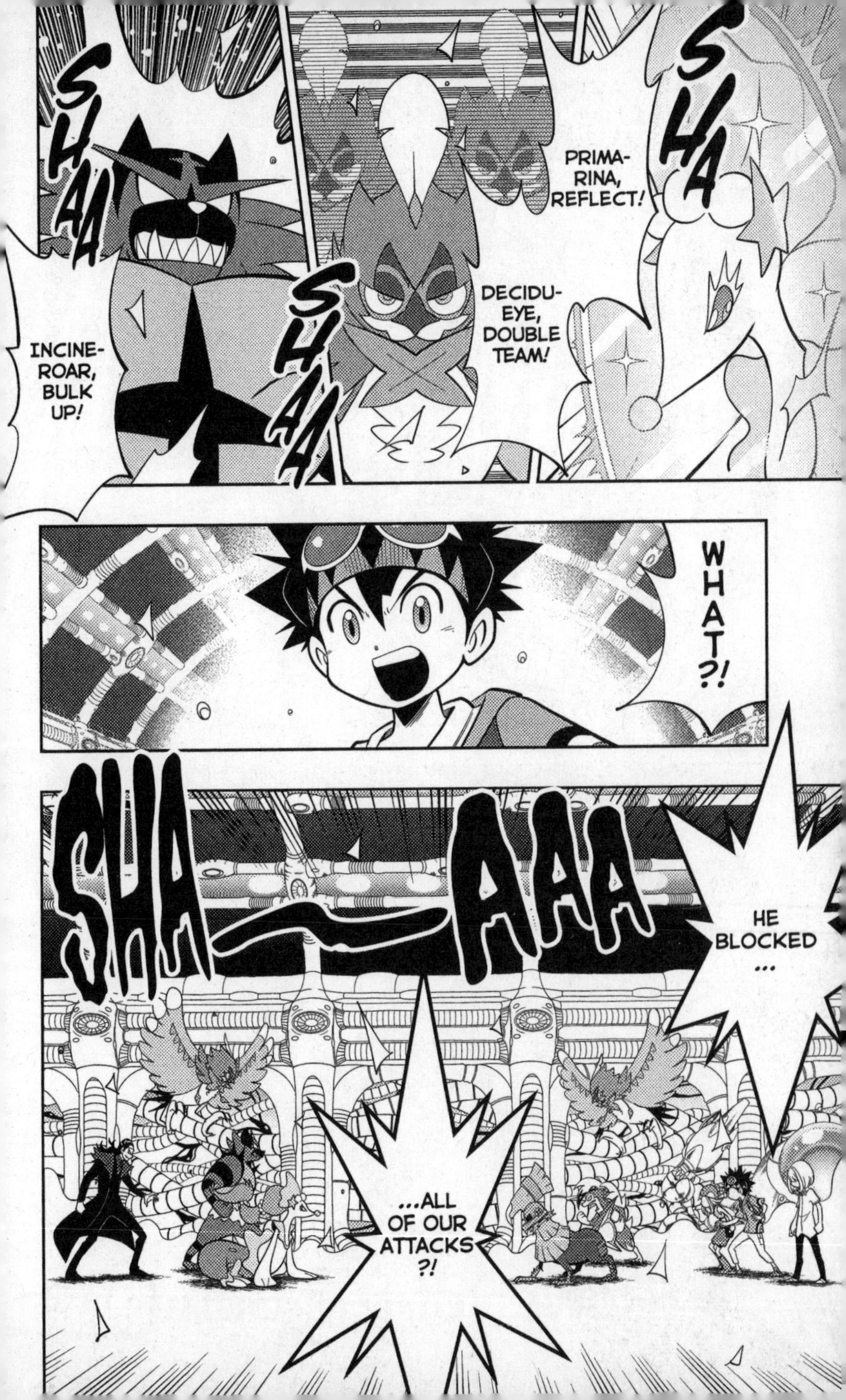

SHUA
PRIMARINA, REFLECT!
SHUAAA
DECIDUEYE, DOUBLE TEAM!
SHUAAA
INCINEROAR, BULK UP!
WHAT?!
SHA—AAA
HE BLOCKED...
...ALL OF OUR ATTACKS?!

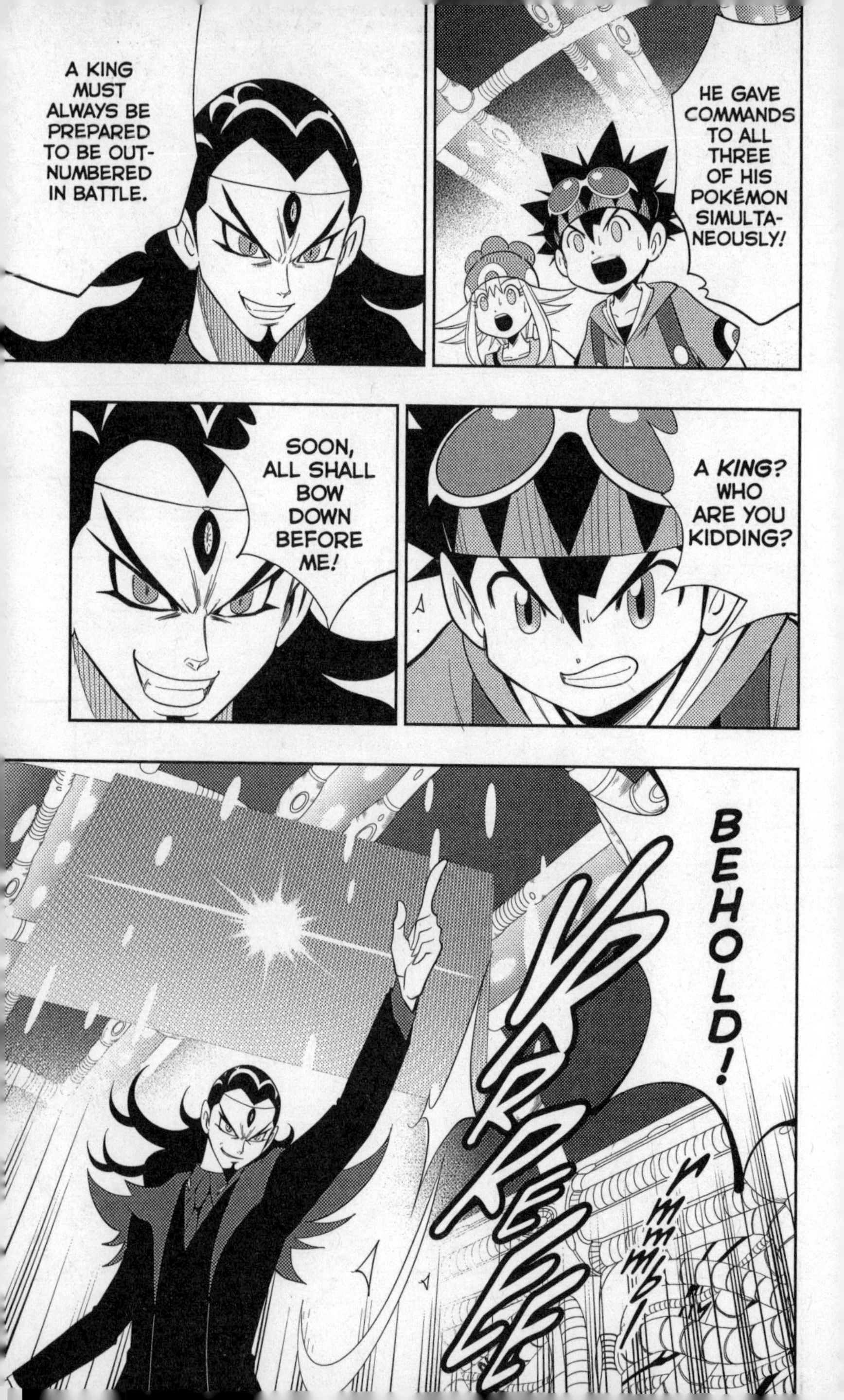
HE GAVE COMMANDS TO ALL THREE OF HIS POKÉMON SIMULTANEOUSLY!
A KING MUST ALWAYS BE PREPARED TO BE OUTNUMBERED IN BATTLE.
A *KING*? WHO ARE YOU KIDDING?
SOON, ALL SHALL BOW DOWN BEFORE ME!
BEHOLD!

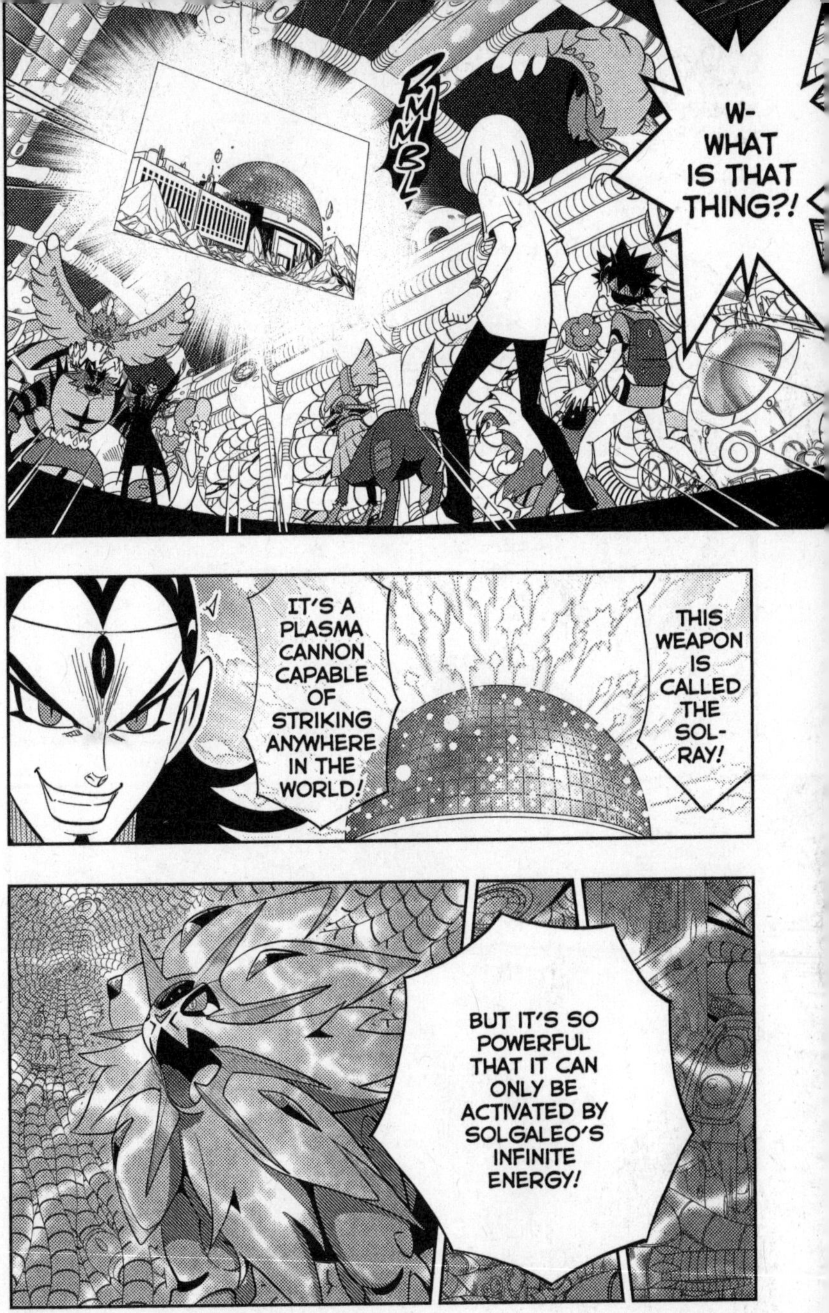
W-WHAT IS THAT THING?!
RMMBL
THIS WEAPON IS CALLED THE SOL-RAY!
IT'S A PLASMA CANNON CAPABLE OF STRIKING ANYWHERE IN THE WORLD!
BUT IT'S SO POWERFUL THAT IT CAN ONLY BE ACTIVATED BY SOLGALEO'S INFINITE ENERGY!

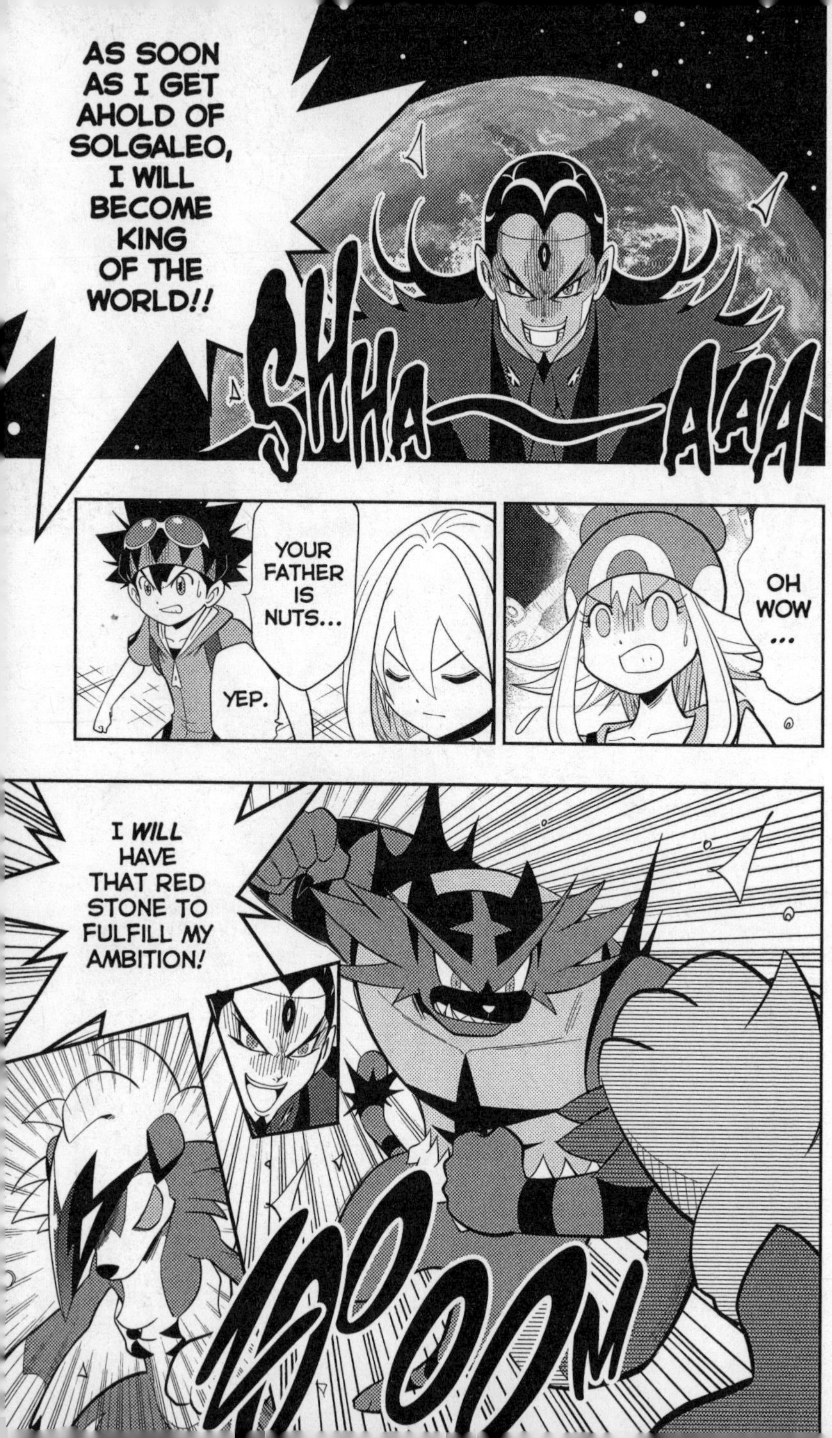
AS SOON AS I GET AHOLD OF SOLGALEO, I WILL BECOME KING OF THE WORLD!!
SHHA—AAA
OH WOW ...
YOUR FATHER IS NUTS...
YEP.
I WILL HAVE THAT RED STONE TO FULFILL MY AMBITION!
VROOOM

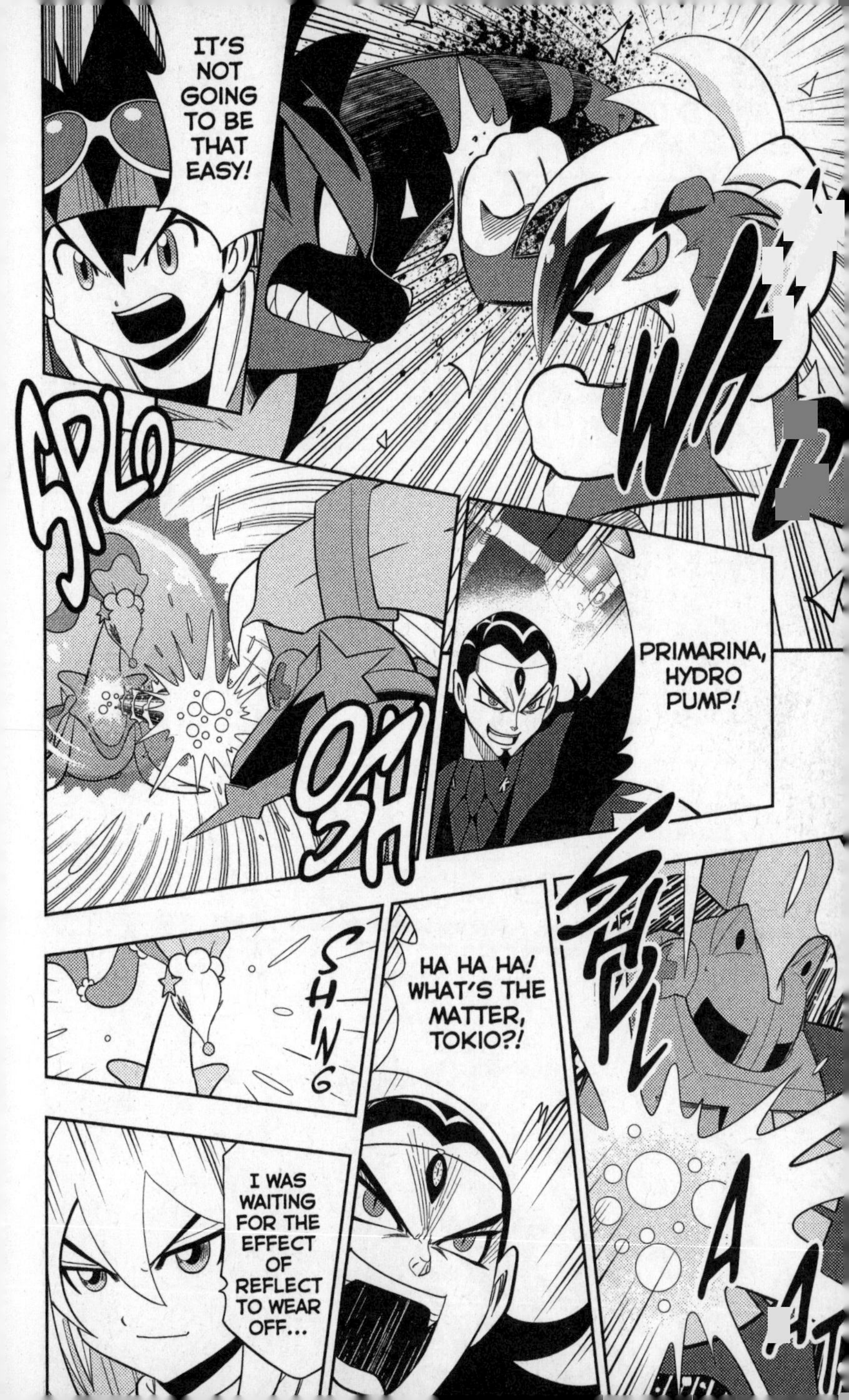
IT'S NOT GOING TO BE THAT EASY!
PRIMARINA, HYDRO PUMP!
SPLO
OSH
HA HA HA! WHAT'S THE MATTER, TOKIO?!
SHING
I WAS WAITING FOR THE EFFECT OF REFLECT TO WEAR OFF...

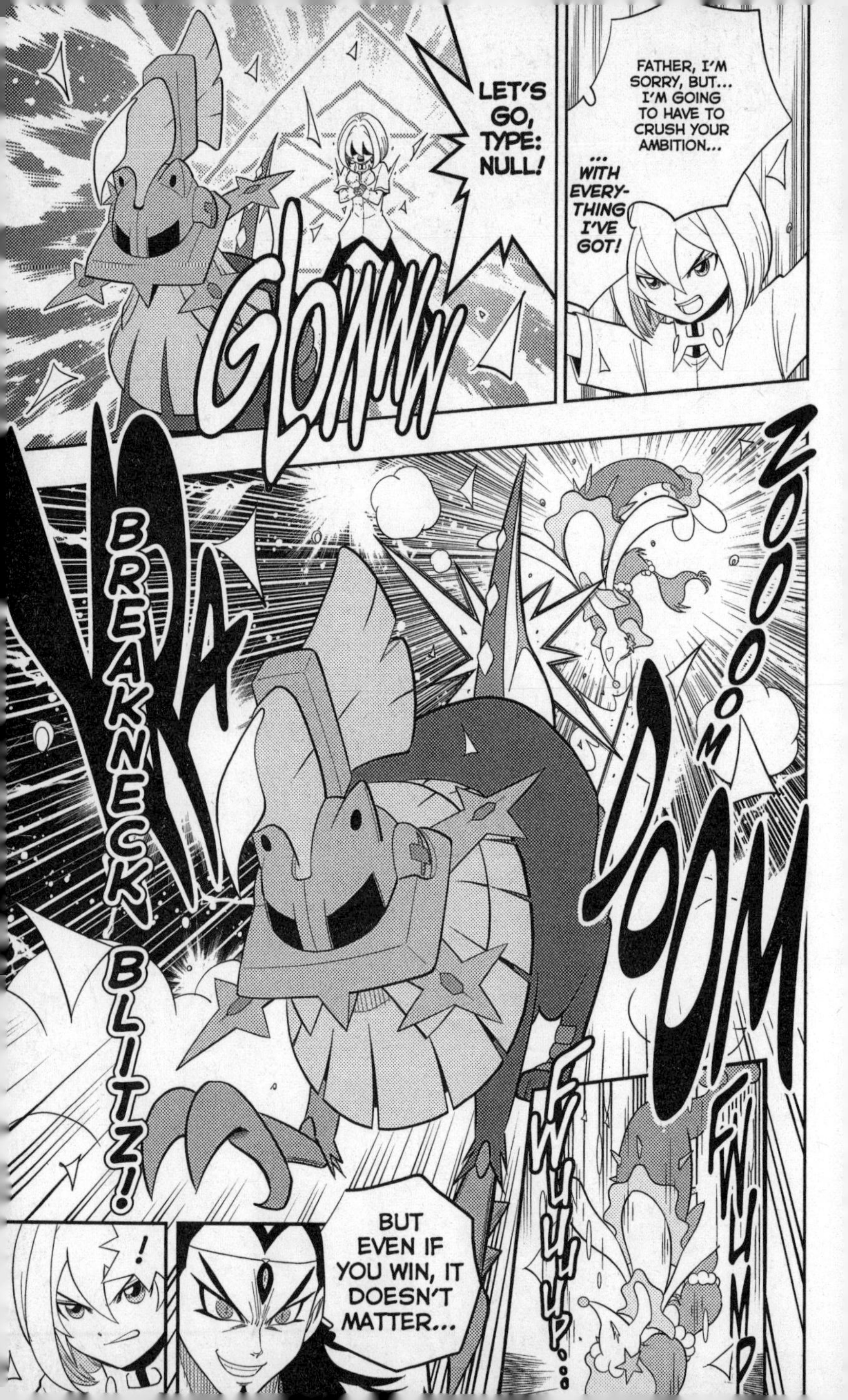
FATHER, I'M SORRY, BUT... I'M GOING TO HAVE TO CRUSH YOUR AMBITION...
...WITH EVERYTHING I'VE GOT!
LET'S GO, TYPE: NULL!
GLOWWW
ZOOOOOOM
DOOM
FWUMP
BREAKNECK BLITZ!
FWUMP...
BUT EVEN IF YOU WIN, IT DOESN'T MATTER...
!

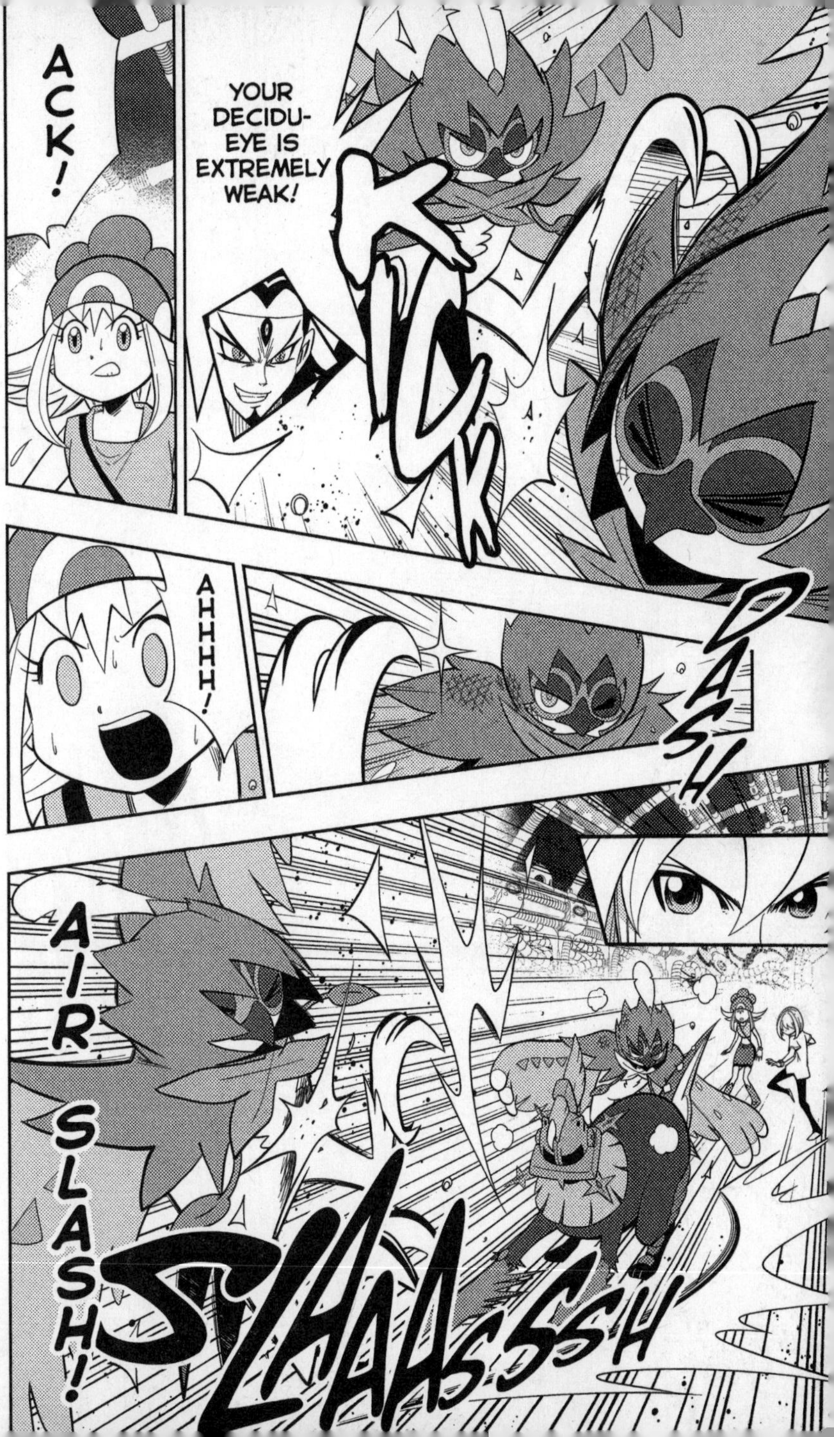
YOUR DECIDU-EYE IS EXTREMELY WEAK!
KICK
ACK!
DASH
AHHHH!
AIR SLASH!
SLAAASSSH

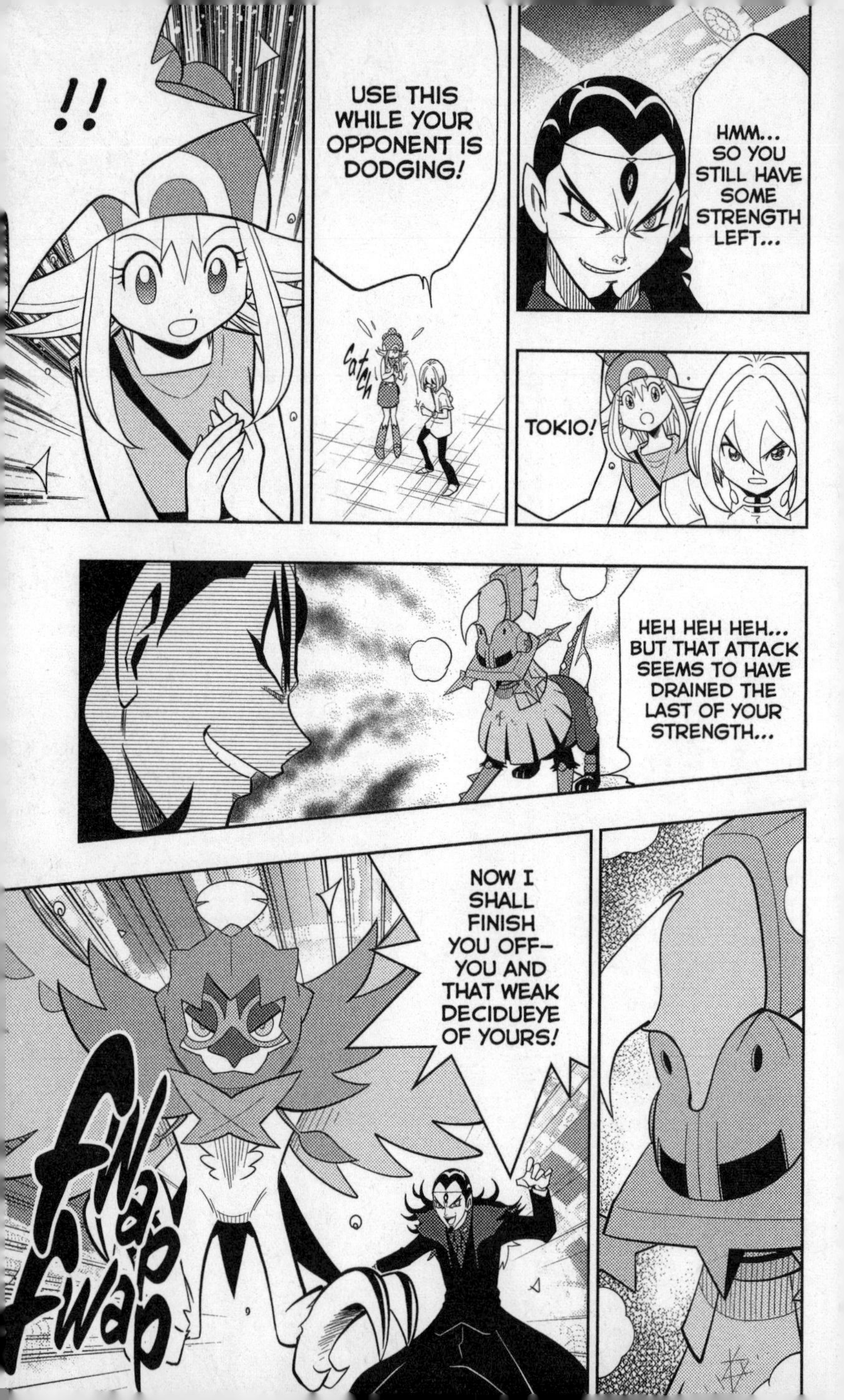
HMM... SO YOU STILL HAVE SOME STRENGTH LEFT...
TOKIO!
USE THIS WHILE YOUR OPPONENT IS DODGING!
catch
!!
HEH HEH HEH... BUT THAT ATTACK SEEMS TO HAVE DRAINED THE LAST OF YOUR STRENGTH...
NOW I SHALL FINISH YOU OFF— YOU AND THAT WEAK DECIDUEYE OF YOURS!
FWap
FWap

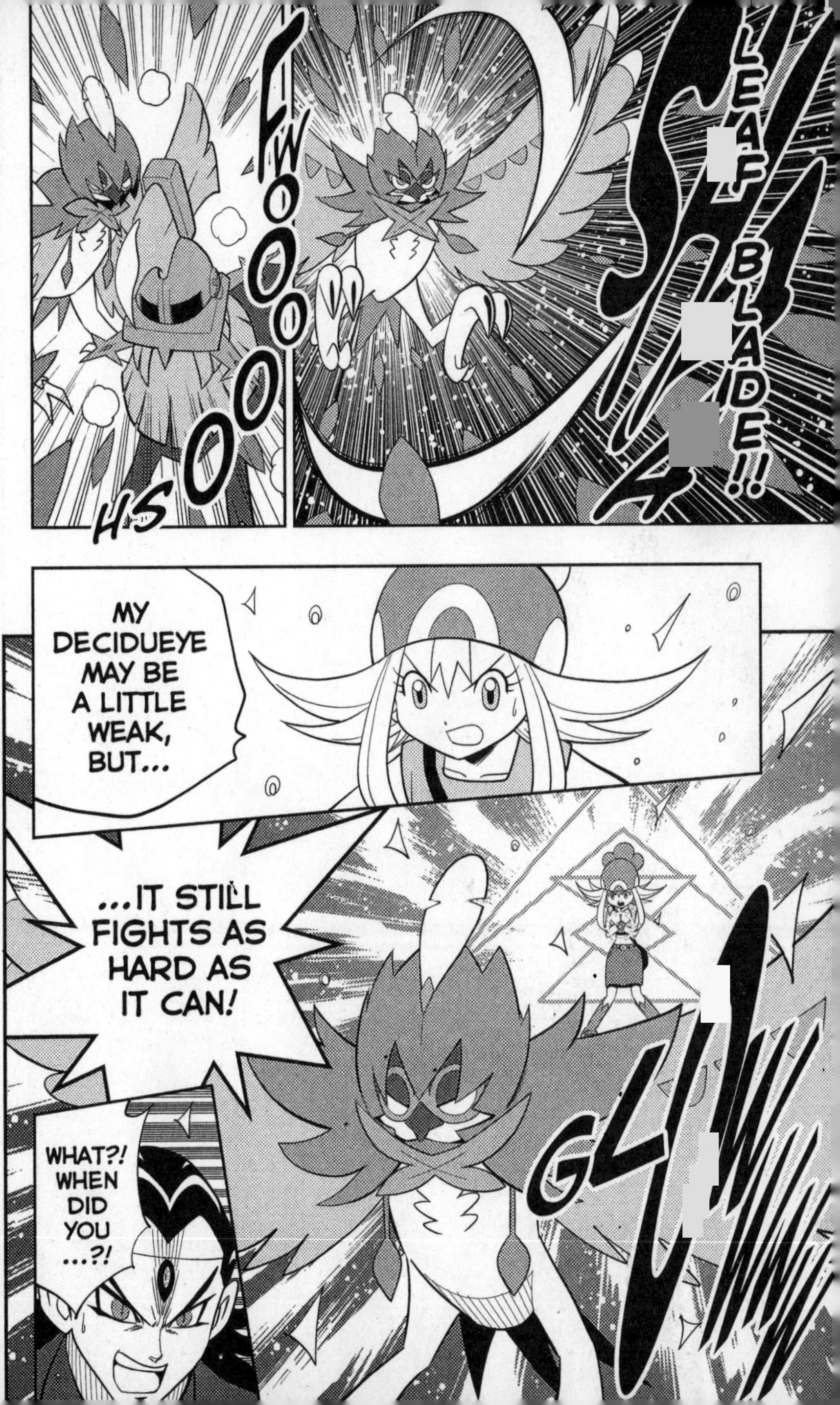
LEAF BLADE!!
MY DECIDUEYE MAY BE A LITTLE WEAK, BUT...
...IT STILL FIGHTS AS HARD AS IT CAN!
WHAT?! WHEN DID YOU ...?!

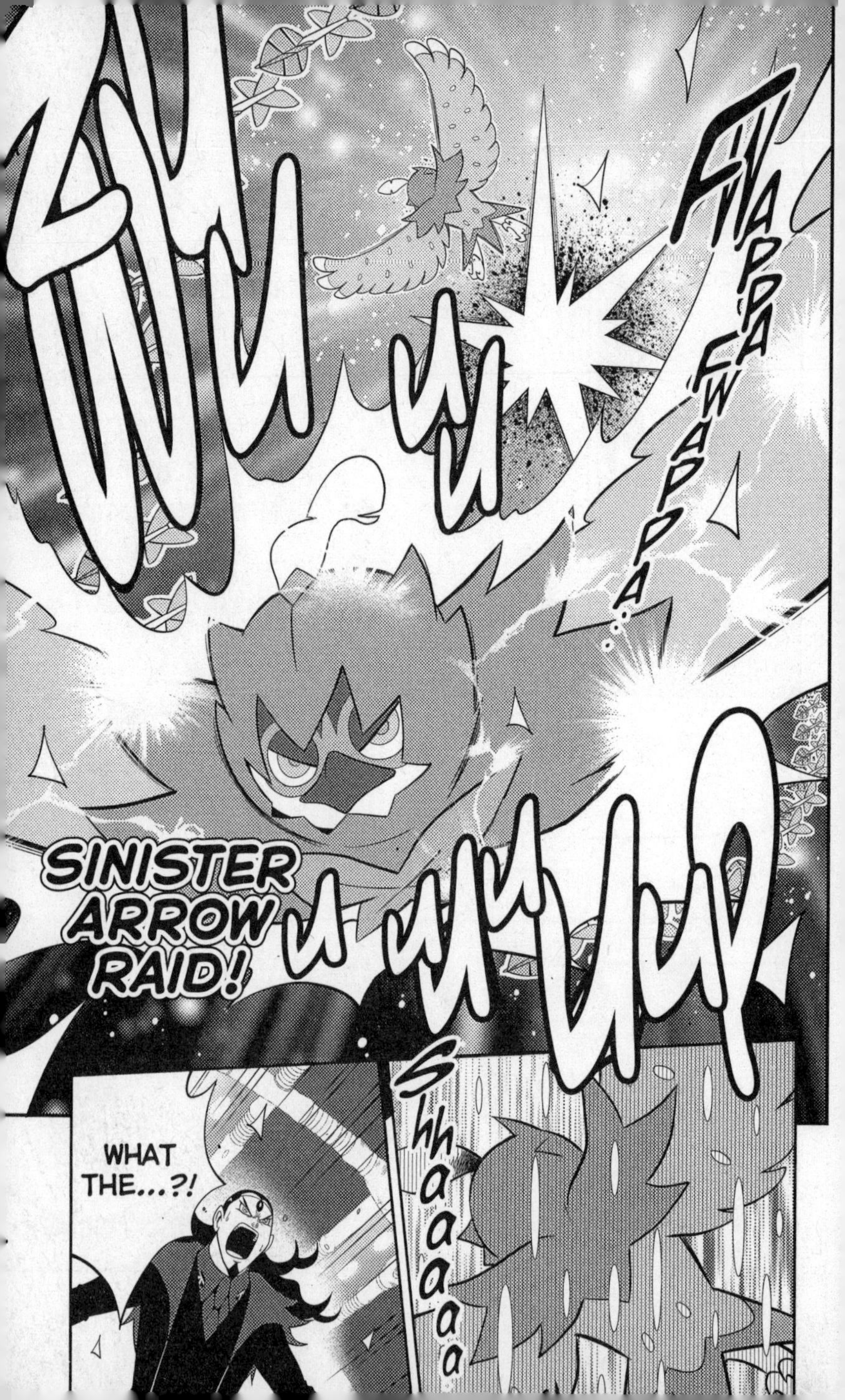
FWAPPA FWAPPA...
SINISTER ARROW RAID!
Shhaaaaaa
WHAT THE...?!

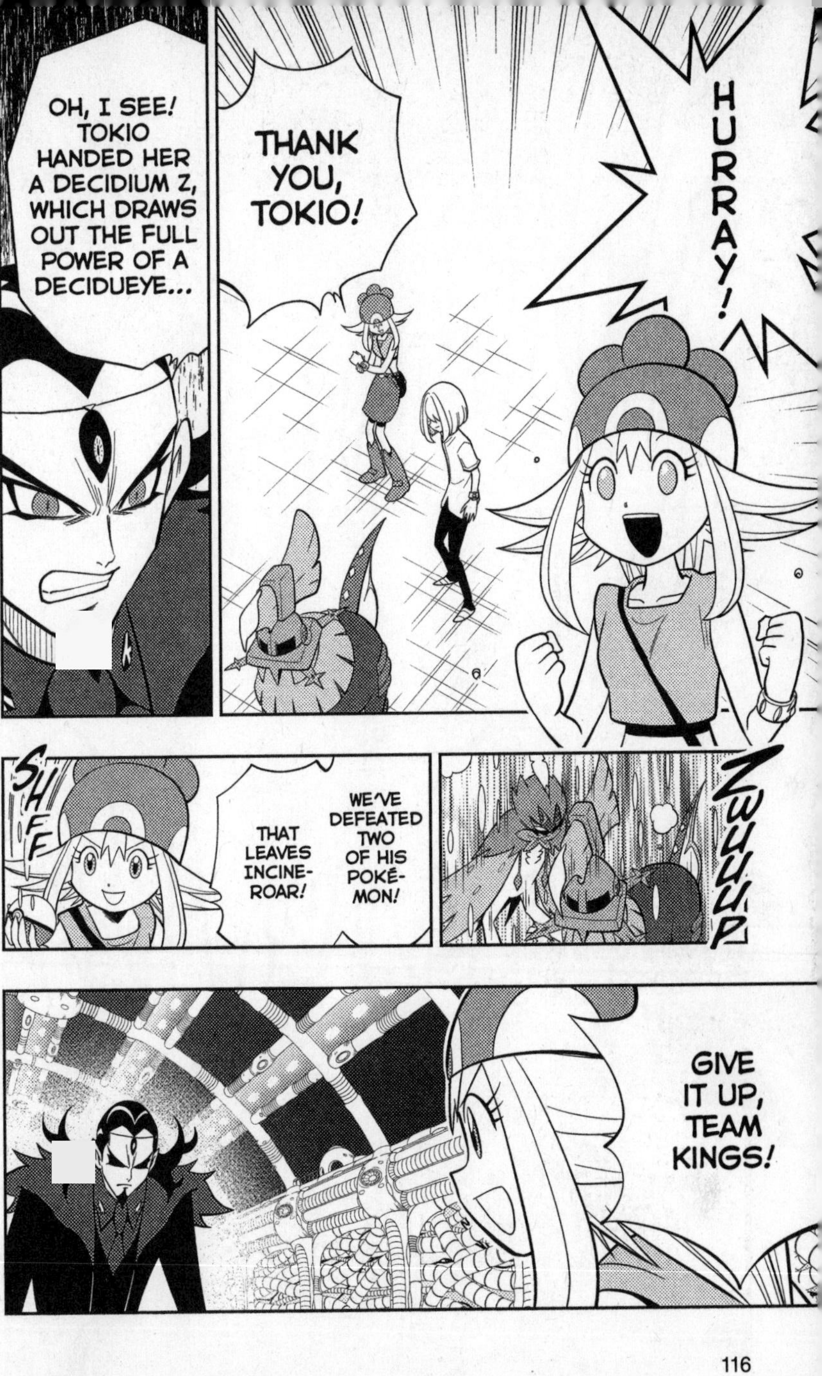
HURRAY!
THANK YOU, TOKIO!
OH, I SEE! TOKIO HANDED HER A DECIDIUM Z, WHICH DRAWS OUT THE FULL POWER OF A DECIDUEYE...
ZWUUUUP
WE'VE DEFEATED TWO OF HIS POKÉ-MON!
THAT LEAVES INCINE-ROAR!
SHFF
GIVE IT UP, TEAM KINGS!

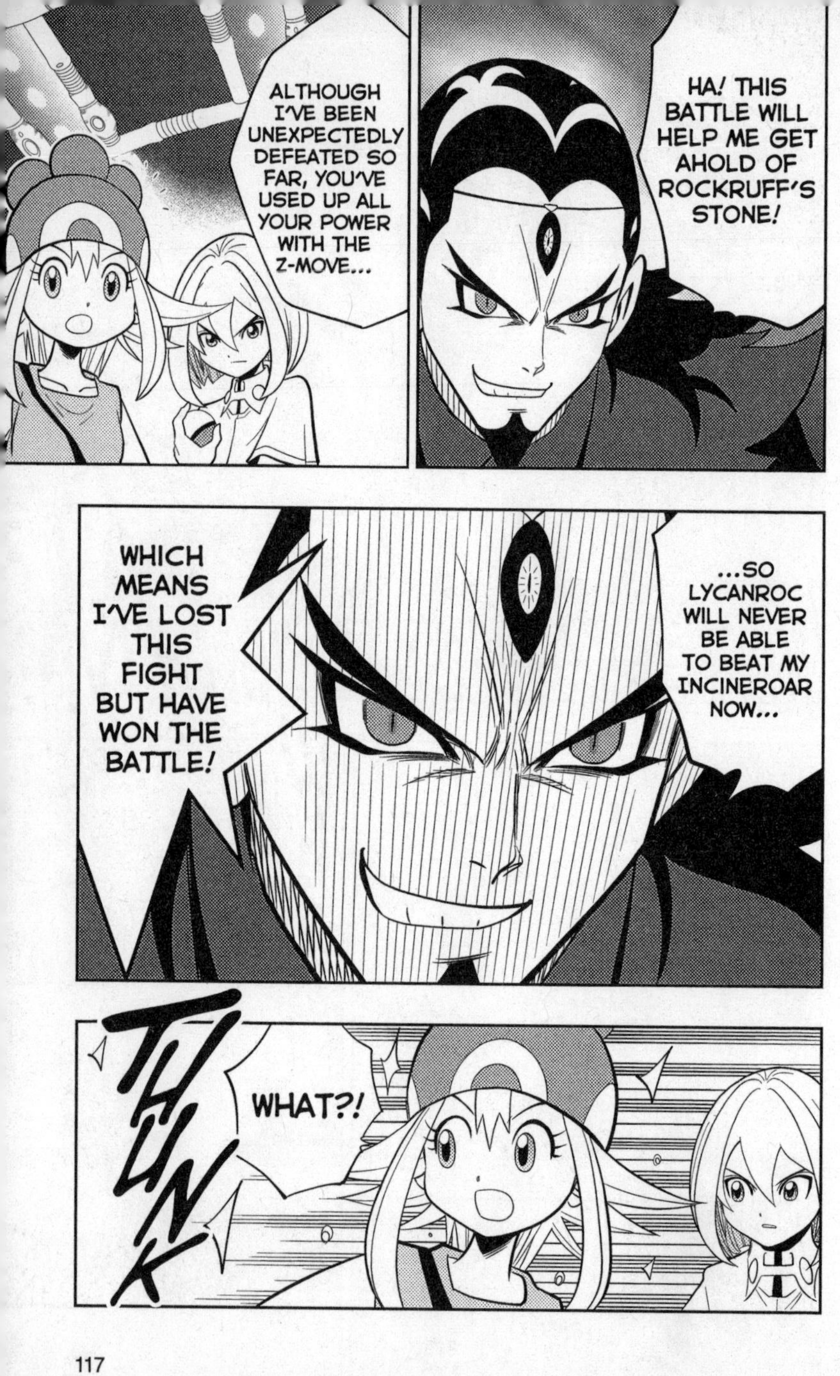
HA! THIS BATTLE WILL HELP ME GET AHOLD OF ROCKRUFF'S STONE!
ALTHOUGH I'VE BEEN UNEXPECTEDLY DEFEATED SO FAR, YOU'VE USED UP ALL YOUR POWER WITH THE Z-MOVE...
...SO LYCANROC WILL NEVER BE ABLE TO BEAT MY INCINEROAR NOW...
WHICH MEANS I'VE LOST THIS FIGHT BUT HAVE WON THE BATTLE!
WHAT?!
THUNK

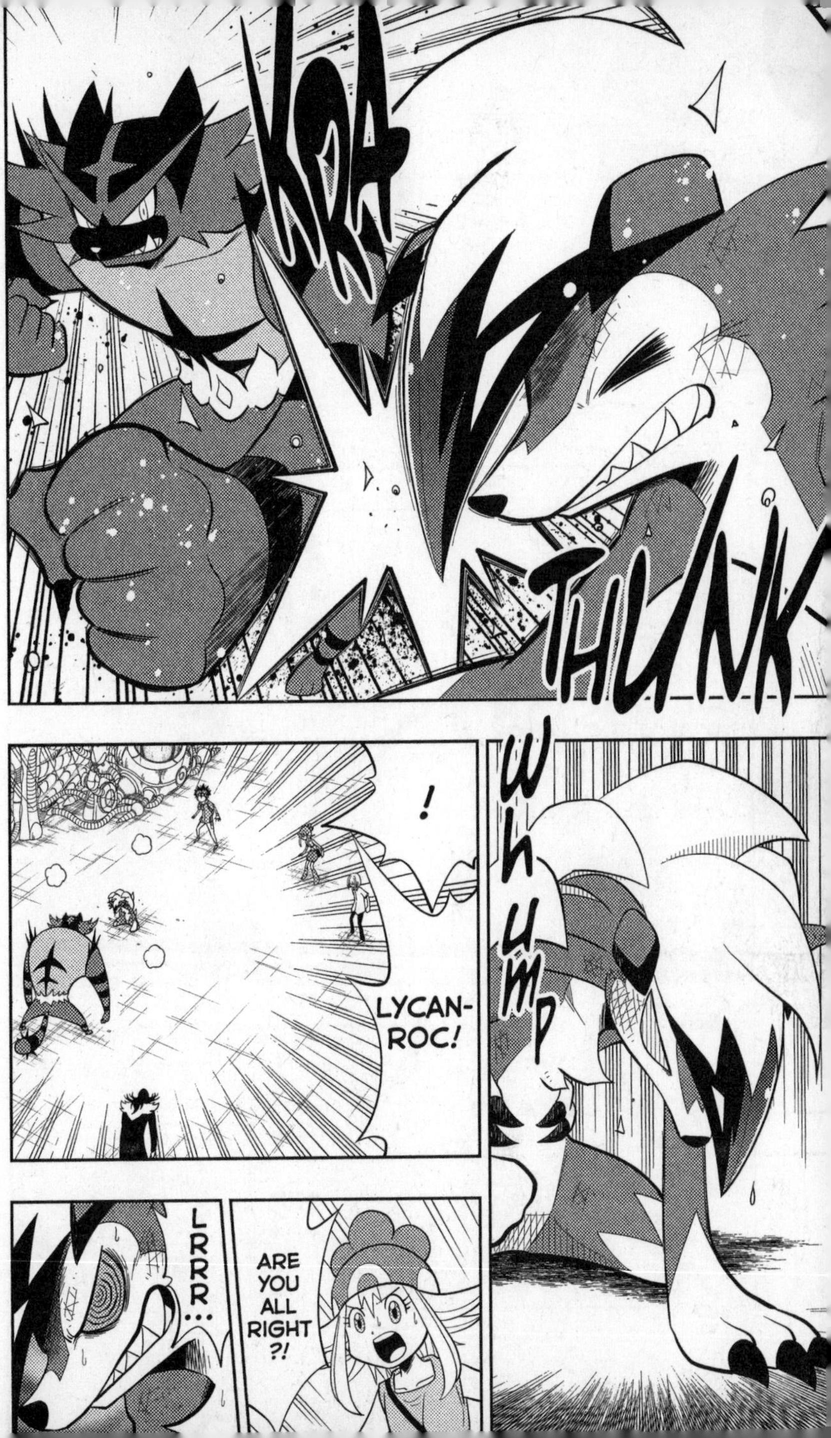
THUNK
WHUMP
!
LYCAN-ROC!
ARE YOU ALL RIGHT ?!
LRRR...

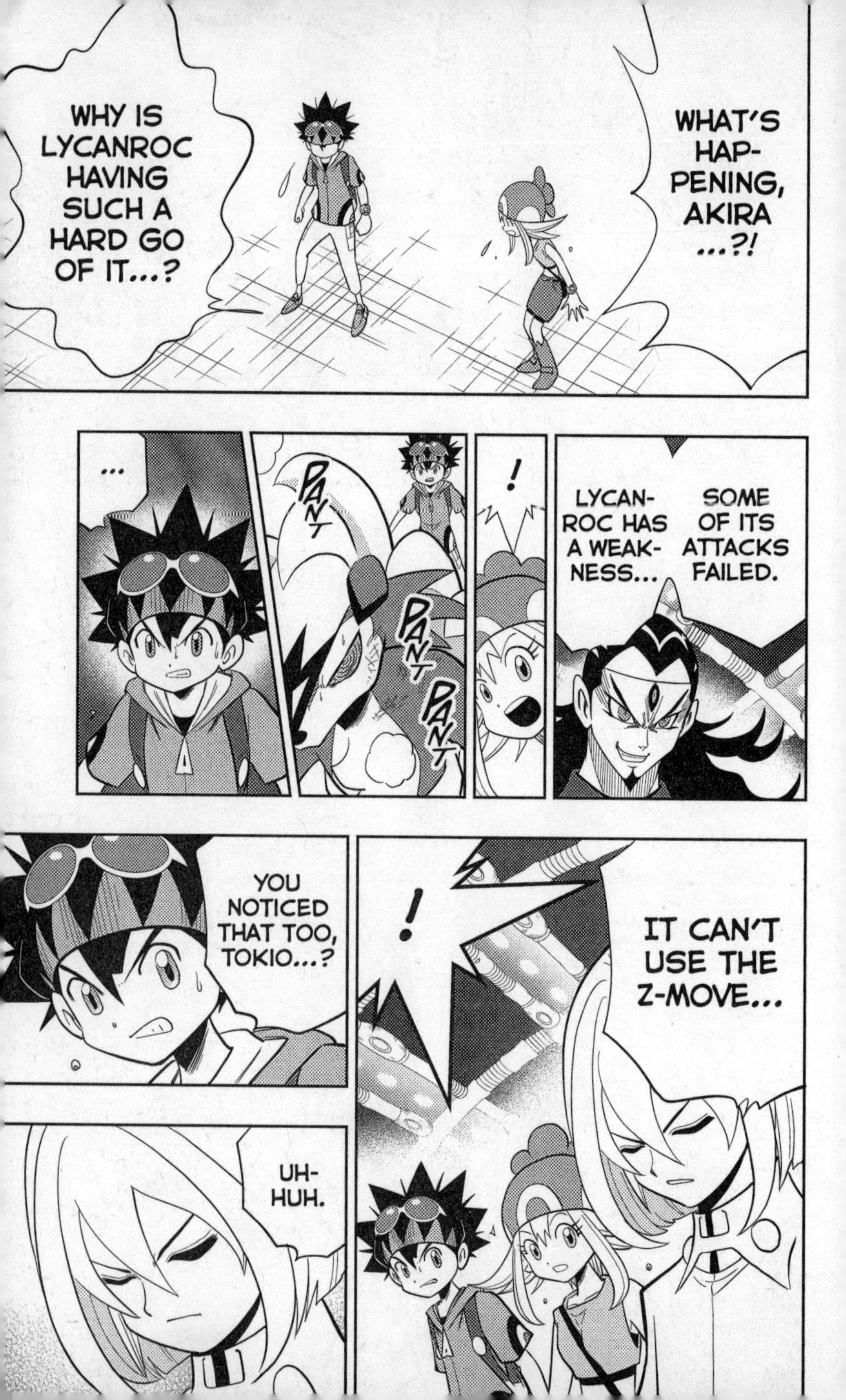
WHAT'S HAP-PENING, AKIRA ...?!
WHY IS LYCANROC HAVING SUCH A HARD GO OF IT...?
SOME OF ITS ATTACKS FAILED.
LYCAN-ROC HAS A WEAK-NESS...
!
PANT
PANT
PANT
...
!
IT CAN'T USE THE Z-MOVE...
YOU NOTICED THAT TOO, TOKIO...?
UH-HUH.

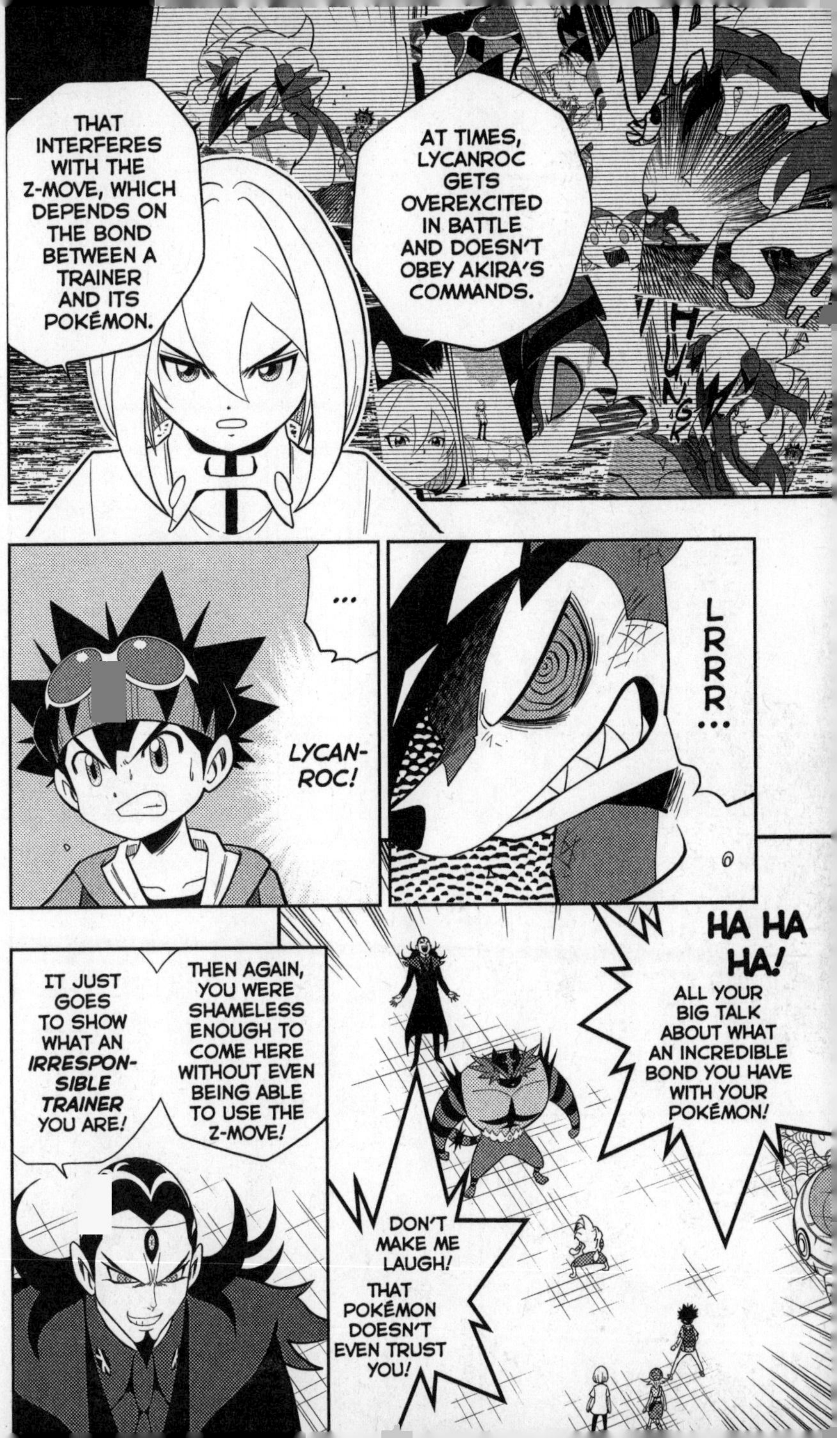
HUNGK
AT TIMES, LYCANROC GETS OVEREXCITED IN BATTLE AND DOESN'T OBEY AKIRA'S COMMANDS.
THAT INTERFERES WITH THE Z-MOVE, WHICH DEPENDS ON THE BOND BETWEEN A TRAINER AND ITS POKÉMON.
LRRR...
...
LYCAN-ROC!
HA HA HA!
ALL YOUR BIG TALK ABOUT WHAT AN INCREDIBLE BOND YOU HAVE WITH YOUR POKÉMON!
DON'T MAKE ME LAUGH!
THAT POKÉMON DOESN'T EVEN TRUST YOU!
THEN AGAIN, YOU WERE SHAMELESS ENOUGH TO COME HERE WITHOUT EVEN BEING ABLE TO USE THE Z-MOVE!
IT JUST GOES TO SHOW WHAT AN *IRRESPONSIBLE TRAINER* YOU ARE!

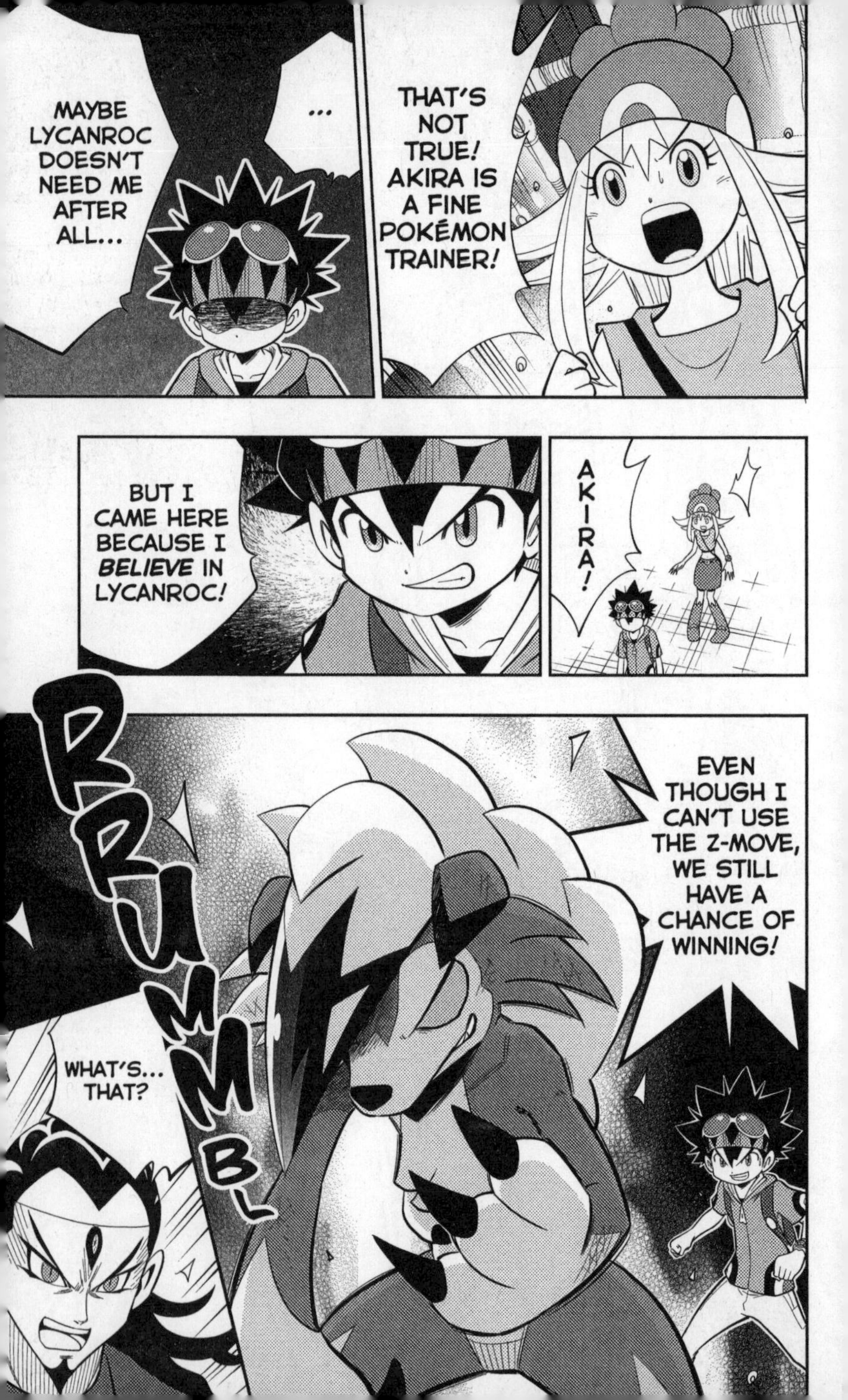
THAT'S NOT TRUE! AKIRA IS A FINE POKÉMON TRAINER!
...
MAYBE LYCANROC DOESN'T NEED ME AFTER ALL...
AKIRA!
BUT I CAME HERE BECAUSE I *BELIEVE* IN LYCANROC!
EVEN THOUGH I CAN'T USE THE Z-MOVE, WE STILL HAVE A CHANCE OF WINNING!
RRUMMMBL
WHAT'S... THAT?

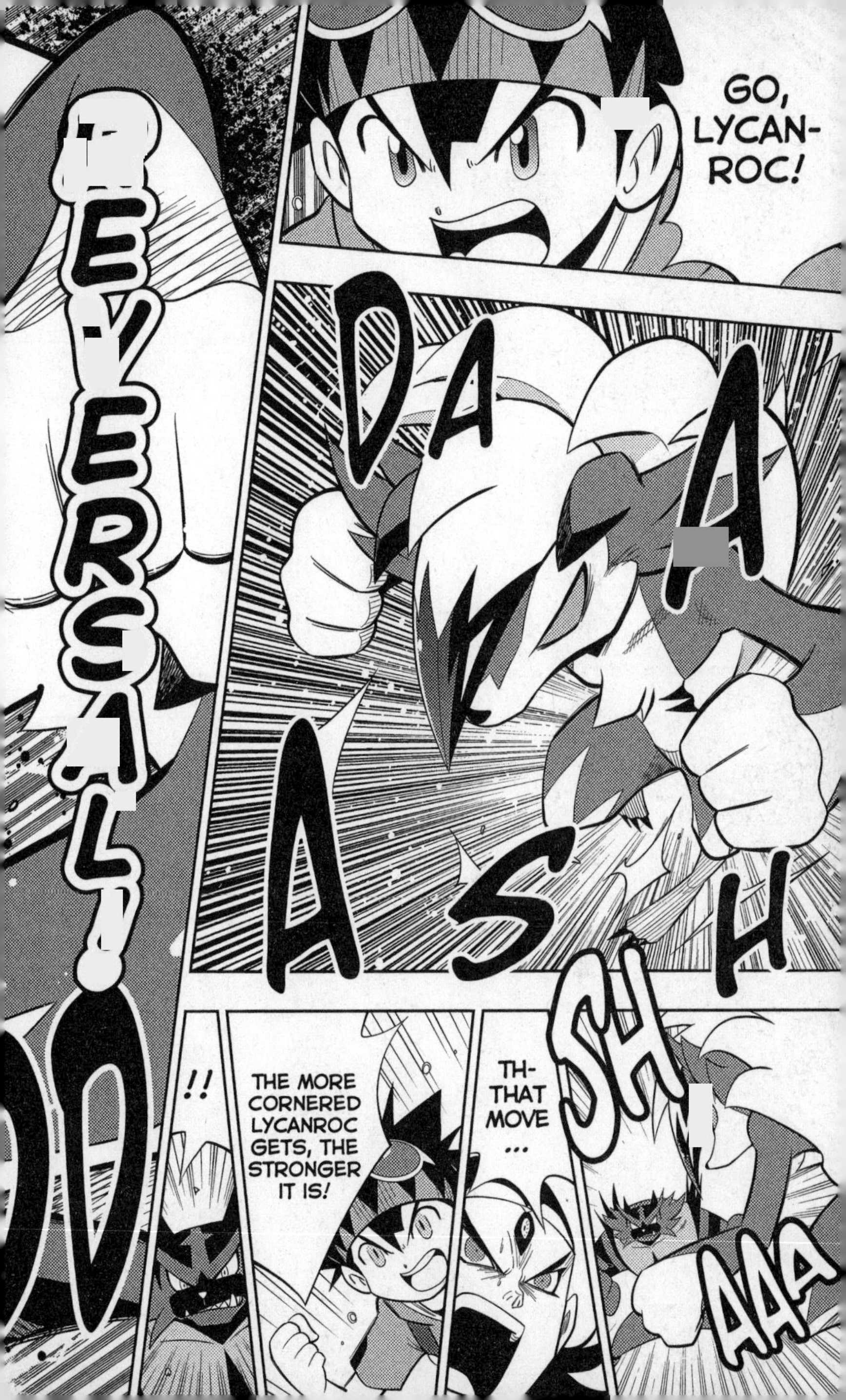
GO, LYCAN-ROC!
DAAASH
SHAAA
TH-THAT MOVE...
THE MORE CORNERED LYCANROC GETS, THE STRONGER IT IS!
!!
EVERSAL

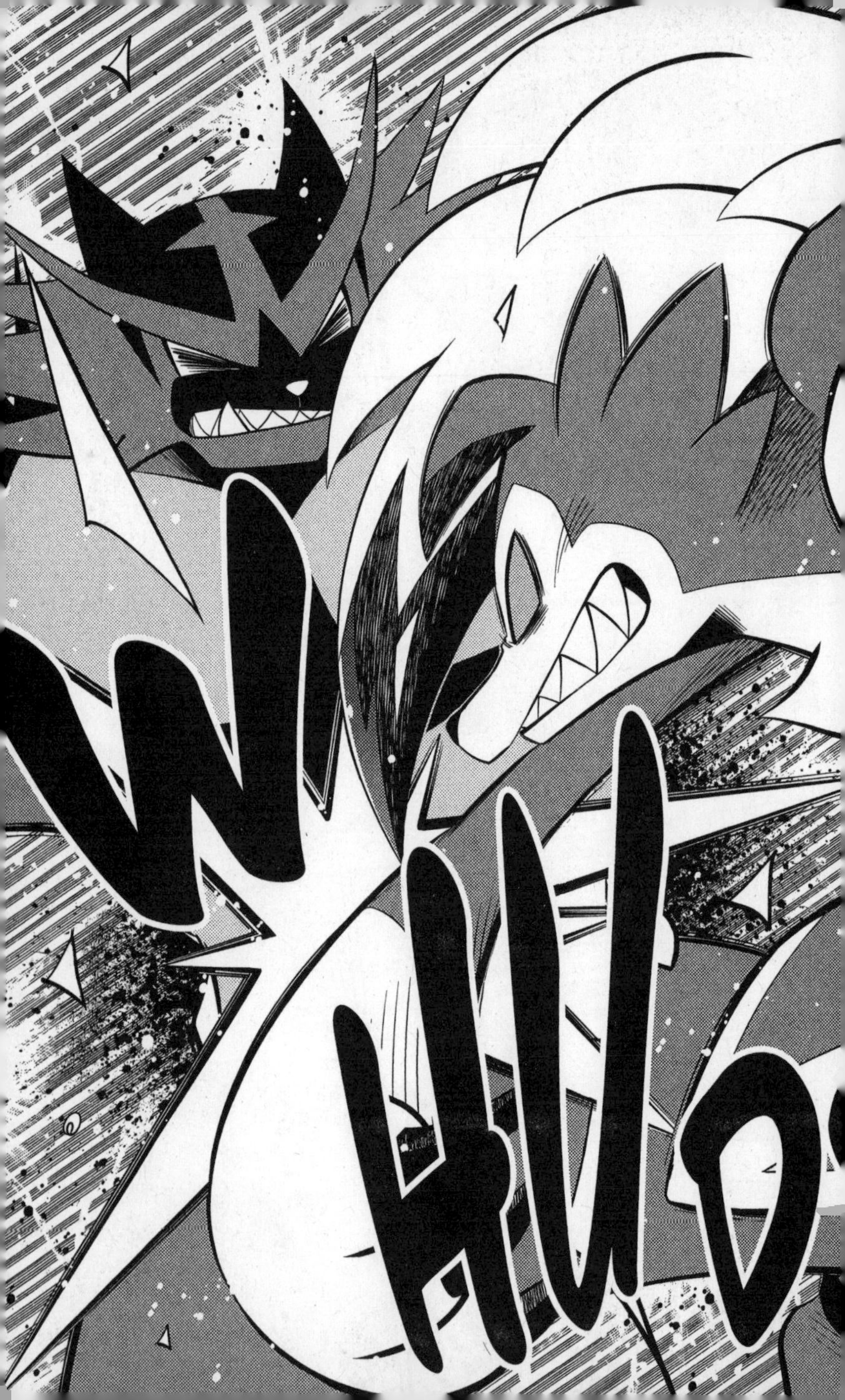

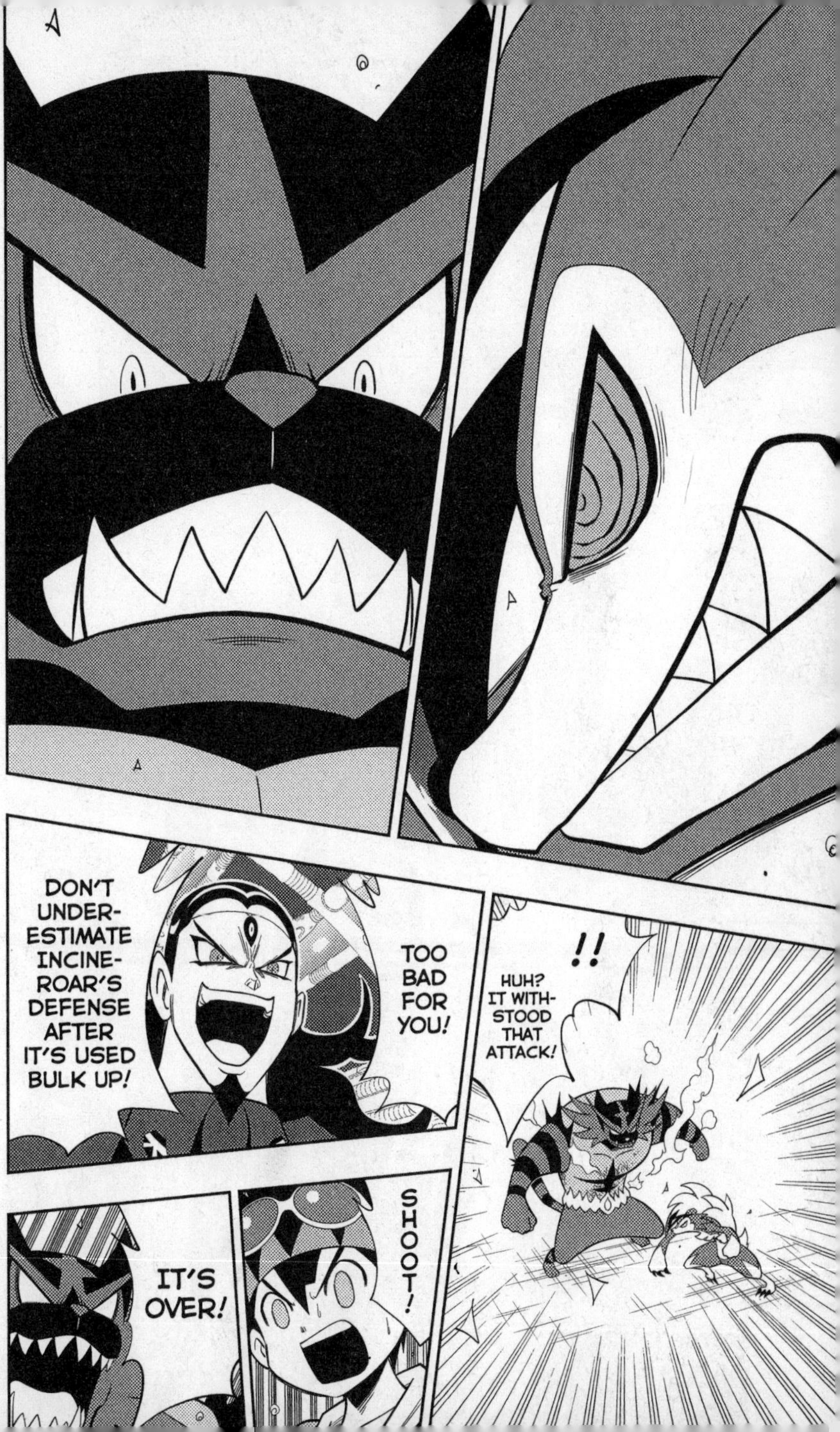
!!
HUH? IT WITH-STOOD THAT ATTACK!
TOO BAD FOR YOU!
DON'T UNDER-ESTIMATE INCINE-ROAR'S DEFENSE AFTER IT'S USED BULK UP!
SHOOT!
IT'S OVER!

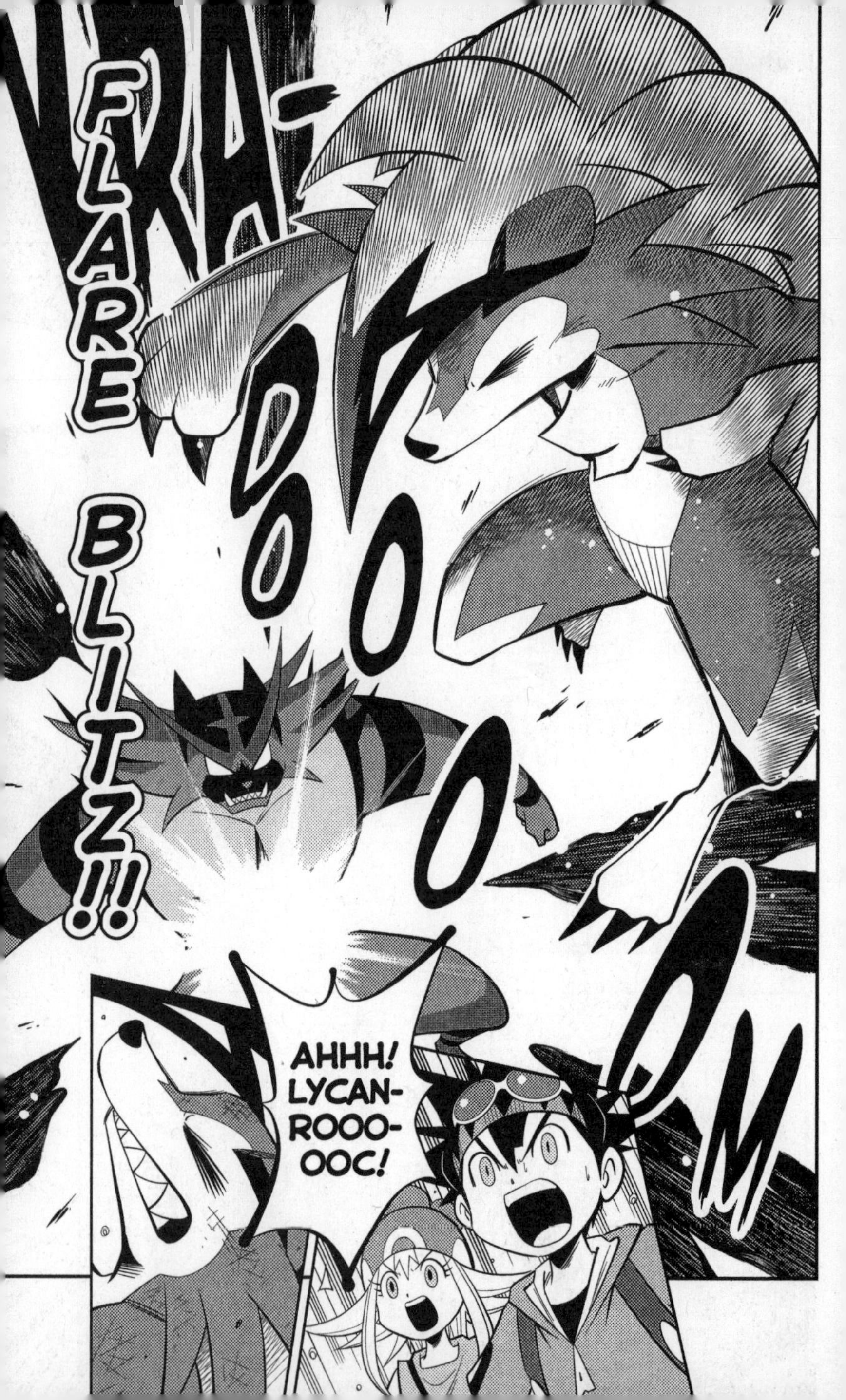
FLARE BLITZ!!
VRA-
DOOOOOOM
AHHH! LYCAN-ROOO-OOC!

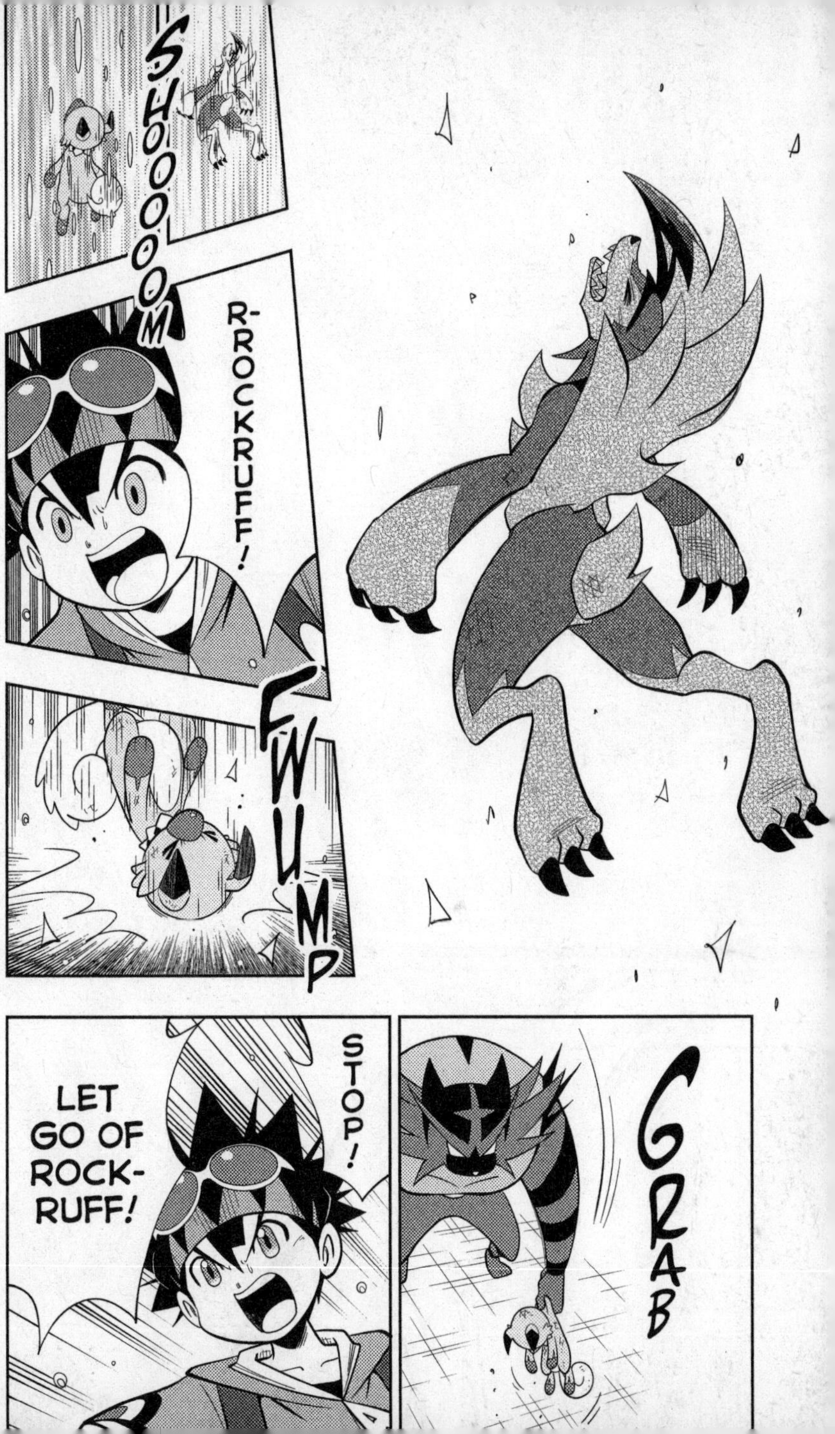
SHOOOOOOM
R-ROCKRUFF!
FWUMP
GRAB
STOP!
LET GO OF ROCK-RUFF!

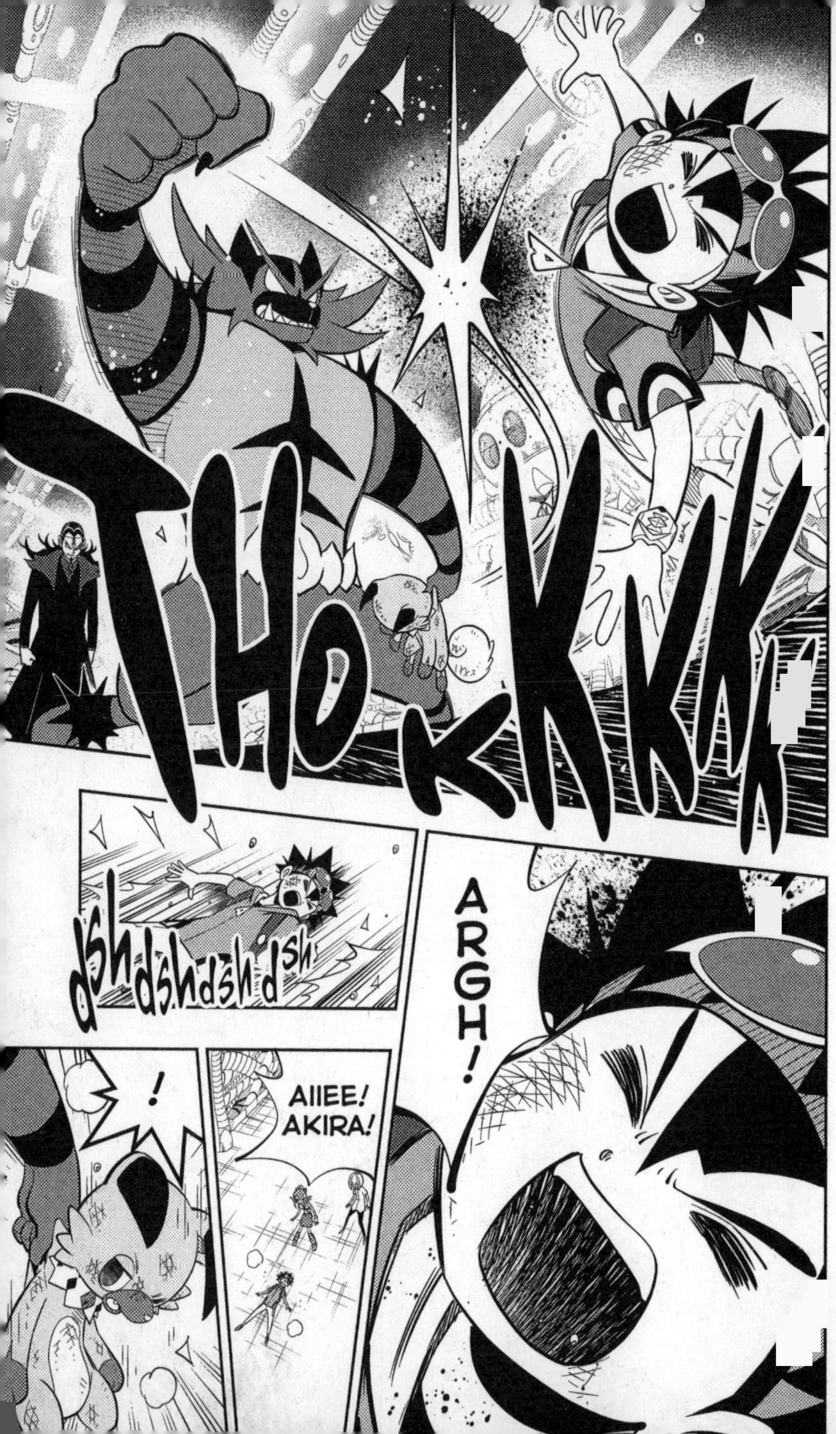
THOKKKK
ARGH!
dshdshdshdsh
AIIEE! AKIRA!
!

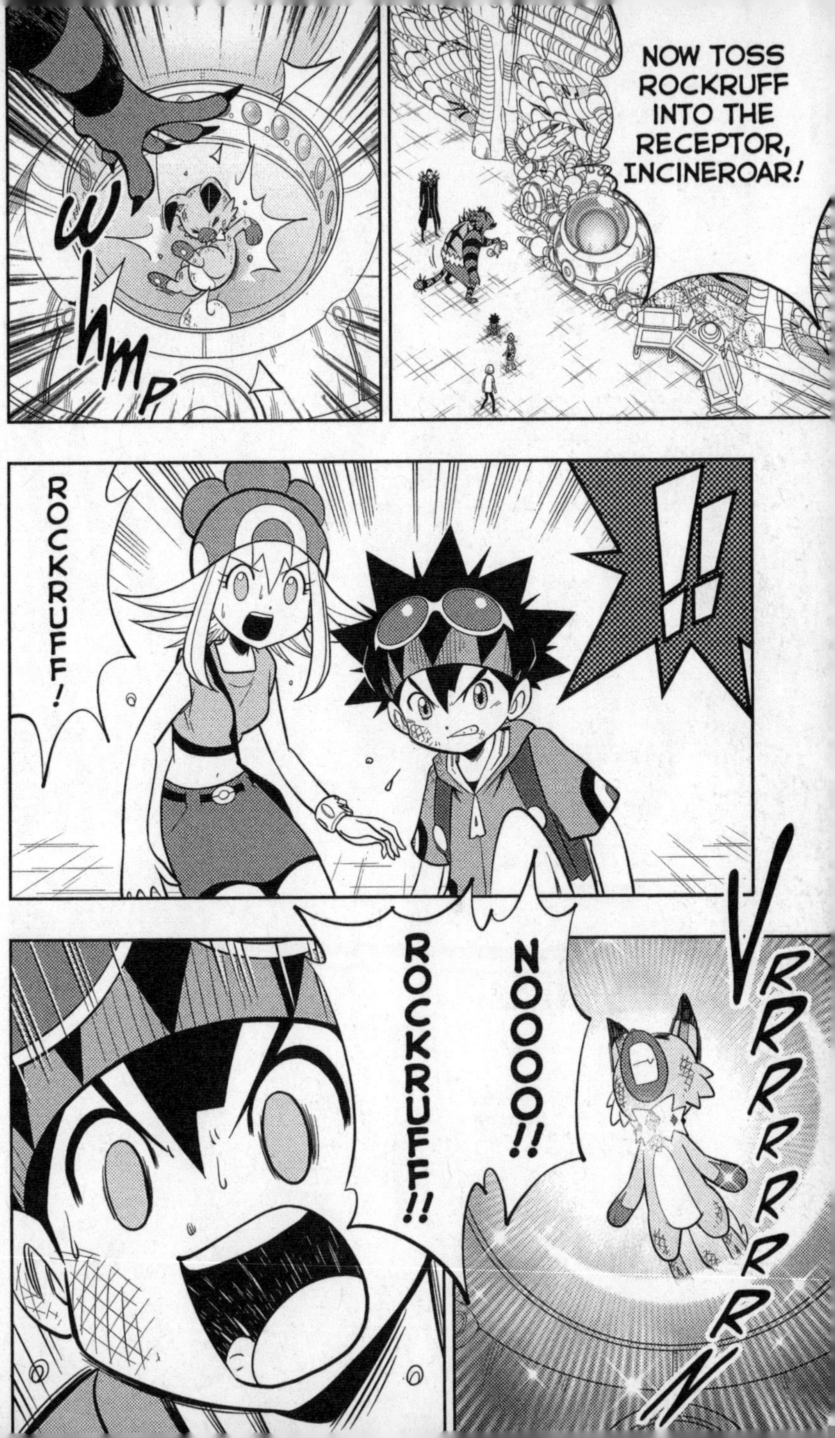

NOW TOSS ROCKRUFF INTO THE RECEPTOR, INCINEROAR!
WHMP
!!
ROCKRUFF!
VRRRRRRRN
NOOOO!! ROCKRUFF!!

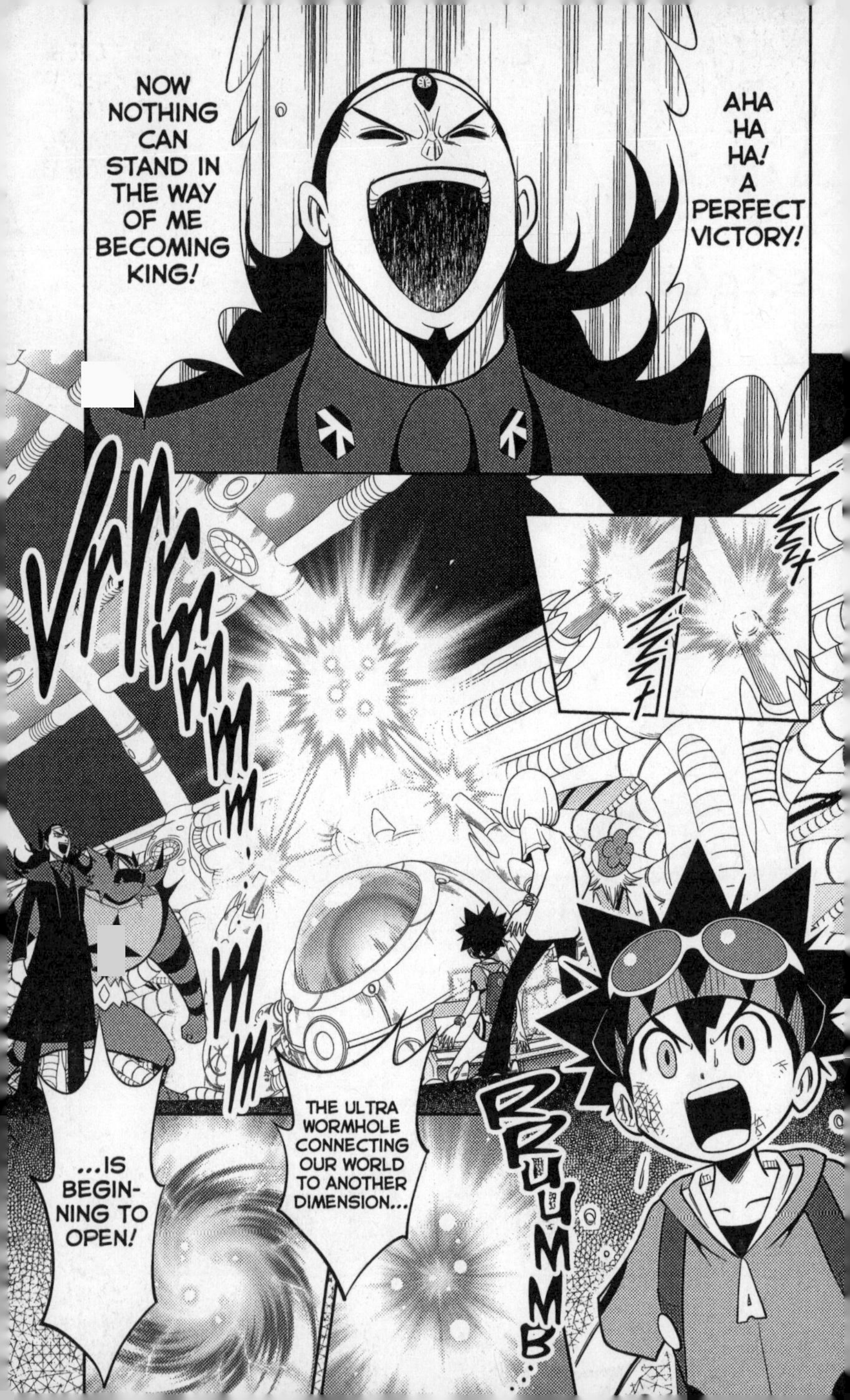
AHA HA HA! A PERFECT VICTORY!
NOW NOTHING CAN STAND IN THE WAY OF ME BECOMING KING!
THE ULTRA WORMHOLE CONNECTING OUR WORLD TO ANOTHER DIMENSION...
...IS BEGIN-NING TO OPEN!

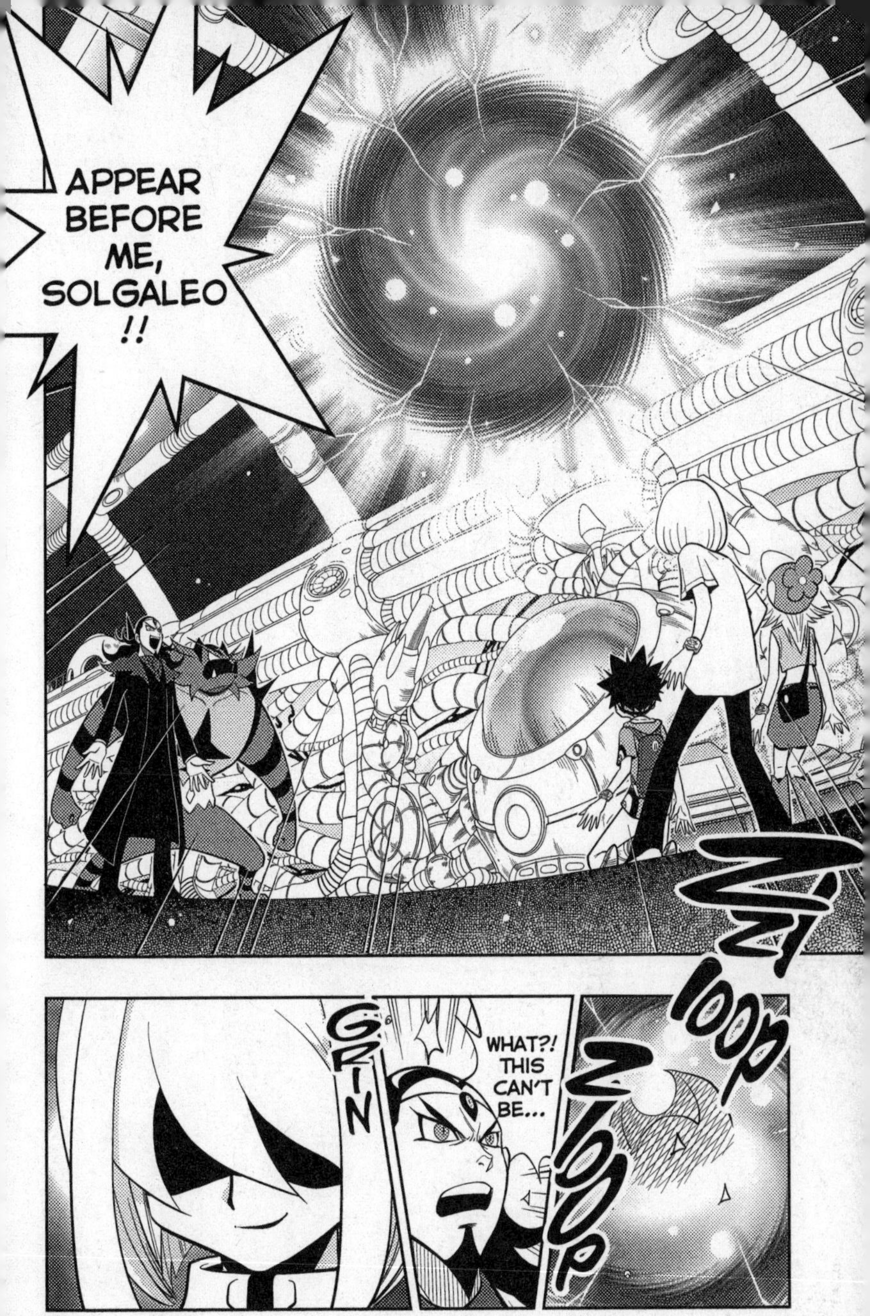
APPEAR BEFORE ME, SOLGALEO!!
ZWOOP
ZWOOP
WHAT?! THIS CAN'T BE...
GRIN

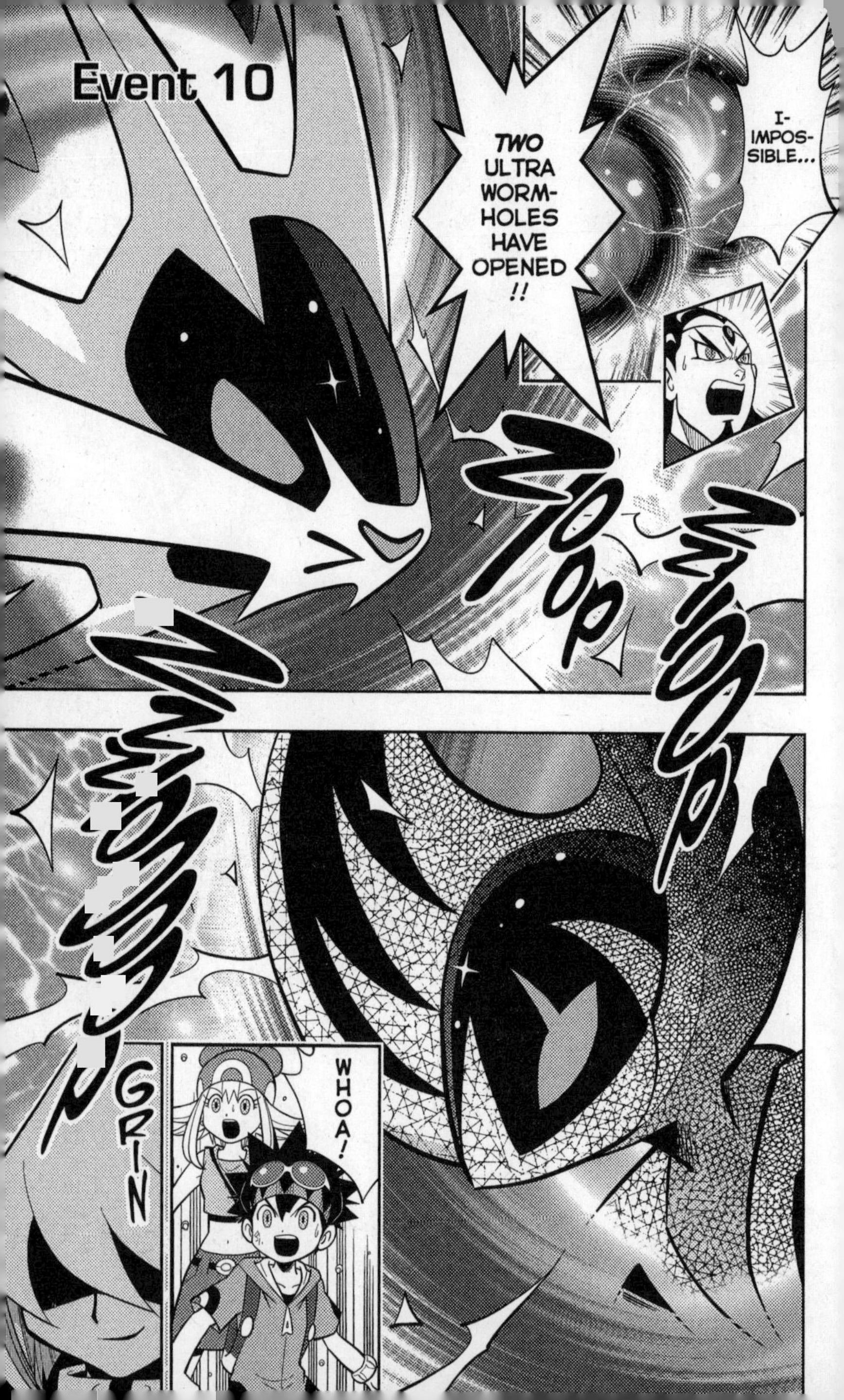
Event 10
I-IMPOSSIBLE...
TWO ULTRA WORMHOLES HAVE OPENED!!
ZWOOP
WHOA!
GRIN

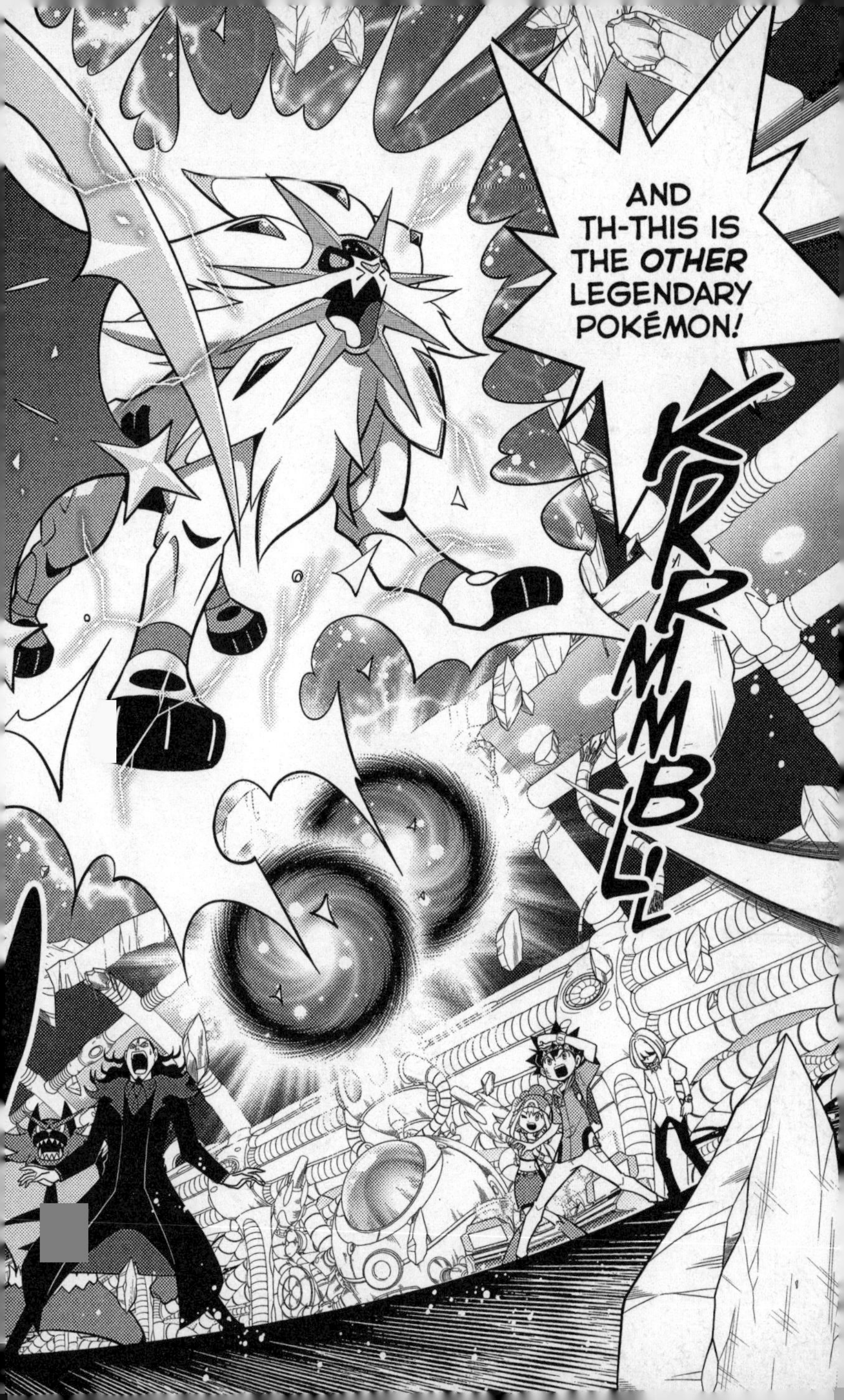
AND TH-THIS IS THE *OTHER* LEGENDARY POKÉMON!
KRRMMBLL

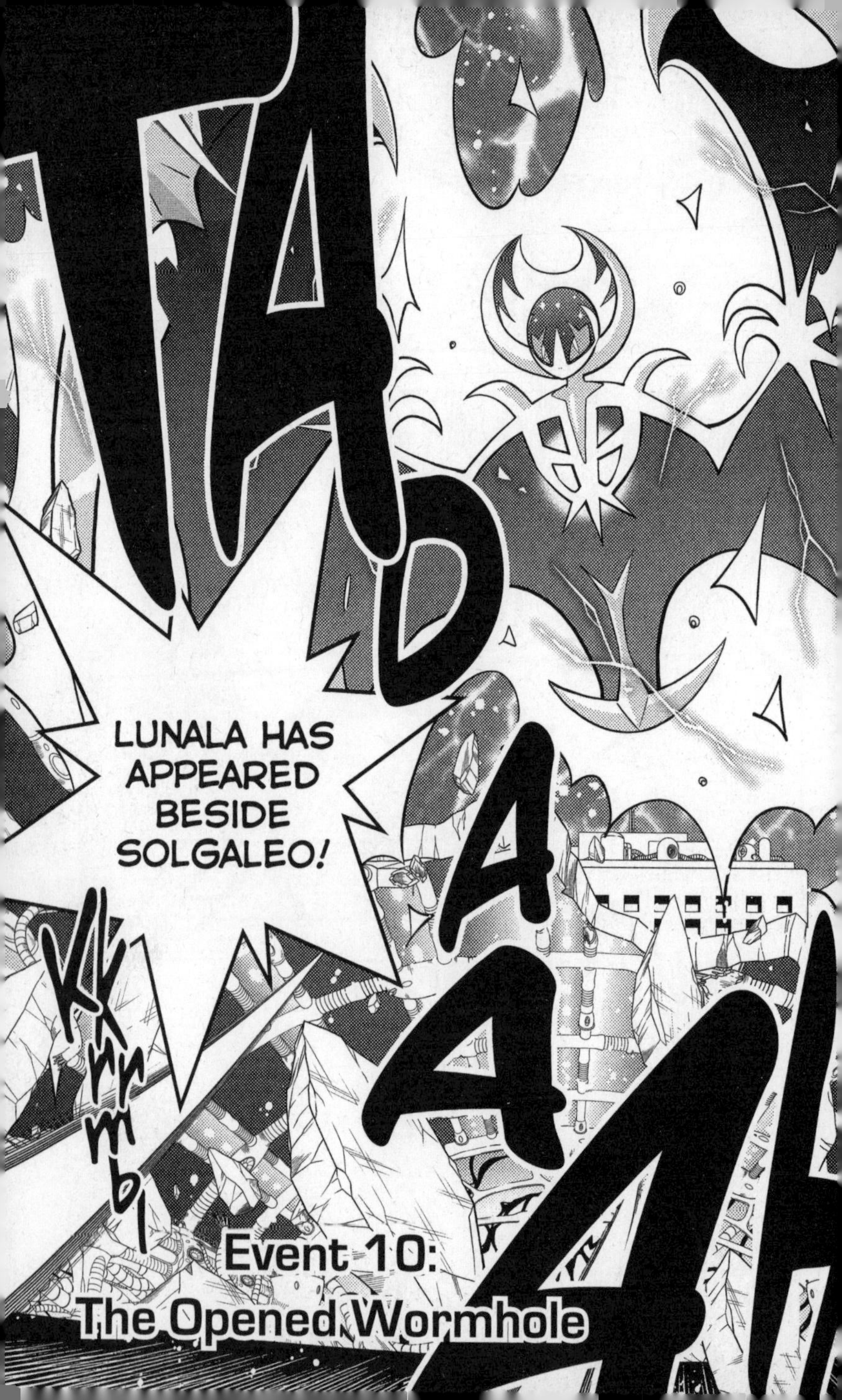
LUNALA HAS APPEARED BESIDE SOLGALEO!
Kkrrmbl

Event 10: The Opened Wormhole

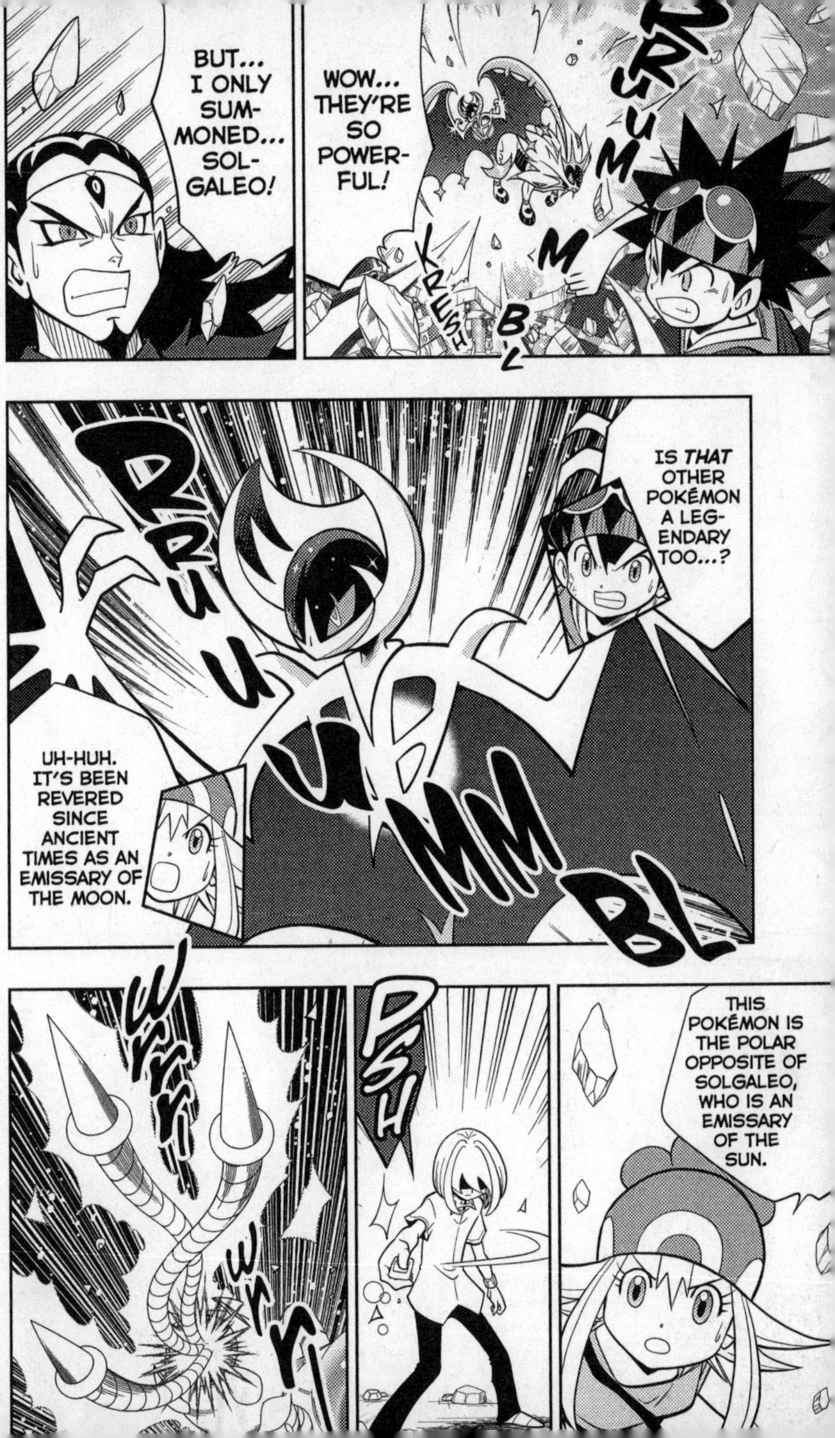
KRUMMMBL
KRESH
WOW... THEY'RE SO POWERFUL!
BUT... I ONLY SUMMONED... SOLGALEO!
RRUUMMBL
IS THAT OTHER POKÉMON A LEGENDARY TOO...?
UH-HUH. IT'S BEEN REVERED SINCE ANCIENT TIMES AS AN EMISSARY OF THE MOON.
THIS POKÉMON IS THE POLAR OPPOSITE OF SOLGALEO, WHO IS AN EMISSARY OF THE SUN.
PSH
WRRR
WRRR

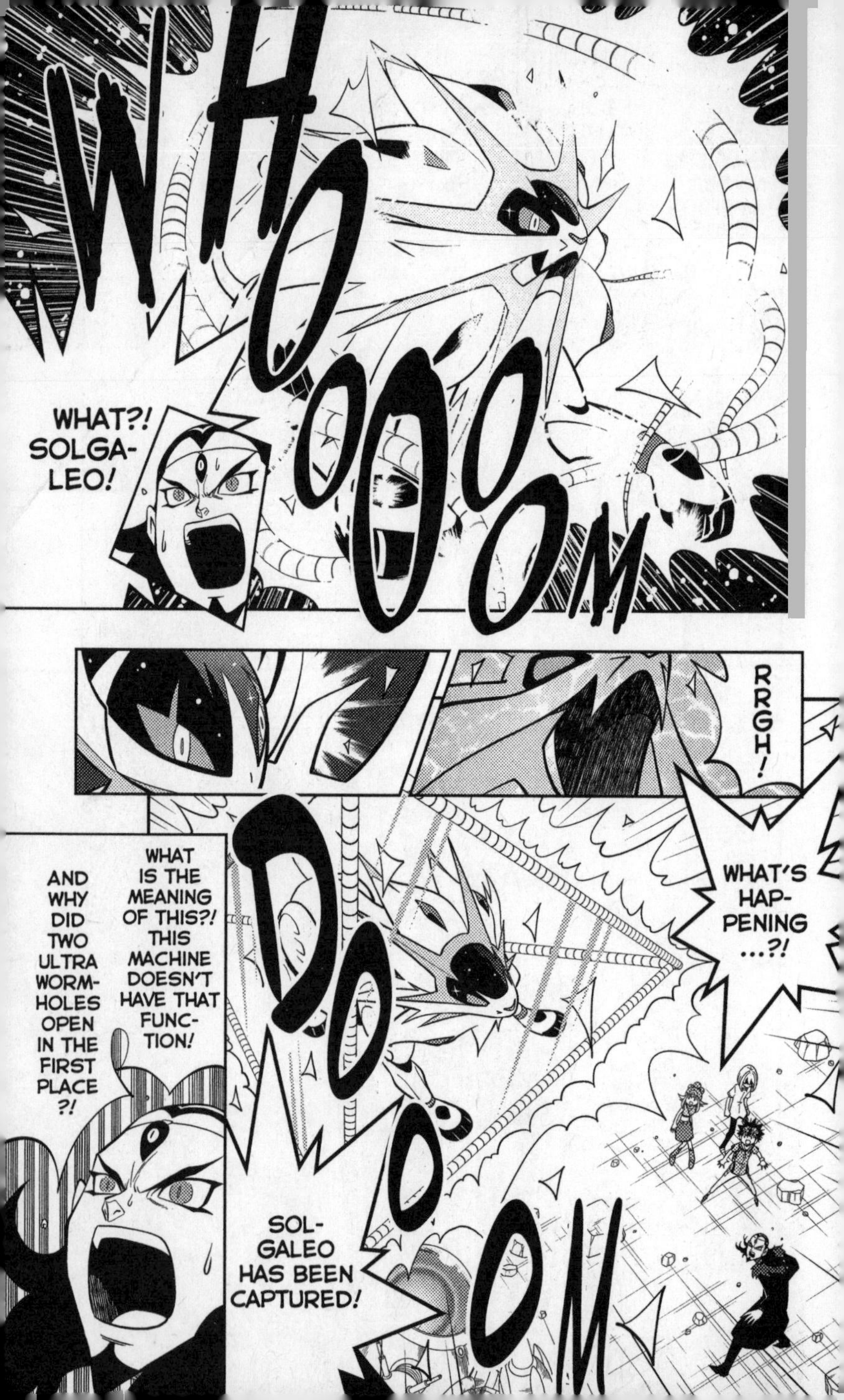
WHOOOOOM
WHAT?! SOLGALEO!
RRGH!
WHAT'S HAPPENING...?!
WHAT IS THE MEANING OF THIS?! THIS MACHINE DOESN'T HAVE THAT FUNCTION!
AND WHY DID TWO ULTRA WORMHOLES OPEN IN THE FIRST PLACE?!
SOLGALEO HAS BEEN CAPTURED!
DOOOOOM

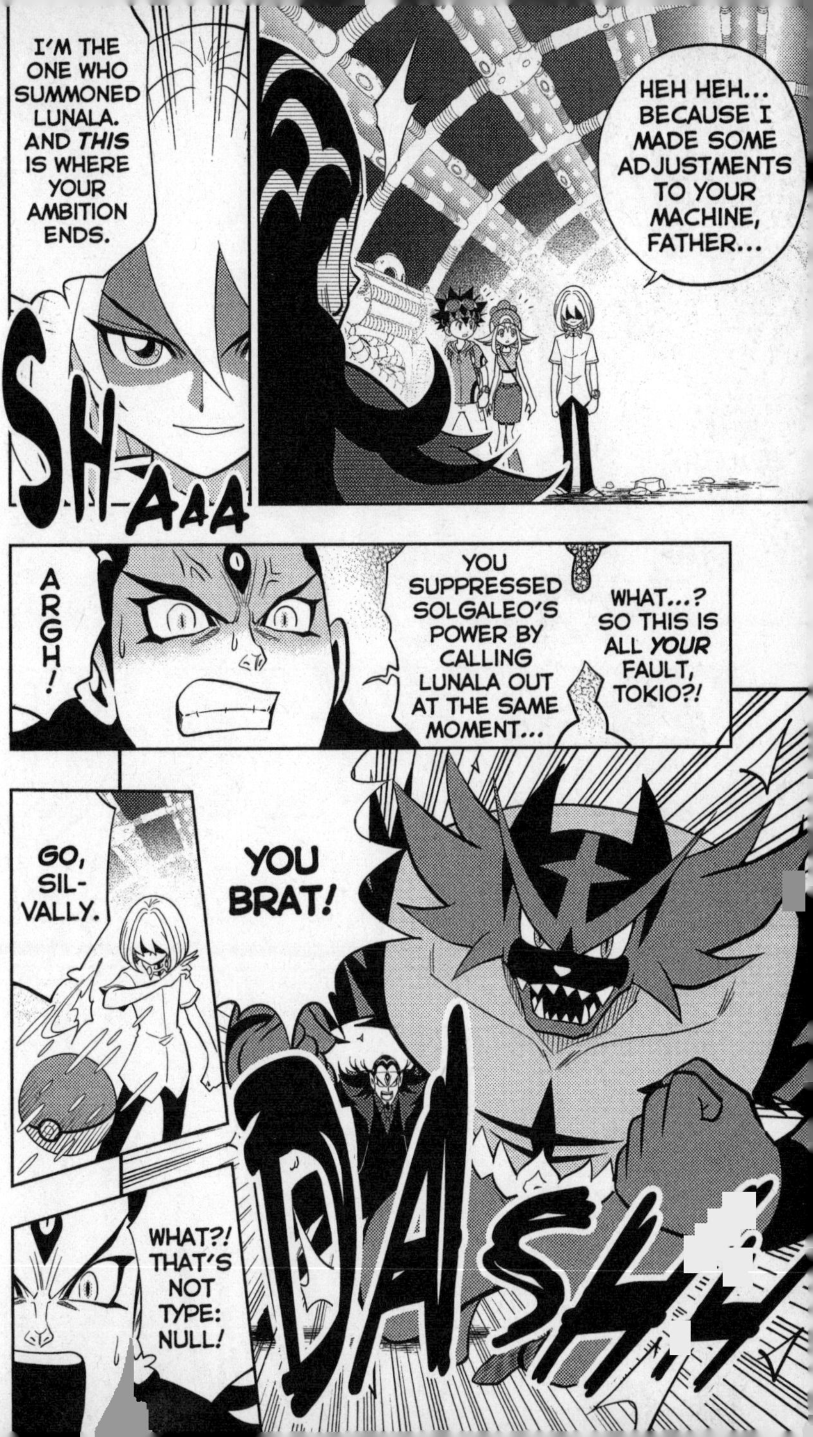
HEH HEH... BECAUSE I MADE SOME ADJUSTMENTS TO YOUR MACHINE, FATHER...
I'M THE ONE WHO SUMMONED LUNALA. AND *THIS* IS WHERE YOUR AMBITION ENDS.
SHAAA
WHAT...? SO THIS IS ALL *YOUR* FAULT, TOKIO?!
YOU SUPPRESSED SOLGALEO'S POWER BY CALLING LUNALA OUT AT THE SAME MOMENT...
ARGH!
YOU BRAT!
DASH
GO, SIL-VALLY.
WHAT?! THAT'S NOT TYPE: NULL!

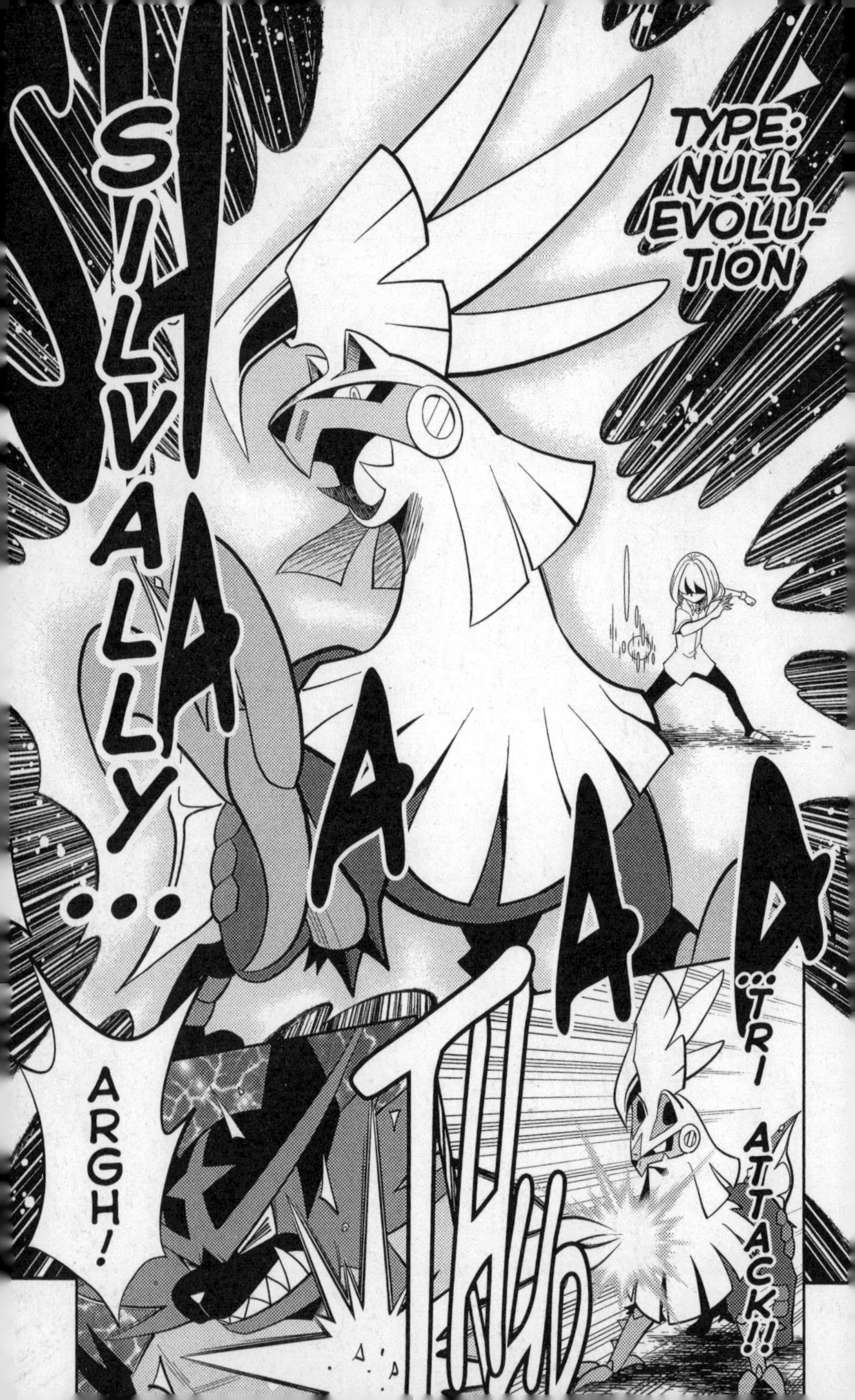
TYPE: NULL EVOLUTION
SILLVALLY...AAAA
...TRI ATTACK!!
ARGH!

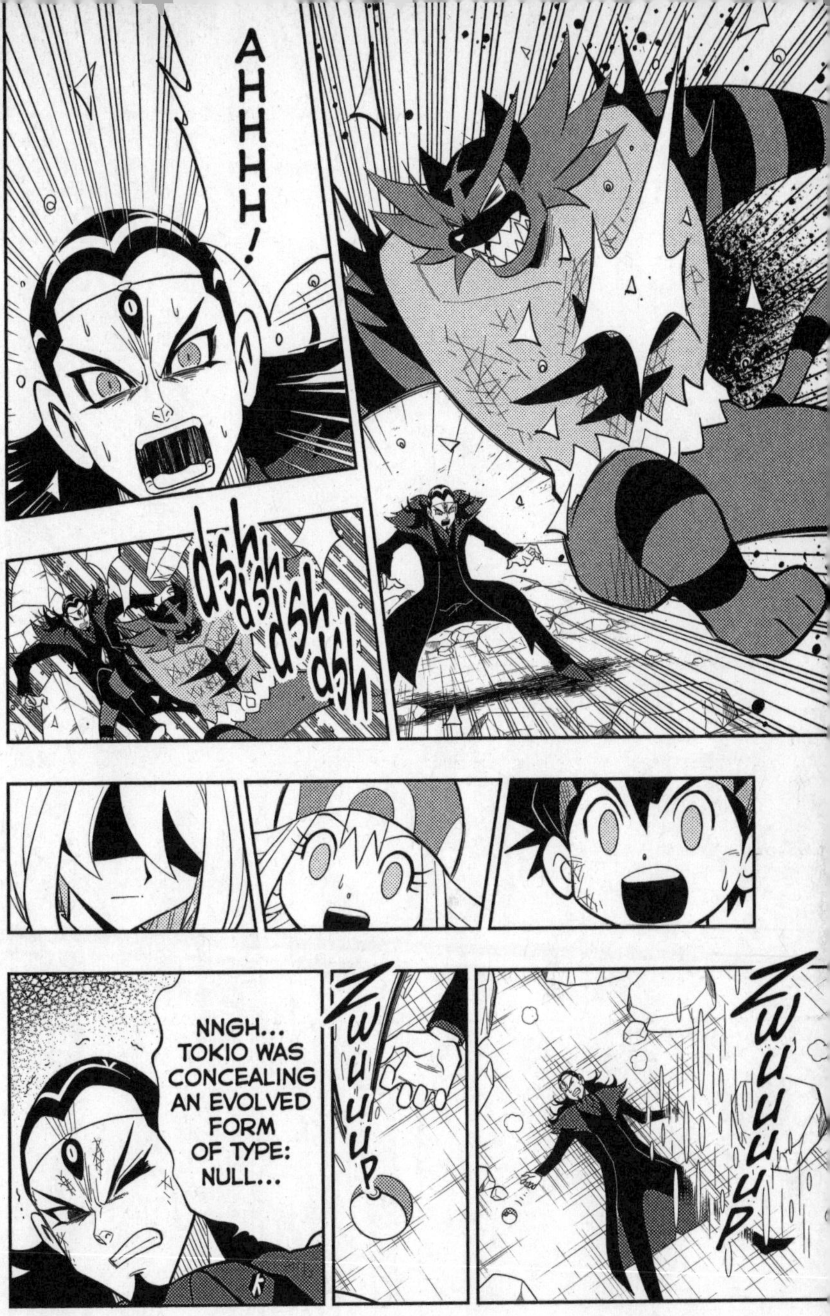
AHHHH!
dsh dsh dsh dsh
ZWUUUUP!
ZWUUUUP!
NNGH... TOKIO WAS CONCEALING AN EVOLVED FORM OF TYPE: NULL...

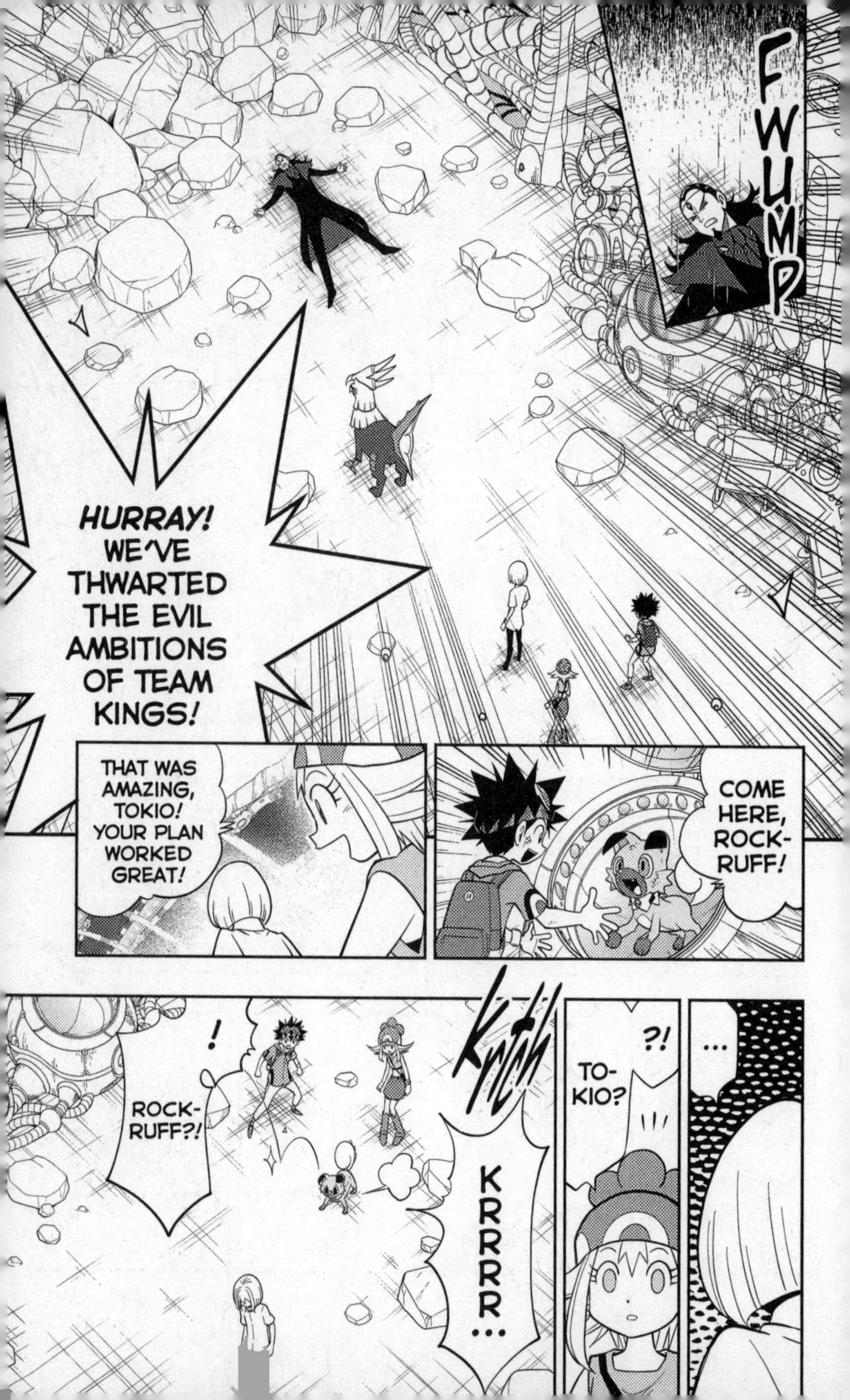
FWUMP
HURRAY! WE'VE THWARTED THE EVIL AMBITIONS OF TEAM KINGS!
COME HERE, ROCK-RUFF!
THAT WAS AMAZING, TOKIO! YOUR PLAN WORKED GREAT!
...
?!
TO-KIO?
Krtch
KRRRR..
!
ROCK-RUFF?!

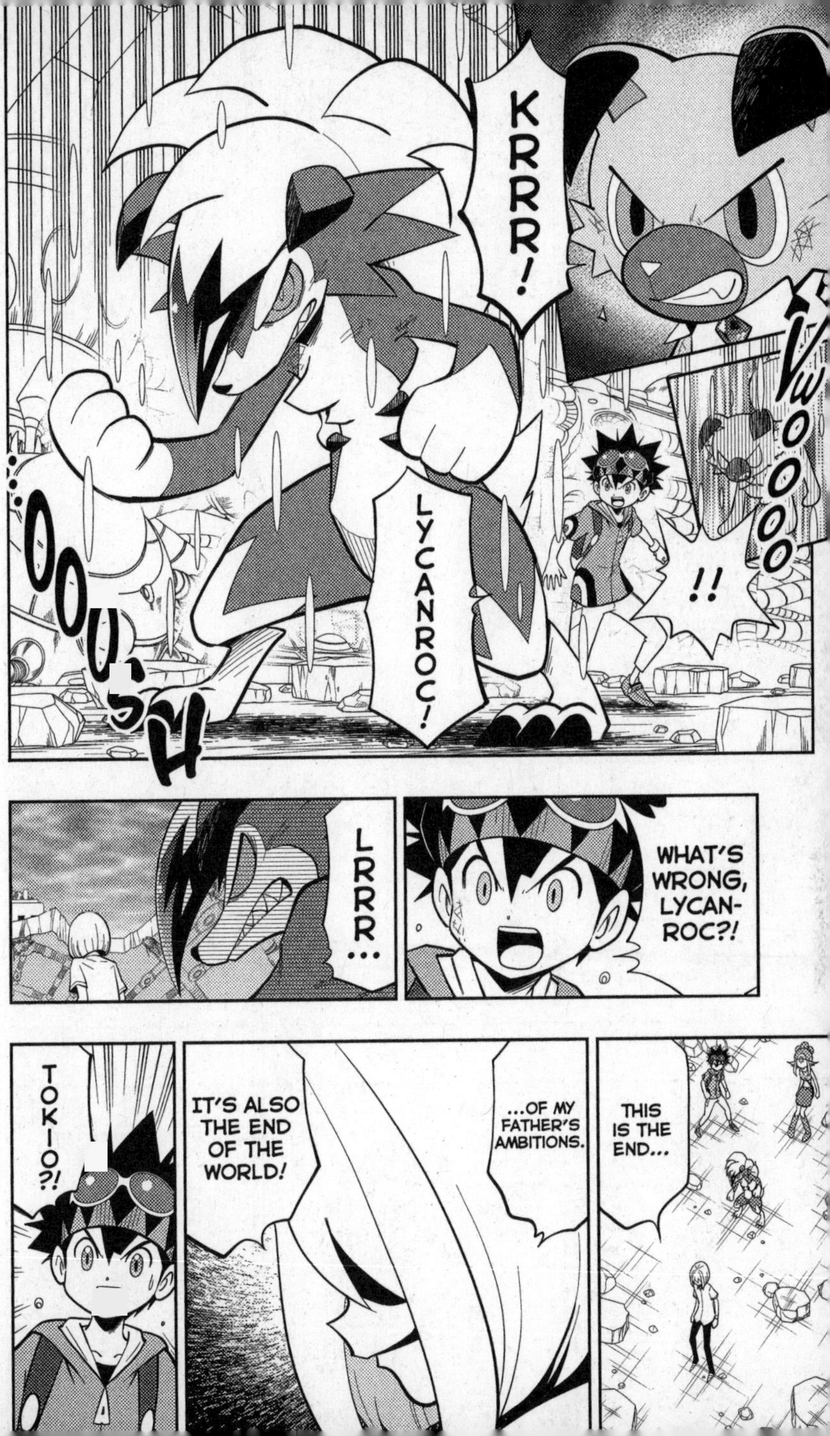
VWOOOOOO
KRRR!
!!
LYCANROC!
...OOOOSH
WHAT'S WRONG, LYCANROC?!
LRRR...
THIS IS THE END...
...OF MY FATHER'S AMBITIONS.
IT'S ALSO THE END OF THE WORLD!
TOKIO?!

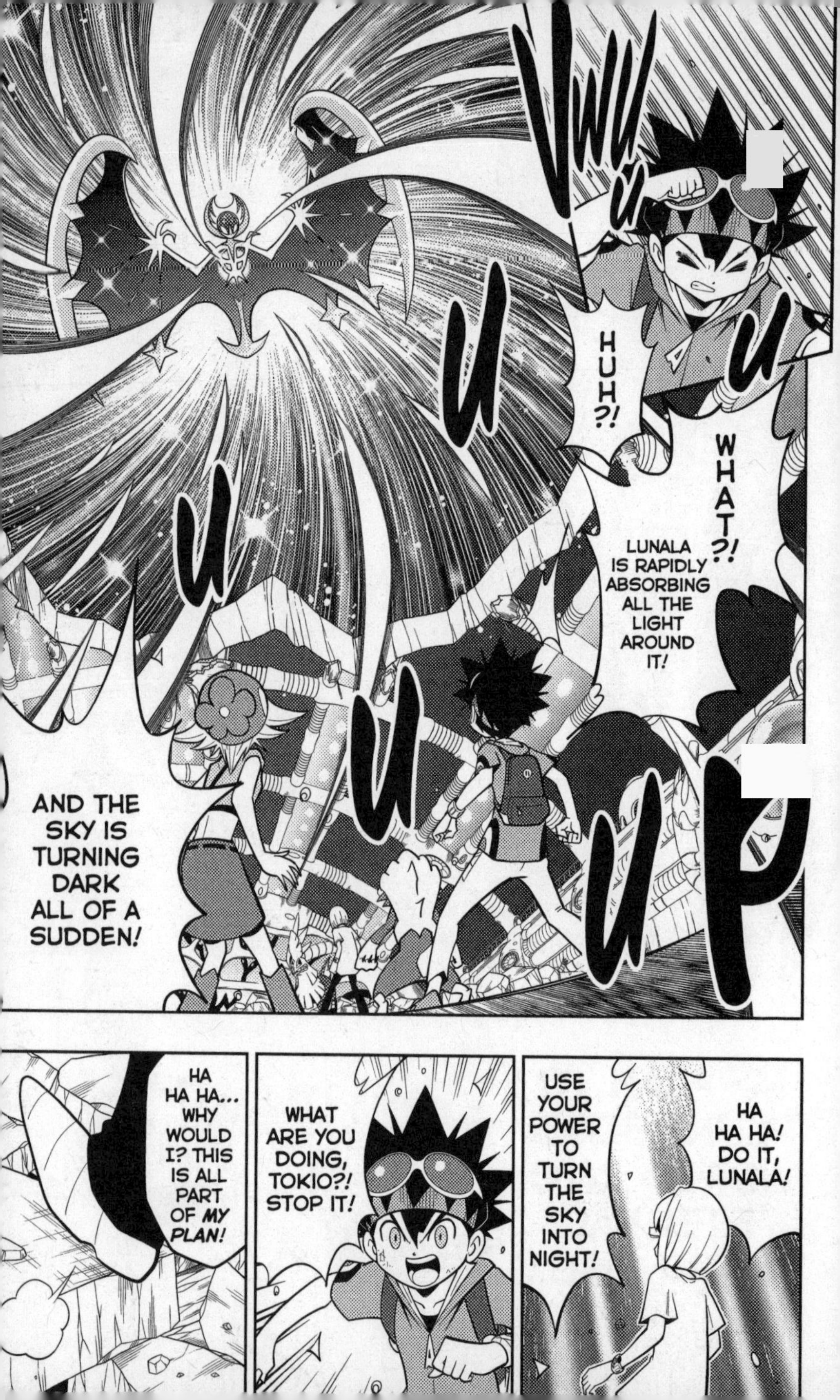
HUH?!
WHAT?!
LUNALA IS RAPIDLY ABSORBING ALL THE LIGHT AROUND IT!
AND THE SKY IS TURNING DARK ALL OF A SUDDEN!
HA HA HA! DO IT, LUNALA!
USE YOUR POWER TO TURN THE SKY INTO NIGHT!
WHAT ARE YOU DOING, TOKIO?! STOP IT!
HA HA HA... WHY WOULD I? THIS IS ALL PART OF *MY PLAN*!

SHAAAAAAAAAA
MY PLAN TO PLUNGE THE WORLD INTO ETERNAL DARKNESS!

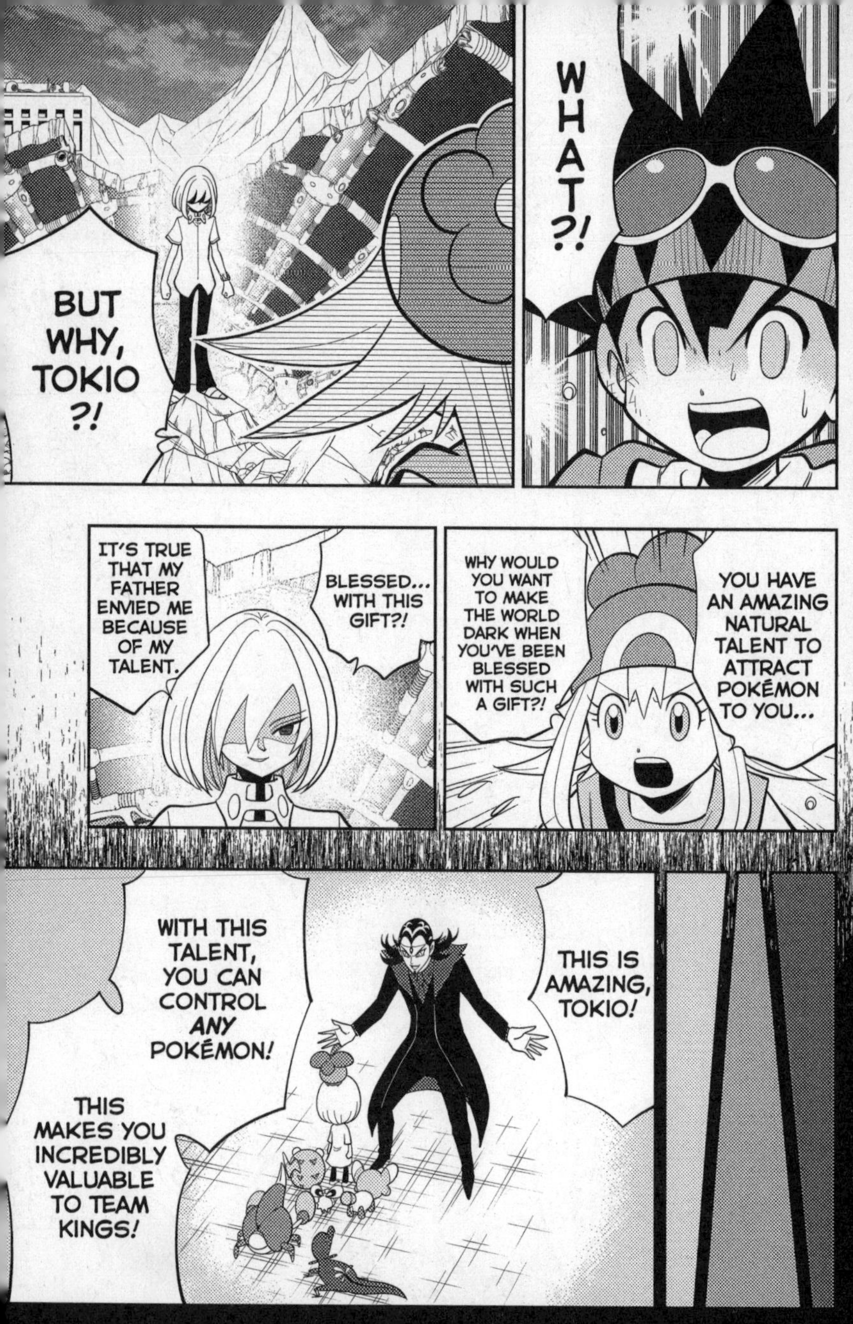
WHAT?!
BUT WHY, TOKIO?!
YOU HAVE AN AMAZING NATURAL TALENT TO ATTRACT POKÉMON TO YOU...
WHY WOULD YOU WANT TO MAKE THE WORLD DARK WHEN YOU'VE BEEN BLESSED WITH SUCH A GIFT?!
BLESSED... WITH THIS GIFT?!
IT'S TRUE THAT MY FATHER ENVIED ME BECAUSE OF MY TALENT.
THIS IS AMAZING, TOKIO!
WITH THIS TALENT, YOU CAN CONTROL *ANY* POKÉMON!
THIS MAKES YOU INCREDIBLY VALUABLE TO TEAM KINGS!

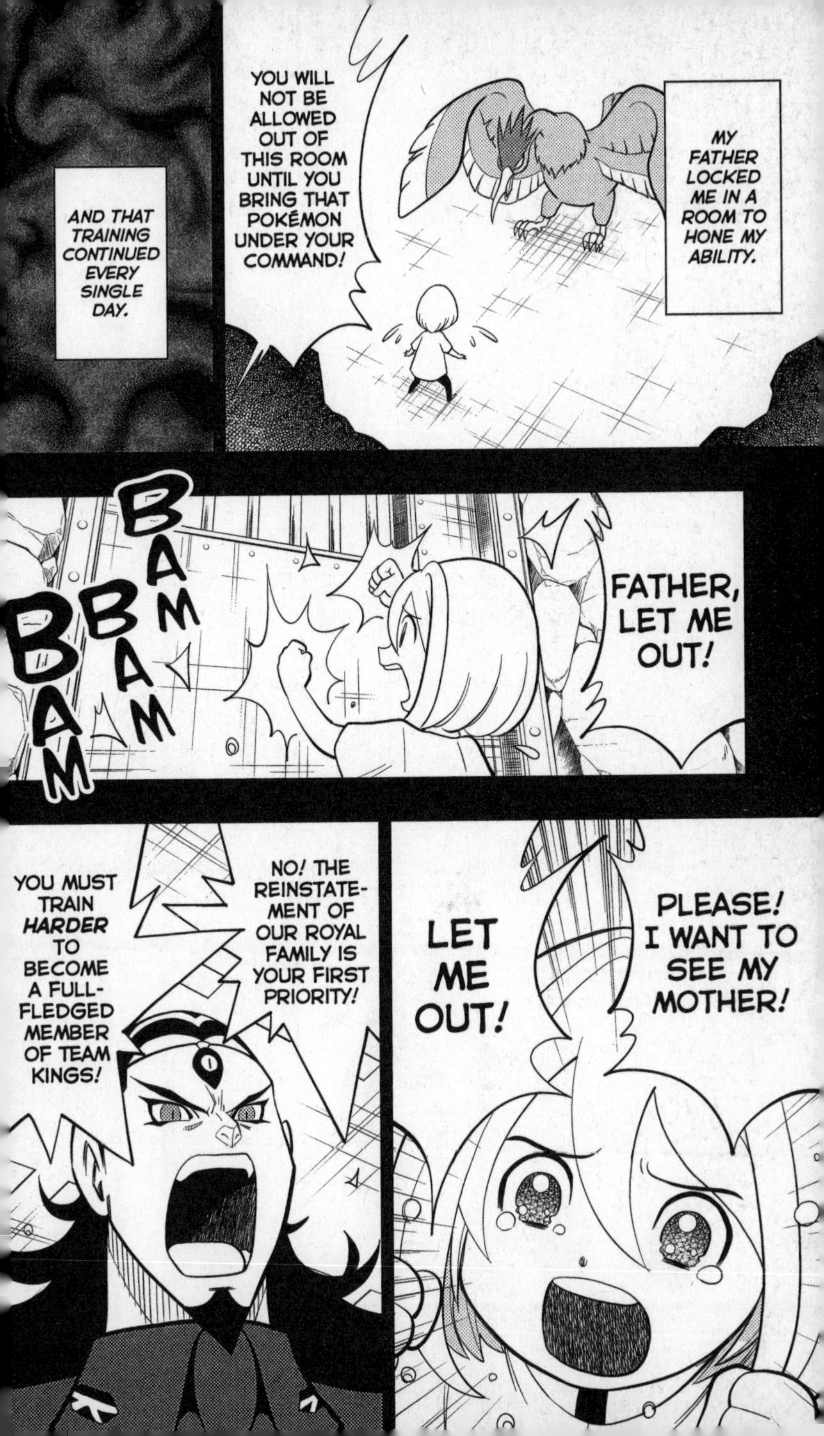

MY FATHER LOCKED ME IN A ROOM TO HONE MY ABILITY.
YOU WILL NOT BE ALLOWED OUT OF THIS ROOM UNTIL YOU BRING THAT POKÉMON UNDER YOUR COMMAND!
AND THAT TRAINING CONTINUED EVERY SINGLE DAY.
FATHER, LET ME OUT!
BAM
BAM
BAM
PLEASE! I WANT TO SEE MY MOTHER!
LET ME OUT!
NO! THE REINSTATE-MENT OF OUR ROYAL FAMILY IS YOUR FIRST PRIORITY!
YOU MUST TRAIN *HARDER* TO BECOME A FULL-FLEDGED MEMBER OF TEAM KINGS!

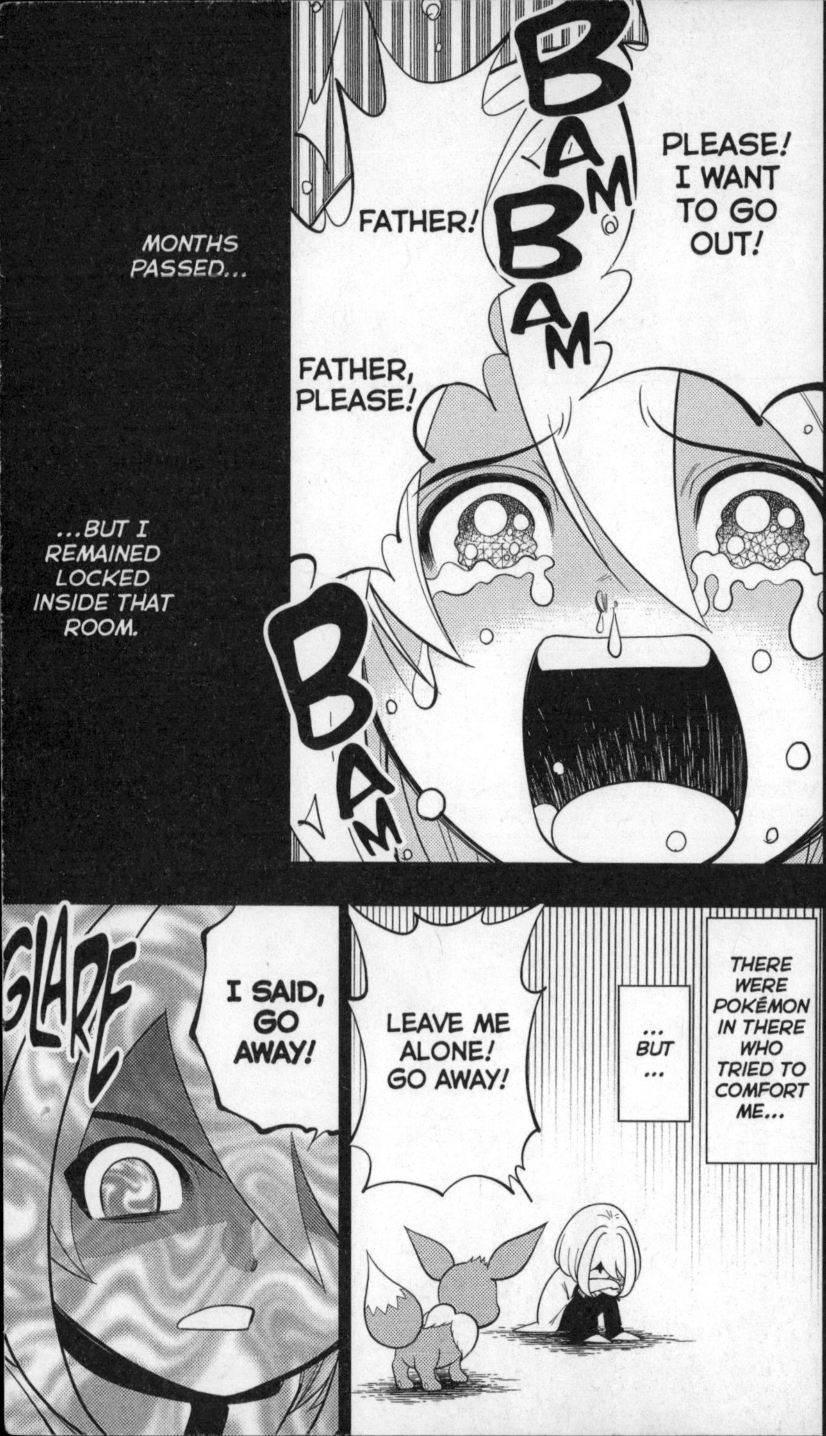
PLEASE! I WANT TO GO OUT!
BAM BAM
FATHER!
FATHER, PLEASE!
BAM
MONTHS PASSED...
...BUT I REMAINED LOCKED INSIDE THAT ROOM.
THERE WERE POKÉMON IN THERE WHO TRIED TO COMFORT ME...
...BUT...
LEAVE ME ALONE! GO AWAY!
I SAID, GO AWAY!
GLARE

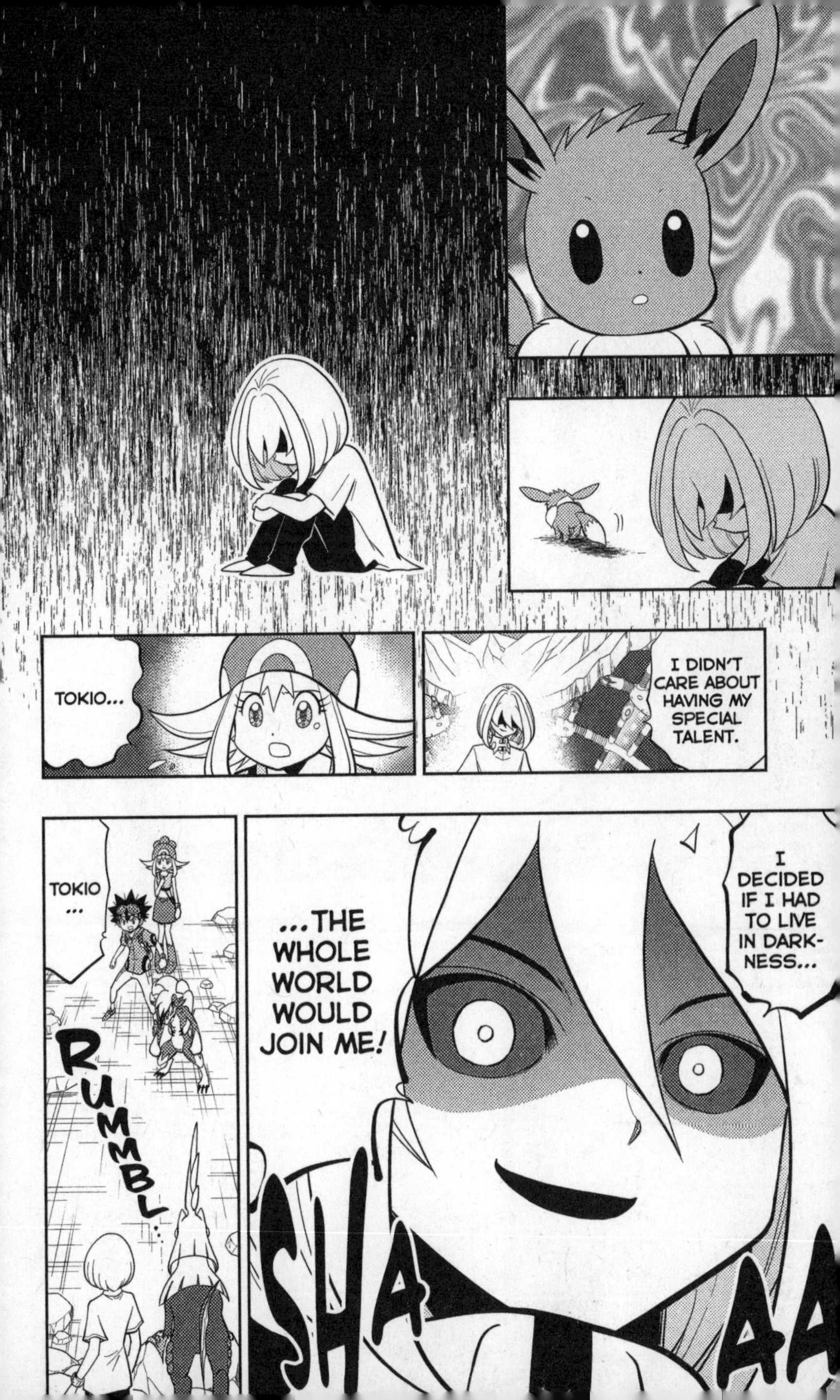
I DIDN'T CARE ABOUT HAVING MY SPECIAL TALENT.
TOKIO...
I DECIDED IF I HAD TO LIVE IN DARKNESS...
...THE WHOLE WORLD WOULD JOIN ME!
SHA
AA
TOKIO...
RUMMBL...

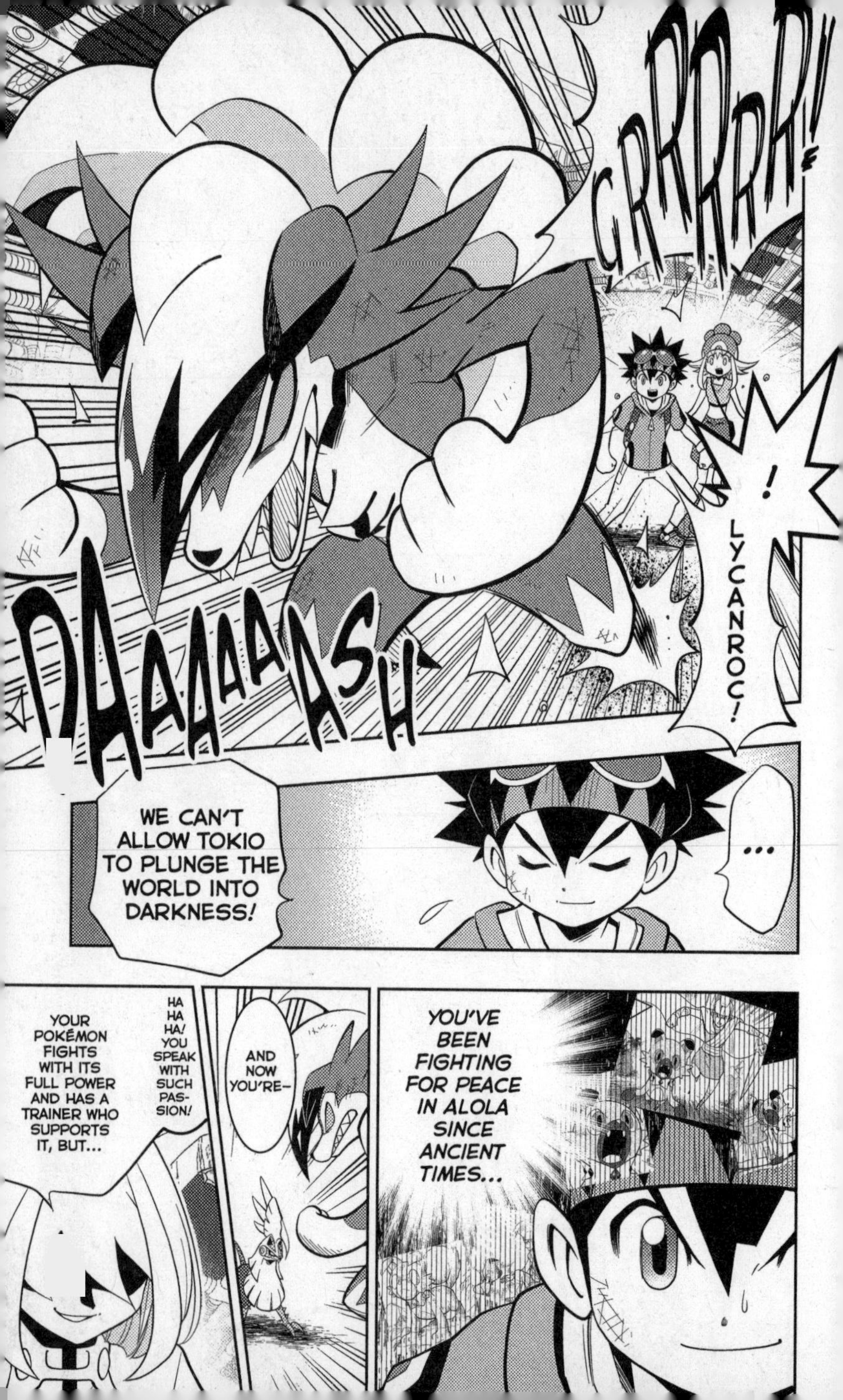
GRRRRAH!!
LYCANROC!
DAAAAASH
...
WE CAN'T ALLOW TOKIO TO PLUNGE THE WORLD INTO DARKNESS!
YOU'VE BEEN FIGHTING FOR PEACE IN ALOLA SINCE ANCIENT TIMES...
AND NOW YOU'RE–
HA HA HA! YOU SPEAK WITH SUCH PASSION!
YOUR POKÉMON FIGHTS WITH ITS FULL POWER AND HAS A TRAINER WHO SUPPORTS IT, BUT...

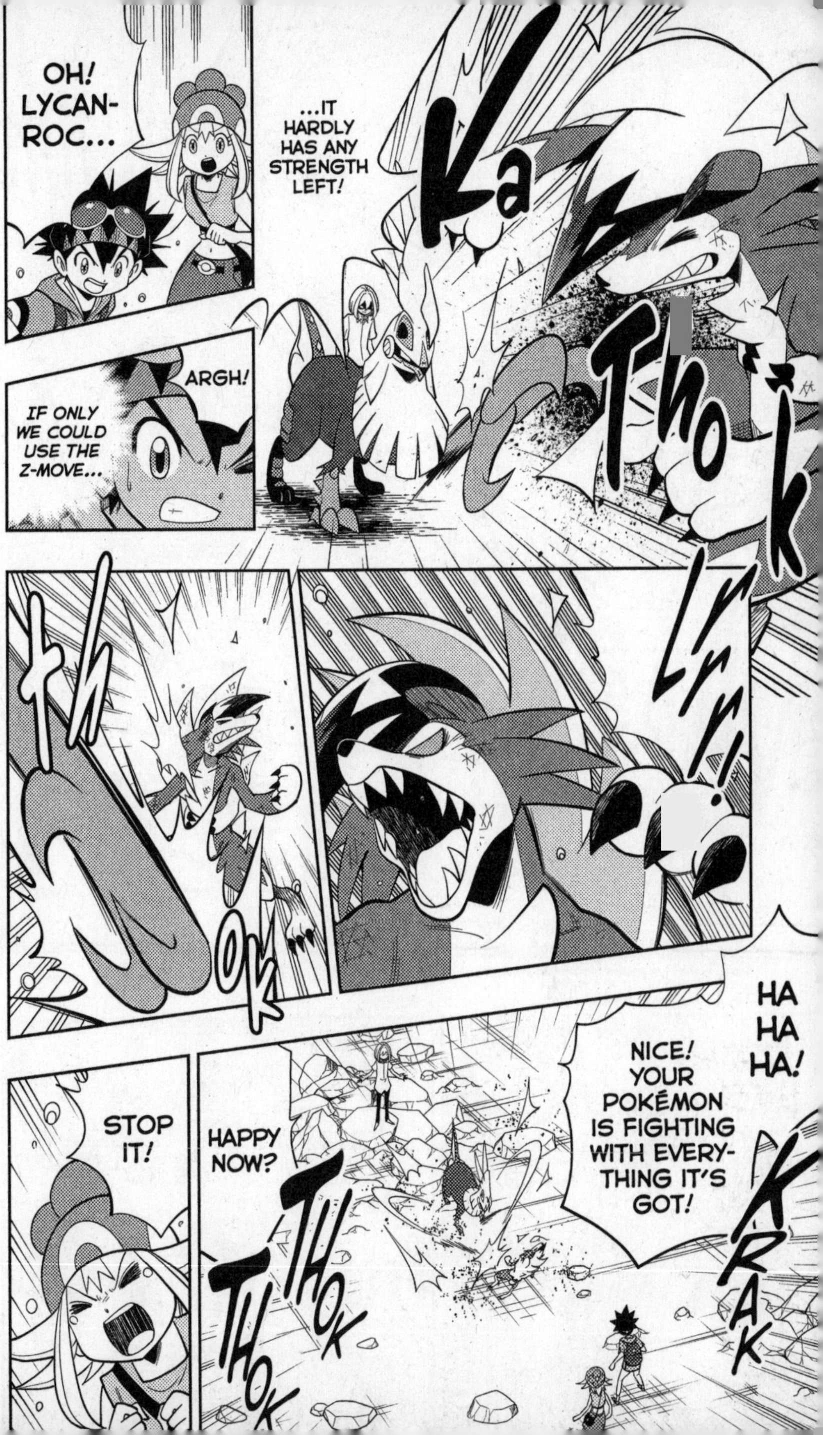

Ka
Thok
OH! LYCAN-ROC...
...IT HARDLY HAS ANY STRENGTH LEFT!
ARGH!
IF ONLY WE COULD USE THE Z-MOVE...
Thok
HA HA HA!
NICE! YOUR POKÉMON IS FIGHTING WITH EVERY-THING IT'S GOT!
KRAK
HAPPY NOW?
THOK
THOK
STOP IT!

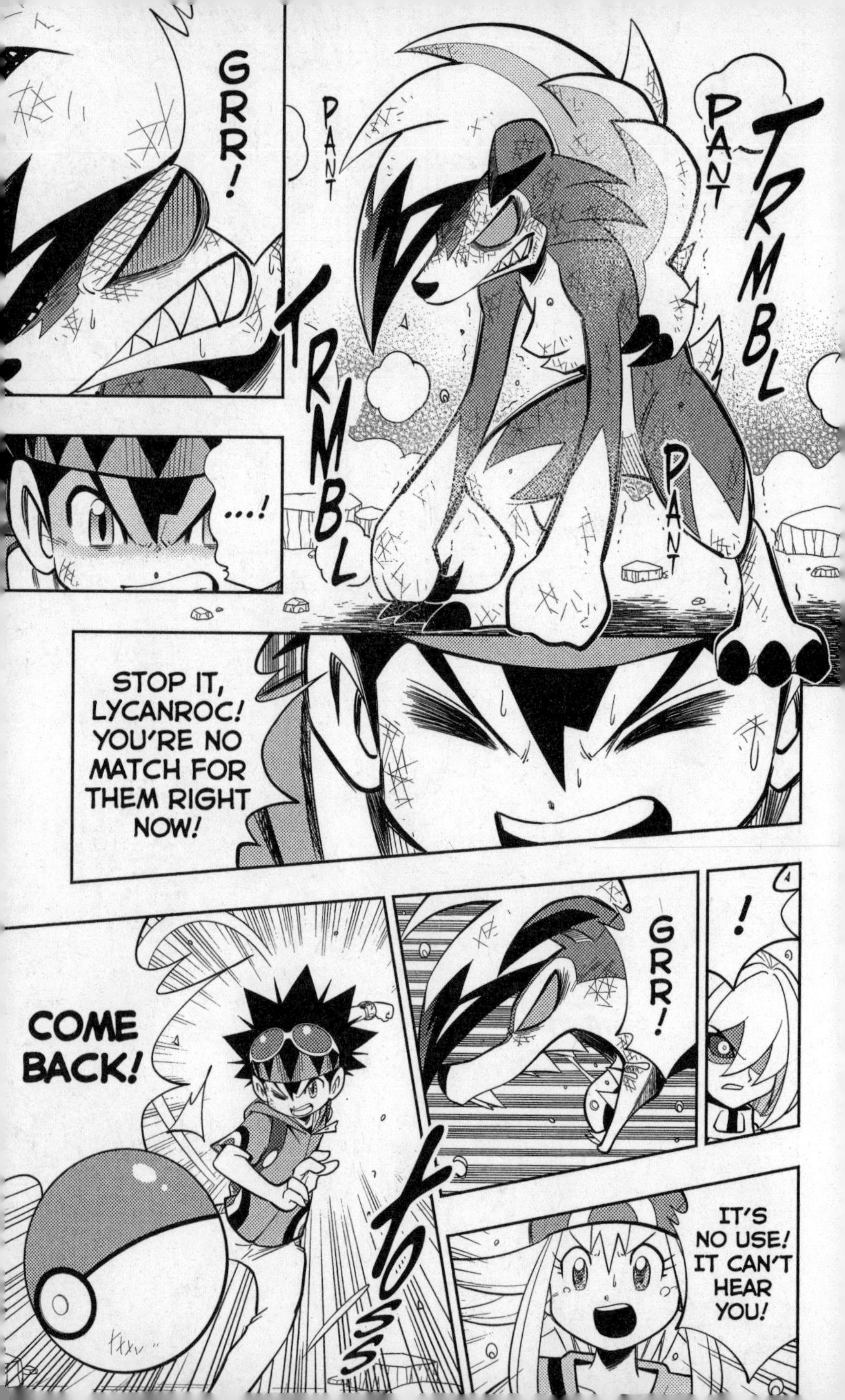

TRMBL
PANT PANT
PANT
TRMBL
PANT PANT
GRR!
...!
STOP IT, LYCANROC! YOU'RE NO MATCH FOR THEM RIGHT NOW!
!
GRR!
IT'S NO USE! IT CAN'T HEAR YOU!
COME BACK!

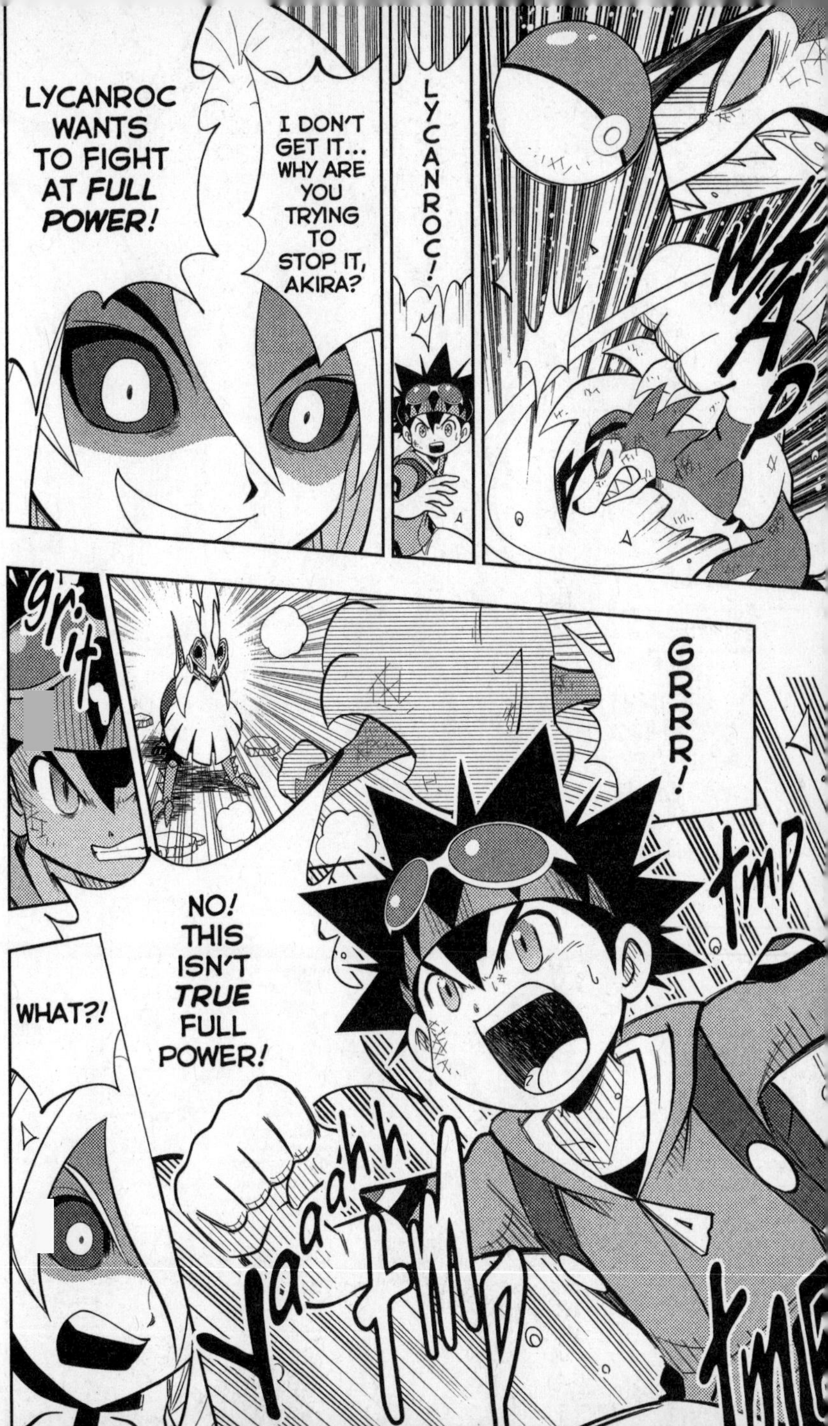
WHAP
LYCANROC!
I DON'T GET IT... WHY ARE YOU TRYING TO STOP IT, AKIRA?
LYCANROC WANTS TO FIGHT AT *FULL POWER!*
GRRR!
grit
tmp
NO! THIS ISN'T *TRUE* FULL POWER!
tmp
Yaaahh
tmp
WHAT?!

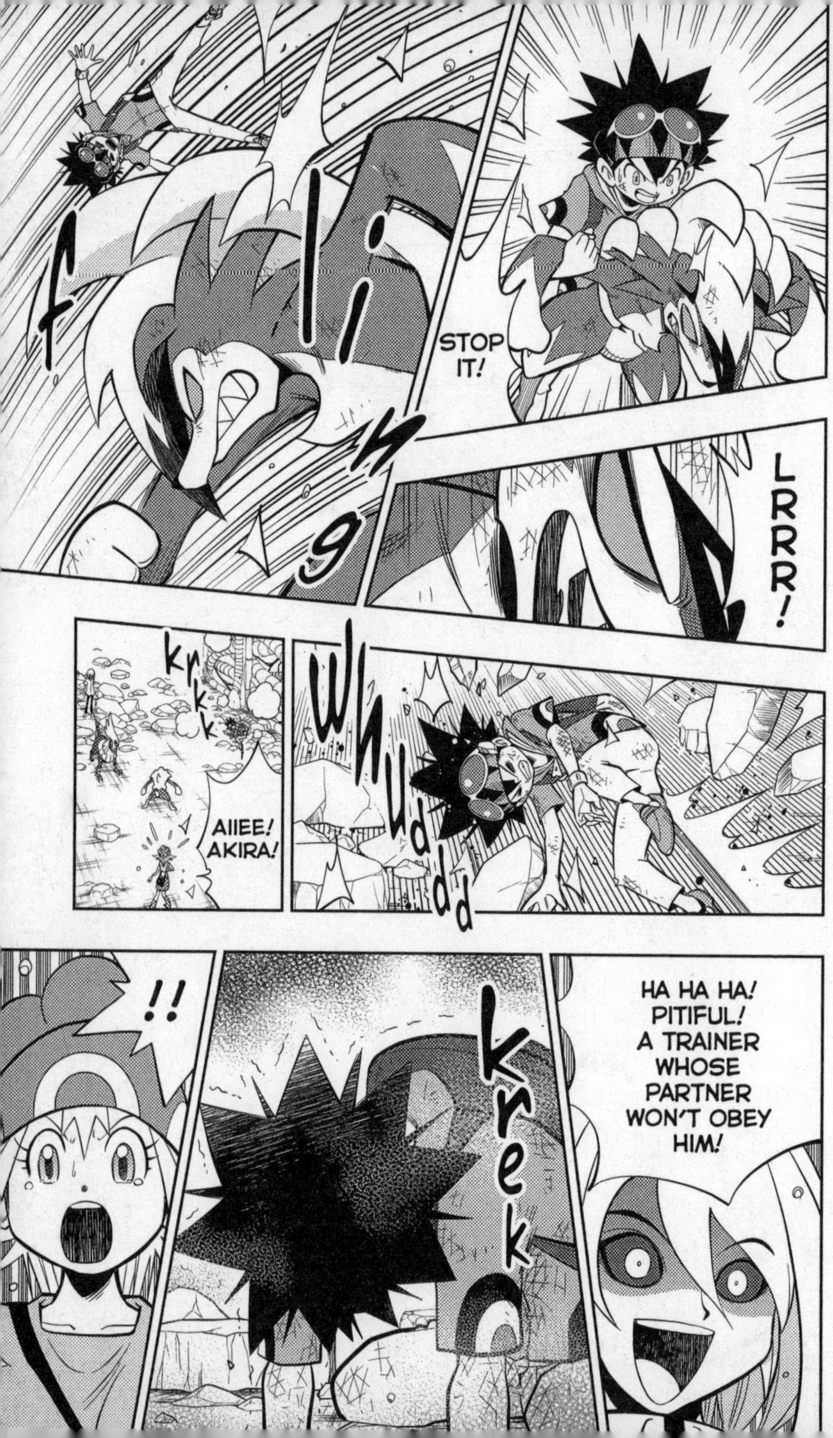
STOP IT!
fling
LRRR!
whuddd
krkkk
AIIEE! AKIRA!
HA HA HA! PITIFUL! A TRAINER WHOSE PARTNER WON'T OBEY HIM!
krek
!!

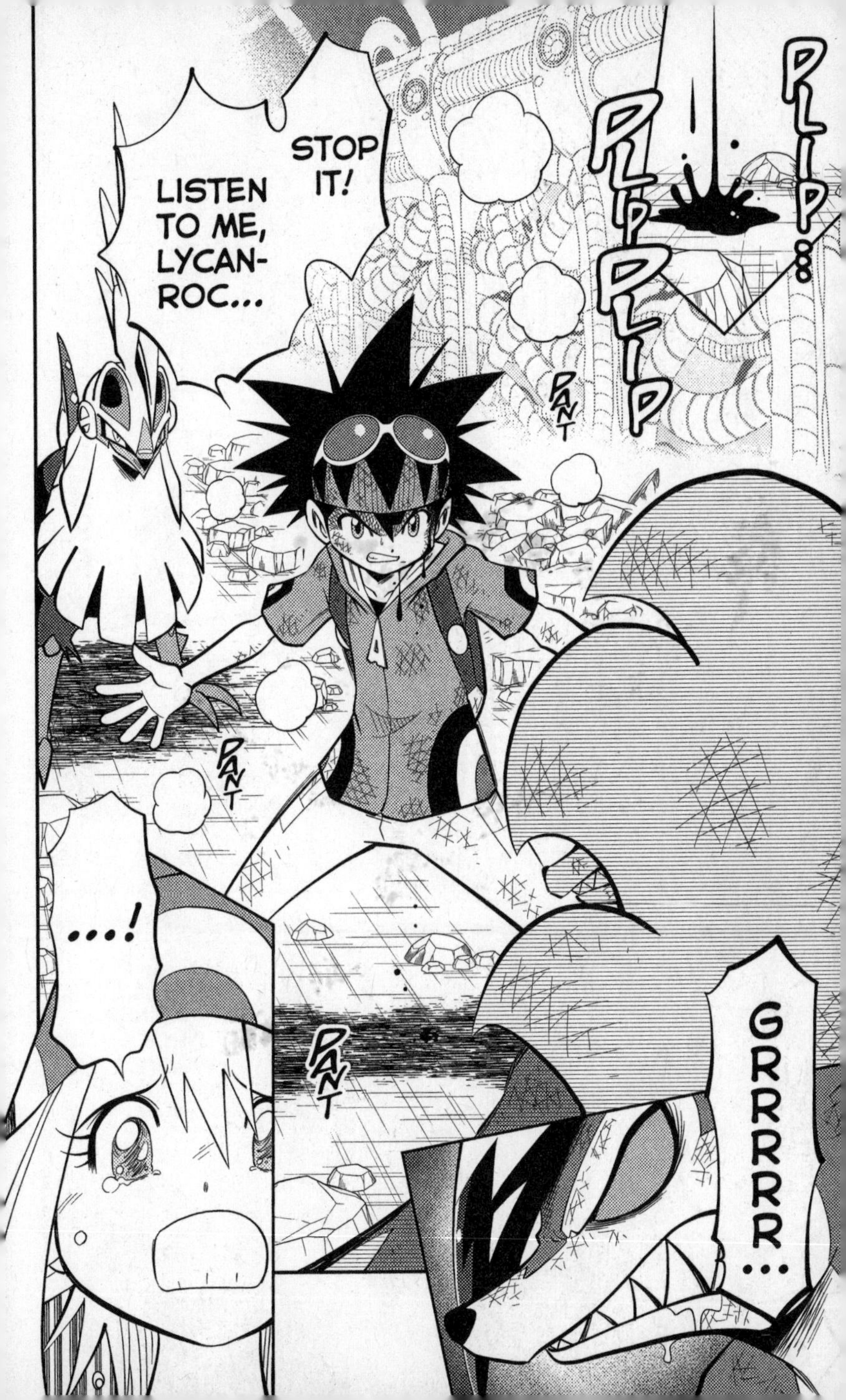
PLIP..
PLIP PLIP
PANT
STOP IT!
LISTEN TO ME, LYCAN-ROC...
PANT
GRRRR...
PANT
...!

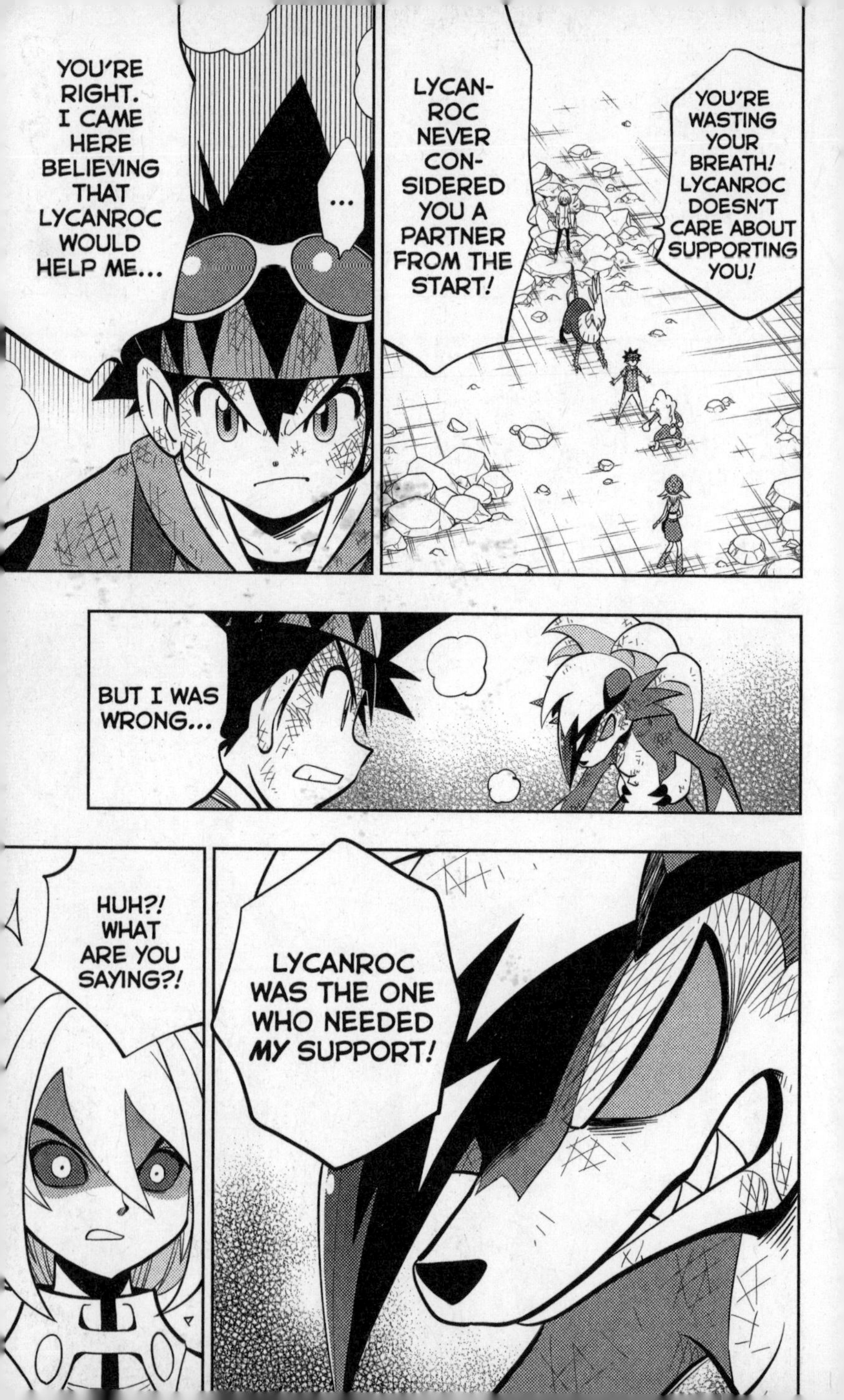
YOU'RE WASTING YOUR BREATH! LYCANROC DOESN'T CARE ABOUT SUPPORTING YOU!
LYCANROC NEVER CONSIDERED YOU A PARTNER FROM THE START!
...
YOU'RE RIGHT. I CAME HERE BELIEVING THAT LYCANROC WOULD HELP ME...
BUT I WAS WRONG...
LYCANROC WAS THE ONE WHO NEEDED *MY* SUPPORT!
HUH?! WHAT ARE YOU SAYING?!

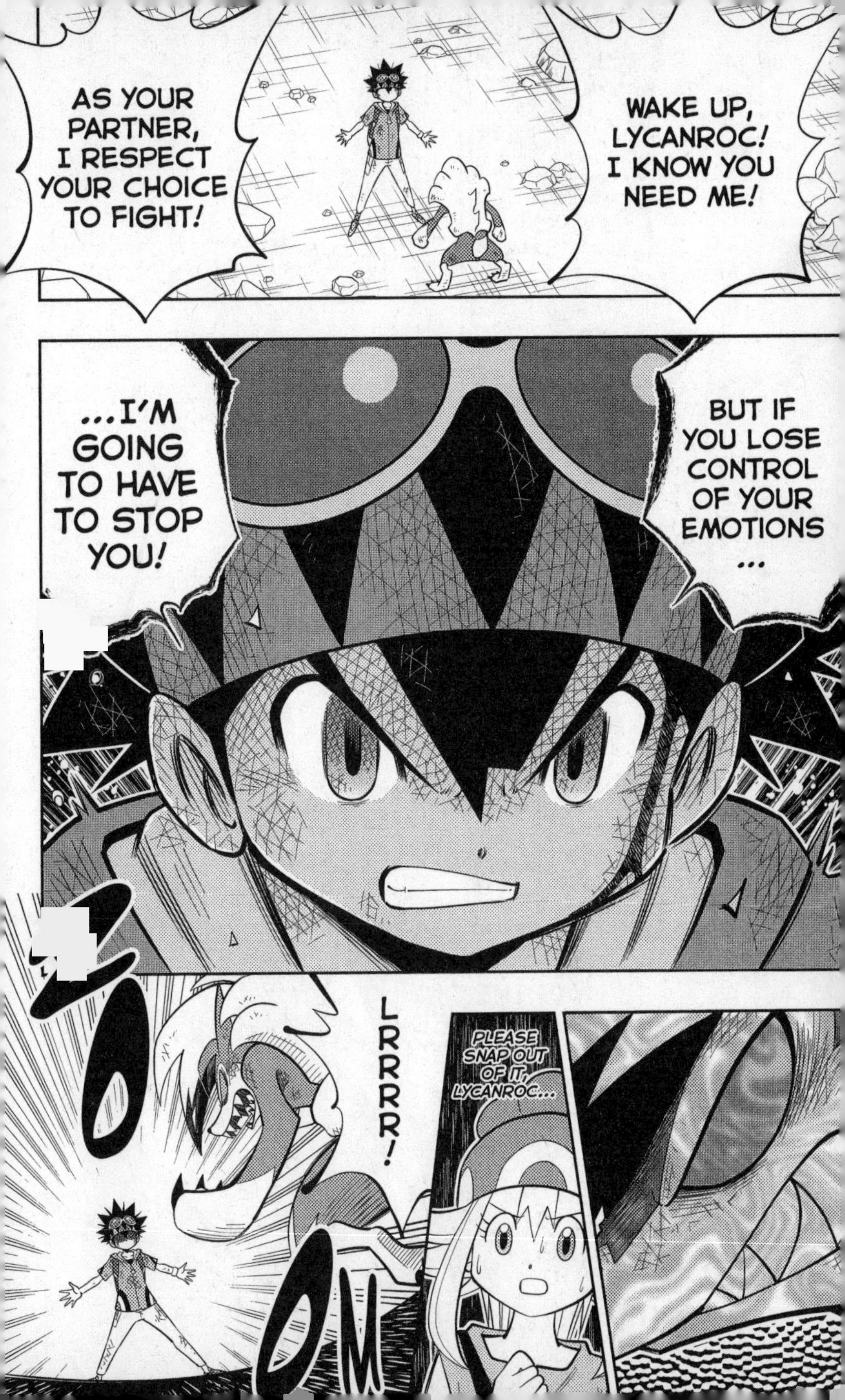
WAKE UP, LYCANROC! I KNOW YOU NEED ME!
AS YOUR PARTNER, I RESPECT YOUR CHOICE TO FIGHT!
BUT IF YOU LOSE CONTROL OF YOUR EMOTIONS ...
...I'M GOING TO HAVE TO STOP YOU!
PLEASE SNAP OUT OF IT, LYCANROC...
LRRRR!

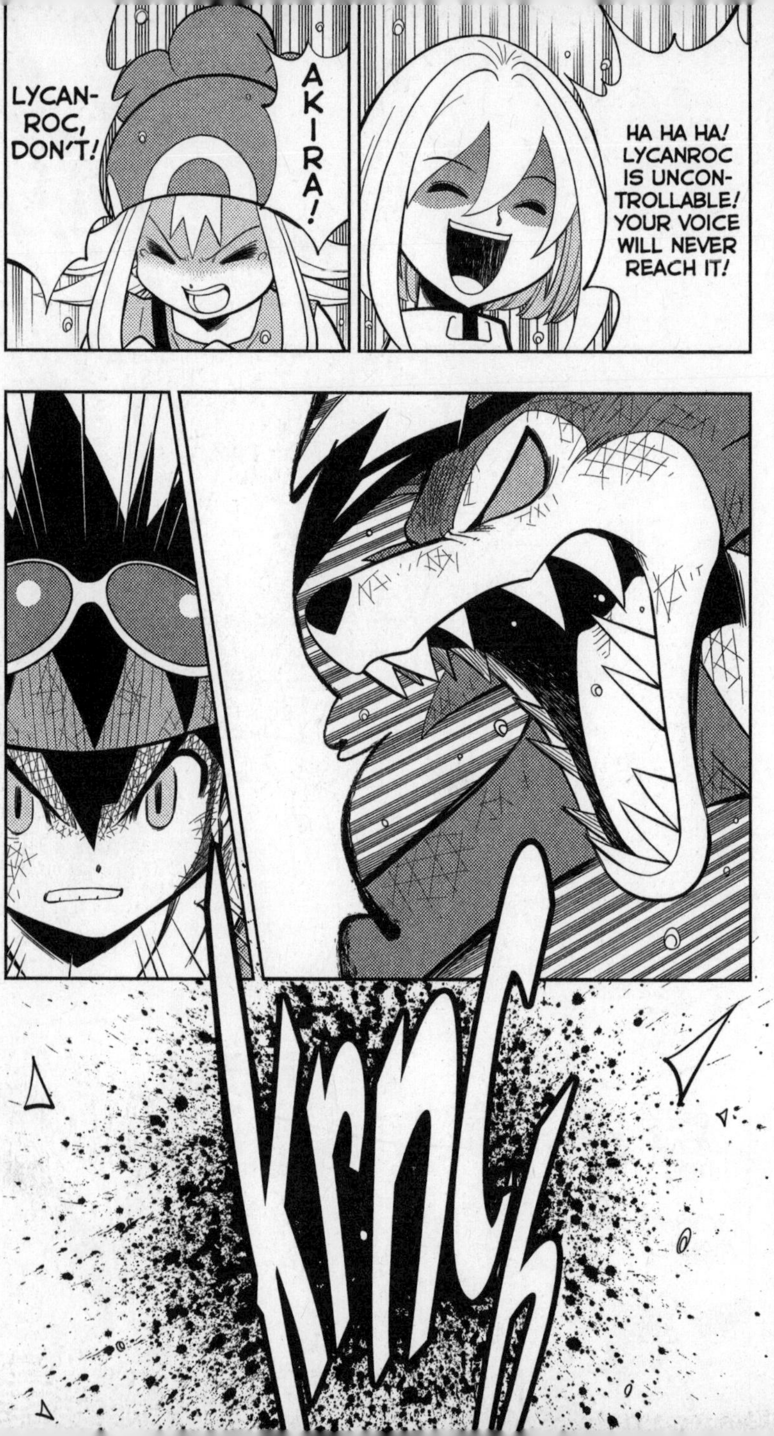
HA HA HA! LYCANROC IS UNCONTROLLABLE! YOUR VOICE WILL NEVER REACH IT!
AKIRA!
LYCANROC, DON'T!

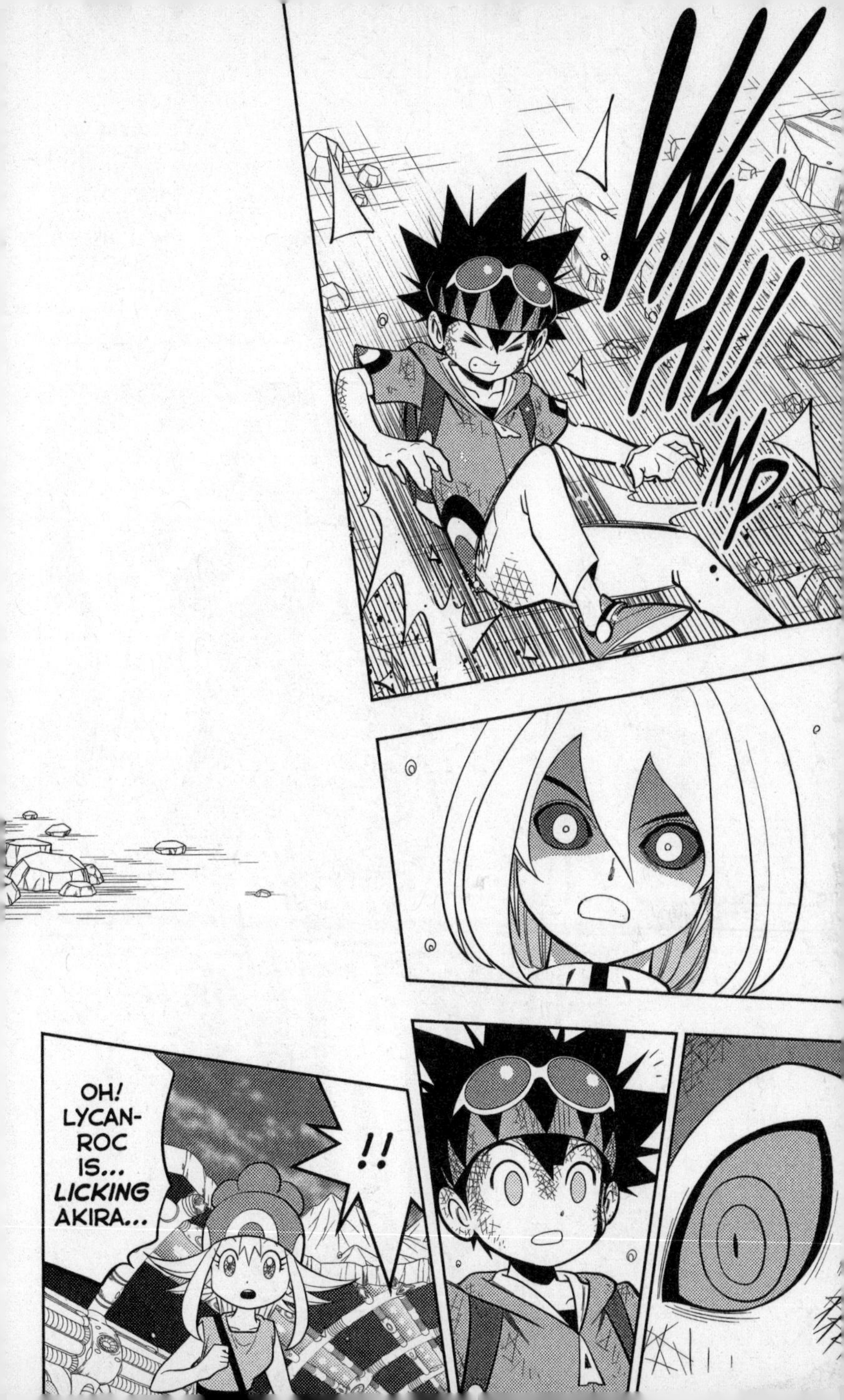
WHUMP
!!
OH! LYCAN-ROC IS... LICKING AKIRA...

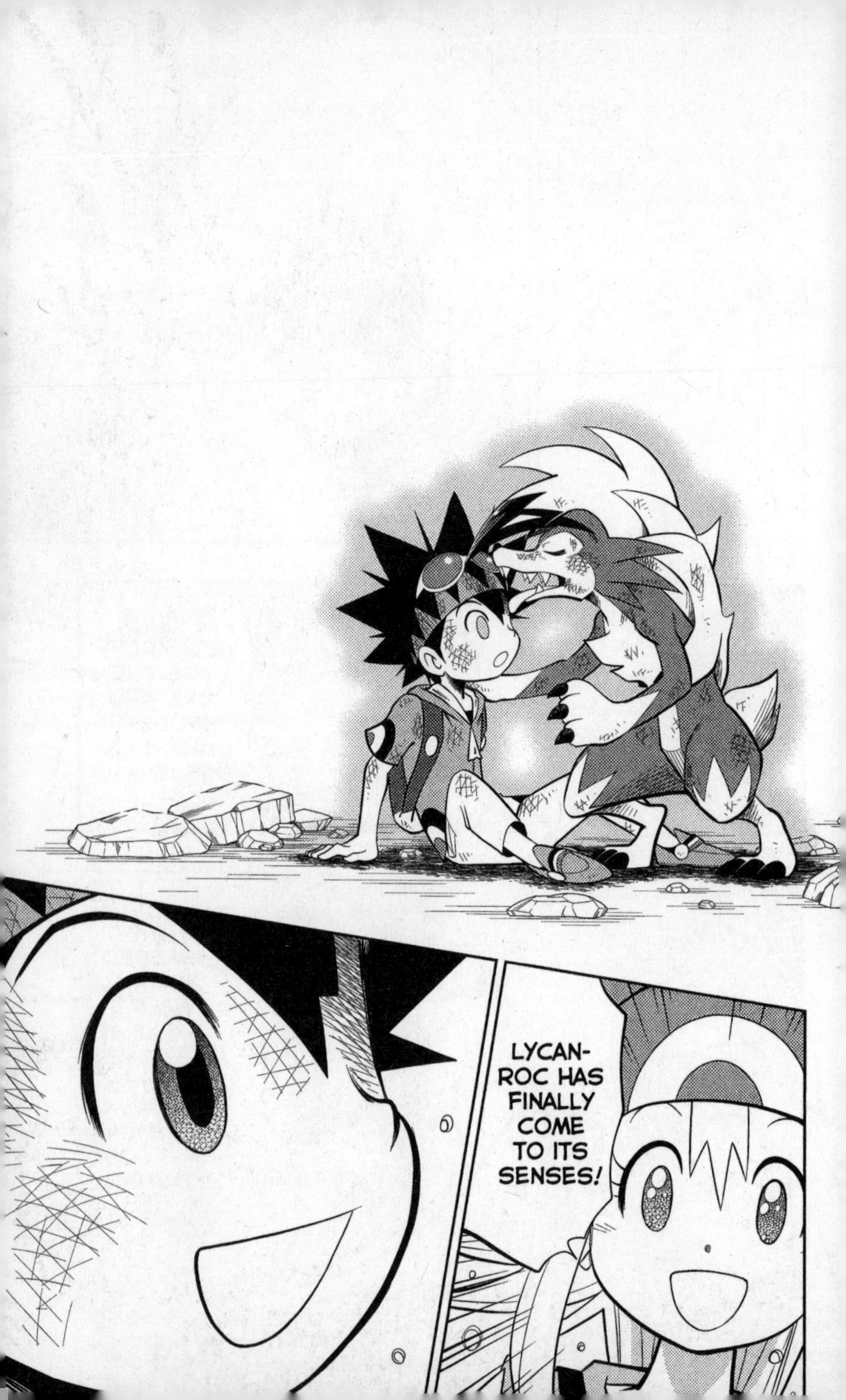
LYCAN-
ROC HAS
FINALLY
COME
TO ITS
SENSES!

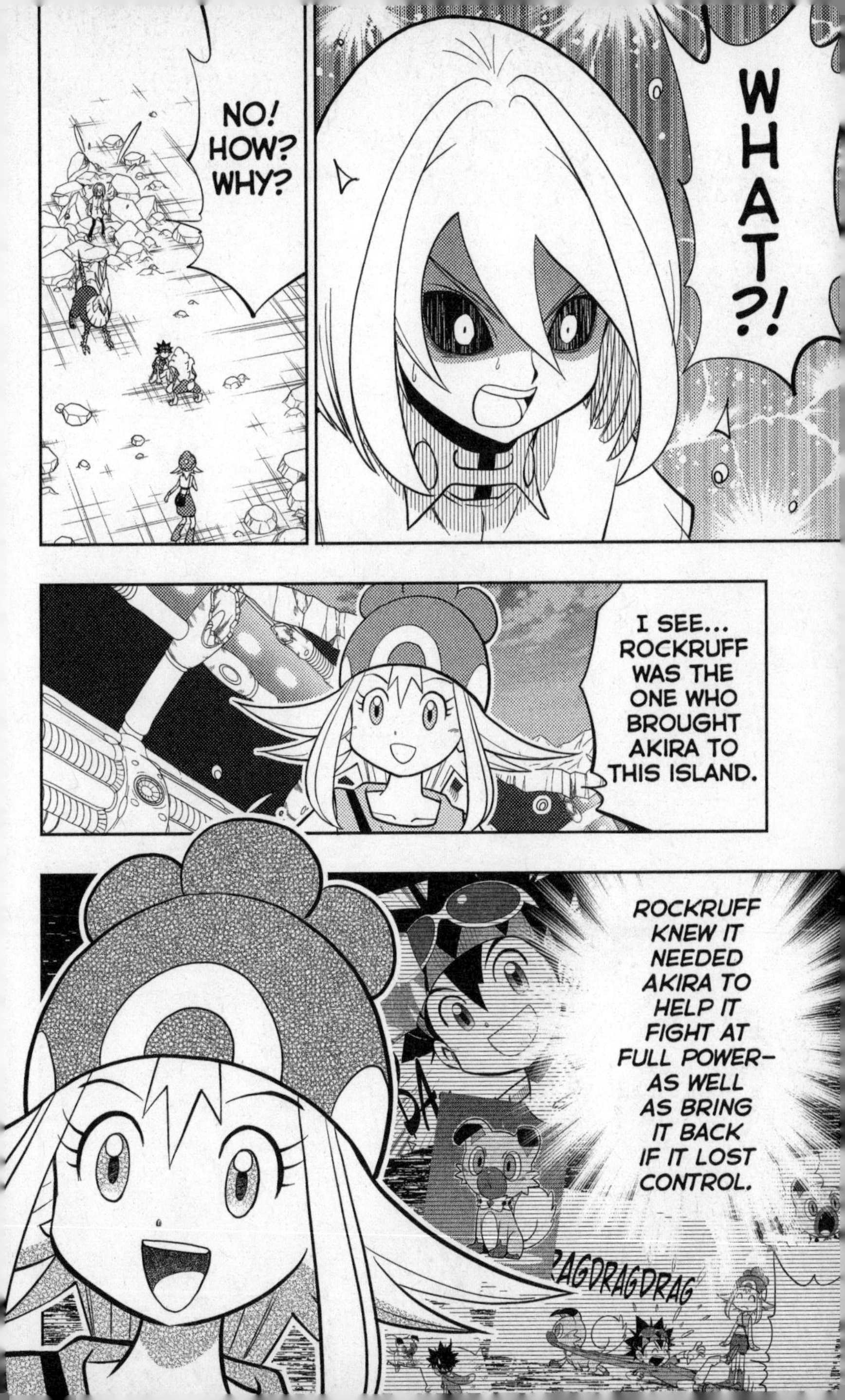
WHAT?!
NO! HOW? WHY?
I SEE... ROCKRUFF WAS THE ONE WHO BROUGHT AKIRA TO THIS ISLAND.
ROCKRUFF KNEW IT NEEDED AKIRA TO HELP IT FIGHT AT FULL POWER—AS WELL AS BRING IT BACK IF IT LOST CONTROL.
RAGDRAGDRAG

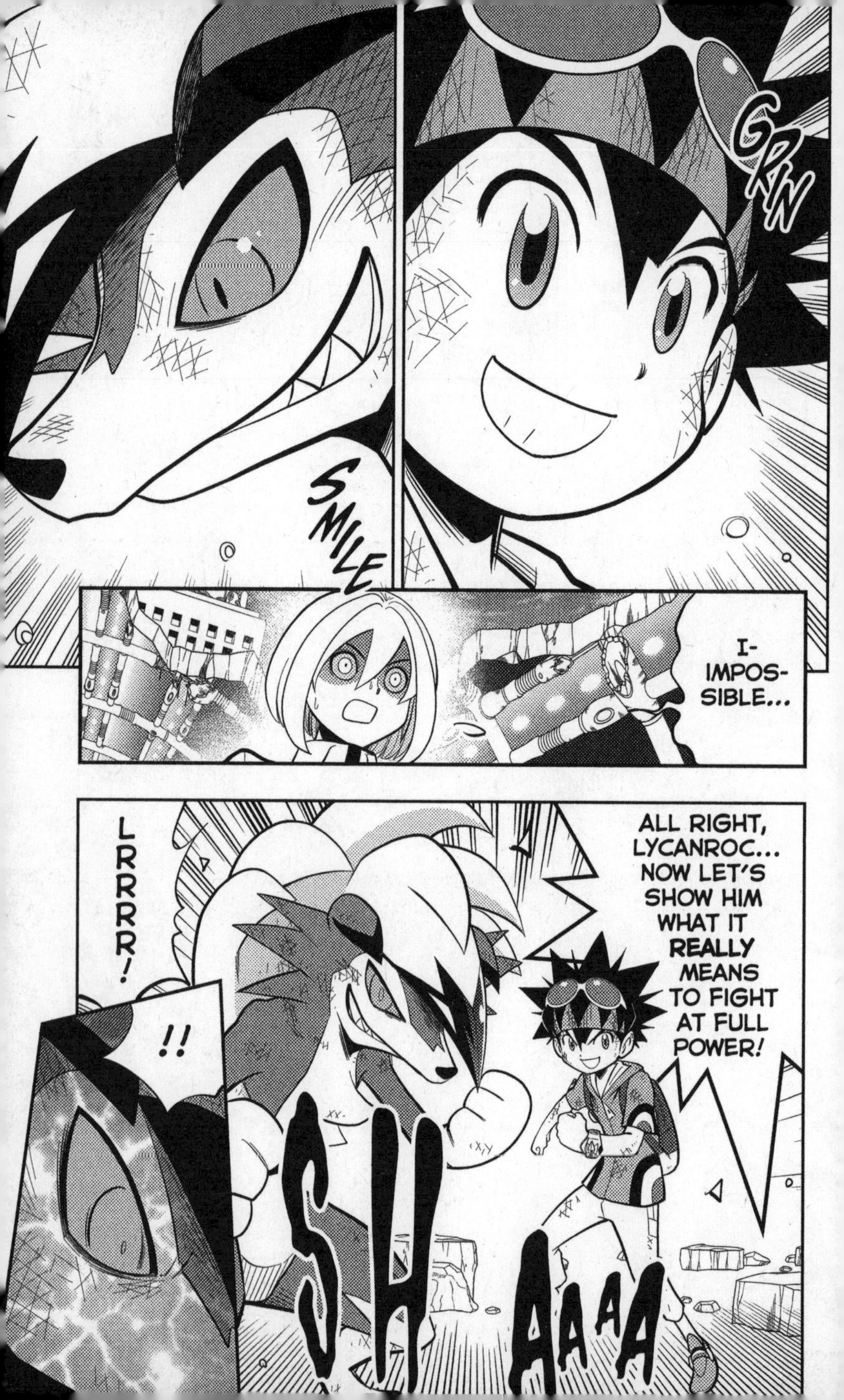
GRIN
SMILE
I- IMPOS- SIBLE...
ALL RIGHT, LYCANROC... NOW LET'S SHOW HIM WHAT IT REALLY MEANS TO FIGHT AT FULL POWER!
LRRRR!
!!
SHAAAA

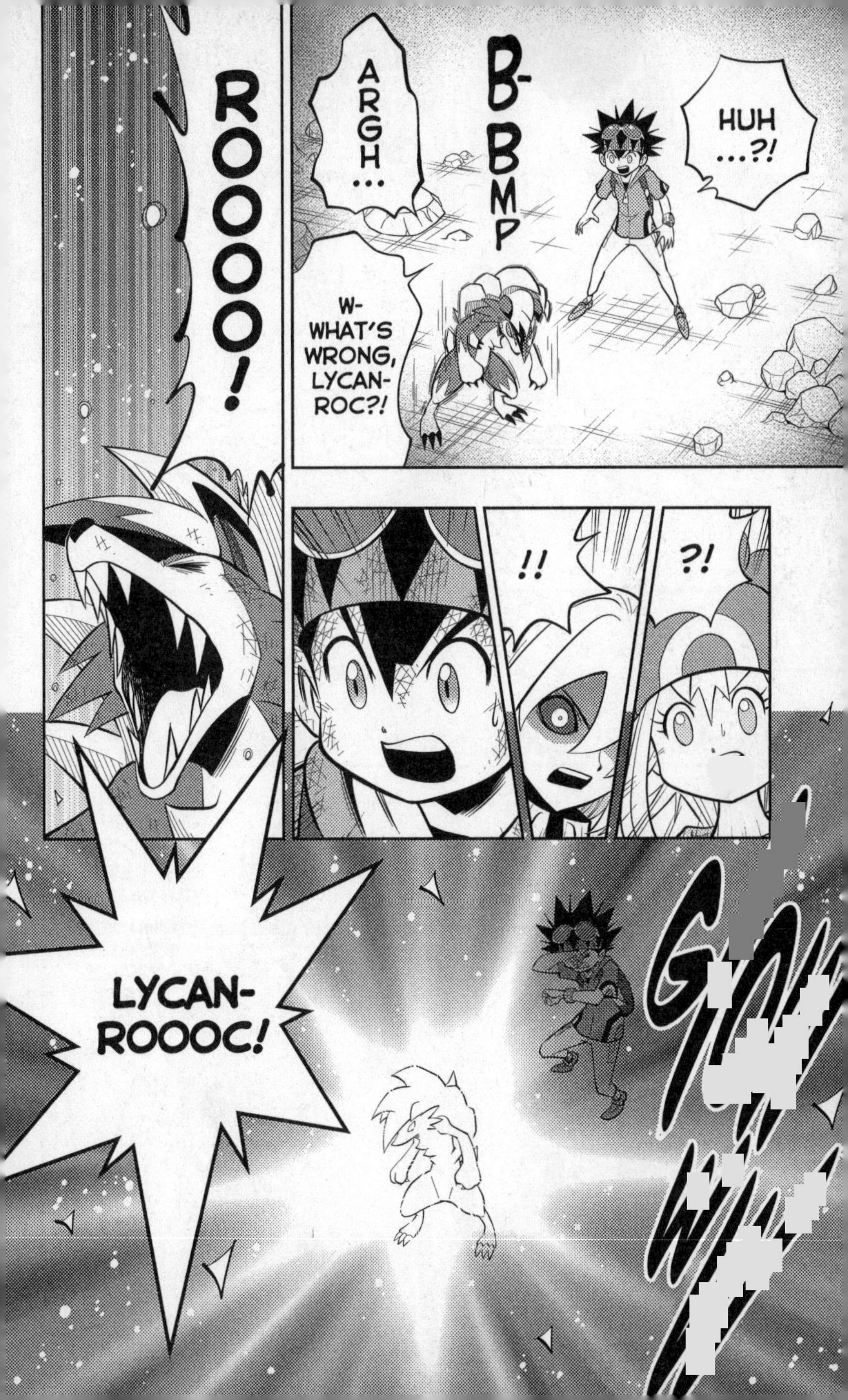

HUH ...?!
B-BMP
ARGH...
W-WHAT'S WRONG, LYCAN-ROC?!
?!
!!
ROOOOO!
LYCAN-ROOOC!

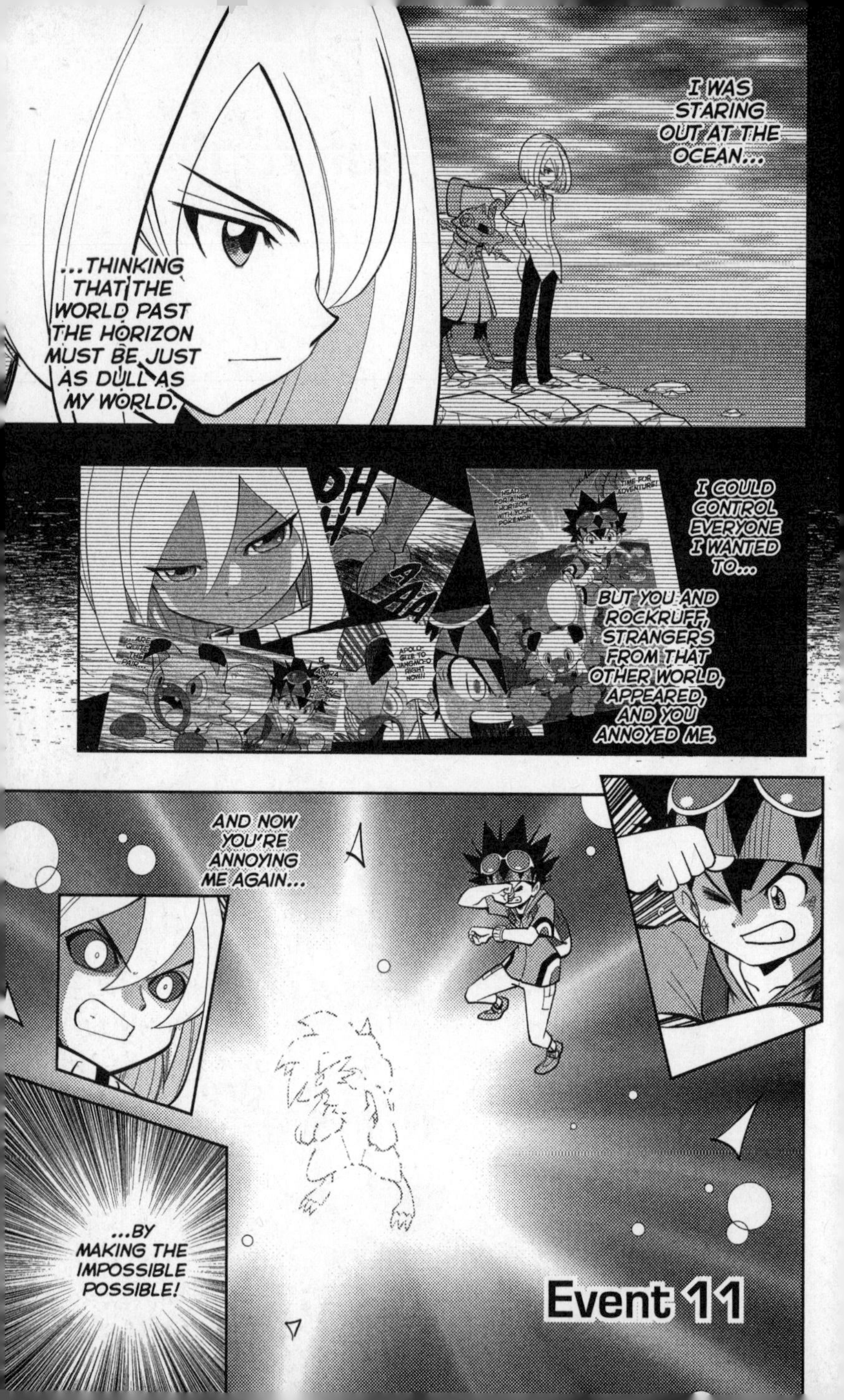

I WAS STARING OUT AT THE OCEAN...
...THINKING THAT THE WORLD PAST THE HORIZON MUST BE JUST AS DULL AS MY WORLD.
I COULD CONTROL EVERYONE I WANTED TO...
BUT YOU AND ROCKRUFF, STRANGERS FROM THAT OTHER WORLD, APPEARED, AND YOU ANNOYED ME.
AND NOW YOU'RE ANNOYING ME AGAIN...
...BY MAKING THE IMPOSSIBLE POSSIBLE!
Event 11

Event 11: To a New Horizon!

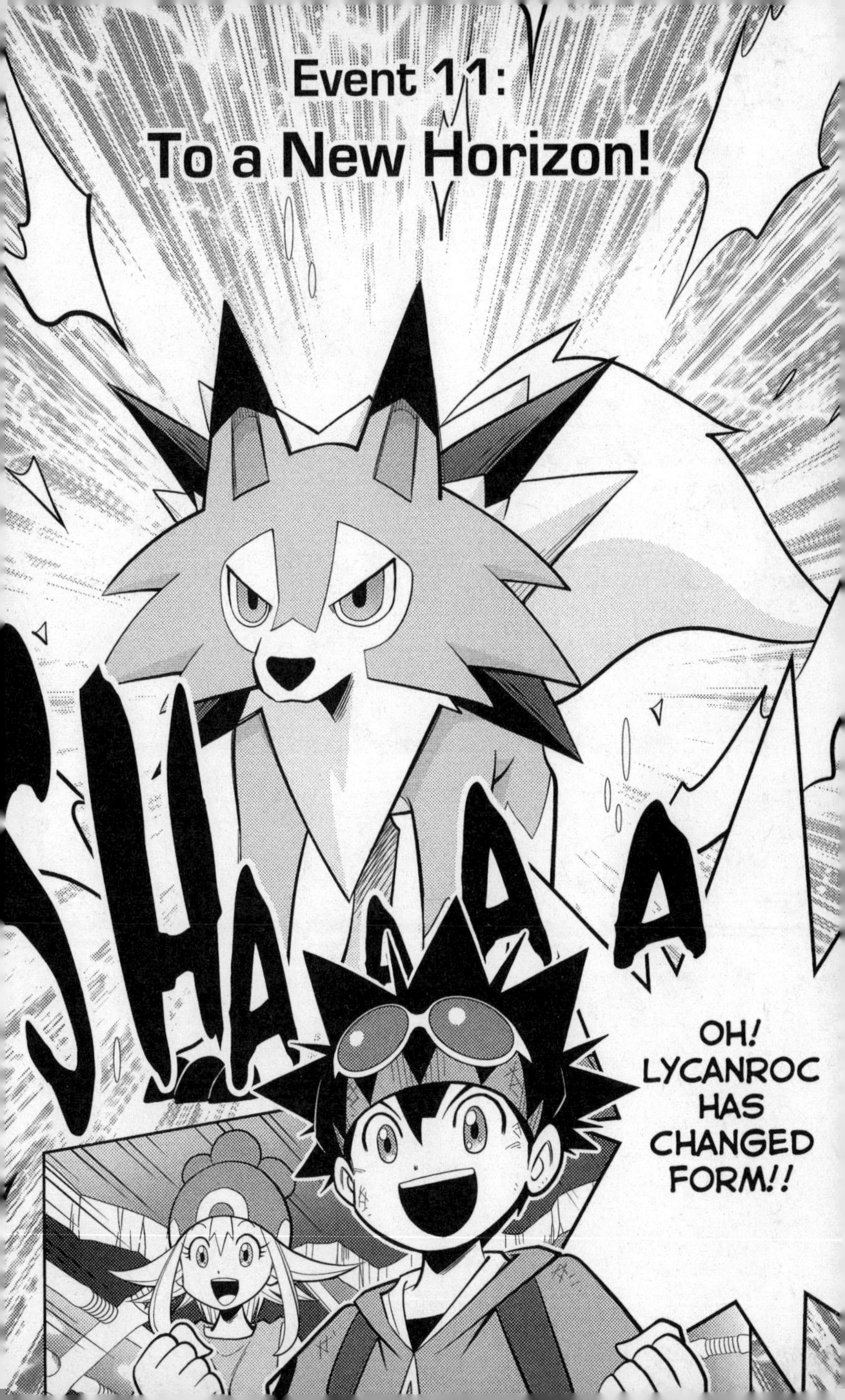

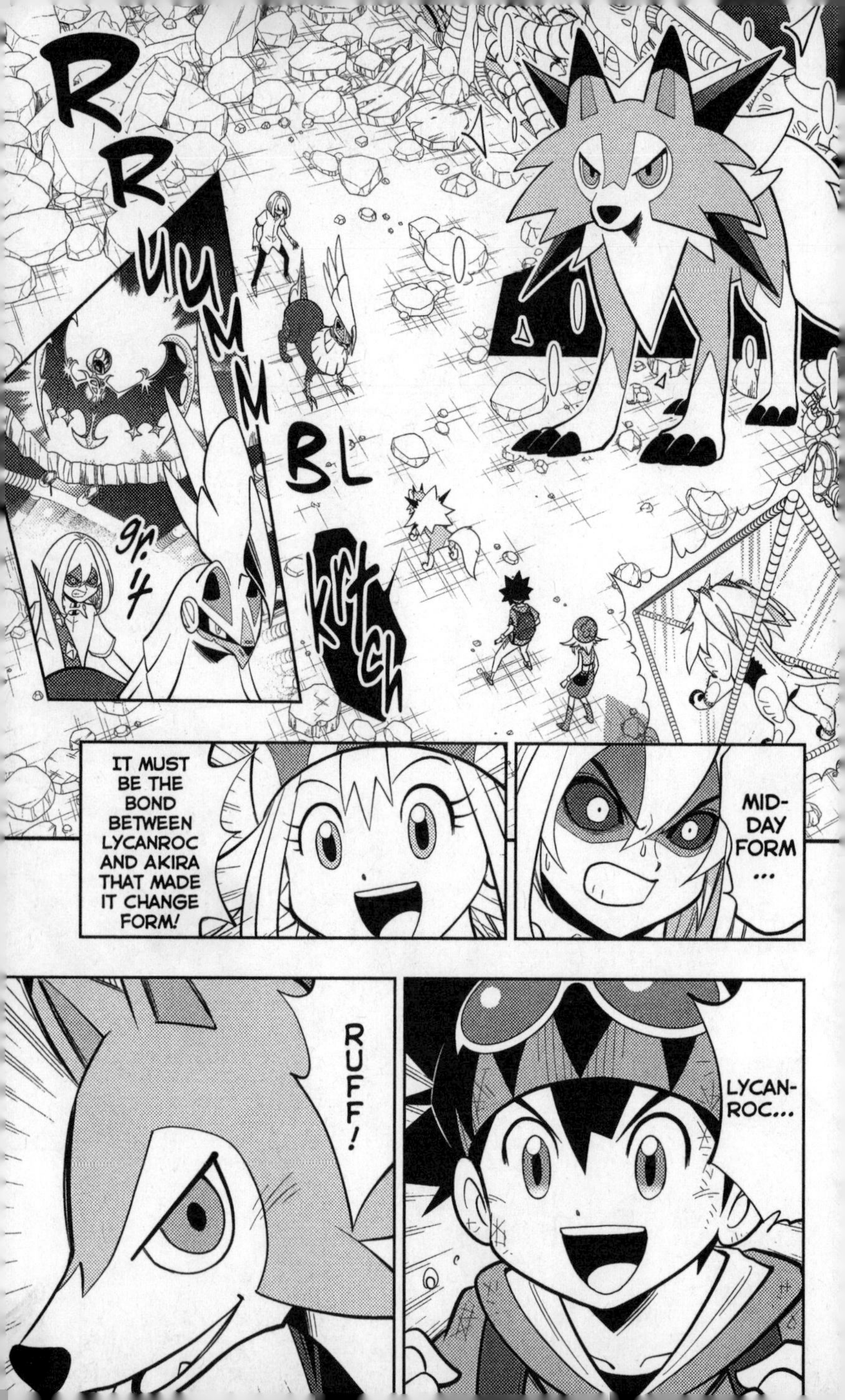
RRUUMMMBL
krtch
MID-DAY FORM...
IT MUST BE THE BOND BETWEEN LYCANROC AND AKIRA THAT MADE IT CHANGE FORM!
LYCAN-ROC...
RUFF!

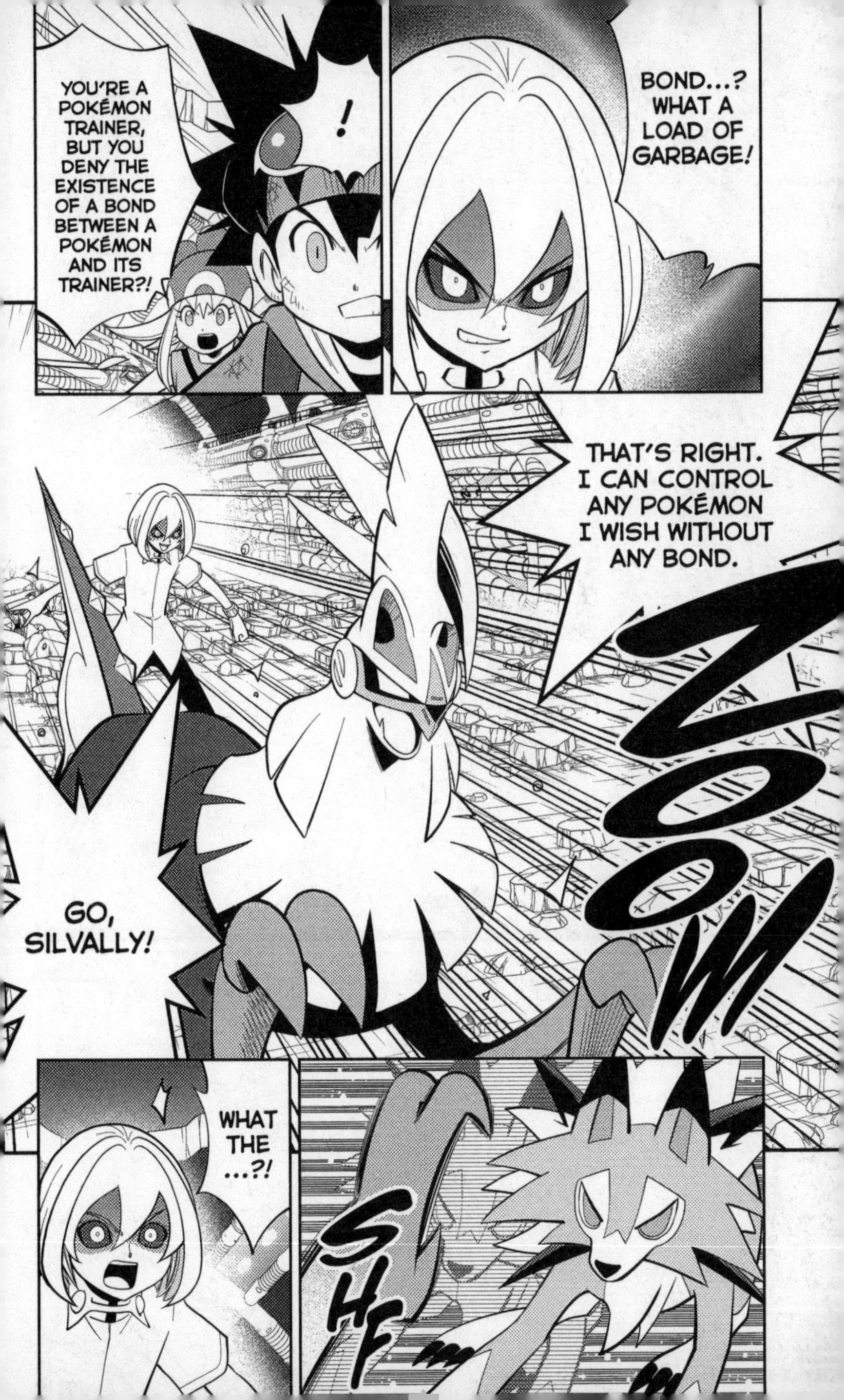
BOND...? WHAT A LOAD OF GARBAGE!
!
YOU'RE A POKÉMON TRAINER, BUT YOU DENY THE EXISTENCE OF A BOND BETWEEN A POKÉMON AND ITS TRAINER?!
THAT'S RIGHT. I CAN CONTROL ANY POKÉMON I WISH WITHOUT ANY BOND.
ZOOM
GO, SILVALLY!
SHF
WHAT THE ...?!

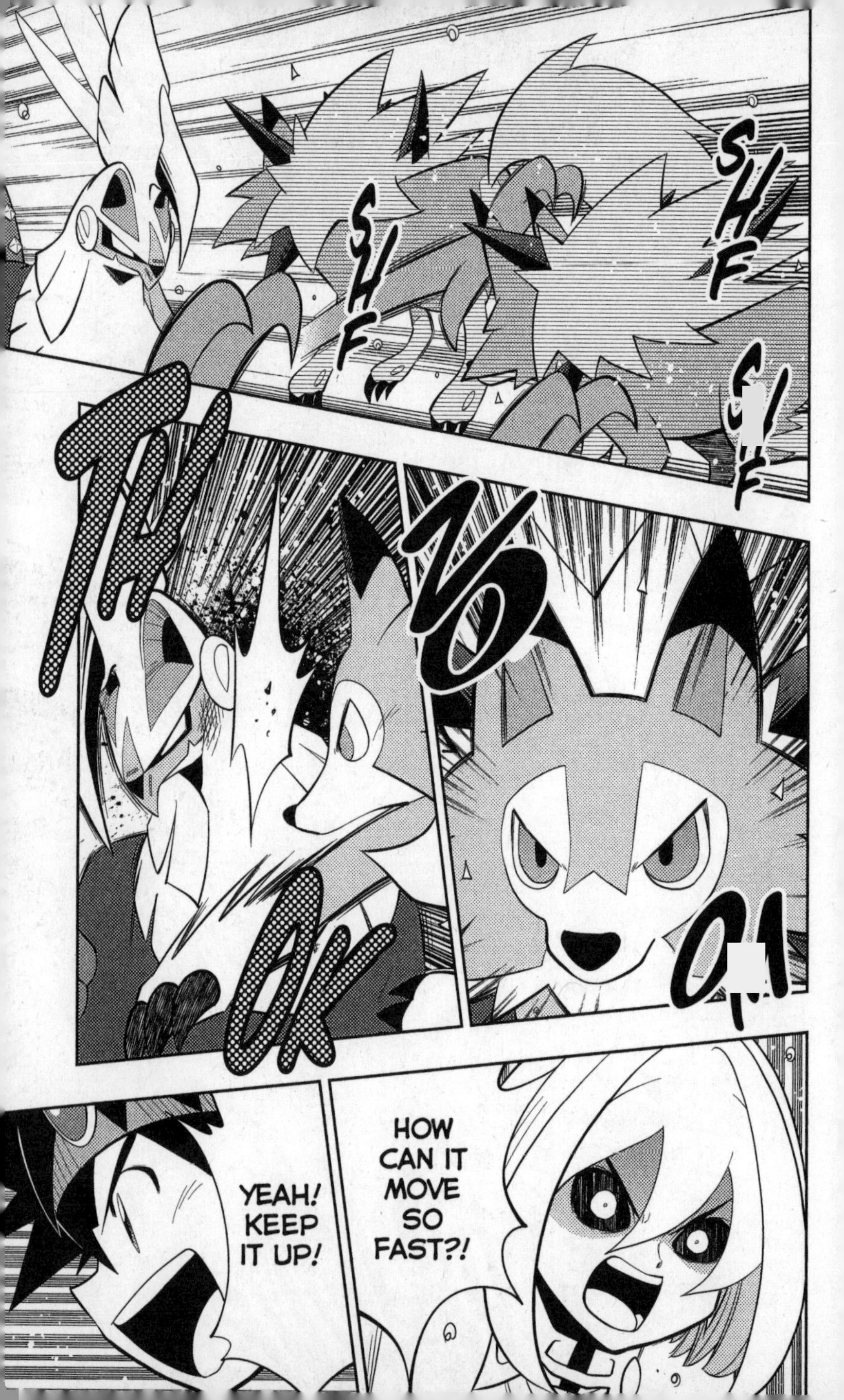
SHF
SHF
HOW CAN IT MOVE SO FAST?!
YEAH! KEEP IT UP!

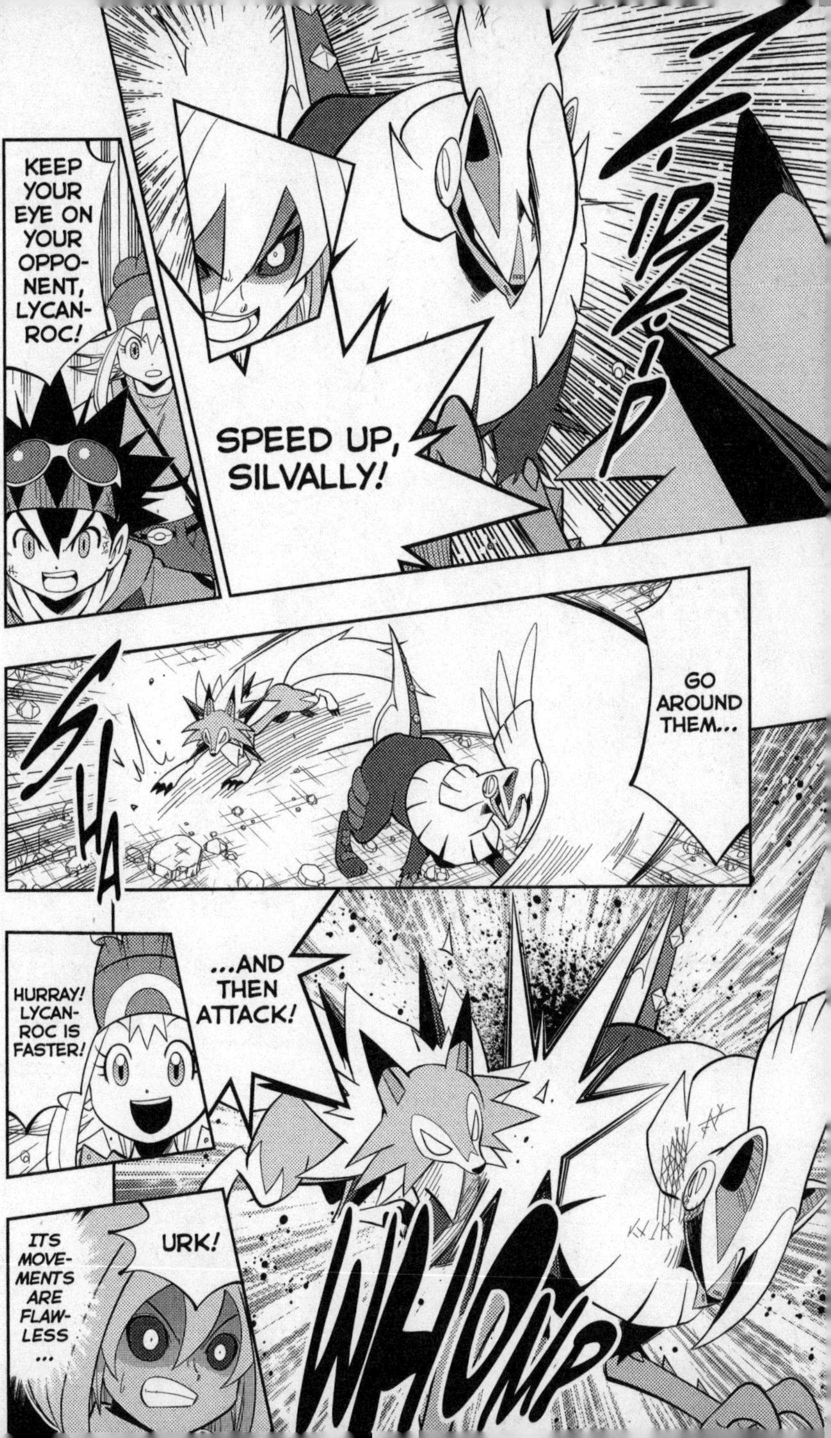
SPEED UP, SILVALLY!
KEEP YOUR EYE ON YOUR OPPONENT, LYCANROC!
GO AROUND THEM...
SHA
...AND THEN ATTACK!
WHOMP
HURRAY! LYCANROC IS FASTER!
URK!
ITS MOVEMENTS ARE FLAWLESS...

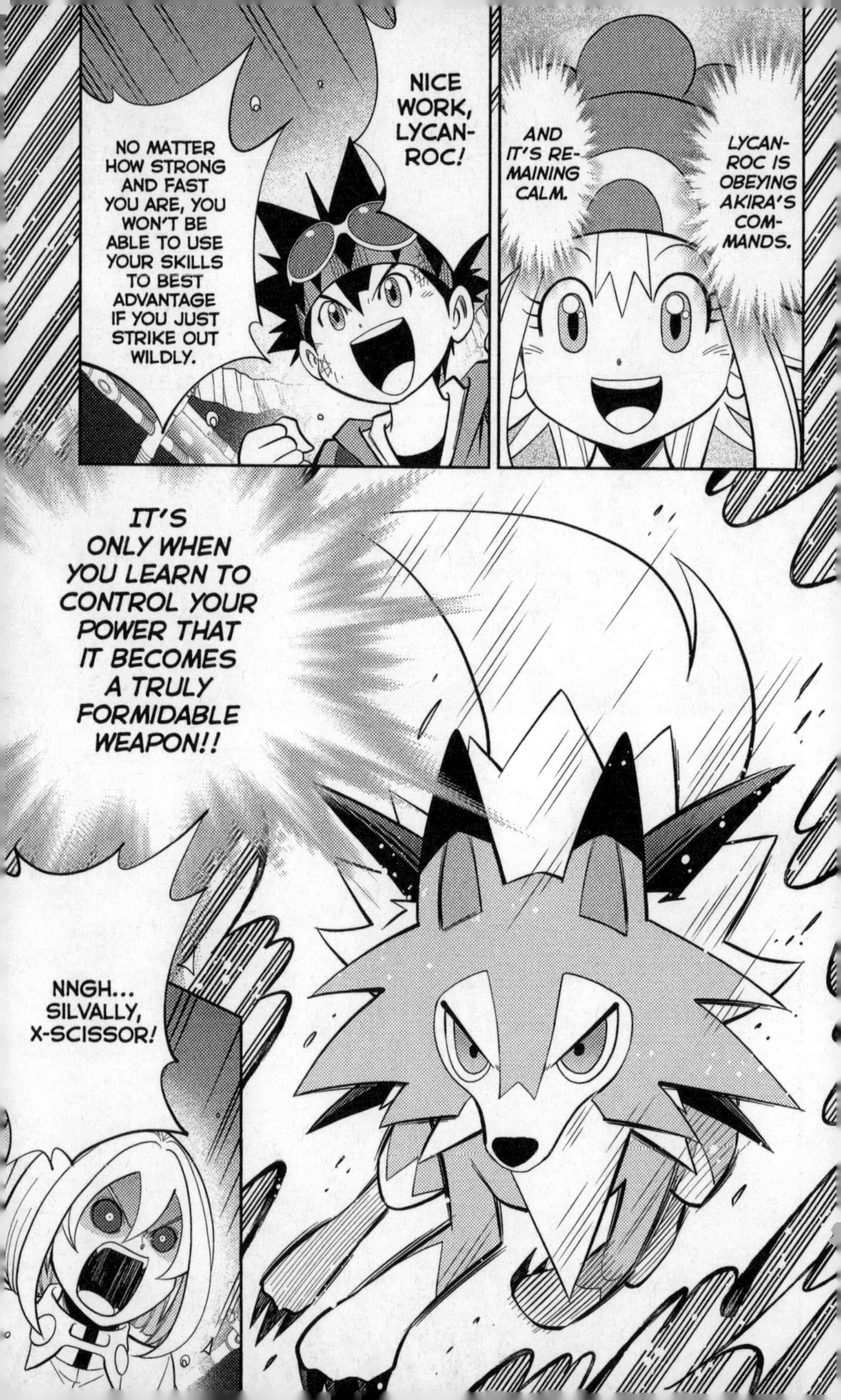
LYCANROC IS OBEYING AKIRA'S COMMANDS.
AND IT'S REMAINING CALM.
NICE WORK, LYCANROC!
NO MATTER HOW STRONG AND FAST YOU ARE, YOU WON'T BE ABLE TO USE YOUR SKILLS TO BEST ADVANTAGE IF YOU JUST STRIKE OUT WILDLY.
IT'S ONLY WHEN YOU LEARN TO CONTROL YOUR POWER THAT IT BECOMES A TRULY FORMIDABLE WEAPON!!
NNGH... SILVALLY, X-SCISSOR!

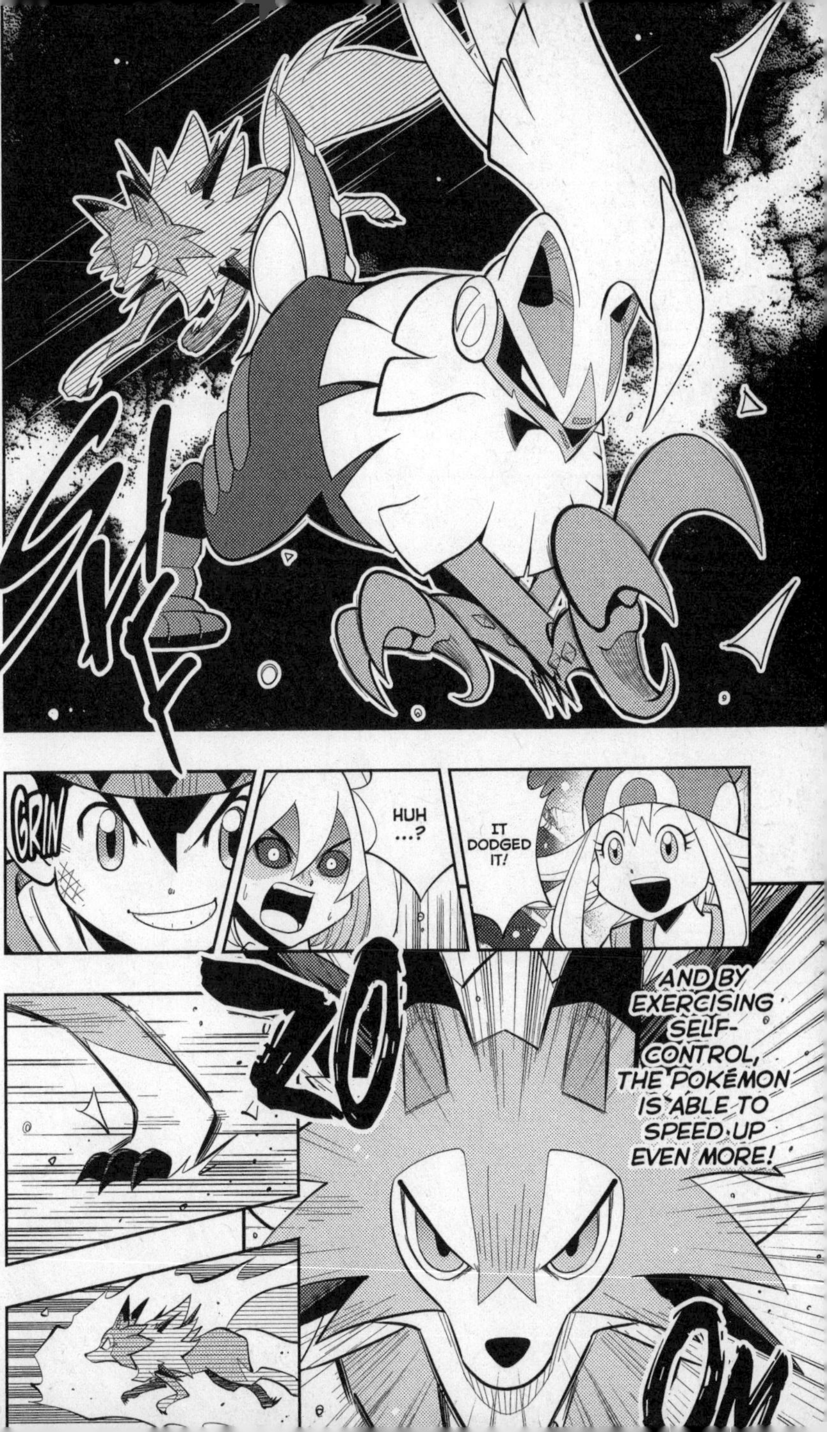
IT DODGED IT!
HUH ...?
GRIN
AND BY EXERCISING SELF-CONTROL, THE POKÉMON IS ABLE TO SPEED UP EVEN MORE!
ZO
OM

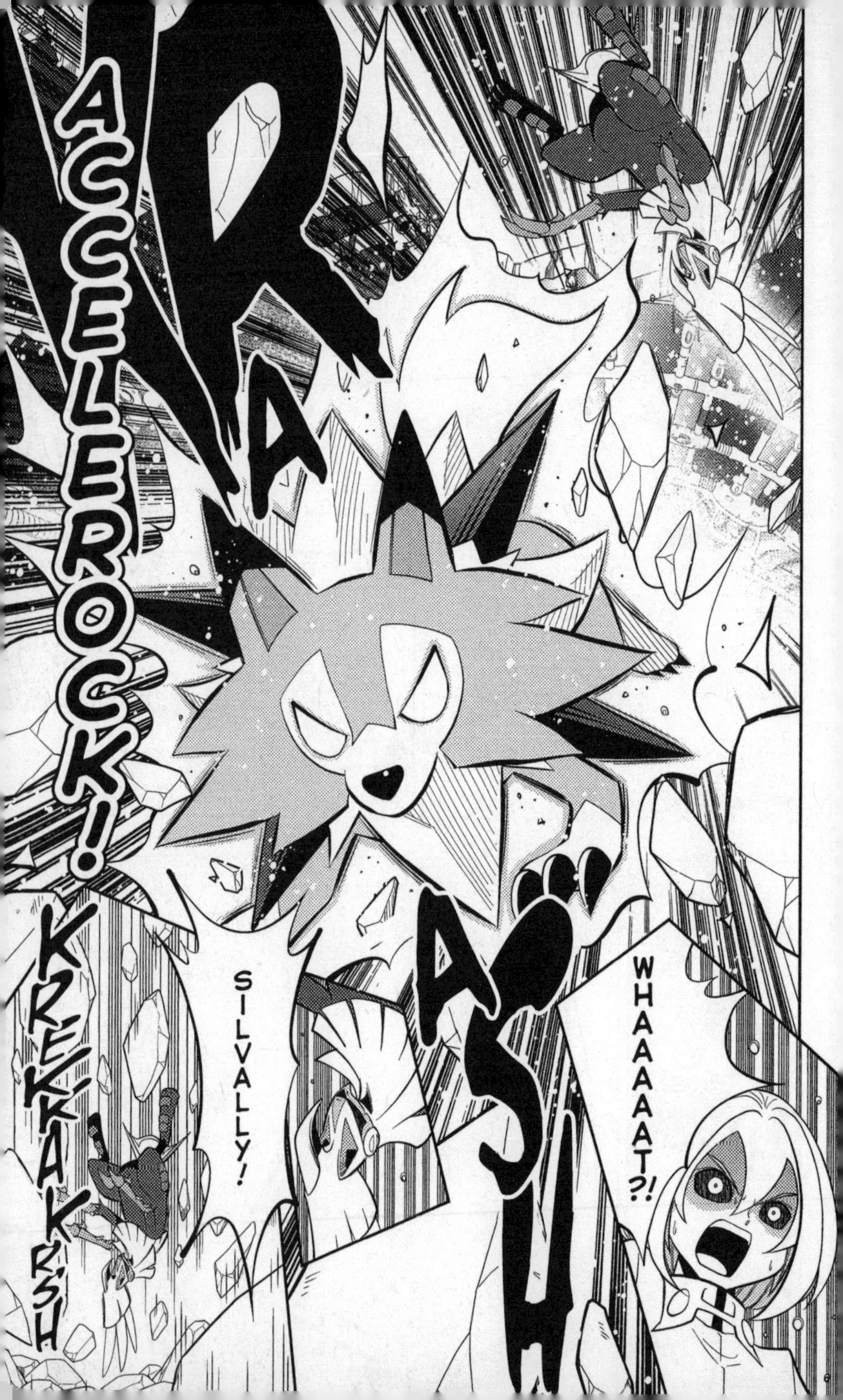
ACCELEROCK!
AAASH
WHAAAAAT?!
SILVALLY!
KREKKAKRSH

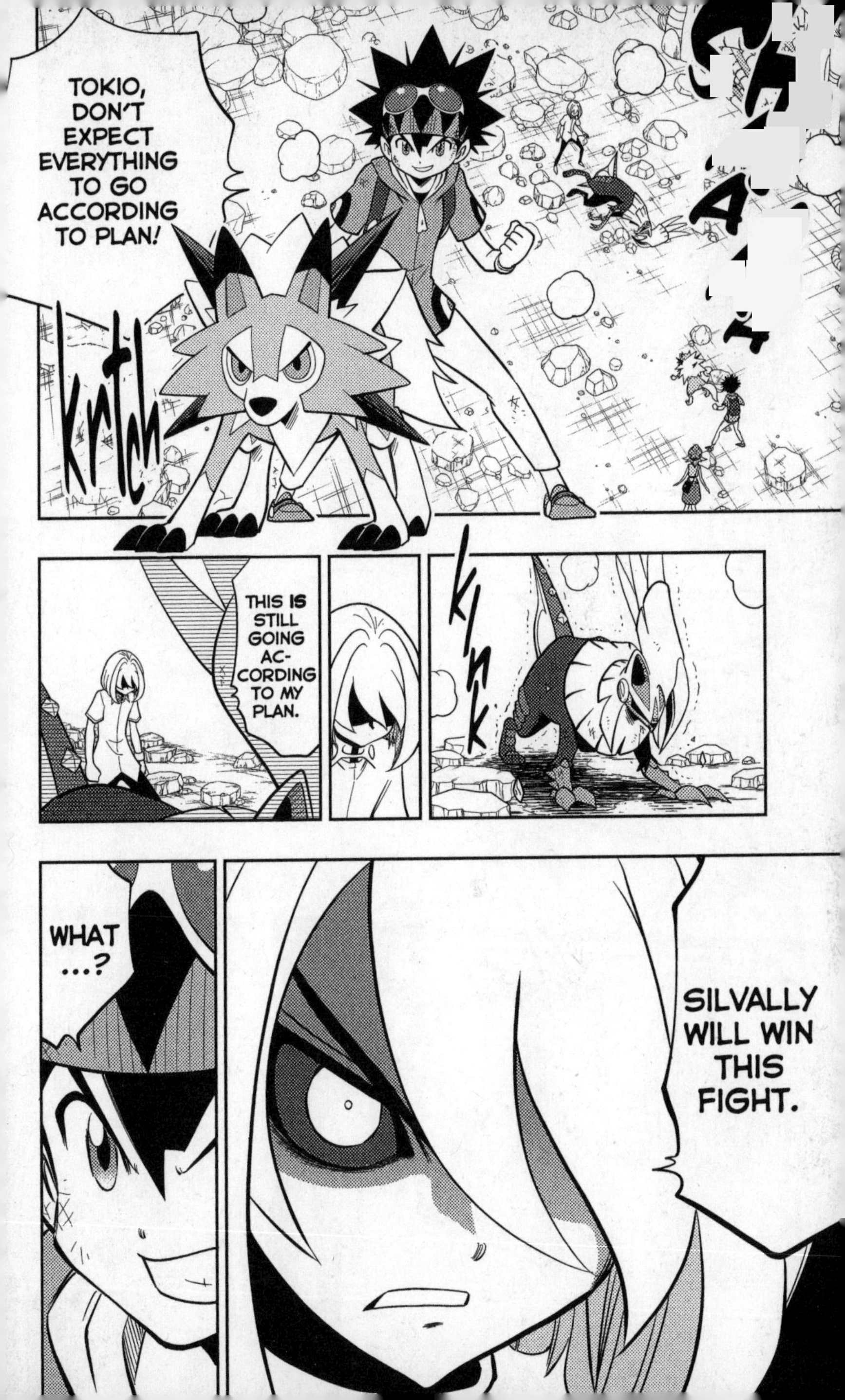
TOKIO, DON'T EXPECT EVERYTHING TO GO ACCORDING TO PLAN!
krtch
klink
THIS IS STILL GOING AC-CORDING TO MY PLAN.
SILVALLY WILL WIN THIS FIGHT.
WHAT ...?

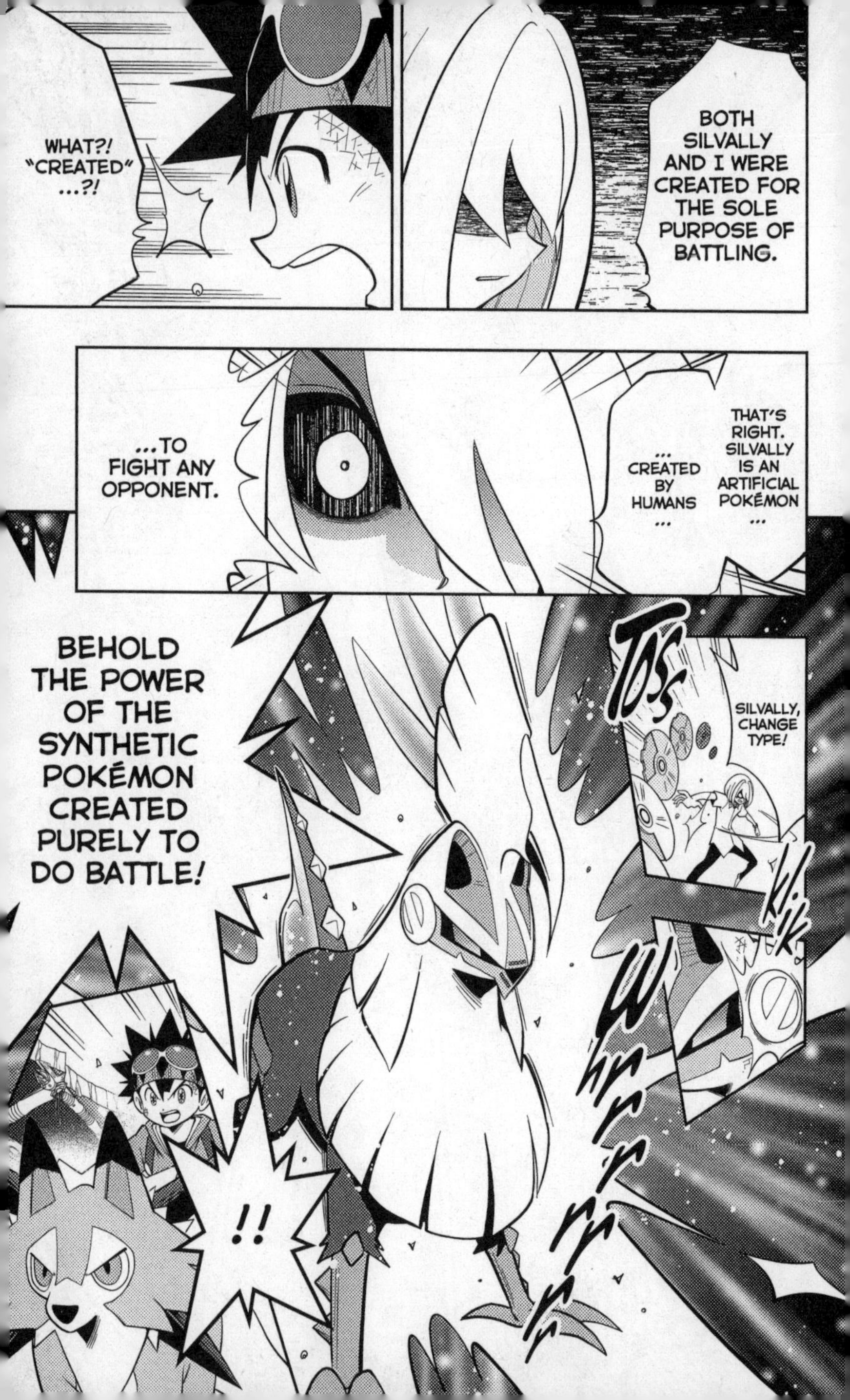
BOTH SILVALLY AND I WERE CREATED FOR THE SOLE PURPOSE OF BATTLING.
WHAT?! "CREATED" ...?!
THAT'S RIGHT. SILVALLY IS AN ARTIFICIAL POKÉMON ...
... CREATED BY HUMANS ...
...TO FIGHT ANY OPPONENT.
TOSS
SILVALLY, CHANGE TYPE!
KLIK
BEHOLD THE POWER OF THE SYNTHETIC POKÉMON CREATED PURELY TO DO BATTLE!
!!

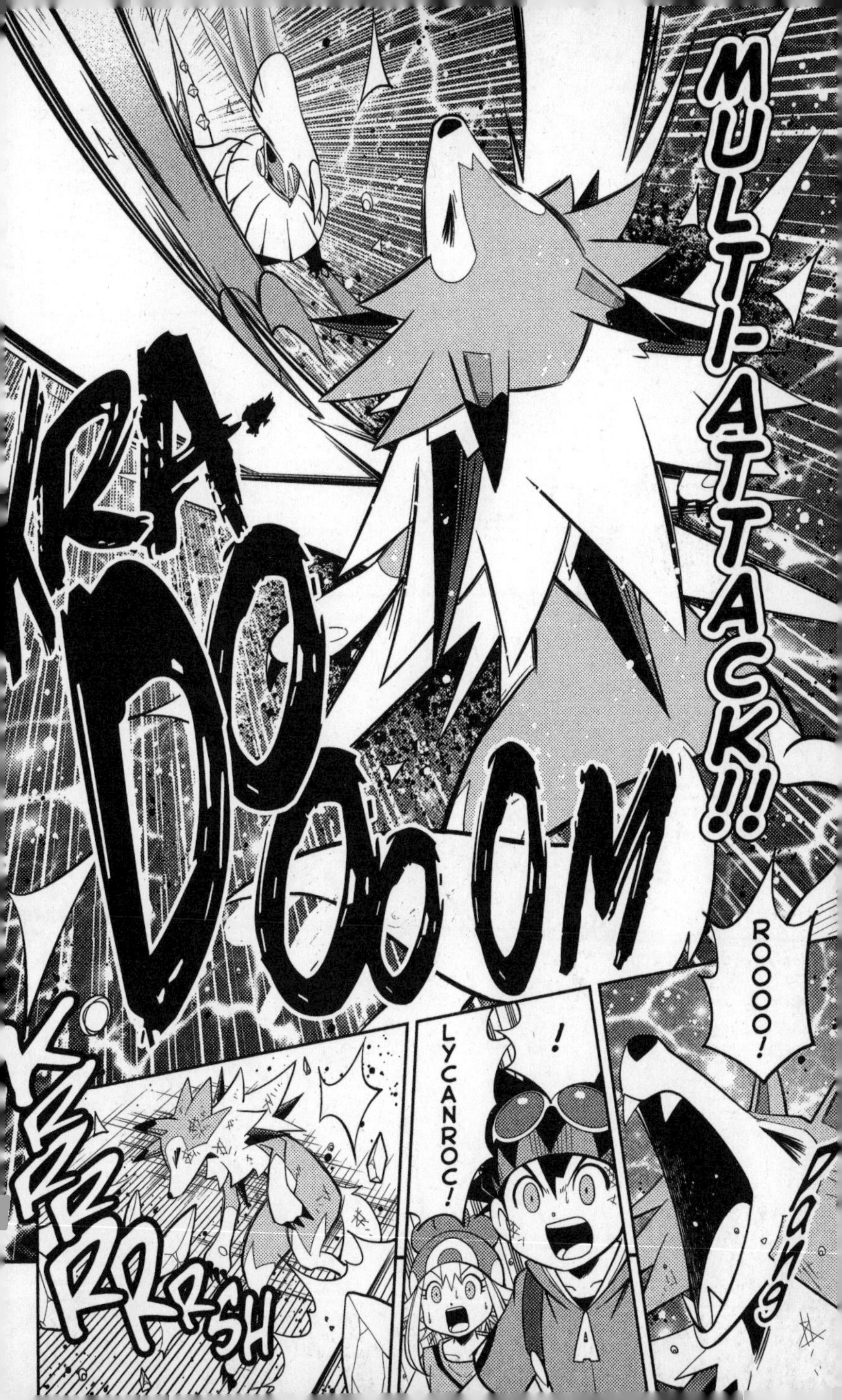
MULTI-ATTACK!!
KA DOOOOM
ROOOO!
chang
LYCANROC!
!
KRRRRRASH

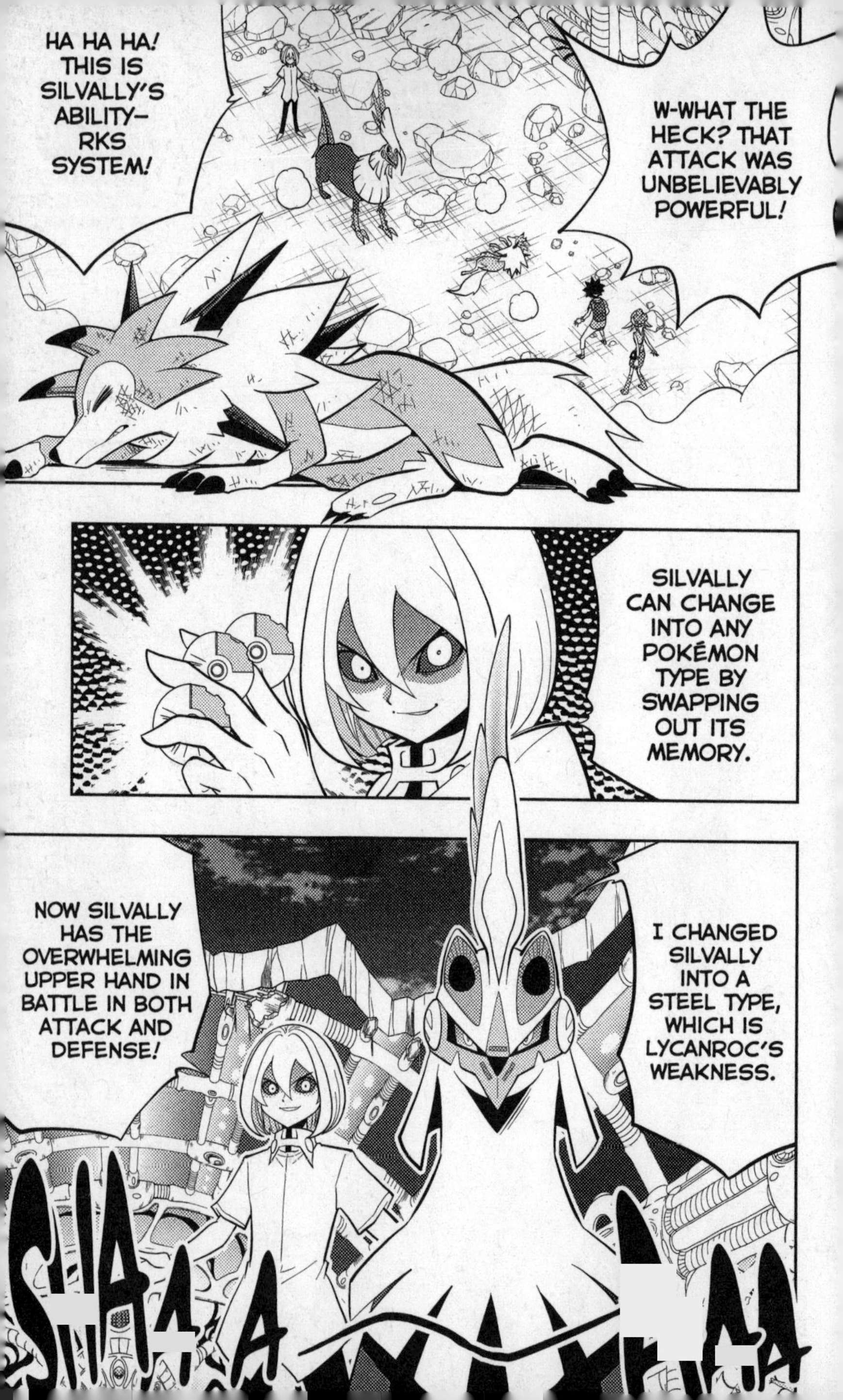
W-WHAT THE HECK? THAT ATTACK WAS UNBELIEVABLY POWERFUL!
HA HA HA! THIS IS SILVALLY'S ABILITY—RKS SYSTEM!
SILVALLY CAN CHANGE INTO ANY POKÉMON TYPE BY SWAPPING OUT ITS MEMORY.
I CHANGED SILVALLY INTO A STEEL TYPE, WHICH IS LYCANROC'S WEAKNESS.
NOW SILVALLY HAS THE OVERWHELMING UPPER HAND IN BATTLE IN BOTH ATTACK AND DEFENSE!

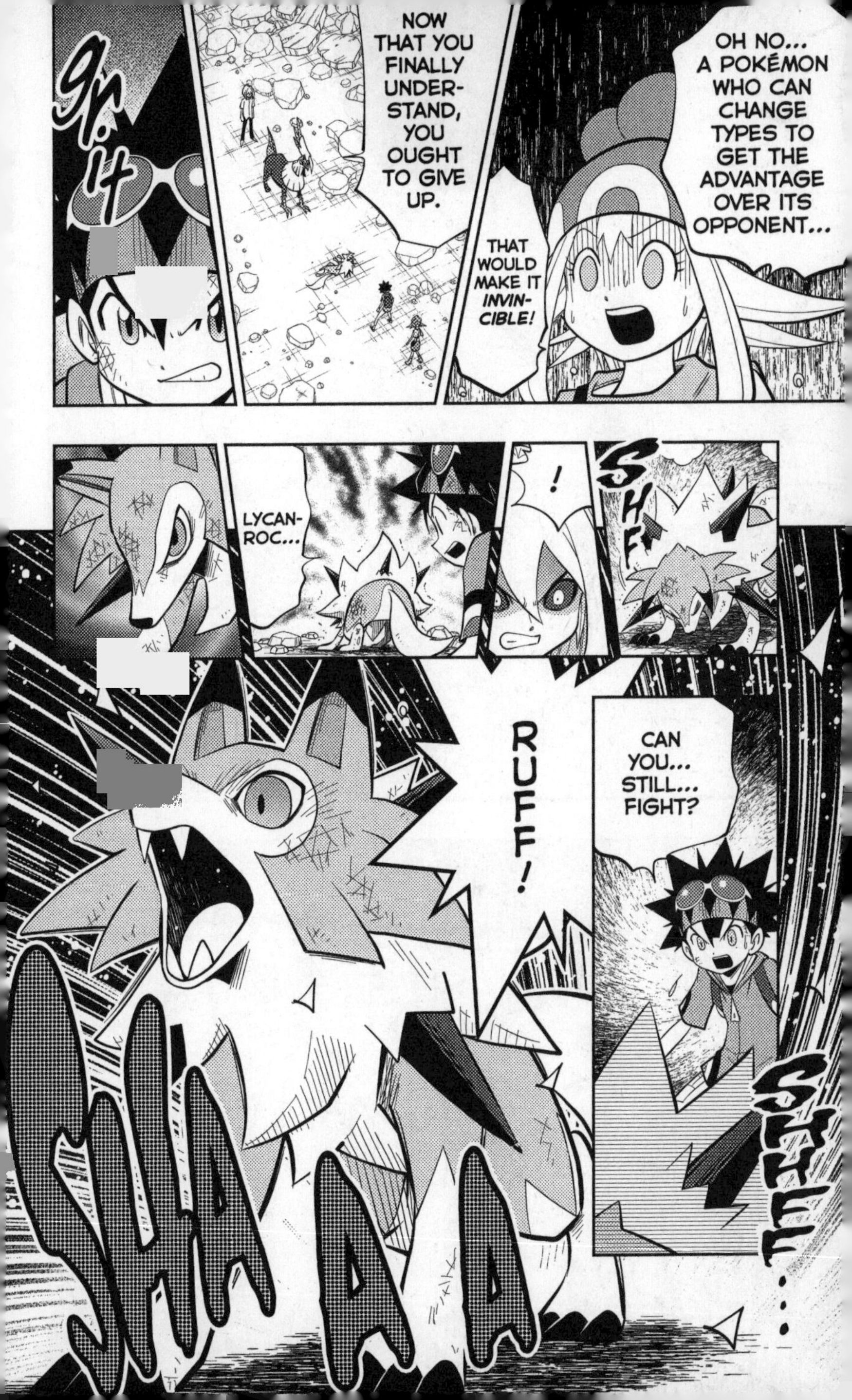

OH NO... A POKÉMON WHO CAN CHANGE TYPES TO GET THE ADVANTAGE OVER ITS OPPONENT...
THAT WOULD MAKE IT INVINCIBLE!
NOW THAT YOU FINALLY UNDER-STAND, YOU OUGHT TO GIVE UP.
grit
SHF
!
LYCAN-ROC...
CAN YOU... STILL... FIGHT?
SHHF...
RUFF!
SHAA

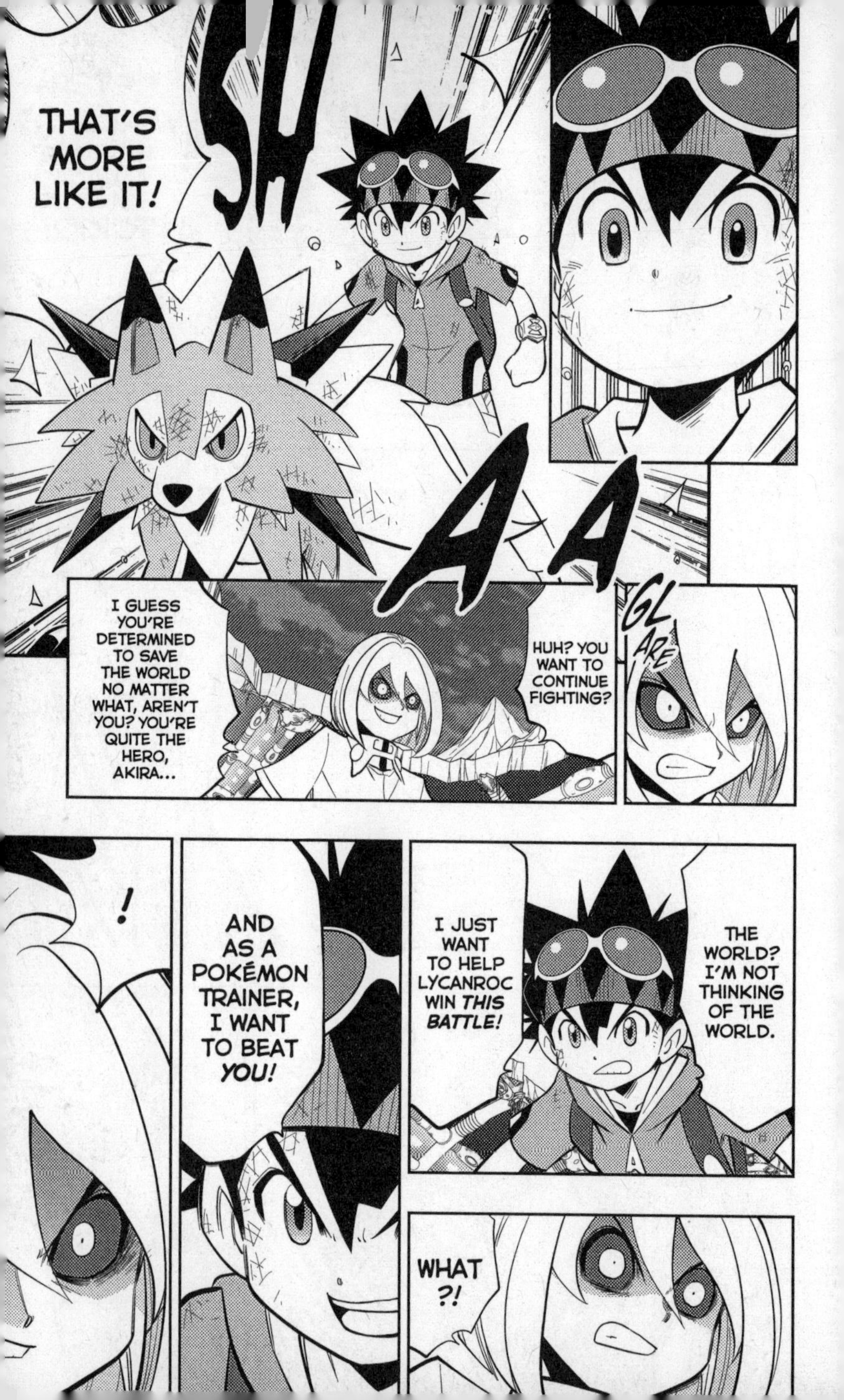

THAT'S MORE LIKE IT!
SHAA
GLARE
HUH? YOU WANT TO CONTINUE FIGHTING?
I GUESS YOU'RE DETERMINED TO SAVE THE WORLD NO MATTER WHAT, AREN'T YOU? YOU'RE QUITE THE HERO, AKIRA...
THE WORLD? I'M NOT THINKING OF THE WORLD.
I JUST WANT TO HELP LYCANROC WIN *THIS BATTLE!*
WHAT?!
AND AS A POKÉMON TRAINER, I WANT TO BEAT *YOU!*
!

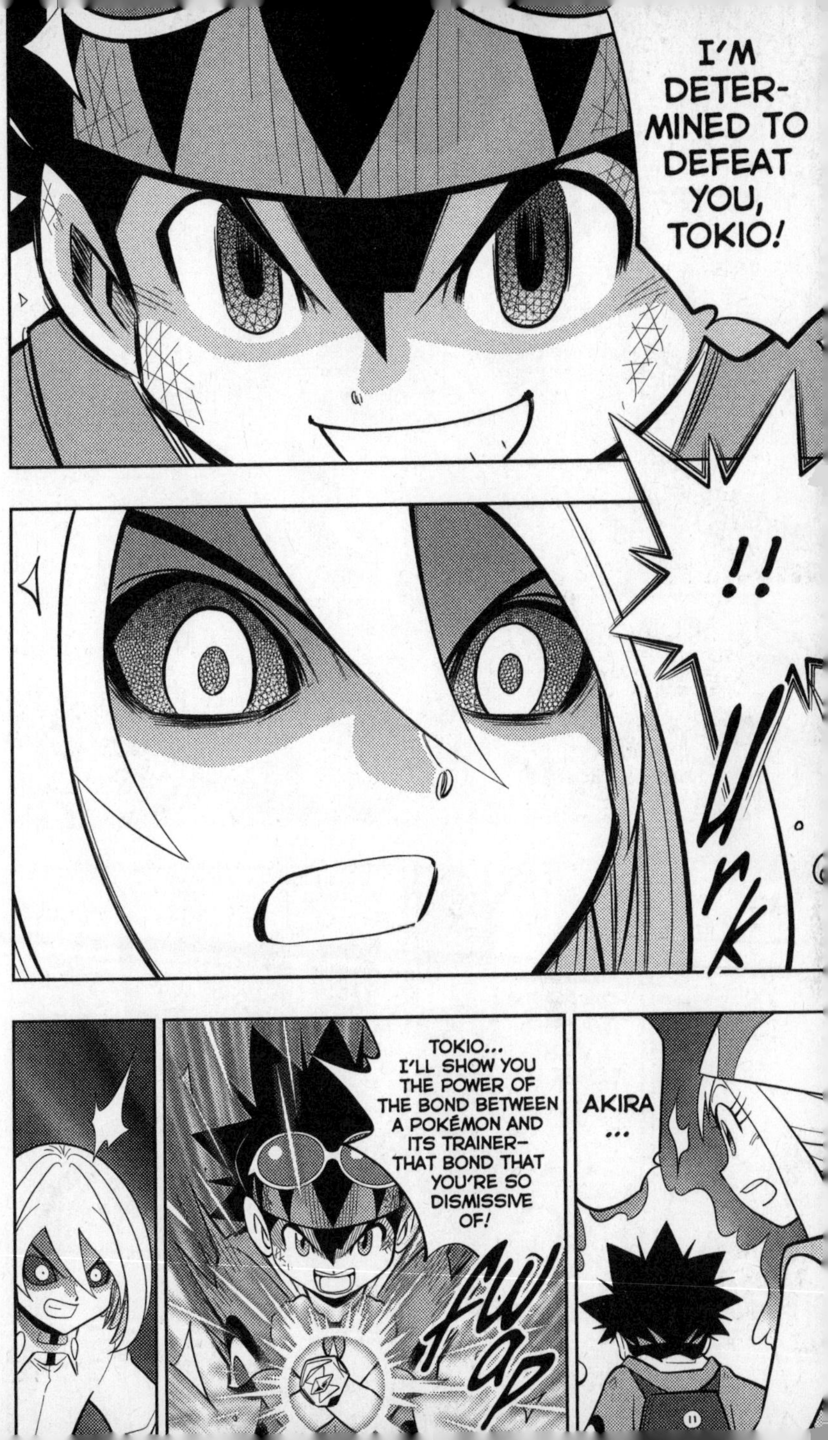
I'M DETERMINED TO DEFEAT YOU, TOKIO!
!!
UNK
AKIRA...
TOKIO... I'LL SHOW YOU THE POWER OF THE BOND BETWEEN A POKÉMON AND ITS TRAINER—THAT BOND THAT YOU'RE SO DISMISSIVE OF!
FWAP

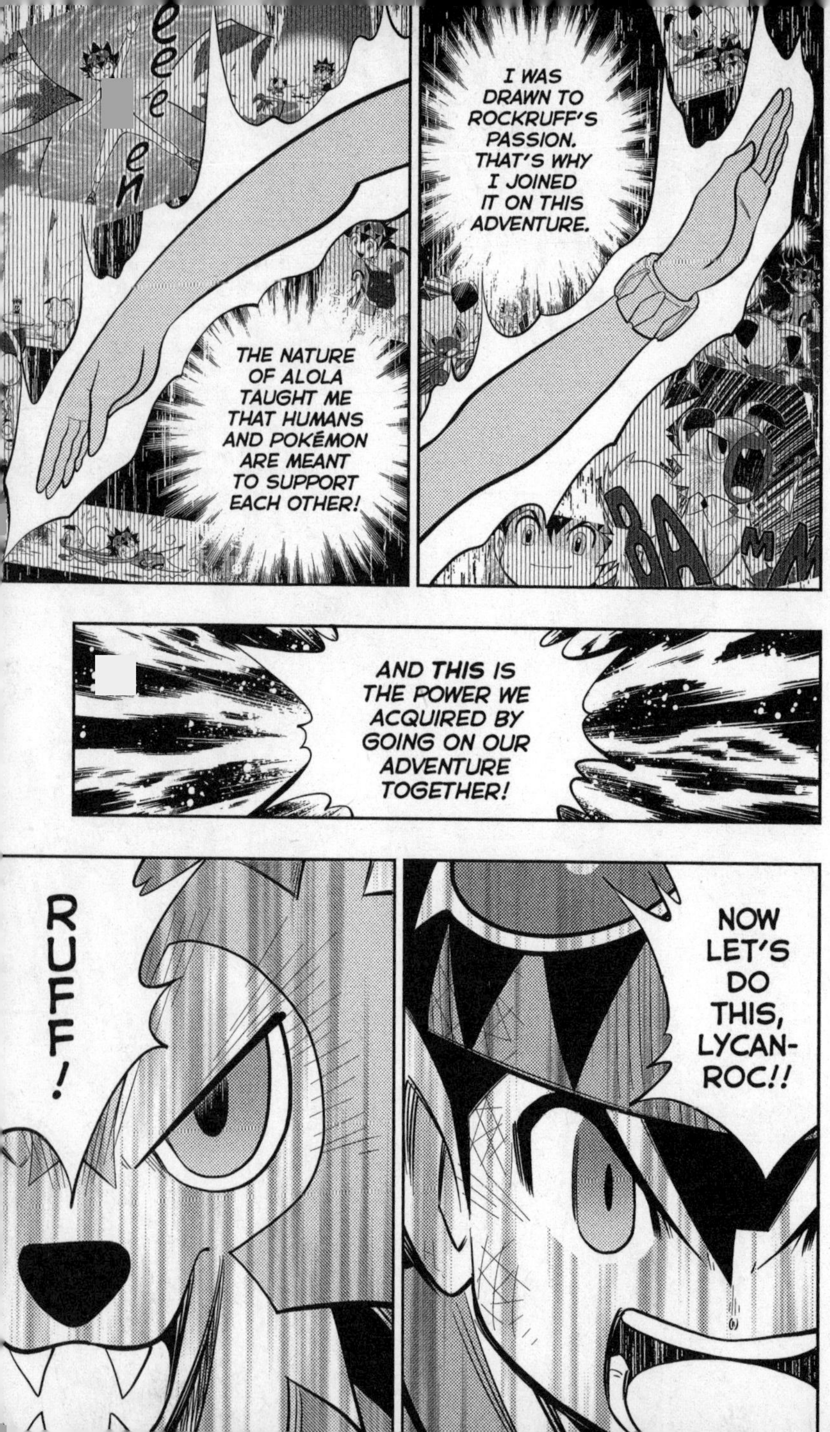
I WAS DRAWN TO ROCKRUFF'S PASSION. THAT'S WHY I JOINED IT ON THIS ADVENTURE.
BAMM
THE NATURE OF ALOLA TAUGHT ME THAT HUMANS AND POKÉMON ARE MEANT TO SUPPORT EACH OTHER!
AND THIS IS THE POWER WE ACQUIRED BY GOING ON OUR ADVENTURE TOGETHER!
NOW LET'S DO THIS, LYCAN-ROC!!
RUFF!

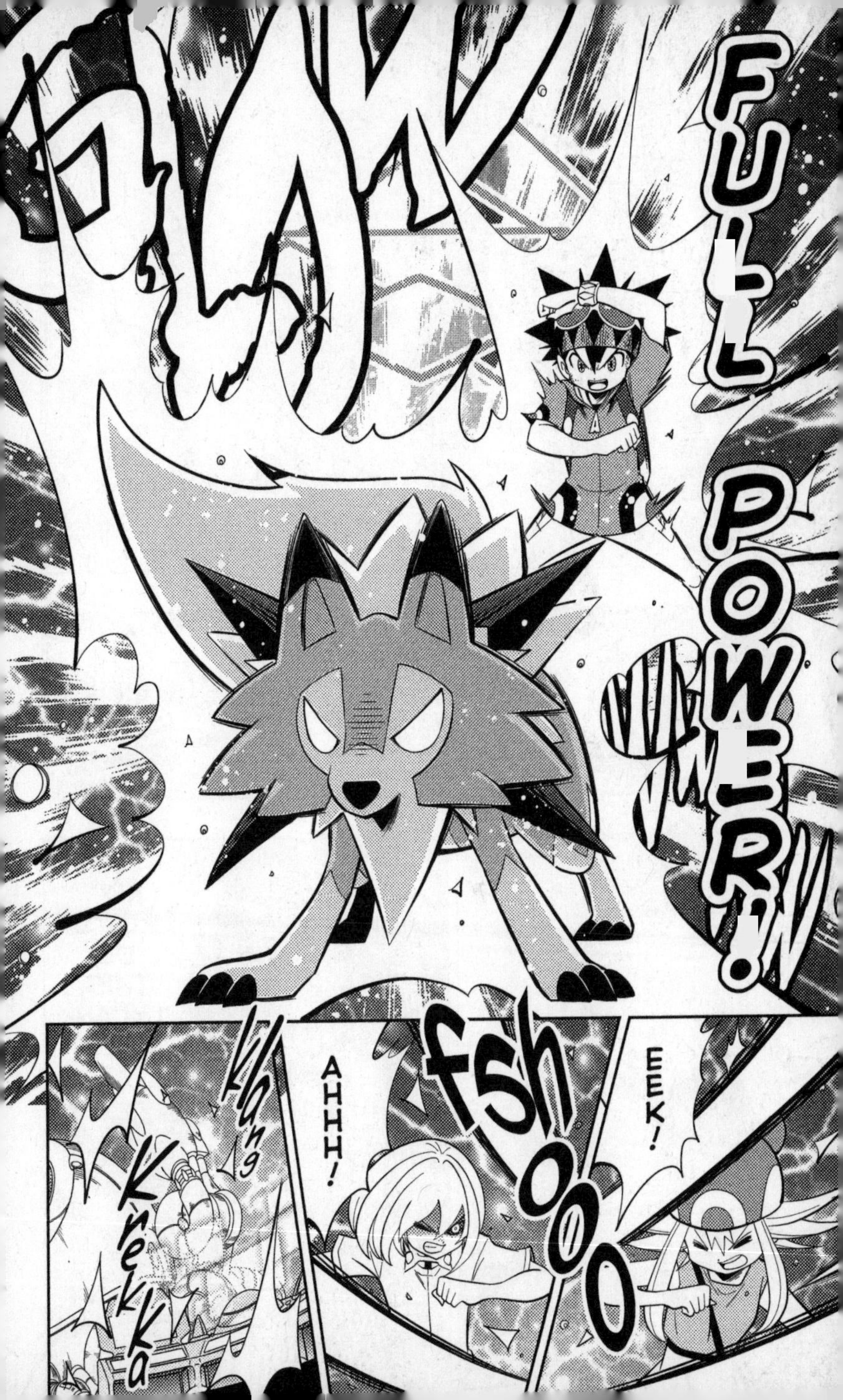
FULL POWER!!
EEK!
fshoooo
AHHH!
klang
krekka

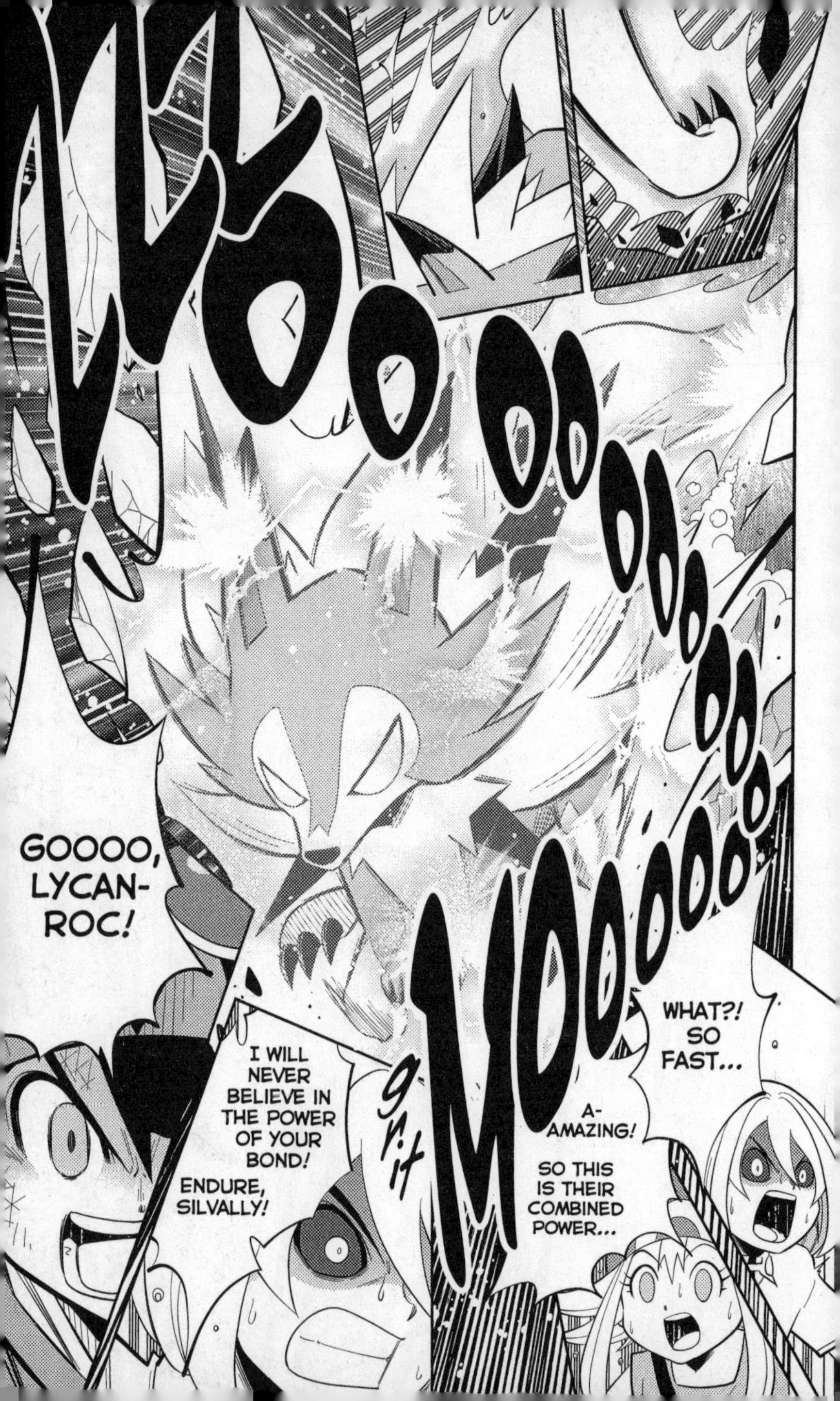
WHAT?! SO FAST...
A-AMAZING!
SO THIS IS THEIR COMBINED POWER...
I WILL NEVER BELIEVE IN THE POWER OF YOUR BOND!
ENDURE, SILVALLY!
grit
GOOOO, LYCAN-ROC!

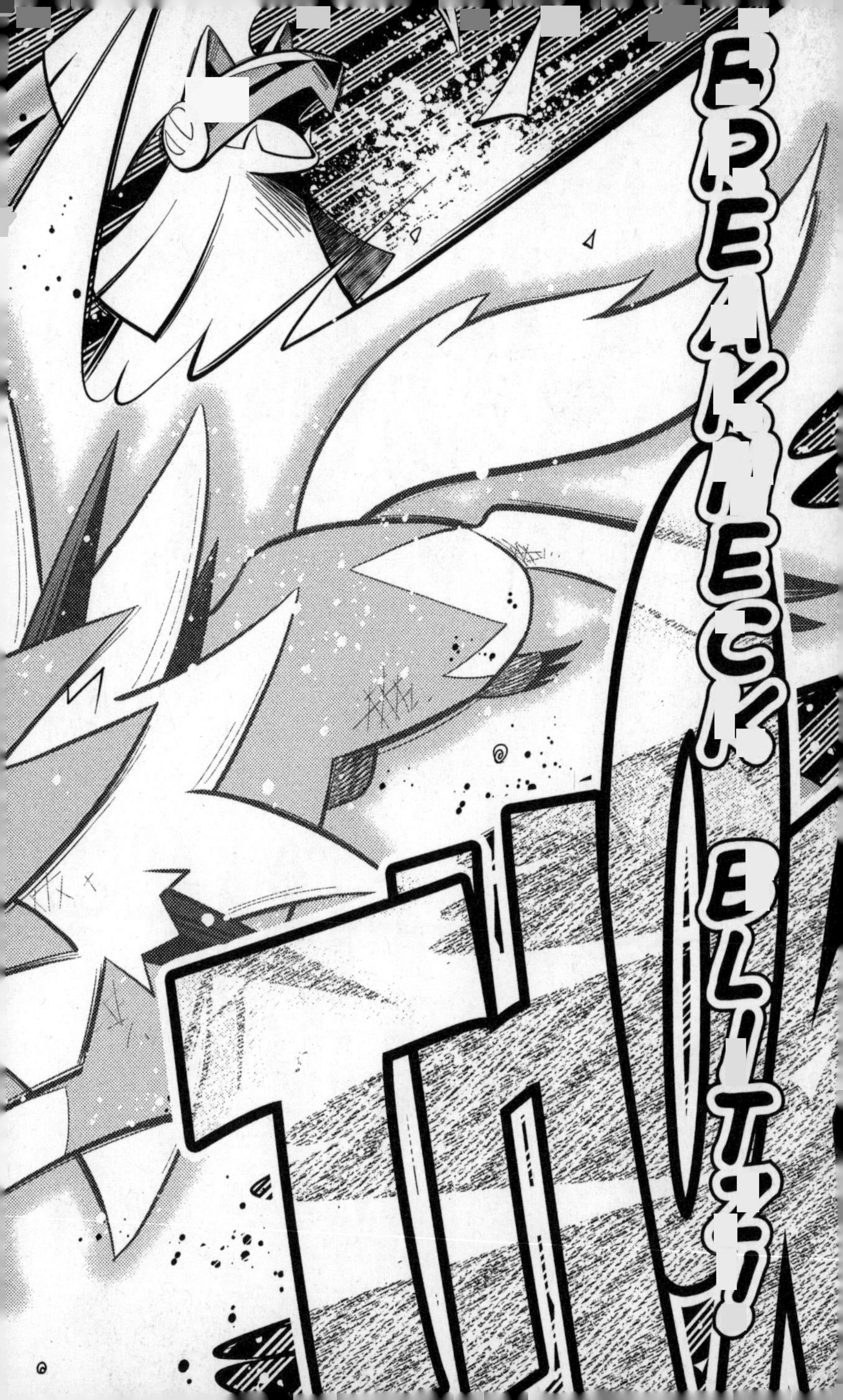
BREAKNECK! BLITZ!

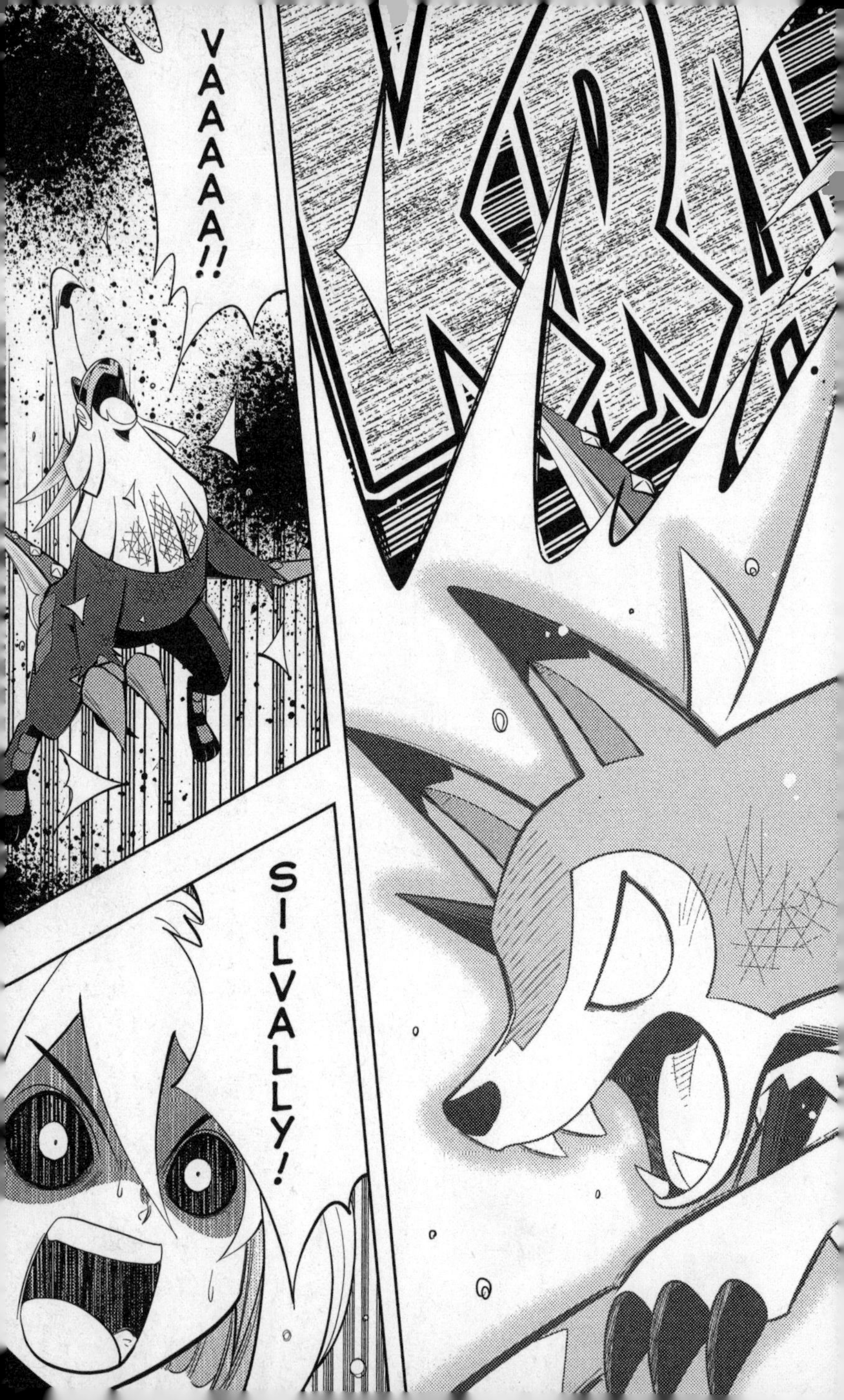
VAAAAA!!
SILVALLY!

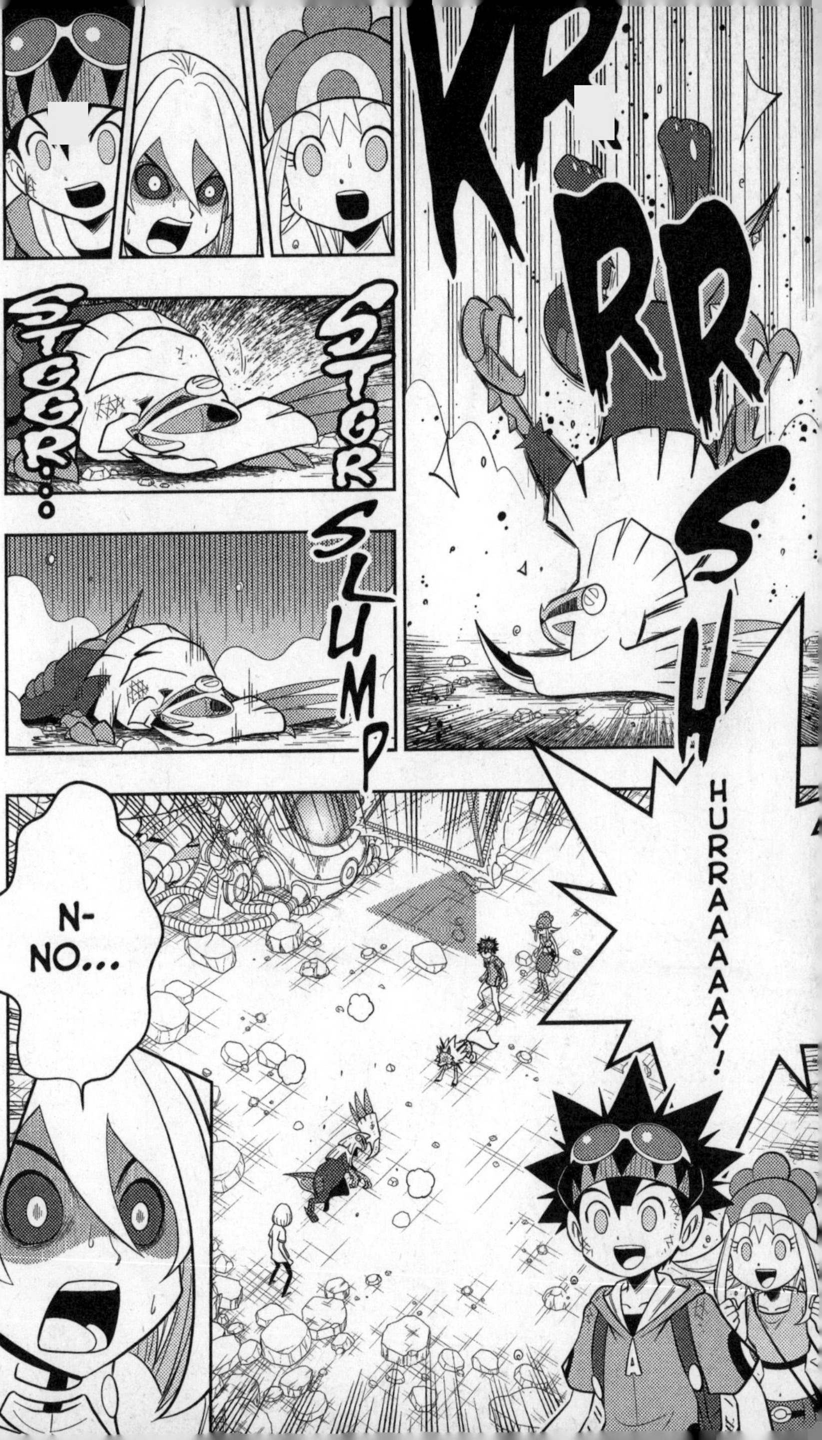
KRRR
SH
STGR
STGGR...
SLUMP
HURRAAAAAY!
N-NO...

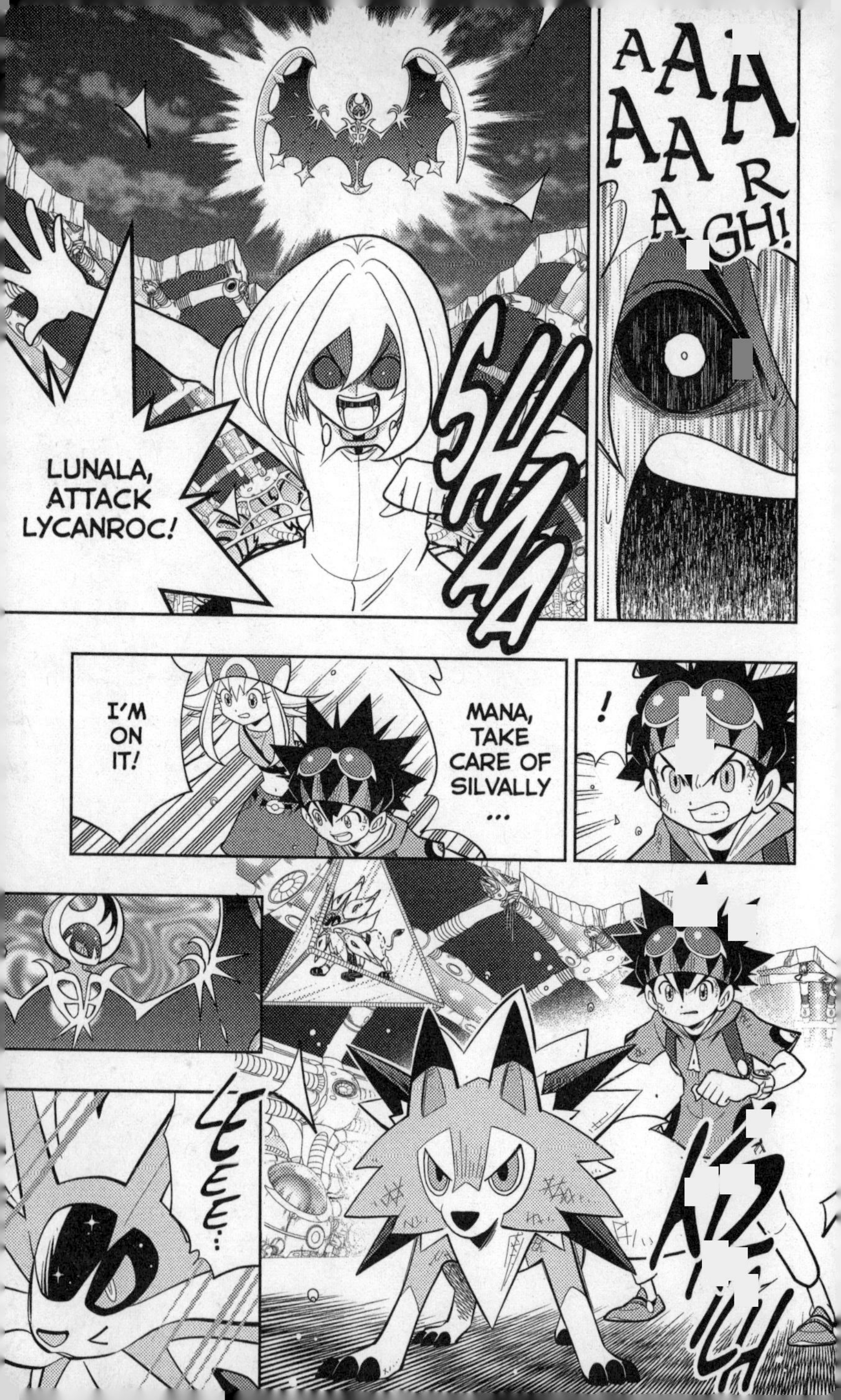
AAAAAAARGH!
LUNALA, ATTACK LYCANROC!
!
MANA, TAKE CARE OF SILVALLY...
I'M ON IT!
EEEE...

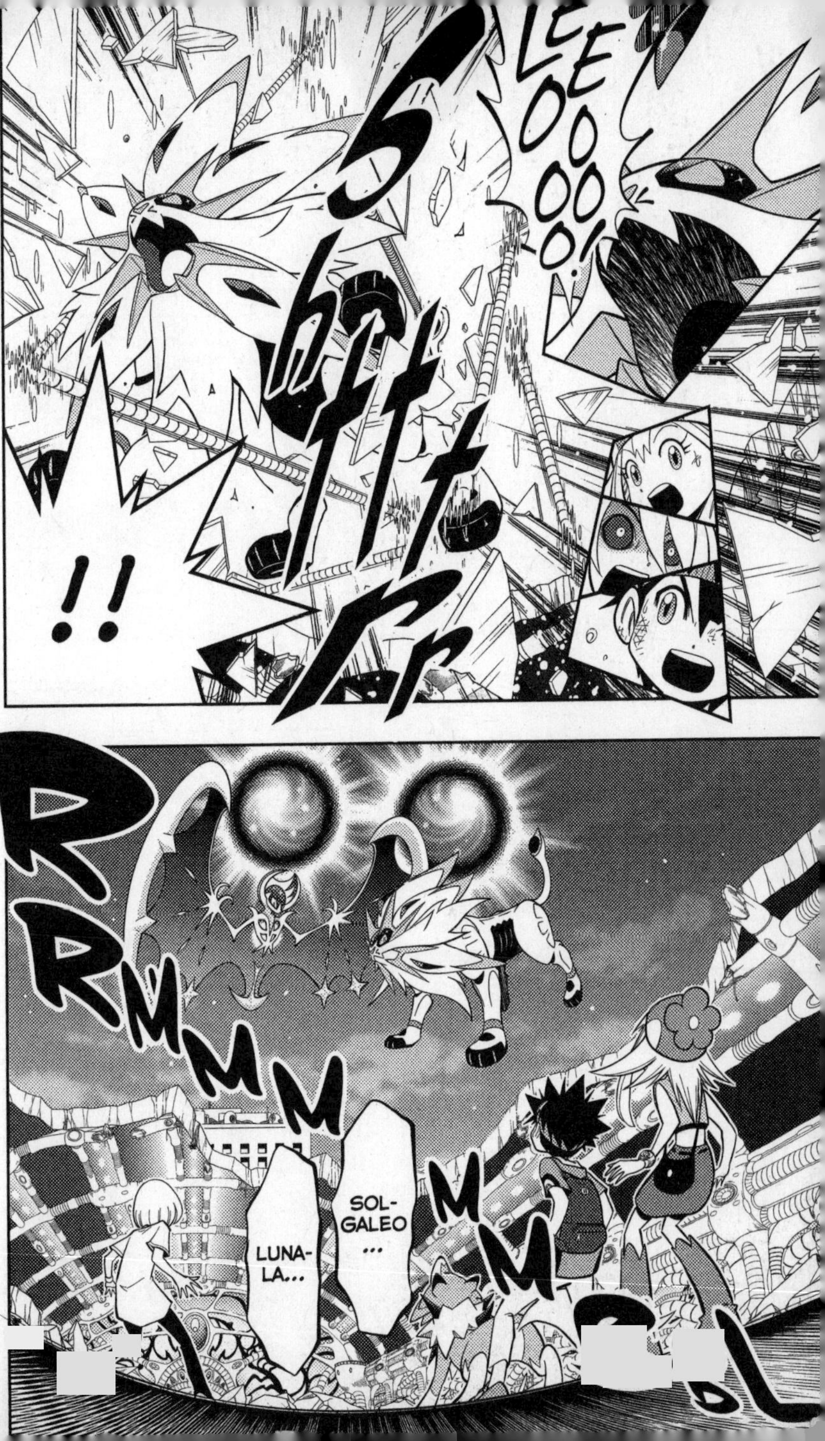

LEEOOOOOO!!
!!
SOL-GALEO...
LUNA-LA...

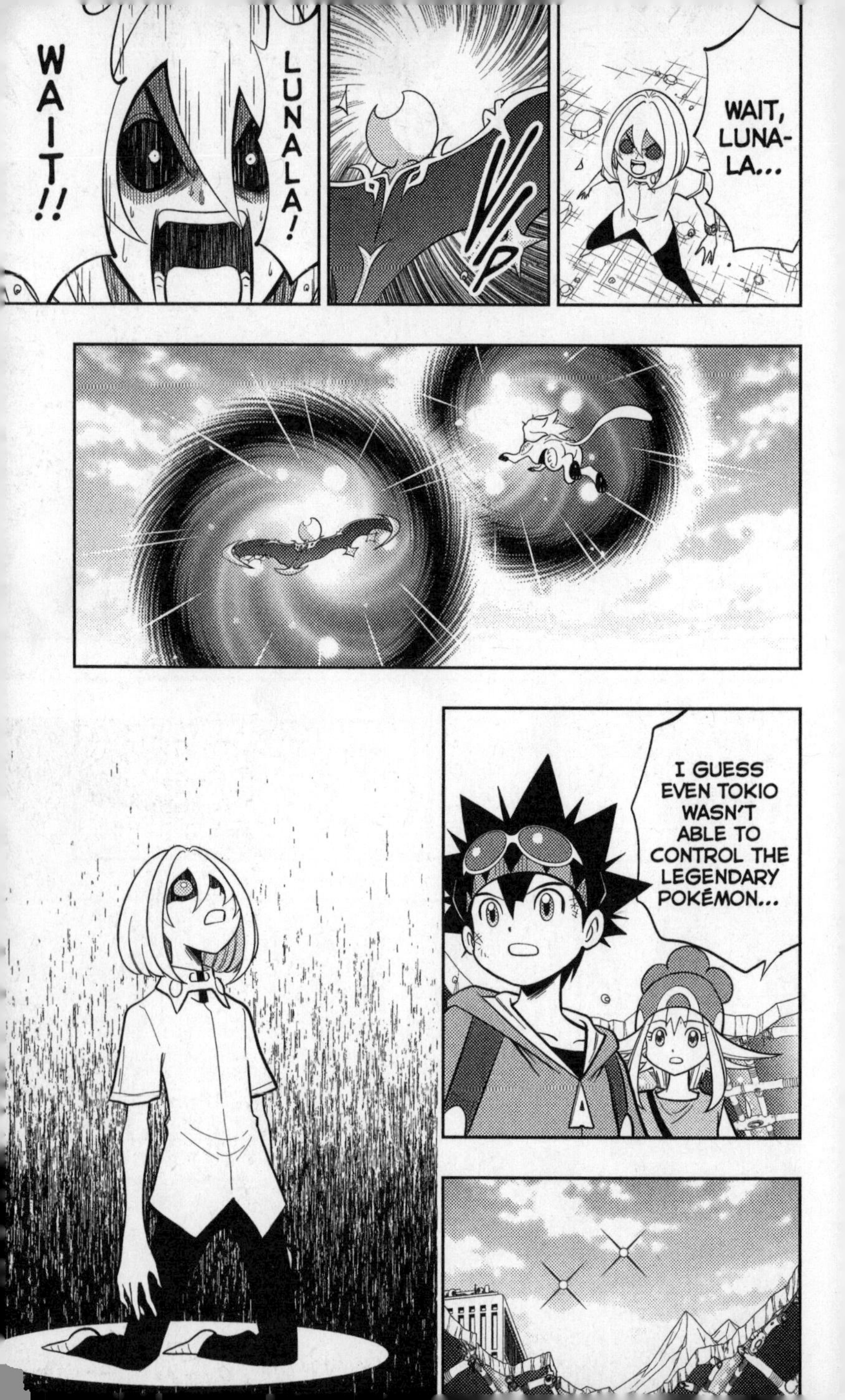
WAIT, LUNA-LA...
LUNALA!
WAIT!!
I GUESS EVEN TOKIO WASN'T ABLE TO CONTROL THE LEGENDARY POKÉMON...

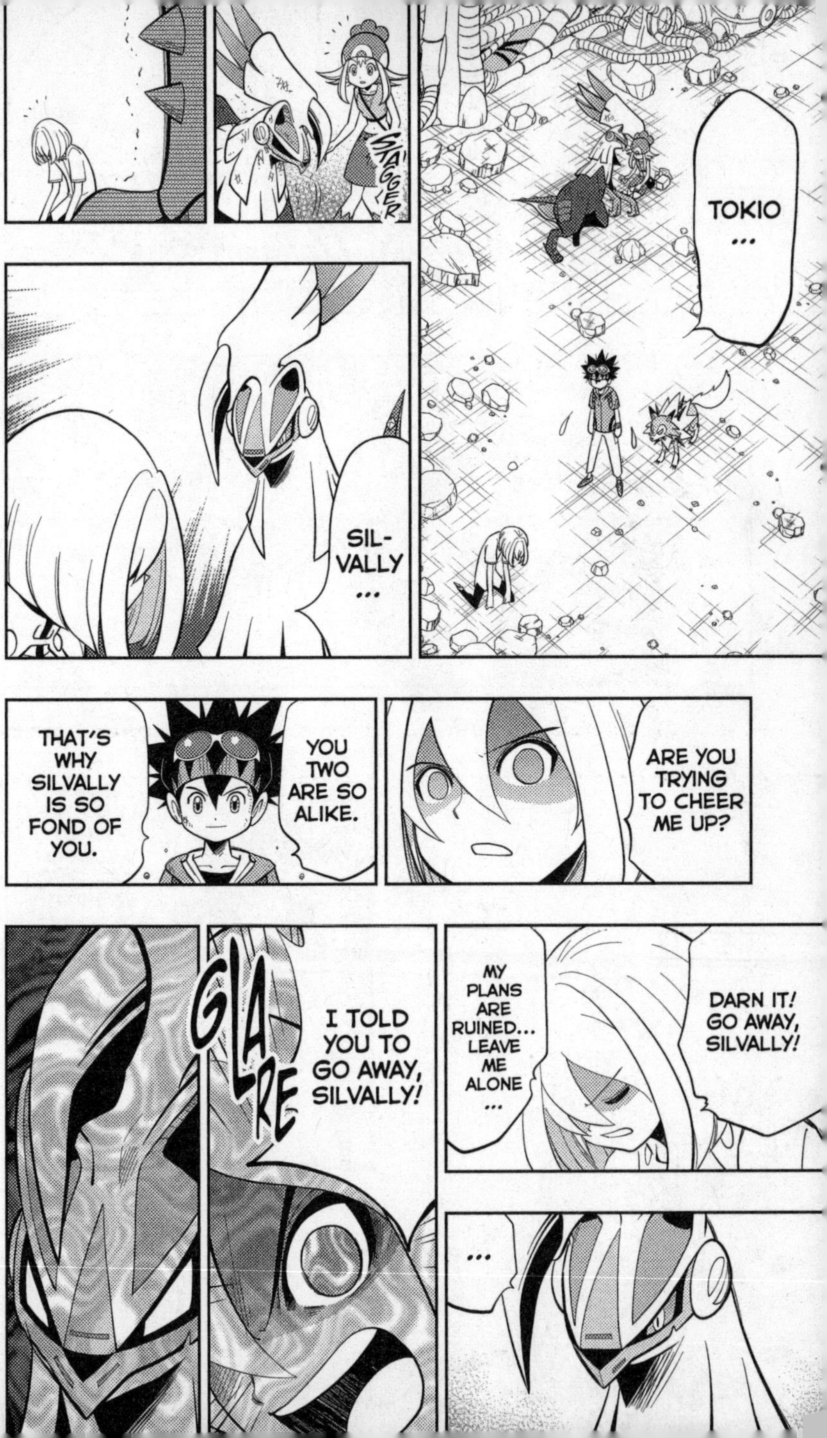
TOKIO ...
STAGGER
SIL-VALLY ...
ARE YOU TRYING TO CHEER ME UP?
YOU TWO ARE SO ALIKE.
THAT'S WHY SILVALLY IS SO FOND OF YOU.
DARN IT! GO AWAY, SILVALLY!
MY PLANS ARE RUINED... LEAVE ME ALONE ...
...
I TOLD YOU TO GO AWAY, SILVALLY!
GLARE

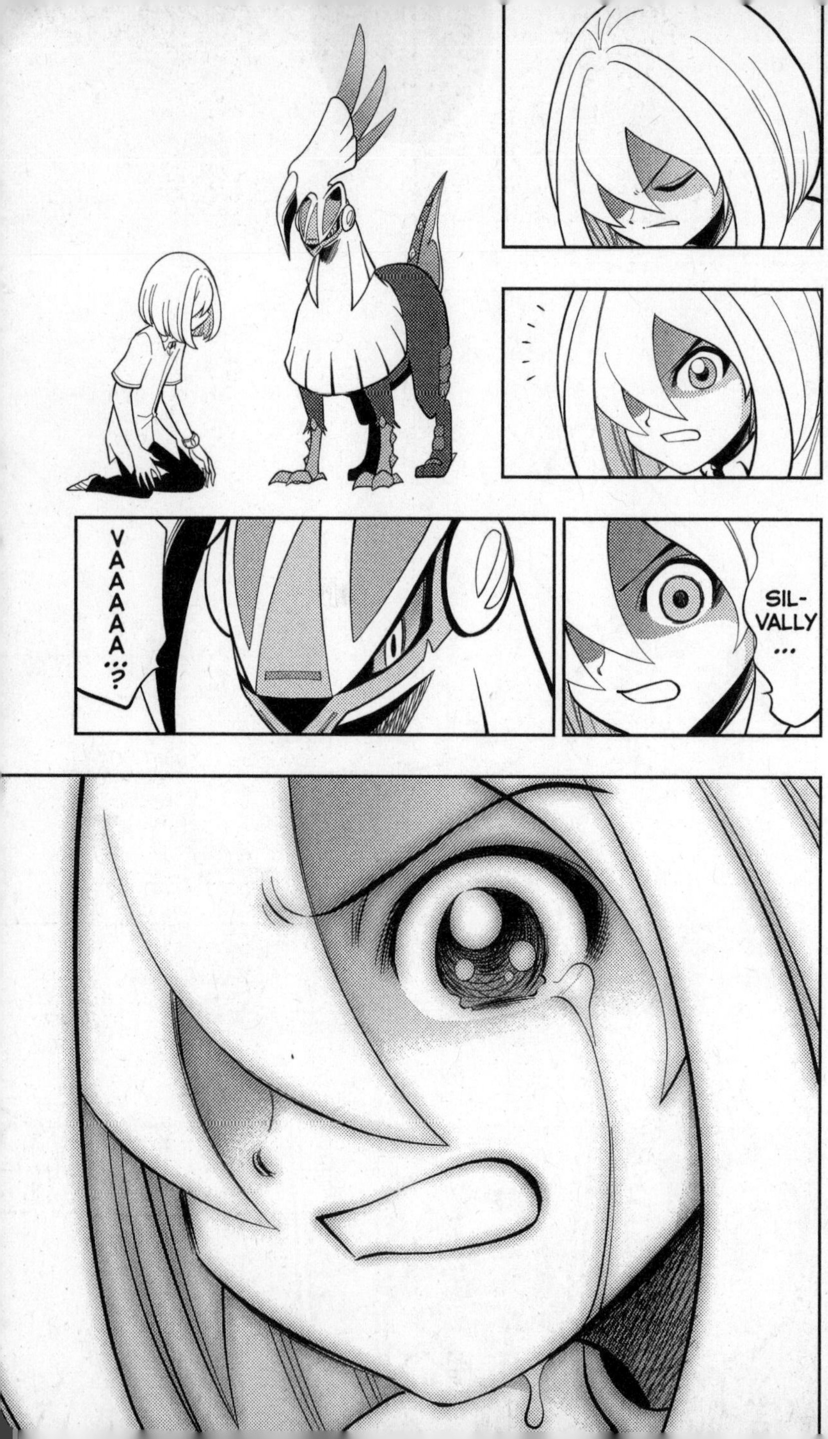
SIL-
VALLY
...
VAAAAA...?

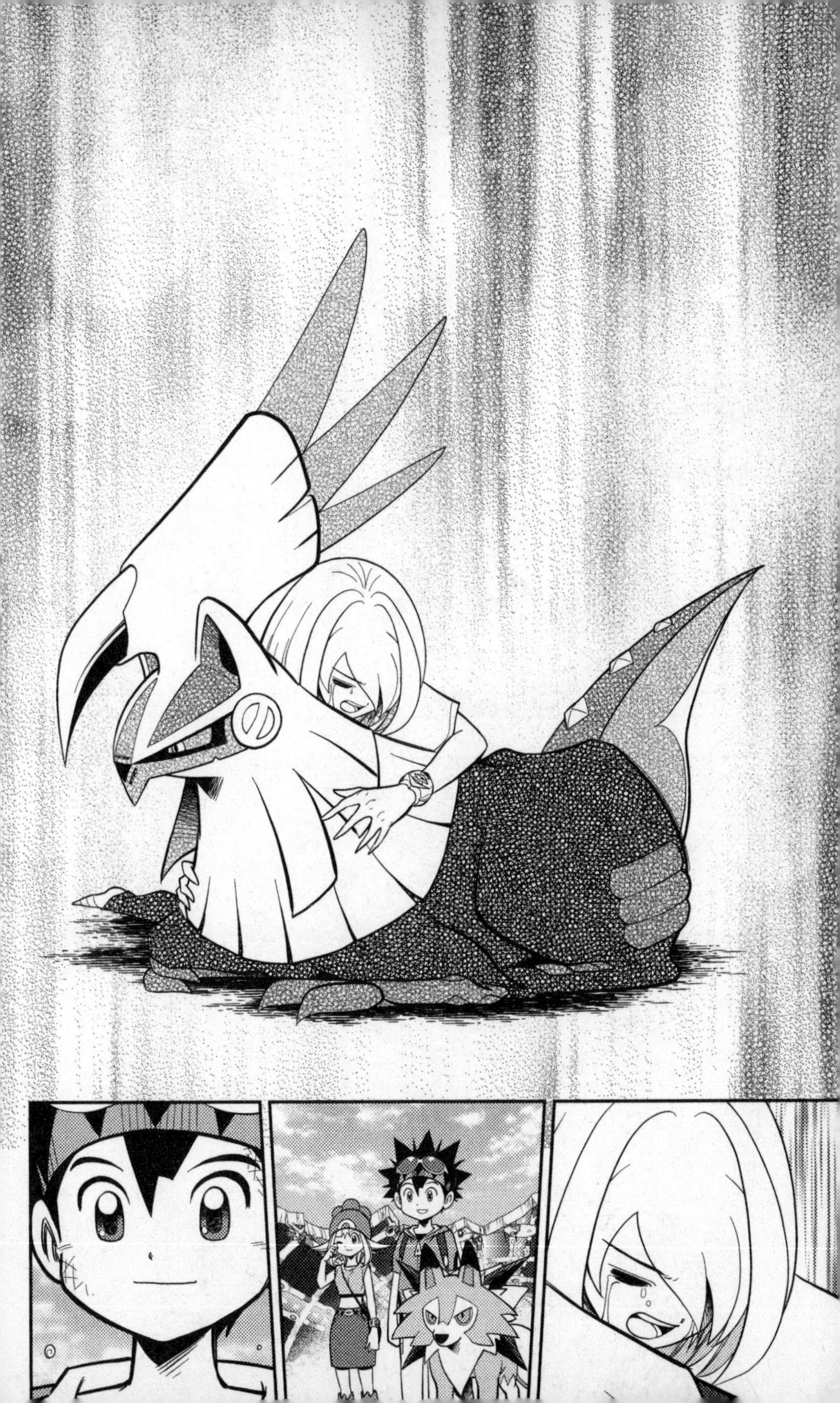

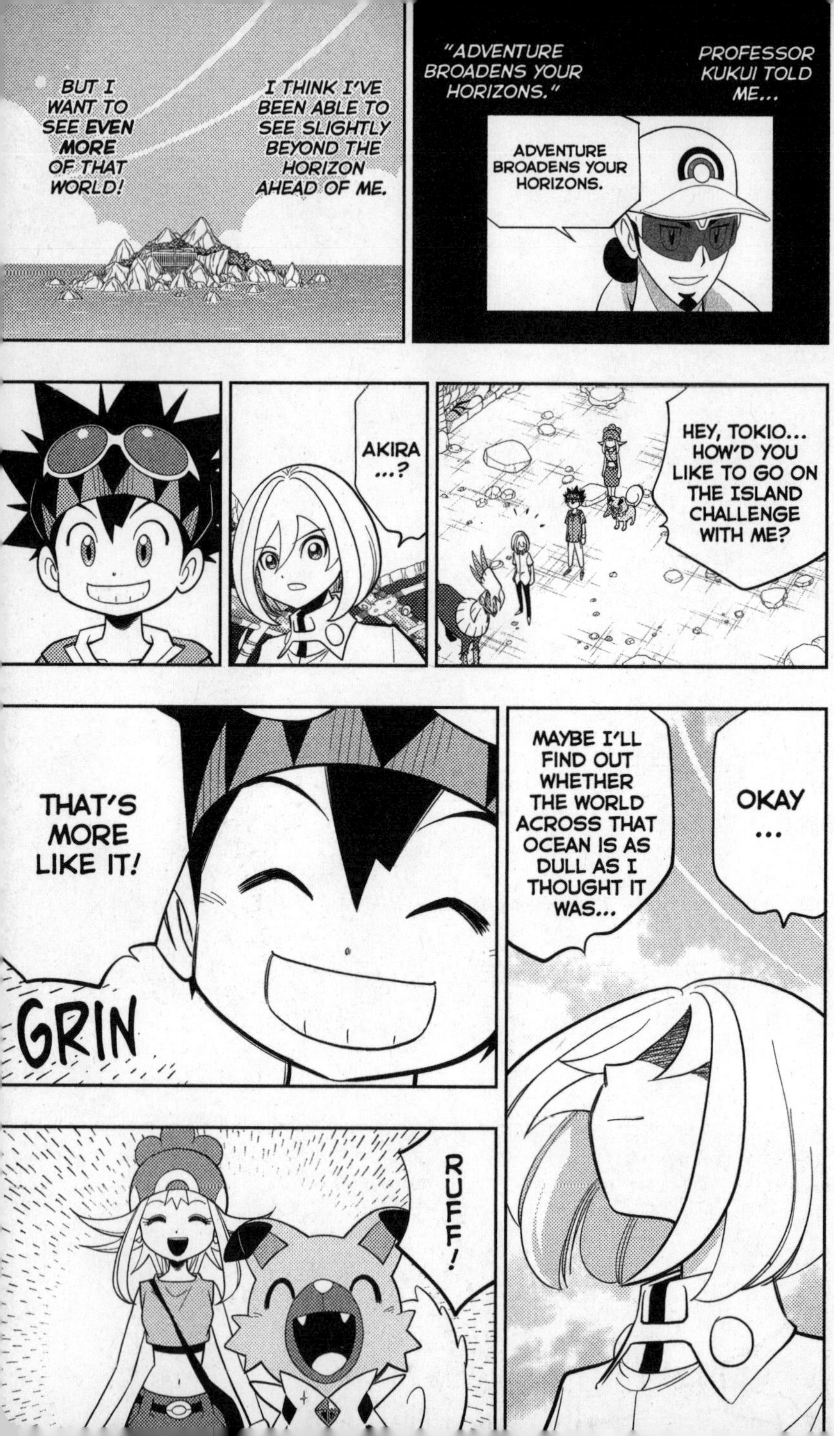
PROFESSOR KUKUI TOLD ME...
"ADVENTURE BROADENS YOUR HORIZONS."
ADVENTURE BROADENS YOUR HORIZONS.
I THINK I'VE BEEN ABLE TO SEE SLIGHTLY BEYOND THE HORIZON AHEAD OF ME.
BUT I WANT TO SEE EVEN MORE OF THAT WORLD!
HEY, TOKIO... HOW'D YOU LIKE TO GO ON THE ISLAND CHALLENGE WITH ME?
AKIRA ...?
OKAY ...
MAYBE I'LL FIND OUT WHETHER THE WORLD ACROSS THAT OCEAN IS AS DULL AS I THOUGHT IT WAS...
THAT'S MORE LIKE IT!
GRIN
RUFF!

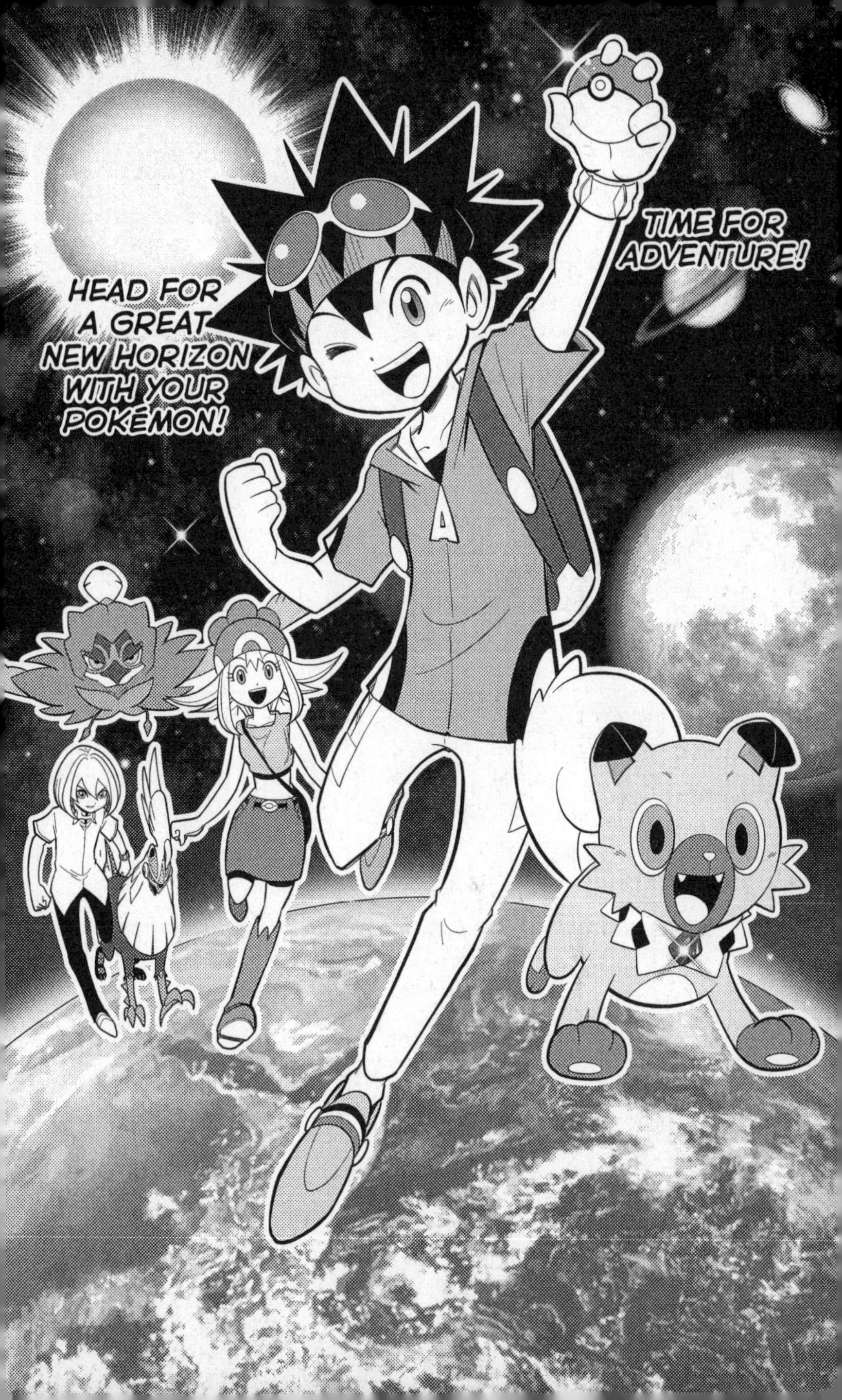
TIME FOR ADVENTURE!
HEAD FOR A GREAT NEW HORIZON WITH YOUR POKÉMON!

———— POKÉMON HORIZON ————
ARTWORK STAFF

Matsubara

Taeko Yabe

Nishiguchi Tanken Taicho
(West Exit Expedition Captain)

Junnosuke Ishi
(Ishii)

———— SUPERVISED BY ————

GAME FREAK Inc.

The Pokémon Company

———— EDITOR ————

Keiten Matsumoto

(Honorifics abbreviated)

Thank you very much.

Tenya Yabuno

THE END!

Tenya Yabuno

What do you need to draw out your partner's full power?! Your Pokémon will teach you that!

Born in Tokyo, Tenya Yabuno made his manga debut in 1990 with his one-shot manga story *Jonetsu no Clipper*. He received the 34th Kodansha Manga Award and 57th Shogakukan Manga Award with *Inazuma Eleven* in *CoroCoro Comics*. His other works are *Ultra Eleven* and *Botch Waiwai Misaki E*.

Pokémon Horizon: Sun & Moon
Volume 2
VIZ Media Edition

Story and Art by TENYA YABUNO

©2018 The Pokémon Company International.
©1995–2017 Nintendo / Creatures Inc. / GAME FREAK inc.
TM, ®, and character names are trademarks of Nintendo.
POKÉMON HORIZON Vol. 2
by Tenya YABUNO
© 2017 Tenya YABUNO
All rights reserved.
Original Japanese edition published by SHOGAKUKAN.
English translation rights in the United States of America, Canada,
the United Kingdom, Ireland, Australia and New Zealand arranged
with SHOGAKUKAN.

Original Cover Design/Takuya KUROSAWA

Translation/Tetsuichiro Miyaki
English Adaptation/Annette Roman
Touch-Up & Lettering/Susan Daigle-Leach
Design/Julian [JR] Robinson
Editor/Annette Roman

The stories, characters and incidents mentioned in this
publication are entirely fictional.

Printed in the U.S.A.

Published by VIZ Media, LLC
P.O. Box 77010
San Francisco, CA 94107

10 9 8 7 6 5 4 3 2 1
First printing, November 2018

PARENTAL ADVISORY
POKÉMON HORIZON: SUN &
MOON is rated A and is suitable
for readers of all ages.

viz.com

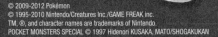

The adventure continues in the Johto region!

POKÉMON™
ADVENTURES
GOLD & SILVER BOX SET

Includes POKÉMON ADVENTURES Vols. 8-14 and a collectible poster!

Story by
HIDENORI KUSAKA

Art by
MATO,

SATOSHI YAMAMOTO

More exciting Pokémon adventures starring Gold and his rival Silver! First someone steals Gold's backpack full of Poké Balls (and Pokémon!). Then someone steals Prof. Elm's Totodile. Can Gold catch the thief—or thieves?!

Keep an eye on Team Rocket, Gold... Could they be behind this crime wave?

VIZ media
www.viz.com

PERFECT SQUARE

POKéMON

ΩRUBY αSAPPHIRE
OMEGA ALPHA

POKéMON

POCKET COMICS

STORY & ART BY SANTA HARUKAZE

BLACK & WHITE

LEGENDARY POKéMON

X•Y

A Pokémon pocket-sized book chock-full of
four-panel gags, Pokémon trivia and fun quizzes
based on the characters you know and love!

THE ART OF

STORY AND ART BY
Satoshi Yamamoto

A collection of beautiful full-color art from the artist of the Pokémon Adventures graphic novel series! In addition to illustrations of your favorite Pokémon, this vibrant volume includes exclusive sketches and storyboards, four pull-out posters, and an exclusive manga side story!

![Pokémon Adventures HeartGold & SoulSilver]

Story by **HIDENORI KUSAKA**
Art by **SATOSHI YAMAMOTO**

In this **two-volume** thriller, troublemaker Gold and feisty Silver must team up again to find their old enemy Lance and the Legendary Pokémon Arceus.

Available now!

YOU'RE READING THE WRONG WAY!

This book has been printed in the original Japanese format in order to preserve the orientation of the original artwork. Have fun with it!

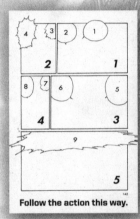

Follow the action this way.